The Mystery of the Lost Crypt

From the same Autor :

- *Meurtres au Méan Martin (French Version)*, June 2022
- *Le Jeu de Quilles en Or (French Version),*   Nov. 2022

Gaël EBER

Thriller

THE MYSTERY OF THE LOST CRYPT

Translated from French by Laurence EBER

Copyright

The Mystery of the Lost Crypt

© Gaël EBER, July 2023

ISBN 9798852515650

All rights of reproduction, translation and adaptation reserved for all countries.

« History is truth that is distorted,
the legend of the fake that is incarnated. »

Jean Cocteau

Preamble

**Moselle, Lorraine, France
Thursday 13th August 1914**

The mist that covered the Lorraine plateau was slow to dissipate in the middle of the morning. In this muggy and stifling atmosphere, two silhouettes crept stealthily between the groves and the cornfields. Second Lieutenant Jean Lestrades accompanied by Private First Class Michel Ducasse had gone on a reconnaissance mission to report on the exact position and size of the German 6th army. According to the latest information provided, it was amassed fifteen kilometers behind the border defined at the time of the Frankfurt Treaty of 1871. The two soldiers, who were sailing through German territory, intended to find refuge on a hillock covered by dense forest, the highest point in the region, where the church and the few houses of the village of Marimont stood at its foot. Following the declaration of war on August 4 between the two countries, the few remaining inhabitants had evacuated the village and only the French-born priest of the church of Saint-Denis had taken the risk of staying on and continued his daily masses before a German military audience that had taken up his cause.

The place would be ideal for spying on the enemy.

But as they were not the only ones to have had this idea, described in all modesty as genius by the very entourage of General Castelnau in charge of the 2nd Army, enemy units were already occupying this strategic promontory. Lestrades had never doubted this for a second. The two soldiers would therefore have to deploy all their skill and cunning to reach this area. A task made all the more difficult by the fact that their clothing did not really help them. That was the least that could be said. While the German, English and Russian armies had all opted for much more discreet colours, the traditional French outfit had remained unchanged since the Second Empire. Old and above all too conspicuous, it looked more like a parade outfit than a war outfit. In particular, their red trousers, known as 'garance', their bluish 'iron grey' capote, closed by two rows of buttons, and their kepi with a madder turban and blue headband. All of this was complemented by equipment that was considered far too cumbersome and uncomfortable. All these elements worked against them in their attempt to go unnoticed in this annexed country.

Hiding in the woods at the entrance to the village since the beginning of the afternoon following the dissipation of the fog, they waited patiently for nightfall to complete their final advance. They took advantage of this to rest and lighten their shoulders, which were bruised by their packs. This was an opportunity to get to know each other better. It was also a way to get rid of the stress of the mission. When the time came, they entered the village through the cemetery behind the church. Warned by some villagers they had met on the way to their homeland, they decided to go to the priest's house, hoping that he would be able to help them. They strolled towards the rectory next to the church. A blood-curdling owl call frightened the two men as they passed. It sounded as if it had been raised to signal a presence. A faint glow came through the wooden shutters on the ground floor. Ducasse noticed a gaping hole in the low wall separating the church from the presbytery. He signaled it to his partner with a wave of his hand and then stepped into it. He gently opened the gate, but paid no attention to the high step that followed. He placed his right foot on the edge of the wet stone, which immediately slipped. His ankle slid. He lost his balance and was dragged by the weight of his pack towards a flower bed where he sprawled out.

A group of German soldiers patrolling nearby were alerted by the noise and two of their number came to recognition. Lestrades lifted his sidekick by the arm to get him to his feet and they both ran with long strides towards the door of the presbytery. They had just time to open the door and rush in before the Germans appeared at the edge of the garden. Inside, the parish priest, who was sitting down to dinner, was so frightened that he dropped his spoon full of soup onto his cassock.

'Who are you?' he asked in bewilderment, staring at them as if he were seeing ghosts.

'Don't be afraid, Father...'

'But what are you doing here, my braves?' he said as he stood up, discovering their nationalities by their attire.

Before they could reply, the front door thundered with several bangs and a man shouted 'Öffnet die Tür! in Goethe's language, making all three of them flinch. A commotion followed. Already alerted by the intrusion of the two soldiers, the priest took them to hide in the adjoining room.

'Quick, get in here and don't get noticed. If they see you, we're not going to have a party,' he whispered.

Then he went to open the door before the German patrol lost patience. After endless discussions in a mixture of the two languages and despite their suspicion, the priest managed to get rid of them. He wiped his forehead with his handkerchief before letting his unexpected guests out of their hiding place. He invited the two Frenchmen to sit down, gave them each a glass and poured them wine to recover from their emotions. All three gulped it down.

The priest asked them again his initial question.

Lestrades took the risk of telling him why they were here so that he could possibly help them in their mission. In any case, they had nothing to lose. Alone, they would not get very far without being caught. The area was swarming with Germans and for good reason, the outposts were stationed there. They had simply thrown themselves into the lion's den.

The clergyman readily agreed to help them and told them the best way to reach the top of the small hill. He also told them of a rumor that had been circulating in the village since the dawn of time concerning the probable existence of an underground passage at the foot of the mound that would allow them to reach the summit in absolute discretion. According to the village elders, this tunnel was the only remains of an old medieval castle which has almost disappeared from the surface and of which only a few sections of the walls of the keep and the enclosures still remain. But as is often the case in legends, everyone seemed to know of its existence, but no one had seen it with their own eyes.

The two soldiers were not overconfident and concluded that it was better not to rely on such gossip. Their time was limited. They would simply follow the path indicated by the clergyman, hide during the day where they could under branches and dead leaves, gather all the information expected by their staff and then turn back the next night. They had a great responsibility and could not fail in their mission. They thanked the priest for his support and then slipped out the back door of the building.

It was one o'clock in the morning.

The mist was already beginning to fall. Added to the total absence of light in the the cottages due to the lack of inhabitants and the dark moon forecast for the following day, they sailed blind. The perfect camouflage in spite of everything. But what seemed to be an advantage soon became a handicap when they had to find their way to the edge of the wood.

A small path on the north side, a hundred meters above the watering hole, the priest told them.

'You can't see anything here! Impossible to orientate yourself...'

'So much for the path and the watering hole. We'll go up that way,' replied Lestrades, who had briefly spotted himself by the light of the torches as the German patrols passed.

They arrived safely at the bottom of the hill on the north side and began their ascent, lurking on the ground as much as possible so as not to take any risks. A warm breeze caressed their faces. They could hear the voices of the enemy units positioned at various points on the ridge very clearly. The chants and loud laughter were no indication of an imminent attack by French forces. The atmosphere was serene and insolently relaxed. An optimism characteristic of the German army. This enraged the French all the more...

They crawled side by side as unobtrusively as possible, in a mixture of country scents, an assortment of mushroom, flower, humus and lichen fragrances. Having no landmarks in this darkness, they had to step over stones, tree stumps and upright branches, frequently clinging to one of them with their imposing backpacks. Above all, they could not avoid the mass of nettles which they crossed from end to end. The jagged, stinging leaves scourged every inch of bare skin on their hands and heads. Ducasse scratched himself until he bled to relieve himself, but nothing did. On the contrary. His inflamed face grew puffier as the itching became more intense, verging on the unbearable. He couldn't stop himself from swearing like a trooper.

'Why on earth did I accept this mission? I'd rather receive a rain of shells...'

'I suspect it will come soon, if that's any consolation. In the meantime, don't scratch yourself. It will only make it worse,' whispered Lestrades. 'And please, stop blaspheming!'

A specialist in medicinal plants when his civilian schedule allowed him to do so, in the middle of the day he would immediately have found the right plants to administer to his comrade to relieve him. But in the dark it was more complicated.

Despite this thorny episode, they resumed their task. Once the nettles had passed, it was the turn of the impatient ones to bother them. These plants, which Lestrades knew as Himalayan Balsam, had fruits in the form of capsules which, when rubbed or touched, burst and spread the seeds around. As they passed, all the capsules exploded. It was like a miniature battlefield orchestrated by

Lilliputians. The seeds entered every orifice, stuck to each part of skin and even penetrated the sleeves and neckline. Eyes, mouth, nose, ears. Everything went through it. But this inconvenience was much less than the previous one. An idea then sprang to mind for Lestrades. Instead of plantain, ideal for relieving nettle stings, he could always use the leaves of these balsamines as a substitute, which he simply rubbed on the skin to calm the stinging fire. Admittedly less effective, but the result would still be convincing. He passed the word to his companion who immediately tore off whole bunches of leaves which he rubbed frantically. The action was immediate. The itching and swelling disappeared as if by magic. He took a few handfuls and put them inside his jacket. Just in case he needed it. There was still a long way to go and many more pitfalls...

As they continued their slow but cautious ascent, Ducasse put his elbow into a small cavity which gave way partially under his weight and made him lose his balance. His chin hit the ground and he bit his tongue. More swearing ensued. But something intrigued him immediately. The surface had given way with a slight creak of wood. Not just branches or twigs. Planks seemed to have been laid down there, all covered with vegetation. Very old, rotten planks that had not stood the test of time as they had immediately given way. He stretched his arm inside the hole, but did not touch any of the walls. It seemed deep. Lestrades, standing back, came crawling up to him.

'If we haven't discovered the entrance to the famous tunnel, we might be able to hide there,' Ducasse said excitedly.

'It would be necessary to be able to inspect the interior to be sure. But that would require the use of a light source, and I'm reluctant to take that risk. With all those Fritzes around, getting caught so close to the goal would be too stupid.'

'I don't think we have much choice, Lieutenant. And who knows, it could be the entrance to the underground. You heard what I heard from that old priest.'

'That's what worries me. He was so drunk that he could have told us nonsense. This space may be a simple hiding place made by the inhabitants to avoid the Germans from wiping out their property. Or even a natural cavity. Who knows? Besides, we don't have much time to visit. We have to be back in two days. We have to hurry.'

He thought for a moment. He hesitated. Then finally gave in.

'Okay, we'll take a look, but quickly!'

So they took the risk of striking a match to make sure that the pit was habitable. While Ducasse enlarged the entrance hole by carefully removing a plank, Lestrades reached into his left jacket pocket and pulled out a small box of matches. He took one, leaned the front of his body forward, Ducasse counterbalancing him on his legs so that he would not topple over into the void, and then struck it. It flared up instantly, dazzling him at the same time. His eyes had long since adapted to the darkness. When he opened them again, he discovered a much larger cavity than he had expected. The bottom was partly flooded, while the ceiling was a tangle of roots. He let it burn down to his fingertips and then let go of the remains, which were extinguished before they even reached the surface of the water.

'So, what did you see Lieutenant,' asked Ducasse impatiently and above all frustrated at not having been able to check for himself.

'It does indeed seem large enough to house us,' Lestrades reported.

But suddenly, just as Ducasse wanted to step forward to try to see something too, both men felt the ground give way. Everything collapsed in less time than it took them to understand what was happening. Ducasse fell full-length into the excavation while his companion managed to hold on to some roots by chance. Fearing that the plant ceiling would collapse under his weight, he slowly let himself fall. But neither of them had anticipated such high water and Ducasse was given a full bath. He was soaked to the skin. He almost drowned. He fell on his back, his bag of more than ten kilos weighed him down and he had all the difficulty in the world to turn around to get up. The water penetrated his boots, and his trousers and long woolen top, both soaked with water, became heavy. Nothing was spared. Neither his rifle, nor his haversack with its spare clothes and various utensils, and even less his two bags filled with food. Once he was back on his feet, he groped the surface of the water for his kepi, which he could not find. As for the lieutenant, he was wet up to his thighs, sparing at least his equipment and food.

The cracking of the wooden slats and their fall into the pond was partly muffled by the dense vegetation, but not enough as a passing German patrol reacted immediately. Three soldiers pointed their rifles at the source of the noise. A fourth, the leader, pointed a torch and scanned the area thoroughly.

'Gibt es jemanden?'[1] shouted the Bavarian NCO.

The two French soldiers, their senses heightened tenfold, remained hidden away in their hole, holding their breath.

The stagnant water in which they waded was cold and foul, caused by the rotting of many plants and rodents. The stench filled their nostrils.

The enemy soldiers were still on the lookout when a large hare came through the beam of light.

'Verdammt noch mal. Es war nur ein Hase!'[2] said one.

'Warum schießt du nicht Franz?'[3] asked another.

'Bist du verrückt? Man wird sich auffinden und einschließen lassen! Behalt lieber deine Patronen für die Froschfresser!'[4]

A general burst of laughter followed, relieving the pressure that they had only dealt with a hare. They slung their rifles again and continued their rounds.

'Let's wait another five minutes until they move away...'

---

1. *Who goes There?*
2. *For God's sake. It was only a rabbit!*
3. *Why don't you shoot Franz?*
4. *Are you crazy? We'll be spotted and arrested! Save your cartridges for the frog eaters!*

Gradually the voices of the Teutonic soldiers faded away. With the danger over, the lieutenant took his torch from the side pocket of his haversack and turned it on. He stealthily scanned the space around him and then lingered on the state of his companion. He couldn't help but chuckle.

'Oh, my poor Michel, you are well arranged... you remind me of my cat when I took it out of the well.'

'Ah, that's all right, spare me your sarcasm!' he replied, quite annoyed.

By the light of the lamp he saw his kepi still floating not far from him, wrung it out and put it back on his head.

The lieutenant continued his inspection of the area. Behind a natural wall of roots, a tunnel extended. While Ducasse, soaked to the skin, went to retrieve his bag which had remained outside, Lestrades continued by picking his way through the prolific vegetation and the numerous spider webs.

As the path climbed, the water had quickly disappeared. Its advance frightened away rats and small rodents that had built their nests in the damp walls.

An old crenelated and riveted iron gate blocked the access. He took a stone and struck a large rusty padlock, which offered no resistance.

He continued on his way and was then bewildered by the sight before him. The gallery was now entirely vaulted with stones from bottom to top. His companion came to join him.

'It's a work of goldsmiths. The craftsmen of this tunnel seem to have taken care to shape it so that it lasts as long as possible,' says Ducasse, sweeping his weak lamp over both ends.

Some stones had not survived the pressure of the invading flora and lay on the ground where the two companions stumbled, when they did not slide on the slippery steps. Caution was called for.

'I don't know why but I have a feeling this place will be our grave. If we don't get caught by the Krauts, we'll be buried alive here,' grumbled the Private First Class.

'Stop bitching and move on. Need I remind you that you were the one who wanted to come?'

'Only fools don't change their minds. We don't even know where this tunnel leads. We're going to waste precious time playing archaeologist...'

'We'll soon find out, you grumpy bastard...'

After only a few meters came the first difficulty. An iron door with bars blocked their way. But the lock, completely eaten away, offered no resistance. On the other hand, the pile of stones behind the door, due to a collapse of the vault at this point and itself most probably caused by the growth of roots that had blown up the structure over the decades, prevented it from opening sufficiently to allow them to squeeze through. They both pushed on the gate like mad, but the door still offered as much resistance. They still had to clear a large number of stones to hope to free it. They hung their lamp on an old root and used their rifles to pry the stones through the bars with their arms alone and push them back as far as they could.

'At least the guns are of good quality. You can't blame them for that in command,' said Ducasse teasingly.

They succeeded, not without difficulty, in their task and opened the door with one last heavy blow. It gave way with a creak that put them on the alert again and with a crash that shook the already weakened ceiling. Dust and dirt were sprinkled on them. But nothing happened. No collapse and no possible alerting of an enemy patrol outside.

'And a past obstacle! I hope the list doesn't get any longer. We have other things to do,' commented Lestrades.

They retrieved their packs and the torch and continued down the dark underground gallery. But they soon came to a gallery perpendicular to their own. They had a first choice. The tunnel continued on either side. One going up, on their left, and the other going down, on their right.

'Which way are we going?' asked Ducasse.

'Our objective being to go as high as possible on this hill to spy on the enemy, we go by the left...'

'What did I tell you, eh?' cackled Ducasse, who immediately seemed to forget his previous misadventure.

They had certainly found what they had not dared to hope for. Exactly what the priest had told them.

The legend was brought to life by these two strangers, even if it was by the greatest of coincidences.

The next evening, at the rectory, at the stroke of midnight, the abbot woke up with a start. He picked up the candlestick on his bedside table and opened one of the two shutters to see for himself what could have caused such a noise. But he saw nothing. Just as he was about to close the wooden shutter, a voice called out to him.

'Oh, abbot!'

The latter leaned out again.

'Who is it?' he asked in puzzlement, trying to pierce the gloom with his still-foggy eyes.

'It's me, Ducasse... We met last night.'

'Oh yes. Come on, get in quickly, there are patrols in every corner, you'll get arrested.'

The soldier ran to the door holding his lower abdomen. He had intense abdominal pain. Once the door was closed, he rushed to the bottle of wine on the table, removed the cork and drank directly from the neck. He gulped down the whole of the poor-quality nectar in one gulp. When he had finished, he sat down, looking haggard. The candlelight showed a pallid complexion and swollen eyes. His hands were shaking. His body twitched.

The abbot approached him gently.

'What is happening to you? Something bad must have happened to make you feel this way. Tell me about it.'

But the soldier did not answer. He stared at the wall with his eyes wide open. It was as if he was under a spell.

'What happened on the mound? Where is your friend? Has he been taken prisoner? Is he wounded? Come on, answer soldier!'

Ducasse finally reacted. He came to his senses and recounted everything that had happened since they had left the presbytery the previous evening, interspersed with violent spasms that twisted him with pain. The abbot was hanging on his every word and did not miss a thing that came out of the soldier's mouth.

'I have to go back to my companion. He was in a bad way when I left. A little wine would do him good.'

'But what happened in that tunnel?'

'It is incomprehensible. A door-sized wall was slightly ajar in the tunnel. We pressed it open further to allow us to slip through and see what was there. The lieutenant went first and almost immediately went into violent spasms. Then I saw him collapse. I ran to help him, but my stomach cramped terribly.'

'What was in this second cave?'

'I didn't really have time to see,' he replied laconically. 'But I thought I saw some chests. Six large wooden chests. When I walked back across the porch from the passageway, the door closed immediately. In my haste, I didn't think to mark the place. I don't know if I'll find it again. I put branches in front of the main entrance to the cave.'

He does not say anything else.

'So the treasure really exists. It is extraordinary! So it wasn't just a legend that has been told for centuries from generation to generation. And you discovered it in less than two hours. It was not chance that led you there. God wanted you to find this passage to tell me. I will go with you. I must see this with my own eyes. And above all you must try to save your friend.'

It was then that Ducasse literally changed. He turned and stared at the abbot. His satanic gaze frightened the latter, who backed away. But the madness that seized Ducasse made him uncontrollable. He got up and threw himself on the priest, clutching his neck with his hands. He screamed like a man possessed and pressed harder and harder.

The abbot tried to break free, but was unable to do so. The young soldier's arms were tetanised, hard as iron bars and firmly sealed to his neck. His end was near.

'Memento Finis,' [1] shouted the soldier who, in his delirium, uttered words in Latin that were previously unknown to him.

A German patrol passing by was attracted by the shouting. They ruthlessly broke down the door and saw the priest lying there, his eyes beginning to bulge.

They pointed their rifles at Ducasse. Not letting go of the embrace despite the stream of invectives from the soldiers shouting words that were certainly incomprehensible in German, they had no choice but to shoot him down like a rabid animal and riddled the French soldier with several shots.

His body twitched for a few more seconds on the cold stone of the kitchen before he drew his last breath.

The priest got up, helped by a German soldier. He struggled to catch his breath. He went out of the house to take deep breaths of fresh air. He revealed nothing to the patrol about why the Frenchman was in enemy territory. And even less about the lieutenant who was lying somewhere in the bowels of the mound. He could not have led them there anyway. So it was better to keep a low profile and feign disbelief and total ignorance.

As the patrol dragged the body of the French soldier out of the presbytery, a look of satisfaction came over the priest's face. He took one last look at him and said quietly:

'Now only I know this secret...'

---

1. **'Think of your end'** *from the Christian point of view and* **'Think of your goal'** *from the military side.*

The Mystery of the Lost Crypt

1

Department of History, University of Nancy
Tuesday 7 May 2014, 11:15

The bell rang in the lecture theatre signifying the end of the class. Some of the students who were ready before the end of the class rushed to the exit to go to the next classroom to reserve the best seats. This was not the case for Cyril de Villiers, who had planned to talk to the professor.

This thirty-two-years-old university student, blond with green eyes, quite tall and a fitness enthusiast, had returned to his studies late in life after a career of almost seven years in the parachute commandos of the 1er Hussars Regiment based in Tarbes and then in the Hubert commando in Saint-Mandrier-sur-Mer in the Var, in the south of France. He took part in numerous missions, from Kosovo to the Ivory Coast, via Haiti, Senegal, Chad and Afghanistan. Then weariness and too many thrills got the better of his dream of serving his country. He had seen enough colleagues off in metal boxes covered with the French flag and realized that one day it might be his turn. He felt that his patriotic duty had been fulfilled and that it was time to turn the page. Or almost, since he was still a reservist. To return to a quieter life. He had therefore resumed his studies four years ago. A radical career change or rather a move back to his first love, archaeology and medieval history.

Cyril walked down the steps of the amphitheater two at a time and approached the desk perched on the platform.

'Hello Professor!'

'Ah, it's you Cyril. So, did you like my lecture?' replied Visconti, having surreptitiously raised his head to see who was calling out to him, while continuing to put his lessons away in his little leather bag.

'Very much so. And I will be able to put it into practice this weekend. This course was just in time!'

'Oh, and what are your plans for the weekend?'

'Don't you remember? I'm going to the countryside with some friends. We're going to study an old castle mound. To see what is left of it or what can be recovered. We discussed it last week. It's related to my thesis...'

'But yes, of course. What am I thinking... probably planning my new digs this summer in the south of France,' he joked to make up for it.

'Without a doubt...,' Cyril continued, winking at him, but went unnoticed.

'And what can I do for you, young man?'

'I wanted to talk to you for a moment to share my latest research on the subject. So as not to get off on the wrong foot.'

'It is the historian's job to keep looking for the right path. Many colleagues have been wrong, sometimes all their lives, and have run their whole career after elements or even sites that in the end never existed or that they may never have found. All this is due to a mistranslation, fictitious information, misinterpretation, false indications. Or sometimes just bad luck. That is the difficulty of our job, my dear Cyril.'

'Yes, it is. But that's precisely what I like about this job. The constant search for the truth to achieve one's goals. The pleasure is all the greater.'

'Yes... you can join me for lunch. I always eat in my hutch. Today it's chicken cutlet and tabbouleh. My wife prepares my meal. And there's enough for two! She always makes too much for fear there won't be enough. Then we can discuss your research in more detail.'

'I don't like to intrude like this, Professor...'

'Come on, don't be so formal. You're not bothering me, or I wouldn't have asked you. Unless the meal doesn't suit you?' he asked, looking sternly at me.

'Yes, yes, it will fit me fine. It's perfect! It's perfect.'

'It's rather my wife you should thank. A real little cordon bleu...'

The University was a labyrinth, and an uninitiated person could easily get lost. The two men walked down various corridors, out the back of the building, through beautifully manicured gardens where students and professors lounged in their free time, to the university library. They went down one more flight of stairs and up the entire corridor to reach their destination.

'And this is my cubbyhole,' he said, opening the door.

He gave a glimpse of a small basement room with no windows, which the Dean of History had asked for to have some peace and quiet.

'You really have to be passionate about your job to want to work here," he liked to remind him. I'll never be able to remember where it is by myself.'

'Think again. This place is ideally located. It's just a stone's throw away from the manuscripts and archives, and above all it's free of noise. So I can be concentrated at all time. I chose the place myself. It's a bit messy for some people, but as long as I can find my way around, that's the main thing. Isn't that the main thing?'

'Absolutely...'

'Well, pull up a chair, we'll have a bite to eat.'

The professor took the open book from the desk, which by the looks of it must have been a few centuries old, and placed it carefully in the central drawer, marking the open page with a sheet of paper showing an alphabet and hieroglyphics.

Cyril looked around the room and tried to find a vacant chair. But the only chair in the room was crammed with a pile of books, each one older than the next.

'Where should I put them?' he asked embarrassed. 'They look so old I hardly dare touch them.'

'Put them where there is still some room!'

'I wouldn't want to make a mess of your office...,' he continued with a touch of mockery.

'But no. Don't worry. I'll find an elephant in a cage. He kicked the chair hard and knocked over the whole pile of books, some of which flew open, crumpling pages. There, now it's free.'

Cyril stood dumbfounded.

'They seemed so fragile...'

'Probably, but without much historical value.'

Visconti rummaged in one of the cupboards and unearthed a second plate, which he dusted with the back of his sleeve, as well as some cutlery. Then he took out of his bag half a loaf of bread, a runny Camembert from a Tupperware that quickly filled the room with a strong smell, and two salad bowls that he placed on his desk. He also pulled a bottle of wine from his bag.

'Smell that fresh mint. I love it! How about a little Gigondas? It's probably not the best match for our meal, but I had a whole load of it delivered and I wanted to try it. Well, make yourself useful, Cyril, and take care of it.'

'Yes, of course. Shall I serve you?'

The professor looked him straight in the eye.

'But what a question! Of course. We can't just look at this tabbouleh!'

The young man laughed. He knew Visconti's humor.

'You are right, Professor. Better to eat it.'

In the midst of a cathedral-like silence for the past ten minutes, Visconti finally spoke up.

'Yummy, really good! So, tell me about it. What exactly are you planning to do next weekend?'

'On Friday afternoon we will drive to Marimont-Lès-Bénestroff, to a B&B located in the village, until Sunday evening. Two friends will accompany me. I might as well combine business with pleasure. And the more the merrier...'

'I see. History students both?'

The Mystery of the Lost Crypt

'One of them is. Oh, and I forgot, my dog too.'

'A student too, I suppose?' smiled the professor. 'Joking aside, didn't I tell you to look in Southern Alsace for this castle?'

'In fact it is rather ambiguous, because there is another castle with almost the same name in the south of Moselle, but I have gathered little information on the internet and in the archives. It turns out that there is a castle mound unlike the other one in the Sudgau in Alsace. Between Marimont and Morimont, formerly Mörsperg and Morsperg. The one I am interested in had several different names such as Morsperc, Moresperch, Marienberg, Morsberg or Mœrsberg depending on the period and the language used. In short, I am a bit lost in the few surviving writings. Do they refer to the castle I am looking for or to one of its namesakes? It is difficult to determine...'

'Ah, I was expecting some extraordinary news on that score. I'm a little disappointed that I offered to share my meal with you... no, don't worry, I'm joking,' he laughed. 'But don't expect me to help you any further. It's up to you to find out which one is the right one.'

'Yes, of course. Far be it from me,' he lied.

He had hoped for his support, but that seemed compromised.

'Now, from what you tell me, I recognize that you have not inherited the simplest. The proof. I have misled you. Your research will be all the more interesting. And then sometimes, at the turn of an old abbey or in the archives at the bottom of an attic or a cellar, you find a rare gem. Writings or stories from the period that put you on the right track. Persevere, Cyril, you have great abilities. Don't give in to the easy way. Don't just look on the internet, there is a lot of nonsense on there. I have given you the most interesting subject. Do not disappoint me. I have great faith in you.'

Cyril was not a little proud of this last sentence which seemed to come from the bottom of his heart. The great dean of the Faculty of History of Nancy, a historian known throughout the world for his numerous medievalist works.

'Yes, you are absolutely right. I must persevere.'

'So, how do you like this tabbouleh?'

'Quite exquisite.'

'I warned you that she was a real cordon bleu.'

Seeing that he should not expect any help from him, Cyril changed the subject. During the meal he had tried to look at the books and documents lying around, but almost all of them were written in Latin and his limited knowledge of Latin could not help him decipher anything.

'And you, professor, tell me, what are you working on at the moment?'

The latter was not expecting this question and almost swallowed his sip of wine the wrong way.

'I'm on so many things at once,' he began, stammering, before pulling himself together. 'But I'm not in the habit of discussing my research with students. And then I'm asked to do so much that I find it hard to get on with my own work.'

The academic student quickly understood the message and did not insist. He left a good quarter of an hour later, at the insistence of the professor who seemed to be in a hurry, but who did not fail to announce a final recommendation.

'Cyril, if you find out anything important, please let me know immediately. And nobody else but me. Is that understood?'

'Roger that, Professor.'

2

**Via Condotti, Pincio, Rome
Friday 14 June 2013, 3am
A year earlier...**

A black limousine drove up the street in the pouring rain. At this late hour of the night, the place was emptied of its uninterrupted flow of tourists who assailed this district during the day and especially this famous shopping street where boutiques, each more luxurious than the next, and internationally renowned shops followed one another. Only the city services were busy cleaning up the place in order to give it back all its attractiveness and cachet for the weekend that was to follow.

In the background stood the majestic church of the 'Trinité des Monts', overlooking the Place of Spain with its gigantic staircase and illuminated by the multiple spotlights that highlighted it. It was easily recognizable thanks to its two symmetrical bell towers dating from the end of the fifteenth century, with an Egyptian obelisk in the foreground. In daylight, its whiteness dazzled the back of the narrow street and contrasted with the walls of the dark and polluted buildings. Dedicated to 'Saint-Louis of the French', its particularity lay in the fact that its maintenance was entirely the responsibility of the French state.

The Grand Chancellor never tired of looking at her.
But that evening, his thoughts were elsewhere.
A mixture of incomprehension and amazement animated him.

The car suddenly turned left at Via Condotti 68, which was the headquarters of the Sovereign Military Hospitaller Order of St. John of Jerusalem of Rhodes and Malta, better known by the synthetic name of the Order of Malta, and rushed into the palace. The two leaves of the large solid wooden entrance door closed immediately, hiding the white eight-pointed cross engraved on the cobblestones of the small courtyard. A butler with a large umbrella rushed to open the door and led the guest to the porch of the Magistral Palace, avoiding as much as possible the puddles that were forming here and there.

'His Most Eminent Highness the Prince and Grand Master Fra' Bertrand de Villaret awaits you in his office.'

'Thank you, Giuseppe,' he replied, already rushing up the imposing stairs.

His Excellency, the Venerable Bailiff Fra' Giacomo Carlo Borgia, appointed Grand Chancellor by the Sovereign Council at the beginning of the year following the death of his predecessor, was, as Head of the Executive, also Minister of Foreign Affairs and Minister of the Interior. Born in Rome in 1938 and a direct descendant of Fra' Alessandro Borgia, Lieutenant of the Grand Magisterium from 1865 to 1872, he had studied history at Saint John's College, one of the thirty-one and most renowned colleges of the University of Cambridge, and was a graduate of the Harvard Business School. He joined the Order of Malta in 1973 and held various positions both within the Order and in the Grand Priory of Lombardy and Venice, before taking his perpetual vows in 1981 and becoming a Professed Knight. He had known the Grand Master for many years and was not in the habit of disturbing him in the middle of the night. This impromptu visit at such a late hour was of his own accord and made his importance all the greater. Borgia knocked on the slightly ajar door. The light was very dim, contrasting with the brightness of the chandeliers in the hallway and on the grand staircase.

'Come in, Giacomo!' said Villaret in a hoarse voice, immediately clearing his throat to find a more fluid tone. 'But don't turn on the ceiling light, my light eyes can't stand it. I hope you have a valid reason for waking me up in the middle of the night,' he teased.

'Yes, of course. I am sorry to disturb you at this time of night, but something very serious has just happened.'

'Tell me more...' he stammered, worried.

Borgia got straight to the point.

'... the Virgin of Philerme has just been stolen!'

'What... what are you saying? Stolen? If this is a joke, it's in very bad taste, Giacomo,' replied the Grand Master in a grumbling voice, rising abruptly from his chair.

'My informant is not the kind of person to make this kind of joke in the middle of the night. And I'm even less so.'

'It is incomprehensible. I thought she was under guard at the museum in Cetinje?'

'Yes, that's right, but it had just been quietly transferred back to the Monastery. A report was to be made shortly on all the relics there. She was only supposed to stay there for a few days. Someone took advantage of this. Someone who seemed to be well informed...'

It was a real burden that fell on the shoulders of the Grand Chancellor.

'But who would want to own such an icon? A collector? A worshipper? '

'This may be the case. But paradoxically the parcel of the Holy Cross and the relic of the hand of St. John the Baptist remained in place. The thief seemed only interested in the painting.'

'It is the Order's most precious possession. This relic belongs to the original Order, which belongs to us, and which came into being over nine centuries ago. Is there anyone who seeks to harm us and destabilize us? Or perhaps they will demand a ransom in exchange. A blackmailer? This icon of Byzantine origin was found by the Order of St. John of Jerusalem on the island of Rhodes where they settled with the Templars following their escape from the Holy Land and the Battle of St. John the Acre in 1291, defeated by the Mamluk Sultan Al-Ashraf. According to the Rhodians, who worshipped her even before the arrival of the

Knights, the Madonna of Philerme, named after the sanctuary on Mount Phileremos in Rhodes, was painted by the hand of Saint Luke and came to the island from Jerusalem more than four hundred years earlier. From then on, the icon never ceased to survive, without respite, the numerous wars and sieges of the different cities of the Order, exiles, revolutions or fires.'

'I know his story. But it could be anyone. Several other orders in the world also claim to be direct descendants of the Hospitallers of Jerusalem. I would see it as an act on their part rather than a blackmailer or Sunday thief. Who else would be interested in such a relic?'

The Grand Master was stunned. He fell back in his chair, totally distraught.

'My God. What can we do?'

'Conducting our own investigation and recovering what is ours at all costs. '

'But how are we going to do it? There is no one here who can do it. I don't have the strength anymore.'

'Think again. There are a few knights who are ready to fight like in the old days and who only need a little action to match their prestigious ancestors. A matter of honor and pride. But we cannot do it without the support of the Holy See. Their networks and resources are much more powerful and important than ours.'

'You are right. We must not lament our fate and act as quickly as possible. But we must try to keep the news to a minimum. Only the members of our Sovereign Council and the knights you are going to include in your team should know about it, as well as the Holy See. Make sure that there is no leakage from the Monastery of Cetinje. We will send our copy there tomorrow. You have my consent for all decisions and methods of action that will enable you to carry out your mission. We will draw on the Order's special funds. I will take care of erasing all traces of future expenses. I will give you a first envelope to meet the first costs.'

'I'm going to tell the people involved right away and then I'll be off to the Vatican and talk to the Cardinal Patronus[1], His Eminence Reverend Alfredo Coppuci, and the Prefect of the

Gendarmerie Luca Armendi. The latter is in touch with the secret services and could give us some interesting information. You never know. This must not be the work of an unbalanced person, but rather of a disciplined organization with a very specific goal. And that's what we have to find out.'

'Do what you have to do and bring me back our Philerma Virgin as soon as possible. I could not live long with the idea of her wandering in the wilderness. She is so fragile and has already suffered so much.'

'We'll hunt down the thieves' day and night to the end of the world if we have to, but we'll find it. I give you my word.'

Borgia took the time to have breakfast in the palace kitchens, collected the envelope full of euros and dollars that the Grand Master had given him, and left at about six o'clock. The day was dawning. A busy day lay ahead.

As agreed earlier, he set up his battle plan. To begin, he called each of the three future members of his elite knight unit. The game would not be easy, but it did not matter. They knew the rules.

They belonged to the Order of Malta.

An organization that had remained faithful to its founding principles for almost a thousand years. Even if it had become totally pacified in the last few decades and was now only active in humanitarian activities, which had allowed the order to survive since its creation compared to all the other organizations with a purely military vocation that were dissolved when their objectives were achieved, The turn of events that occurred tonight would force its members to reconsider their vision and principles, which was not to the displeasure of some, thus regaining their two primary functions dear to their motto 'Tuitio Fidei et Obsequium Pauperum'[2].

---

1. *Représentant du Pape auprès de l'Ordre de Malte.*
2. *'Défense de la foi et assistance aux pauvres'*

Borgia knew their answer before he even called them. All three were unstoppably discreet and faithful. Two Knights of Grace and Devotion in Obedience who were not religious and therefore did not take the three evangelical vows of obedience, chastity and poverty as did the Professed Knights, but who nevertheless formulated vows committing themselves to live the Christian and moral precepts of the order. And a Lady of Grace and Devotion, who did not take any religious vows, but who also committed herself to the principles of the church and the order.

All three would accompany him in his quest for justice. The honor of the Order had been sullied and put to the test. This affront had to be properly cleansed.

They were dynamic people who fitted in very well and whose loyalty and bravery he had already been able to assess during a mission of much lesser importance, but representative of their commitment and devotion to the order. Both men were in their late fifties. The woman would soon be in her thirties. But her belonging to one of the most illustrious and ancient families of the organization, which had produced two Grand Masters and a number of Professed Knights, gave her ipso facto a high title and rank within the brotherhood despite her youth. A sort of eternal recognition.

Even though the current members, from knights to volunteers, came from all walks of life and nationalities, the order still retained its old noble values and was extremely attached to its traditions. And the Virgin of Philerme was an integral part of these traditions.

3

Marimont-lès-Bénestroff, Moselle
Friday 10 May 2014, 1pm

The dreadful weather that had been raging throughout France since the official start of spring reached its peak at the end of the week. Everywhere rivers, ponds and streams were overflowing, flooding fields and threatening homes. As much rain had fallen in the last three days as had fallen all season, according to meteorologists' statistics.

'We picked the right weekend to go there. It's like the middle of the night,' grumbled Cyril, who was struggling to keep the car on the road with each gust of wind. 'Typical Scottish weather...'

The clouds were so low that they were almost like fog, greatly reducing visibility.

'In the end, no matter how expensive the car, the wipers don't work much better on your BMW than on my old Clio,' said his companion.

Cyril gave a grunt in response.

They had met on the university benches and had been living together for a year. Five years younger than him, of average height and slender build, her long natural blonde hair surrounded a radiant face enhanced by magnificent blue-grey eyes. She had the same passion for medieval history and archaeology and came from a very old family in Périgord whose first recorded ancestors date back to the 11th century.

In the back of the car, Gilles, a childhood friend of Cyril's, was a little stressed and as focused on the road as if he were driving. The quietness in the compartment was suddenly interrupted by Gilles' bellowing.

'Stoooop! It was there on the right!'

Cyril, surprised, instinctively slammed on the brakes.

On the wet road, the car skidded off the pavement into the left lane, eventually coming to rest perpendicular to the way at the lowest point where the road formed a bowl. The hazard warning lights came on automatically after the sudden braking. The three passengers were stunned and took a few seconds to recover.

'But you're completely insane for shouting like that! You nearly killed us,' Natasha said, still trembling, turning back to Gilles.

'Well, I was just saying that we should have turned, nothing more,' he replied sheepishly. 'I never said to slam on the brakes.'

When she turned to see Cyril's reaction, she saw his eyes widen. The fear was written all over his face.

'Oh shit... he said.'

She followed his gaze and saw two large headlights appear from what seemed to be a truck and approaching them at high speed. She couldn't help but scream back.

'Oh, God, no!'

The truck was getting dangerously close without moderating its speed. The driver did not seem to see the car in the way, and for good reason, he was concentrating on writing a message on his mobile phone. The impact between the two vehicles was only a matter of seconds. Despite the torrential rain, the outline of the vehicle was becoming increasingly clear. Gilles stammered, frightened:

'It's a tanker! Do something, Cyril, I beg you, get us out of here, he shouted.'

Only a few dozen meters more and the truck would hit them head-on. The impact would be terrible. At the speed the driver was going, it would only take him a handful of seconds to swallow that distance. But Cyril did not panic like his comrades.

He started up again, put the car in reverse and put his foot down as hard as he could on the accelerator pedal. The car took a fraction of a second to react, the rear wheels skidding on the wet road, then jumped and slid into the ditch. The truck passed them in a flash, missing the back of the car by a few centimeters.

The accident was narrowly avoided.

His driver did not even notice the scene, still more preoccupied with his motive than with what was happening on the road. When he looked up to check that his vehicle had not deviated from the straight and narrow road, he was already too late and did not even see the car deliberately drive into the ditch to avoid him. His left-hand mirror and the window were unusable, too fogged up. The clouds of water generated by the wheels on the wet road prevented any rearward visibility. So he continued on his way as if nothing had happened.

In the car, hysteria was at its peak. In the midst of the stress, Natasha let out a few sobs with her hands over her face. Cyril reassured her and soothed her as best he could. The dog, frightened by the brutal maneuver, was howling to death.

'Okay, let's calm down. We come to our senses. Let's take a deep breath. Let's pretend nothing happened,' sighed the young man, who pressed the button to turn off the engine while leaving the hazard lights on.

'OK, said the other two in sync.'

The three of them found it difficult to extricate themselves from the vehicle as the ditch was so deep and raised the front end. The trunk was inaccessible from the outside, so they folded down the rear seats to get the dog out and retrieve their things. As soon as he got out, the faithful companion sped across the field like a madman without stopping. No matter how much Cyril yelled and called him, the Golden Retriever did not react and continued his stampede. After a few minutes, he disappeared into the forest.

'Oh dear... he must be terrified, poor fellow.'

'Don't worry, he'll be back,' Natasha said calmly.

The Mystery of the Lost Crypt

'I hope the village is not too far away. I'll call a garage tomorrow to come and get it out. I hope the side-skirt isn't too badly damaged.'

'In any case, I have to admit Cyril that it starts at the quarter turn, unlike mine,' she acknowledged.

'There has to be an explanation for the big difference in price,' he replied with a touch of mockery in his turn.

'And you, Gilles, don't ever do that again,' she threatened, glaring at him.

'But what? I just said turn left, now stop...'

'It's okay, it's okay, stop the spat. I told you before that we wouldn't talk about it anymore. '

They returned to the junction they were supposed to have taken before their unfortunate incident. The sign indicated the location of the village a little less than two miles away. But in the pouring rain, it seemed to be on the other side of the world.

After three small bends, the road passed into the forest. The trio entered it, still in single file, with their heads down to avoid the wind and the drops whipping their faces. The branches of the oaks covered the entire top of the road, forming a natural canopy. But this green roof was not waterproof and made the place even darker. From time to time, Cyril called out his dog's name, hoping that it would obey his call. But without success.

'It's like November,' said Gilles to break the ice a little.

But all he got in return was a small 'yes'. The resentment seemed to be still there.

The trees were oozing monstrous drops of water that came crashing down on the heads and shoulders of the two young men who prayed each time that it would be the last. Gilles raised his head to admire this green and shimmering nature and caught one in his right eye, disabling him for a short time. He couldn't help but let out an expletive of which he had the secret.

As for Natasha, she had been a little more far-sighted in bringing her pocket umbrella. She tried several times to give it to her companion, but the latter, out of self-respect for his former job as a commando as well as out of purely male and macho

The Mystery of the Lost Crypt

solidarity with his friend, declined the offer, which she openly enjoyed.

'Hey, it's wet in the rain, don't you think, boys?' she said, a little mockingly.

But she got no answers. Their humor seemed surprisingly extinct.

Halfway through the short passage in the forest, they heard the roar of an engine. Gilles, who was walking last, turned around to look at the road. He saw a car approaching at a slow pace. He instinctively held out his arm, sticking out his thumb like a hitchhiker, and signaled with his other arm to slow down. But rather than stop, the car accelerated and did nothing to avoid the large puddle that had formed at their level, splashing them from head to toe.

'You bastard!' shouted Gilles, raising his fist.

'Can you confirm that it does get wet in the rain?' Cyril retorted, hilariously, addressing Natasha, who was soaked from head to toe, holding her umbrella turned upside down by the spray and the car's blast.

'Not even funny...'

'I don't think you need your umbrella anymore. '

When they emerged from the forest, they found fields on their right where a property flanked by turrets at its entrance, stood. There were barns attached to it and a pond at the front with wild reeds almost entirely surrounding its circumference.

'Very beautiful house... it even looks like a castle,' remarked Natasha.

'Yes, it looks like it, but the one we're looking for doesn't exist anymore and it's supposed to be at the top of this hill,' he said, pointing to it on his left. 'They probably used the stones to rebuild this mansion. That was extremely common in those days. Many medieval castles were reduced to mere quarries and were dismantled in order to recover the materials for new constructions, of course to keep costs down and to facilitate their transport. The original castle in this hamlet must have suffered the same fate.'

They walked another hundred meters or so and came to a junction of two roads. The village church stood straight ahead of them, slightly higher than the road.

'Do you remember the address?'

'No, but in a village of fifty inhabitants and less than fifteen houses, one will quickly find it. The owner of the gite had told me that it was located at the exit of the village. And given the poor internet reception, it will be quicker than searching on Google Maps.'

'Beautiful and big church for such a small village,' said a surprised Natasha.

'I learned that about two thousand people lived here when the medieval castle was still standing. There must not have been the forest that there is today.'

'Oh, that much! It doesn't look like it.'

'Well, there are two main routes,' Gilles continued, anxious to get dry as quickly as possible. 'So there are still three possibilities, I suggest we do them in order.'

'On the right, you can see the village sign crossed out, so it's already the end on this side. You can go and see over there if the house is the B&B you're looking for,' Cyril pointed at him. 'We're waiting for you, it's not worth it to go all the way...'

Gilles obeyed without saying a word. He had understood that this was not the time for him to engage in any kind of power struggle or even to upset them, especially if this would allow him to be forgiven in their eyes. The two lovers watched him leave, amused and happy to see that he complied without flinching. But he soon returned. They had to continue their wandering. They went on across the road, passing between the church and what looked like the village square with three large trees in the middle surrounding a table and two benches. As they walked along the square, Cyril's gaze, turning left and right to discover the surroundings, came to rest before a house where he recognized the car that had showered them in the forest. At the same time a shadow appeared behind the curtain of a bay window.

'Look, someone is watching us,' he said.

The Mystery of the Lost Crypt

'I'd go and ring the bell to smash that bastard's face in,' replied Gilles.

'If I were a guy, I would do the same,' the young woman added.

'Let's avoid being too conspicuous. Every village has its idiot. We've probably had the honor of meeting him...'

They continued on their way and soon found themselves at the end of the village where two houses faced each other on either side of the road and a farmhouse a hundred meters in front of them. The gite was on their right. The characteristic 'Gîtes de France' sign stood at the entrance to the property under a huge chestnut tree.

They had finally arrived. Soaked to the skin, but happy to be safe and sound. At the same time, the sky decided to calm down.

Cyril had been worried about his dog ever since he fled and ran wild through fields and forests. He had not obeyed any of his calls.

'He'll come back,' said Natasha, who felt he was down. 'Give him time to calm down. He was traumatized by what happened in the car. We'll keep looking for him tomorrow.'

The Mystery of the Lost Crypt

4

Vatican City, Rome
Friday 14 June 2013, 6am

Giacomo Borgia's limousine pulled up in front of the Porte Sainte-Anne. Usually the busiest of all the entrances, it was still deserted at this hour. Two Swiss Guards in blue uniforms and 'Alpine' berets opened the two doors of the large iron gate. The car moved slowly through the city under the benevolent gaze of the two eagles which stood on the tops of the pillars on either side of the portico. On their right, at the bottom of the steps leading to the main door of the Church of St Anne of the Palestinians, Luca Armendi, the prefect of the Vatican gendarmerie, was stoically waiting for them. He waved his hand to signal the driver to stop, closed his umbrella and climbed into the back of the vehicle. A crisp, spruce-scented air accompanied him.

'My morning greetings Excellency,' he said, turning his head to the left. 'Bad weather these days. But I'm not going to complain about it. It scares away the tourists and lightens our surveillance duties!'

'Yes, as you say, bad weather...' replied the Grand Chancellor, still lost in thought.

'I have already notified His Eminence Reverend Alfredo Coppuci, as you suggested. He will join us directly at the operational command center.'

'Good. Apart from the two of you and of course His Holiness the Pope if you deem it necessary, our Grand Master does not wish this information to be revealed to anyone else. And even less that it be broadcast by the press or radio. It is still too early. Can we count on your discretion?'

'You can, of course.'

The car turned off into Via Del Pellegrino immediately after the Church of St. Anne and then, still on its right, passed the headquarters of the Osservatore Romano, the daily newspaper published by the Vatican's official information service since 1861, and finally the Gendarmerie Barracks. Armendi accompanied Borgia to the porch of the church of San Pellegrino, which was used by the fire brigade and gendarmes.

He looked at his watch.

'There will be a very short service in less than a quarter of an hour, Your Excellency. I propose that you take part in it. '

'A very good idea. Let us first ask our Lord to give us the necessary strength to face this ignominy that has just struck the Order.'

When mass was over, they both went to the barracks opposite the church. The chief of the gendarmerie opened the lift door and let Borgia in first.

'Couldn't we have taken the stairs? I don't mind a little morning exercise. I do so little.'

'There is no staircase where we go...'

Armendi placed his thumb on the multimodal biometric reader combining finger vein recognition and fingerprinting, then brought his face to the face of the iris scanner.

'You do not skimp on security issues. If everyone applied this strategy, we wouldn't have a problem now.'

'Two years ago, Spanish researchers succeeded in recreating an accurate image of an iris in just a few minutes, thereby trapping VeriEye, one of the most sophisticated biometric verifiers in existence today.'

'But I had always read that it was the most efficient technology?'

'Don't worry. For the time being, it still remains so. Because to be able to recreate this artificial iris, you still need to have the source database. This will inevitably happen one day. At the same time, for even greater security, we have coupled three different technologies.'

'Do many of you have access?'

'No, there are only five of us. Myself, my Director General Vincenzo Giordano, the Cardinalis Patronus Alfredo Coppuci, Colonel Herman Müller, who commands the Pontifical Swiss Guard, and the Secretary of State Mgr. Alessandro Bianchi.'

The authentication of the first two readers allowed him to move on to the third and enter the password while protecting the keyboard with his hand. A green light confirmed the accuracy of the last security level, clearing the way to the basement. The lift took only five seconds to descend. The door opened and faced a new armored code door.

'A real fortress! Even the Pentagon's security would blush...'

'Hence its appropriate nickname the 'Bunker'.'

Buried six meters below ground, the operational command center, with a total surface area of 1,600 square meters, included a large workroom equipped with state-of-the-art, secure and tamper-proof communications and computer equipment. The prefect's office, known as the 'Aquarium', was adjacent to this room and separated by a large bulletproof and blast-proof glass window and essentially comprised the armory. The rest of the area was used as living quarters with bedrooms, kitchens, shower rooms and fitness rooms, allowing about 30 people to live there for several months in case of emergency. The pontiff of course had a small personal suite.

Three gendarmerie officers and a Swiss guard were present on arrival and working at their respective posts.

'Anything you see or hear here is highly confidential. I also rely on your discretion...'

'In return, you can also count on mine. But how did you build all this space?'

The Mystery of the Lost Crypt

'Nothing could be easier. We used the existing space! A crypt discovered by chance when a wall of the barracks' cellar collapsed following successive weakening due to earthquakes and repair work over the centuries. To prevent the whole building from collapsing and to make use of all the newly discovered space, the foundations were seriously consolidated and 'The Bunker' was built and extended a little further.'

'When?'

'It was built a dozen years ago for the 2000 Jubilee. It was enlarged and further modernized following the attacks on the twin towers in New York.'

The great Commander was amazed by so much technology, but more importantly, he had no idea that the Vatican could set up such a device.

'We are in direct contact with the Italian and French intelligence services and with Interpol,' the prefect said. 'Two specialized units were created in 2008. The rapid intervention group, the GIR, specialized in anti-terrorism, as well as a mine-clearing unit.'

'Isn't that a bit disproportionate?'

'The resurgence of inter-religious tensions as well as the conflicts in Africa and the East over the last two decades left us no choice. There were significant risks of reprisals from certain radical fundamentalist communities. Our Holiness receives dozens of death threats every week. Nothing could be overlooked. The past events were the perfect opportunity to create this operational center. The results are rather flattering, even if we would obviously prefer to need it as little as possible.'

The proof is that this special unit has already uncovered various cases such as the Vatican leaks. It was in May 2012, the famous "Vatileaks", which led to the arrest of the personal butler of Pope Benedict XVI or the ongoing investigation into the embezzlement of funds from the Vatican bank by a cardinal.

'I am delighted with your excellent results because, as I told you on the phone this morning, we will need your services very much to solve our case.'

'It should have been done much longer ago. But then, after all, both I and my predecessors are simply carrying out the orders of successive pontiffs.'

At the same time, they were joined by Alfredo Coppuci, the Cardinalis Patronus. He knew nothing yet. The truth was just as terrible for him to hear. But once he had digested his disappointment, he quickly temporized.

'After all, there is no need to worry! This icon is the primary symbol of the order, but it does not change its foundations or its history. And above all the recognition by Pope John XXIII of the current Constitutional Charter. It is not based on the safeguarding of any painting or effigy.'

'Not quite...'

'What do you mean by that?' asked Coppuci.

'After what has just happened, I cannot keep the secret any longer...'

The two men were hanging on his every word, impatient for him to reveal the contents of his secret.

'Two of our professed Knights, eminent historians, had been working for several years on a very special subject. A manuscript dating from the very beginning of the thirteenth century had been found on the site of the church of Saint-Marie-Du Temple, in the former enclosure of the Templars in Paris, the headquarters of the Order in France and above all of their bank.'

'The Maison du Temple was completely destroyed by Napoleon Bonaparte around 1810. Where could such a document have been discovered?'

'When the asphalt of the Rue Perrée was repaved, the foundations of the church, which were still present under the road, were uncovered and excavated for several weeks. To everyone's surprise, a crypt was also discovered there. A passageway was finally opened in one of the surrounding buildings. It was there that this book was taken from one of the Templar tombs. The epitaph mentioned that he was one of the few survivors who fled when his family was arrested by the soldiers of Philip IV the Fair on Friday, October 13, 1307. This would corroborate with certain passages describing the years of imprisonment and torture of the arrested Templars, including the Grand Master Jacques de Molay.'

'What is in this book?'

'This book, partly encrypted, was a kind of biography of the last two decades of the Templar order. From the defeat at Acre in 1291 to its dissolution in 1312. But only a few snippets of this book could be decoded. The encryption system used was extremely complex, surely one of the most ingenious ever used, and only the Templars had the secret. It seemed to be coupled with one or more other codices in order to have the full text. Other books' to be discovered of course...'

'And why are you talking about the book in the past tense?'

'Because the book mysteriously disappeared six months ago!'

'But what does this have to do with the icon?'

'We didn't manage to find out, but the book mentioned it. We were just about to study it when someone seems to have beaten us to it and taken advantage of a very temporary relaxing of the security system to steal it.'

'I see. So it could have been the same people who stole the book and the painting of the Virgin...' Coppuci said worriedly.

'Let's say the same sponsor for sure!'

'If this book is, as one would expect, a biography of the two centuries of the Templars' existence, the end must most probably refer to the continuation or not of the order after its dissolution at the Council of Vienna and the death of the last Master, Jacques de Molay. As well as the fate of all the Order's assets. This is why the King of France wanted to do away with it so much. For the sole reason of seizing their property and preventing them from overshadowing him in the levying of various taxes. And as their usefulness was no longer necessary following their forced departure from the Holy Land, he took advantage of this to put pressure on the Pope.'

'It is well known that all their assets, both the money of the commanderies and the walls themselves, were returned to the

Hospitallers after the dissolution of the Order. What could be left?'

'In France, yes. But the central headquarters of the Order was never in the West, but in Jerusalem, Cyprus or Acre. It was in these successive places that all their goods from pilgrims' donations and treasures of kings from all over Europe were protected. The Templars offered guarantees of security.'

'So it would refer to the Templar treasure?'

'Exactly. The famous treasure of the Templars that has caused so much talk and ink to flow...'

'Pure fantasy of historians and treasure hunters!'

'I don't think so... It is well mentioned in the history books that Philip the Fair had not recovered much.'

'They spent everything on the crusades.'

'Certainly in part. But also helped by the rulers.'

'If I have followed you correctly, this book would tell us the instructions of the last Master of the Order as to the fate of their treasure. Its use, even its location?'

'This is a sensible assumption...'

'Now I understand better how it can make so many other people lust after it. It is indeed more serious than expected. Could the icon provide an answer as to the location of the other books?'

'This is also a possibility.'

'I think it is high time to get to work.'

The Mystery of the Lost Crypt

5

Marimont-lès-Bénestroff
Friday May 10th 2014

The gite that the three academics had booked was made of exposed stone, recently renovated, and covered on one of the side facades by climbing ivy. The house was set in a magnificent wooded park of about fifty acres with a large swimming pool and a jacuzzi. The three friends occupied two of the four available rooms. The weather, which had deteriorated further in recent days, and the alarming weather forecast for the weekend seemed to have discouraged the other tourists who had planned to stay in the other two rooms, preferring to cancel their getaway at the very last moment. So they were alone with the owner couple. In their late sixties and newly retired, they had lived in the village for over forty years. Although their small business had quickly become flourishing, they seemed worn out and weary of constantly looking after their guests and were thinking of selling their residence and moving to the hinterland of the south of France to live out their days in peace to the gentle sound of cicadas. While waiting for a buyer to show up, the pampered tourists were in clover. To sell their business at a good price, they had to maintain these good figures. And to please the public and their regular customers, they had to continue to put on a show.

After relaxing in the bubbling pot and cooling off in the outdoor pool, the trio sat down in front of an open fire where a rabbit stew with white wine and spätzle, a traditional Alsatian pasta, awaited them.

'A real treat. Well done to the cook,' said Gilles as he poured himself a second plate of his own.

'Well, you've got a nice fork,' joked Cyril. 'Better to have you in a photo than in a boarding school...'

They finished their dinner with a mirabelle plum tart and a little digestive for the bravest, homemade Williams pear schnapps, and spent the rest of the evening, slumped in the living room sofas, rehashing the world while warming their rather tired carcasses.

'And what have you come for in the region? As far as I know, there's not much to occupy the evenings of three young people from the city here. Unless there's a rave party in a nearby field?'

'Not at all. We don't go in for this kind of celebration. In fact, I'm preparing a thesis on the disappeared castles of the region and the consequences on the villages or estates attached to them. And this castle mound would be one of them.'

'Oh yes, that, to be part of it, she is indeed part of it. Much to our chagrin.'

'Why is that?' asked Natacha, who was as surprised as her companions at the answer given.

'Because historical monuments impose drastic and, it has to be said, totally crazy standards on us.'

'Just like everywhere else as soon as a place is classified as a historical monument.'

'Let's talk about the historical monuments. I went up there once, many years ago, and apart from a low wall two stones high, there was nothing visible. And that was already thirty years ago. So imagine since then... There's nothing very historic up there. Or maybe it should be reclassified as prehistoric...'

'Yes, seen like that. But we'll see what happens tomorrow.'

'At least you can visit the church. The present building is said to date from the seventeenth century, but its altar is much older, dating from the end of the first millennium. The castle opposite the hill is also said to be over two hundred and fifty years old.'

The Mystery of the Lost Crypt

'You mean the manor house with the little towers near the forest?'

'Yes. It is called 'the castle'. It was probably built from the old one. To be sure, ask the owners. Although, I don't think they're here at the moment. They are from Paris and spend more time there than here.'

Her husband confirmed this with a nod of his head.

'And how did they end up here?'

'Oh, that's a long story. I'll tell you tomorrow if you like. But one thing's for sure, they've got old records. They'll probably let you see them if you ask. They are very friendly.'

'That would be very interesting indeed...'

'And maybe you'll find some clues to the famous underground,' she whispered.

'What underground?'

'The one that runs from the bowels of the castle to, they say, the entrance to a village a few miles from here. And the treasure it would contain,' she giggled nervously.

The young man's eyes opened like a child discovering his Christmas present.

'Nonsense! Stop this nonsense! There never was an underground passage, let alone your treasure, otherwise they would have been discovered long ago,' her husband grumbled.

'And what do you know? This is not nonsense...'

'But of course it is.'

The tone rose to a crescendo between the husband and wife, but deflate like a soufflé when they realized the discomfort caused and the embarrassed look on their guest's faces.

Tiredness and the gentle warmth of the hearth had got the better of the other two, who had been dozing in their armchairs for quite a while and had therefore avoided the fight.

'Well, I've heard enough, I'll leave you with the matron. Have a good time, said the owner of the place, getting up from his brown leather chair.'

'Your husband doesn't seem to share your opinion...'

'Don't mind him. He's a grumpy...'

Cyril remained pensive, staring at the wisps of flame escaping through the vent. He was already imagining himself discovering this tunnel and the famous treasure the manageress spoke of.

'And what kind of treasure would there be?' he continued, wanting to know more about this local legend.

'According to what has been said for ages, it is a game of bowling pins.'

'A what?'

'Bowling pins made of gold.'

'This is not a common type of treasure. I would even say very original. And where would it come from?'

'I have no idea. But it must date from the Middle Ages, as the main castle has been destroyed for a long time now. But as I said, it's only a legend. As much as the existence of an underground is quite plausible, there are some in almost every castle, I have more doubts about this mysterious treasure, the woman smiled. But legends keep dreams and hope alive, that's all that matters.'

Lost in his thoughts, Cyril immediately recalled his lessons on the Middle Ages given by Professor Visconti in the second part of the program. And in particular the one about the underground.

There is not a castle that does not have its own underground passageway, most often of disproportionate length and whose enigmatic entrances have been forgotten by everyone for ages. All these underground passages, which are attached to numerous monuments and ancient sites, are often the subject of ramblings and extravagances in the collective imagination and feature in legends and oral rumors [...].

He couldn't help but make the connection with what the landlady had just said. It was almost word for word his words. But he had also learned that these legends always had some truth in them.

But there is never smoke without fire. Indeed, many places such as castles, abbeys, churches, strongholds, but also medieval towns or villages, had tunnels or galleries for various purposes. Underground refuges, escape tunnels, others for military defensive purposes only, networks of cellars on several levels, etc... But it should be noted that of all these uses, only a few had the sole purpose of escape following a siege. And none of the legendary underground tunnels measuring several kilometers and linking two castles, for example, has ever been discovered. So you might as well get the idea out of your head that you will one day come across a fabulous discovery of this kind. And if that were to be the case, I would validate your diploma on the spot [...]

It was one o'clock in the morning. The landlady had gone to bed, leaving her three young guests alone in the living room. Cyril couldn't help but dream about what he had heard tonight. Perhaps you will find some clues to the famous underground [...] And to the treasure it might contain... He thought of the immediate repercussions of such discoveries. In his thesis, it would certainly be of the greatest effect.

The last log was finishing burning. His eyelids were getting heavier and heavier and the struggle to stay awake was becoming difficult. He decided to wake his two acolytes and succeeded, not without difficulty, in sending them to their beds.

The Mystery of the Lost Crypt

6

Hinterland of Nice
Friday June 14th 2013, 2pm

Comfortably seated in his office chair, which he had tipped backwards, the man had been tapping on his touchscreen tablet for two hours, without any specific goal, without really paying attention to what he was looking for. Simply to kill time. He kept looking at his watch and seemed impatient.

Suddenly a thunderous melody, an extract from Carmina Burana, 'O Fortuna', woke him up from his lethargy. He reached for his mobile phone and immediately recognized the number on the screen.

His long sit up was finally rewarded.

He had been waiting for that phone call for almost a month. Ever since they had planned the operation down to the last detail. In spite of his legitimate anxiety, he did not stifle his pleasure at listening for a few more seconds to the melody he loved so much, whose rapid rhythm and volume were perfectly suited to the situation.

This call, at this very hour, must have meant that everything had gone smoothly and that the caller, with the coveted object, was now halfway along a motorway service area somewhere in Italy.

Eventually he picked up the phone. A strong Slavic accent was heard.

'I've got it. I'll be at your house in less than five hours.'
'Good. Don't take any unnecessary risks. We've been waiting for so long to get it surely we can wait another hour,' he gloated.
'Don't be afraid.'

As soon as he hung up, he dialed another number. This time the call remained in French territory.

The new person immediately picked up the phone.

'That's it, we've got it!'
'What? Do you have it in your possession? Thank God. Can you see it? What's it like? I can't wait to see it with my own eyes.'
'Almost. He is still on his way. It's only a matter of hours now. I'll have it by the time you get here.'
'It's wonderful. I jump on the first plane.'

A Mercedes was heading west into Italian territory.

Ivica Godic, of Montenegrin origin, had just spent a sleepless night and was beginning to feel tired. But he had to keep going. The abnormal overdose of caffeine should do the trick. Once the parcel had been delivered, he would have the luxury of sleeping as much as he wished. And given the substantial bonus promised on delivery, he could even afford to take a few weeks' holiday with the hundred thousand euros he would receive. He had already received forty thousand euros the previous year for all the costs that the operation would generate, but above all as a down payment for the work to be done. A sort of fixed-term employment contract for eighteen months. This was undoubtedly his most profitable mission, given the little effort and risk involved. It was child's play.

He had already travelled more than a thousand kilometers. He still had four hundred and fifty to go. He had set off immediately, swapping his van for a German car, which was more spacious and comfortable for such a long distance, so as to leave no trace in case the monastery guards had spotted the vehicle. He had driven along the Adriatic coast from Dubrovnik to Trieste via Split and

The Mystery of the Lost Crypt

Zadar and then off the coast of Venice before heading inland. He had stopped at a motorway service area near Verona to have another cup of coffee, but above all to telephone his short-lived but generous employer, as he had instructed.

The night had been less eventful than he had feared. A few cameras outside were quickly neutralized thanks to his laptop, two guards whose routine rounds he knew and very rudimentary alarm systems that were easy to bypass. Six months of preparation since the last ceremony where he had already been able to identify and develop his modus operandi. He was still working alone. He had noticed that all the detection systems had not been put back in place for the three days the Monastery hosted the relic within its walls. In short, it was child's play for this experienced thief. In a little less than half an hour, everything had been secured. All he had to do was leave his van in the forest where he had parked the Mercedes that was waiting for him on his long journey.

It passed Brescia, Genoa and then the tunnel marking the French-Italian border between Ventimiglia and Menton. But at the exit, a small surprise awaited motorists and other truckers. The French and Italian mobile customs patrol, nearly a hundred agents in total, were mobilized there and carried out unannounced checks. It was a crackdown operation. This little setback did not worry him. He had planned everything, even this possibility. His scenario was well oiled.

'Good morning, sir, customs control. Do you have anything to declare?' engaging conversation in Italian.

'Hello, officer. No, absolutely nothing.'

'May I see your papers and those of the vehicle. Where are you going?'

'On holiday for a few days with my brother.'

'And where does he live?'

'In Nice.'

'And where are you from?'

'From Dubrovnik.'

The customs officer scanned the interior of the car. He looked puzzled. He made his decision after a few seconds of reflection and a final look at Ivica. His nervousness did not go unnoticed. These agents had an excellent sense of observation.

'I'm going to ask you to follow my colleague,' he said abruptly, gesturing to another man a little further away.

The customs officers had created a very specific codification. Each sign had a precise meaning, allowing the colleagues in charge of the search to focus their research on a specific goal.

'But why?' replied Ivica, his voice raised.

'Nothing. A simple check. Relax, because you have nothing to be ashamed of. Just a routine check...'

Luck, which had been on Ivica's side until then, seemed to be failing him. He was asked to park in the car park provided for this purpose. Ivica lost his temper. Droplets of water beaded on his forehead, which he immediately wiped off with his sleeve in an attempt not to let anything show.

Come on, take it easy. There's nothing to worry about. They don't know anything about it and there's about as much chance of an agent recognizing the painting as there is of winning the lottery. He's looking more for drugs or counterfeit, he thought inwardly, to reassure himself.

The second customs officer, a Frenchman, asked him to open the trunk. One of his colleagues joined him with a German shepherd who jumped into the trunk, sniffing frantically in every nook and cranny, strongly encouraged by his master.

'Come on, go fetch Flica, fetch!'

But the animal did not seem to be attracted by any particular smell. He did the same in the car's interior and then around the outside, but with no further results.

'Open your travel bag and take out your belongings one by one, the customs officer ordered sharply.'

The Montenegrin complied without flinching. This was not the time to react. In other circumstances, he would not have allowed anyone to speak to him in this way. But here he had to swallow his ego. He took out the icon, wrapped in Kraft paper and tightly tied.

'What is it?'

'A gift. A painting by an artist from my country. An icon of the Virgin Mary.'

He carefully untied the cord and peeled off the two taped flaps, then took it out to show her.

'Did you buy it in an art gallery? Do you have an invoice?'

'No. It was painted by a friend.'

The simplicity of the picture did not seem to interest the agent much.

Quite unfortunately.

'Special. I don't really like anything to do with religion,' he replied dismissively.

Ivica jumped into the breach to regain his composure. After all, if the customs officer didn't care about the painting, he had no reason to feel uncomfortable.

'Yes, as you say. I don't really like it either, but my sister-in-law loves it. To each his own.'

The customs officer finished his search and found that there was nothing to get his teeth into. He finally let him go. Ivica started up again with a great 'wow' of relief and continued his escapade.

He arrived in Nice at around nine o'clock and went straight to the agreed location, a large disused warehouse on the outskirts of the city, to deliver the package.

An old rusty door was ajar.

He rushed in.

Inside, everything was empty. Thousands of square meters that had been teeming with life ten years ago were now emptied of all their substance. Only the oldest workers could still remember the original layout.

A man was already waiting for him there.

Standing in front of his car, he must have entered through one of the large side doors. Ivica could not see his face. He was hooded, as he had been every time they had met before. Not once had he seen his face. But he recognized him by his deep voice. He could have identified this characteristic tone among a thousand, in any circumstance.

'Do you have the icon?' said the man dryly.
'Do you have the money?'
'Of course. Show it first.'

Ivica took the painting out of his briefcase and handed it to him.

The man took out a knife, cut the string and then frantically tore the wrapper.

'How can anyone love this horror!'

Ivica looked at him, speechless.

'You spent so much money to end up saying that it's a horror? I expected anything but that. I must say that I don't understand anything anymore. But after all, that's your business, not mine. Where is the rest of my reward?'

'Here's your fee,' he said, handing him an envelope.

Ivica took it and opened it to see what was inside. His due was there. He could finally enjoy some good weather. He planned to stay in Nice for a few days, enjoy the unseasonably warm sunshine and, if he felt like it, have a dip in the sea. Then he would go back to his country and wait for the next mission which, he hoped, would bring him as much money.

Just as he was about to turn to leave, he noticed an insignia on the shirt of his interlocutor, right above his heart. He thought he saw a yellow cross.

'What's that crest? I've seen it somewhere before.'

The man was embarrassed by the question.

'Nothing at all,' he said, replacing his overcoat.

'I'll leave you to it. It was a real pleasure to work for you. And please don't hesitate to call on me again if you ever have a similar job. You know how to reach me.'

'I've got it,' the stranger replied dryly.

When Ivica turned his back to leave the building the way he had come in, the hooded man put his hand in his right pocket and pulled out a Beretta with a silencer.

But just as he was about to raise his arm and point it at Ivica, a voice was heard at the far end of the hangar.

'What are you doing here? This is private. You have no right to be here,' shouted a security guard escorted by a Rottweiler.

Ivica did not look back and disappeared. The masked man put his pistol away, got into his car and left the scene as well. There was no point in taking unnecessary risks. And even less bloodshed in the middle of town. He would have many more opportunities to achieve his ends.

Ivica, on his way back to his room after a late swim in the hotel pool, got a call on his phone. To his surprise, it was his generous employer again. The telephone conversation was brief. He seemed to want to give him a new assignment. He was getting tired, but given the remuneration offered, he could not refuse.

The first one was already unexpected, a second one as well paid would allow him and his family to be free of need for a while.

He had arranged to meet him in a car park along the Moyenne Corniche road in the hills above Nice. A small, well-protected and isolated area in the mountains, away from prying eyes. Like the last time.

The Mystery of the Lost Crypt

7

Marimont-lès-Bénestroff
Saturday May 11th 2014

Men and equipment were loaded into the three helicopters that took off from the French aircraft carrier anchored off the Somali coast.

'Fifteen minutes before the drop zone,' said one of the two pilots on the microphone.

The twelve members of the Hubert commando checked their equipment one last time. Cyril was pensive. His previous mission in Mali had resulted in one dead and several wounded in their ranks. An ordeal that had left a deep impression on the group. And especially the young man, since the deceased was none other than his roommate. They had learned to deal with these difficult moments during training, but could one really ignore all emotion when it was a close friend? It took a few weeks of enforced rest and sessions with the battalion shrink to get back into the group. Something had changed in him.

'Two minutes...'

They were approaching the area. All the lights on board went out.

The day's mission was not the easiest. A French cargo ship had been boarded a week earlier by Somali pirates and three people, including the captain, were being held hostage in a small fishing village. An exorbitant ransom demand was currently being negotiated with the French authorities for their release, but the government's position in this case remained clear and precise. It would not accept any transfer of funds. The only solution to recover them was to go and exfiltrate them. This task fell de facto to the Commando Hubert, one of the seven commandos of the French Navy and probably the most prestigious of all, specialized in hostage rescue.

'Thirty seconds, get ready!'

The pumas hovered less than ten meters above the perfectly flat ocean surface. There was not a wave to darken the picture. The faint light of the crescent moon reflected off a sea of oil. Ideal conditions for this mission. The commander gave the go-ahead and the twelve men jumped into the void simultaneously. They never returned to the surface. Once underwater, they immediately switched on their handheld underwater scooters, which would pull them to a cove thanks to the machines' GPS, programmed from the positional readings taken by a drone. Evolving in complete darkness, scaring away here and there huge fish as surprised as he was, Cyril felt an apprehension he had never known before. The darkness of the abyss suddenly frightened him. He could make out a figure in front of him, strongly illuminating its surroundings. One detail immediately intrigued him. What turned out to be a man was actually moving underwater without diving equipment. As he got closer, the surprise was total. The skin was lacerated and torn to shreds. Probably one of the Europeans killed by his kidnappers and thrown into the water to make the bodies disappear. But as he passed by, still pulled by his scooter, the dead man's eyes opened and his face lit up.

A vision of horror ran down his spine.

He was looking at Gaëtan, his friend who died in the operation in Mali! It all seemed unreal.

He panicked. He immediately dropped his scooter and lost his regulator. Bubbles escaped from his mouth and he quickly ran out of air. There was no one around to help him. They were already far away. He could only rely on himself. But no matter how hard he tried to reach the surface, he could not. Gaëtan was holding him back and dragging him inexorably towards the depths.

One last bubble and then came the phase of inhaling the water. Then after a few spasms, it was definitely over.

The view became blurred and then the blackout was complete.

Cyril woke up with a start, covered in sweat, struggling to catch his breath.

He looked at his watch. Four o'clock in the morning.

Natasha turned on the reading light on the headboard and reassured him.

'Another nightmare. Always Gaëtan. Like the previous nights. I can't forget him. How long will he haunt me?'

'We'll take care of that when we get back,' said the young woman, stroking his face. 'In the meantime, try to get back to sleep.'

In the early hours of the morning Cyril was the first to wake up, at around nine o'clock, leaving Natacha to enjoy the warmth of the duvet for a few more moments. He had managed to fall back asleep without the slightest nightmare. The disappointment was great when he opened the curtain. The rain had stopped, but the mist had appeared. The castle mound had disappeared under the thick layer of clouds that clung to it like the highest mountain peaks.

'Pfft, what rotten weather!' he muttered.

'What are you saying?' asked Natasha, who hid under her cushion to avoid the sudden brightness.

'I was just saying that it was the perfect day to start our study. At least we won't have any regrets about getting started.'

He barely had time to finish his sentence when she had already fallen back asleep. He got dressed and went downstairs to have breakfast. He knocked as he passed by his friend's door, but no noise disturbed the calm that reigned in the room. So he was even to go alone.

The atmosphere between the two managers did not seem to be good. When he entered the dining room, they were staring at each other. Probably the aftermath of the previous day's heated discussion.

In spite of himself, Cyril had to pay for it.

All he got was a curt "Hello" and an equally cold and distant "Tea or coffee?" The opposite of the charming and welcoming behavior of the day before.

But the young man ignored them and questioned them as if nothing had happened.

'Can we visit the village church?'

'It is locked. Only the mayor and the priest have a set of keys,' said the woman.

'And where do they live?'

'The parish priest looks after several villages in the region, all in the vicinity. It is the community of parishes of Saint Vincent du Haut-Bois. But it would be quicker for you to ask the mayor. He lives at the foot of the hill, after the house that makes the corner at the crossing on the right as you go up. He was recently elected about two months ago.'

'Thank you, I'll check with him.'

'By the way, I'm going to recover your car which is still in the ditch this morning with the help of a neighbor,' says her husband. 'We'll see how the underbody looks. If there's the slightest problem, we'll take it to a garage in the next village.'

'That's very kind of you. I will leave the keys with you before I leave.'

His two companions joined him in dribs and drabs. They looked defeated and walked slowly. They did not seem to be in full capacity to explore the remains and take possession of the place. Cyril couldn't help but chuckle when he saw them.

'Stay here, I won't be long,' he said. 'In any case, given your faces, you won't get very far.'

8

Nice
Saturday June 15th 2013, 4am

Ivica arrived shortly before the scheduled time. He parked at the far end of the car park, away from the other vehicles present. He turned off the ignition and switched off the headlights.

The place was not so deserted after all. Several camper vans, with their flaps up, were parked at the rest area. A mixture of different nationalities crowded together, but fortunately there was no activity at this late hour of the night.

The Croatian chewed his gum frantically and glanced left and right at every suspicious noise. But only a few night birds, rodents and the songs of sleepless cicadas disturbed the peaceful surroundings.

Finally, after a good quarter of an hour of waiting, a car arrived. He called his headlights three times and it pulled up next to the Croatian, after answering the same way, in the opposite direction, so that the driver's side windows could face each other. Ivica immediately lowered his.

'You can't do without me anymore,' the Croatian joked in a low voice. 'How can I help you this time?'

The tinted window of the car that had just parked lowered to half height. He had expected to see a man wearing a balaclava, as he had the day before, and as he had for the two years of collaboration. But it was not to be.

He saw in the half-light of the cabin the face of a man in his forties, square-jawed, with blond hair, but already balding, and menacing blue eyes.

Ivica turned on the light in the ceiling lamp.

'Turn it off now, you idiot! I don't want anyone to notice us. There are more tourists than I thought.'

Ivica immediately noticed that the voice was different from the one he was used to hearing and especially from the one that had left him a message on his mobile the day before. Nothing was going on as usual.

He complied, troubled.

The dark moon, which had been at its height the day before, and the natural wall of bushes behind the two vehicles only accentuated the darkness. Only the buttons and the standby GPS of the two cars gave off a glow that made it possible to distinguish between them.

'Indeed, you are doing a good job. Very good indeed. But my boss never works with the same people twice,' he continued.

'I don't understand. So why bring me here then?' he wondered.

'Just to get it over with.'

Ivica had no time to react. He vaguely distinguished an object coming out of the window opening. A red beam of light glared at him.

He saw nothing else.

The man rolled up his window, got out of his car and, after putting on a pair of gloves, inspected both Ivica's jacket and the passenger compartment where he retrieved the wallet and a couple of other odds and ends. During his thorough search, he was intrigued by a faint beam of light in his face. No sooner did he turn his head away than the line of light disappeared. A few seconds later, the phenomenon happened again. Someone seemed to be watching him. He got out of Ivica's car, picked up his torch and scanned the surrounding bushes. Suddenly he saw a small shadow running into a motor home.

'Hmm, just a little kid,' he grumbled.

He got back behind the wheel of his car and slipped away as quietly as he had come.

In the early hours of the morning, gendarmes, alerted by tourists parked at the rest area, discovered a man in his car shot through the head. The first leads of the investigation favored a settling of scores between mafia gangs, as is too often the case in the region. The number plate of the car, registered in Bosnia, pointed to this first hypothesis. The Bosnian diaspora was very active in the region in the fields of prostitution and petty crime. Enough elements to the taste of the investigators to prevent this case from getting bogged down in the heap of many other similar unsolved cases to date. They could only hope for a hypothetical public claim in order to close it.

While the forensic police were busy in white overalls looking for elements that might help them advance the investigation, a child accompanied by his father approached the inspector in charge of the investigation, Mattéo Piéroni, better known nationally under the nickname 'Le Marseillais'.

'May I speak to you please?'

— Pardon? Oh good mother of Marseille, what is this one gibbering to me. I don't speak English,' said the inspector with his best southern accent.

'And I don't speak French very well.'

'Well, we're not out of the woods yet, buddy!'

He turned to his deputies to find a kind soul to act as a providential translator.

One of his colleagues came to meet them.

'Do you need help, Le Marseillais?'

'I have a small problem with language comprehension. I've stopped English in the twelfth grade, or even before. And then in my beloved rocky inlets, I don't have much opportunity to speak Shakespeare' language.'

'You didn't get that nickname by accident... OK, let me help you out here.'

The conversation with the tourist could finally begin. The latter related that he had found his nine-year-old son prostrate in his bed in the early morning. He had struggled to get him to talk, which he finally succeeded in doing through patience. His story was confusing, but he learned enough to understand that his son had witnessed the murder.

The boy kept staring at his father, looking haggard, with terrified eyes. He was in shock.

'And did he see the killer's face? Could he describe it to us to make a sketch?'

His colleague translated. The father asked him. But the boy remained silent.

'The number plate of the vehicle?'

No more reactions.

'A car brand, a colour?'

He was shaking all over his body.

'I don't think we'll get anything out of him today. He is too shocked. He has probably seen things, but is unable to share them or perhaps even remember them.'

'How can you not remember?'

'A kind of amnesia following an emotional shock. Only a psychologist could remedy this and try to make him recover the memory that has already fled deep inside him. It is a means of self-defense.'

'And it would be a long time before he could remember these details.'

'A few days, a few months or even a few years... there are no precise rules because each person reacts differently.'

'If we have to wait for years, we are in trouble. But in the meantime this would be our only witness. We interviewed all the other tourists in that car park last night and everyone was sawing wood. Ask them if they can come by the station in the next few days.'

'He just said that they are going back to England tomorrow.'

'All the more reason to do it today. Even if it means asking a child psychiatrist to help him. And we'll have to get in touch with our English counterparts so that the youngster can benefit from therapy and they can return the results to us.'

'If the family agrees...'

'Well, look at the child, it would be in their interest. This can only be beneficial in helping the child to overcome this ordeal.'

Just as the father and child were about to return to their camper van to prepare to follow the inspector to the police station for the deposition, another colleague came up to them. A good six feet tall, with a shaved head, a square jaw, dark eyes, an authoritative tone and a confident walk. His nickname 'the tank' was not stolen.

The boy immediately stiffened when he saw him and clutched his father's legs. He was shaking from head to toe. He turned his head away so as not to see him. Inspector Piéroni and his providential interpreter noticed the child's reaction.

They both looked at each other and understood immediately.

Their colleague was in no way responsible for the killing as he was on a stakeout with the inspector himself that night, investigating a drug case, but on the other hand seemed to match the killer's morphology given the boy's reaction.

'We know roughly what our man looks like. We're going to be able to put together a sketch of him. That's a good start.'

Returning from his morning jaunt, Karl pressed the button on the remote control that opened the gate to the residence. He drove up the long white gravel driveway winding through a forest of Aleppo pines and parked in front of a magnificent stone mansion, a former 13th century Cistercian abbey.

Nestled in the hinterland of Nice in an estate of more than twenty hectares, this residence, rebuilt, enlarged and renovated several times over the centuries, consisted of two perpendicular wings, where some of the old arcades had been preserved on the ground floor, opening onto a garden where the original fountain was enthroned in its center. Other vestiges of the original abbey were still present, from a well incorporated into one of the inner rooms to the stone pillars serving as the sub-basement of the former monastery or an access to an underground passageway leading down to the level of the hill allowing the monks to escape.

This place had managed to keep that authenticity so typical of the Mediterranean landscape, which had long since disappeared in the seaside area, subject to urban pressure and transformation into farmland where only the riparian forest in the alluvial plain of the Var was maintained with a relatively diversified hydrophilic flora. White poplars, alders, ash trees, sage, willows and other herbaceous plants were found there. There were also trees more traditionally adapted to the hot and dry climate of the summers, but also mild and wetter in the winters, such as olive trees and prickly pears. Add to this the piercing cries of the various birds of prey and the songs of the cicadas, the property was situated in an extraordinary biodiversity, nestled in the heart of hills and forests.

A real haven of peace which, in addition, had always been spared the numerous forest fires which raged every year in the region.

Just as he entered the huge entrance hall, the owner of the house came down the imposing staircase directly to the left.

'Ah, there you are, Karl. Did everything go as we wanted?'

'Without a hitch, Grand Prior. Everything went well,' he said, handing him a thick kraft envelope. 'I went to his hotel room to clean up all traces of your meeting.'

'Perfect. He hasn't had time to spend anything yet. Everything still seems to be there,' he replied, glancing quickly at the contents. 'Come, follow me, we'll have a nice cup of coffee before you go back to the airport to pick up our venerable Commander. He's arriving in Nice on the first eight o'clock plane. This could be a great moment for the Order if he succeeds. A historic moment even.'

At last, the recognition so long sought after all these years of waiting in the shadow of our usurpers.

9

Marimont-lès-Bénestroff
Saturday May 11th 2014

Natacha and Gilles had just had time to emerge from their lethargy when Cyril appeared.
'Back already! So?' she asked.
'He gave me the key without any opposition. A very nice mayor. Which doesn't seem to be the case for everyone... I met two others who seemed delighted to see me. Some specimens...'
'If you had been here two months earlier, you would have seen a real clan war. The village was divided in two, said the owner of the lodge, who came out of her shell again.'
'That much? So much commotion in such a small village... and what was the reason for it?'
'You may have seen the beautiful, flamboyant town hall on your way in. That is the reason. And this is what the current mayor denounced in his campaign. No one can deny that he was right, except perhaps the big loser in these elections.'
'That's for sure. Well, anyway, we should probably go. Otherwise we're not going to do anything all day...'
Cyril retrieved his backpack, which contained all kinds of tools. Decameters, cords, plumb bobs, carpenter's nails, a folding shovel, a trowel, brushes of all sizes, a sieve, a torch, notebooks, pencils, labels and a small metal detector made up the perfect kit for the amateur explorer that he was. As for Gilles, he carried the

dumpy level and its relatively cumbersome tripod. Natacha took care of the food. Three baskets of food prepared by the hostess. All specialities from the region. A good way of highlighting the local products she was offering for sale.

Only two minutes' walk and they found themselves in the village square, with the church on their left, standing at the top of a steep, wide staircase, and the hillock still lost in the clouds in front of them. There seemed to be no path leading directly to the top over the ruins of the old castle. They approached the bottom of the mound and saw that the whole slope was strewn with brambles, nettles and other thick, tangled thickets. Impenetrable vegetation or too risky for anyone who did not want to tear their clothes. They had no choice but to go around to find a more favorable access. The day before, when they had arrived, while crossing the forest, Cyril had noticed a large number of ruts, most probably dug by the tractors of individuals who had come to cut their wood, thus acting as makeshift forest roads.

They passed the new 18th century castle-farm as the mayor had told them.

'We'll have a look around when we get back,' says Cyril, scanning the area for any human presence.

But for the moment there didn't seem to be anyone around. They entered the forest and began to climb through the first visible ruts. But they quickly got out and tried their luck a little further on. The heavy rain that fell earlier made the ground extremely muddy and slippery. Dirt and leaves quickly clung to the shoes and made the task even more difficult. At times they even had to use the branches, when they were able to grip them, which were also slippery from the damp, to move forward and not go back down to square one every time.

The progress was slow and trying, but they finally reached their goal after a good half hour of hard work. At least they thought so, because indeed, no remains seemed to be visible, confirming what the manager of the lodge had told them.

'What, all this for that!' grumbled Gilles.

'Don't panic. I told you from the start that this castle mound was recognizable only by its name. That's why we have shovels, my dear friend. The aim is to find the remains of the foundations.'

'Well, the advantage is that the soil is loose enough to dig without too much pressure...'

'So let's get to work!'

'And won't we get into trouble if we make holes everywhere?'

'I showed him a document from the university. He fully agrees with our approach and has given me carte blanche. However, if we find anything, we have to tell him beforehand. That's the deal.'

They divided the area between them, leaving a few meters of space between them, and began to shovel.

This allowed Natacha to warm up. It must not have been more than fourteen degrees, not counting the humidity, which made it feel even colder.

Cyril had been able to retrieve a topographical survey of the area during his research at the Nancy history faculty, as well as an old aerial photo where the outline of the old structure could still be seen here and there. He had incorporated all the data he had in his possession into his GPS, enabling them to dig in strategic places where they would be sure to find something.

After a good ten spadefuls, Natacha's shovel came up against an obstacle. Probably a stone. But after clearing the periphery, she realized that the object of the crime was completely rusty in the end. A seal or a pot. She called out to her companions, who came running at once. After having freed it from its earthen prison, Gilles, an amateur specialist in military clothing and armaments from various periods and more particularly from the wars of the last two centuries, quickly recognized its origin.

A German helmet from one of the two world wars.

In rather poor condition, the corrosion after all those years of burial having done its work, but identifiable all the same. The top part was missing and several other holes were visible on the bottom part.

The Mystery of the Lost Crypt

The young woman was quite proud of her discovery. But unfortunately this find did not interest Cyril, who had come for a completely different reason.

'After all the events of the last three great wars, there's bound to be a lot more of the same,' he says. 'At least they'll be able to display them in glass cases in their beautiful town hall...'

To his great satisfaction, Cyril gradually cleared what looked like a low wall. The deeper he dug, the bigger the wall became, revealing old stones cut and polished by centuries of wear and tear, arranged in a staggered pattern. He used a shovel and a pickaxe to rough up the stones, then finished with a broad brush. After a few hours of backbreaking work, the result was striking. A good two meters long and thirty centimeters high were cleared and almost cleaned. Natacha had come to help him. He took care of the rough work, she of the details.

They quickly realized that the task would be titanic.

Especially with three people...

'Do we have plans for next weekend, honey?' he asked with a smirk.

'I can see you coming with your big hooves... but to tell you the truth, I wouldn't mind coming back. On the contrary.'

'The same goes for me!' said Gilles, whose frenzy of future discoveries grew stronger.

The latter was not to be outdone in terms of discoveries.

After Natacha's discovery, his search had shifted somewhat to objects from more recent times. Equipped with a metal detector, which was constantly ringing, he unearthed kitchen utensils, bullets of all calibers, war medals with the swastika and a bayonet. But unlike Natacha's helmet, it was in perfect condition. It was rusty, but it was whole. Scrubbing away the dirt and rust with a brush, he uncovered an inscription engraved on the top of the blade.

Franz ENTNER, 12 August 1914, Marimont

'Look at this,' he said, approaching the couple. 'This German had engraved his name on his bayonet here only days before the battle with the French began. Did he have any idea at the time of the tragic event that would take place in this region a few days later and last for four long years?'

'Franz ENTNER, Marimont. Strange, the name of the village at that time still seems to be in French, even though the region has been annexed to the German Empire for more than thirty years,' Natacha remarked.

'From what I have read, it was not until 1915 and until the end of the war that the village took on a Germanic-sounding name, 'Morsberg'.'

'That's wonderful, Gilles. But it doesn't help my case. If you could go back a few centuries in your research and concentrate on the Middle Ages rather than the Great War, that would help me a lot. Instead, find us a coat of mail, a tile, some sestertium or gold coins. That would be more interesting...'

'You're right, I'm here to help you. I'll continue my personal research next week!' he said, winking at her.

'That's fine. In the meantime, we're going to take a well-deserved break.'

The fog had only partially dissipated and the air was still cool. After only a ten-minute break, Natasha was already freezing. The high level of moisture penetrating her clothes made it feel even worse. She went back to work without delay.

While Gilles was taking stock of his finds, a noise in the distance put Cyril on the alert.

'Please Natasha stop digging for two seconds.'

'Why, what's going on?'

He did not answer immediately and remained on the lookout.

'I heard barking.'

He whistled and called many times.

'Do you expect him to answer you?'

'If only you knew how right you are,' Cyril replied curtly.

The distant noises resumed.

'Indeed, there is no longer any doubt that it is a dog. Perhaps a village dog.'

'I'm sure it's him.'

'But then why doesn't he come to meet us?'

'I don't know. Maybe he's hurt. The barking seems to be coming from the village. Or maybe he's being held in a pen.'

'We will tour the village in the late afternoon.'

They resumed their tasks after this short interval. But a little less serenely for the academic who remained on the alert, listening for the slightest bark.

10

Nice
Saturday June 15th 2013, 8am

Karl arrived at Nice airport and double-parked. He had neither the time nor the inclination to go and park properly in the reserved spots at a five minutes' walk away distance. He scanned the giant arrivals screen. The flight from Paris was delayed by fifteen minutes. He fumed. Strangely, the plane was late every time he picked him up. After thirty minutes of what seemed like endless waiting, he saw him pass through the last gates. Blond hair, blue eyes, a height of about two meters and an extraordinary build, Karl, who had Germanic origins on his father's side and Danish on his mother's, could not go unnoticed.

The traveller had no trouble spotting the Viking giant in the crowd.

'Was your flight pleasant, Commander?' asked Karl in a tone of hypocrisy.

'A horror. Too much shaking with this bad weather everywhere. And the landing was more than a little bumpy.'

'And again, a delay...'

'I hate waiting before boarding. Too boring. Too big a waste of time. That's why I always book my seat in advance,' he says with a smile. 'That way they have to wait for me. I work in the subscriber's area and wait for the last call before the boarding gates close for good to come. Five minutes before take-off. You always have to know how to be long in coming!'

'Always getting on the plane late, one day they will leave without you!'

'I try not to overdo it...'

The two men returned to the car. A Border Police officer was writing him a ticket. Karl approached him with a threatening look. But, unlike most of the time, his attitude did not have the desired effect and did not impress the officer, who was concentrating on his task.

'Yet, the day had started quite well this morning,' grumbled the Prussian giant, who slipped a twenty-euro note into his driving license.

The officer grabbed it, slipped it into his pocket and then tore off the ticket he had just carefully filled in, hurling a more than banal moral at him while a tourist, also badly parked and ticketed, was ranting beside him, witnessing the scene.

On their arrival at the Commandery, the Grand Prior and the Commander embraced warmly. The long-awaited day had finally arrived. Jubilation and excitement were evident on their faces.

'So that's it, it's finally here?'

'It is waiting for you in my office.'

'Have you told the other commanderies?'

'Not yet.'

'You did the right thing. It's better to wait for the results of the research before getting the whole organization together. Make sure we hold all the cards. The surprise will be all the better.'

The two men went up the grand staircase and then to the office of the Supreme Master of the Order.

'A glass of whisky?' he offered his host to keep him a little more on tenterhooks.

'Nine o'clock in the morning... it's still a bit early for an aperitif. But I'll have a coffee,' he said, turning to the butler who came out of the room to prepare it for him. 'Well, enough waiting, let me see it. I'm beginning to lose patience.'

The icon lay on the desk, protected by its wrapping. The Commander saw it and did not hesitate to take it. He and the Grand Prior had known each other for many years and were not above protocol when they were alone together. The Commander tore open the kraft paper.

'And here is the famous Lady of Philermo, the Virgin of Philerme! One of the three sacred relics of the Hospitaller Order, along with the hand of St John the Baptist and a fragment of the Holy Cross. Isn't it beautiful?' he said, a little ironically.

'Be careful though. It is fragile, to say the least. It is over a thousand years old. Handle it with care.'

'Oh, much more than that. This painting is devoutly attributed to St. Luke the Evangelist, companion of the apostle Paul. It is therefore almost two thousand years old. And even if he wasn't the author, it's still a couple of years old. He turned the painting over and began to inspect the back carefully.'

'What are you looking at?'

'If the codex is true, the coding key for the most important passage would be on this table.'

'On this little board?' he said, taken aback, as he approached the Commander.

'Where did you think? I certainly didn't have it brought back to contemplate. But don't ask me where or how, because I haven't got a clue. Don't forget that the Templars' imagination was very fertile in the field of encryption, so I doubt I'll find the solution so easily.'

'Come on, don't be so modest. Your abilities are known and recognized throughout the world. You will have no problem solving the riddle. I am sure of it...'

This is exactly what the commander wanted him to say to flatter his ego. He liked to hear this praise for him.

'It's ironic that they used a fetish icon of their enemy brothers, the Hospitallers, to put in a crucial fact and the Hospitallers never knew it. It was right under their noses, and ours, all along.'

'Perhaps it is a blessing in disguise. Assuming that it concerns the Templar treasure, or even just a part of it, if the Hospitallers had known about it, they would undoubtedly have recovered it long ago. And in the end it would have benefited dear Napoleon Bonaparte...'

The Order flourished on the island of Malta from the time of its acquisition in 1530 with the blessing of Pope Clement VII, building the city and port of Valletta, palaces and churches, a new hospital considered the best in the world, and various medical schools. His fleet also ruled the entire Mediterranean, definitively countering any Ottoman desire to expand into Europe. The hegemony of their fleet was total and lasted for over two hundred and fifty years. But in 1798, General Bonaparte, on his way to Egypt to campaign and capture it and thus block the route to India for the English, passed through the island of Malta. When the Grand Master Ferdinand de Hompesch categorically refused to harbor the French army there for a limited time, Bonaparte took it by force, beating the English, who also had their sights set on this island, which was a strategic position in the Mediterranean. He then took all the Order's wealth and dissolved it at the same time. The knights had to abandon the island again and wander around for a few years before the order finally broke up. Some of them took refuge in Russia with Tsar Paul I and others in Rome, in Italy in 1834. But according to some historians, the Order ceased to exist officially after its dissolution by the future French emperor.

The Grand Prior, quite worried about the fate of the painting his friend had in store for it, flinched at the slightest sudden manipulation by the latter.

'Take it easy... is it the real thing?'

'I can't guarantee in a few seconds that it's the original, but what is certain is that it looks very old. Even if it has been restored several times since then. But we could say that it is the right one... we still have to find this famous coding key.'

'I have complete confidence in you for this. I'm sure you'll find it quickly.'

'My work is already well advanced on this subject. I have a few leads. This icon is a central piece of the puzzle. It will not allow me to solve the enigma of the alleged treasure entirely, but it will be of great help at least concerning its location.'

'Perfect. That's all I wanted to hear. For your return, it might be more appropriate to drive back rather than fly. What do you think?'

'It would indeed be safer. And anyway I had not taken a return ticket. The cargo is far too valuable to be put in the hold. By now, the customs and police authorities must already know about its disappearance. Too dangerous...'

'Good. Karl is ready just now. You can leave whenever you like.'

'The sooner the better. I'll keep you posted on the progress of my research.'

Less than five minutes later, the Mercedes sped off, sending the rear wheels skidding across the gravel.

The Grand Prior, who watched them leave from the window, closed his eyes. A feeling of fulfillment mixed with satisfaction came over him at that moment.

They were so close...

The Mystery of the Lost Crypt

11

Marimont-lès-Bénestroff
Saturday May 11th 2014

Like any archaeologist worthy of the name, they had previously carried out a grid survey enabling Cyril to map the area and also to locate the extraction of any objects found.

They laid out the ground in squares of two by two meters using stakes and ropes. Luc used an aerial photograph dating from 1975 and recovered from the Regional Center for Historic Monuments to judge the approximate location of the foundations of the original castle. A shot of the site cleared of trees where part of the outline of the building was still visible at that time.

He also decided to take photos at regular times throughout the day to see the different phases of the construction site and its progress. Valuable photos that would later be used to fill the 80 pages of his thesis.

The excavation site moved forward at great speed by the middle of the afternoon, with the three neophytes working hard. Several low walls two to three stones high, previously buried under a layer of earth and humus, had already been uncovered. A more than unexpected achievement, given that they had to leave the next evening.

Cyril stopped for a moment. He stepped back, climbed a small pile of wood to get some height and looked at the site as a whole.

He was proud of the work they had done so far. He felt he had made the right choice in choosing this site.

On his way back to his spot, he glanced briefly at Natasha and noticed that something was wrong. She had been looking unfocused and nervous for a few minutes, regularly raising her head and looking around for a few seconds. He approached her.

'You don't look well. Something's wrong?'

'Have you ever had the feeling that someone is watching you? I do at the moment. I feel like we're being watched all the time. She contemplated the surroundings for a moment and scanned every bush or pile of logs that could serve as a hiding place, but saw no one. Nature this year was hasty and leaves were a good month ahead, the forest was already very dense and dark. The mist enhanced the poor visibility.'

'It's likely. We are strangers to them. And strangers are scary, disturbing, intriguing... maybe they're worried that we'll discover something. After all, they can always spy on us and look at us like curious beasts, we have nothing to hide. I don't really care. He raised his arm and pointed his middle finger to the sky...'

'You like making friends...' she laughed.

'Well, at this point, one more or less won't make much difference to our situation.'

'You're right, mate!' said Gilles.

The latter and Natasha made the same gesture in general hilarity before getting back to work.

About an hour later, Cyril made his first discovery. While clearing the earth in front of his low foundation wall, he uncovered a small alcove between two cut stones, the entrance to which, blocked by a smaller stone and not sealed with mortar, fell apart after only two passes with a trowel. He removed it and discovered that an object had been placed and was almost completely filling the cavity. A leather purse, worn out and partly eaten away by moisture.

His first treasure.

'Come here, I've found something,' he gloated like a kid in awe of his birthday present.

'Wow, what a crazy treasure! If it's the one the lady at the lodge was talking about, this 'golden bowling pins' has hit the skids,' Gilles laughed. 'It's not even worth my spiked helmet and my bayonet!'

'such a jealous...' teased Natasha.

'Scandalmonger. We've only just started and already you're hoping to find the Grail,' Cyril added.

'I must admit that patience is not my strong point. And legends, even less... But anyway, it's a good start.'

He carefully took it out and put it in a plastic box. There was no question of checking its contents on the spot. That would wait until they got back to the faculty, where a small laboratory would be available for dissecting and cleaning it.

'It looks full. I'd be curious to see what's inside. He couldn't help but shake the purse slightly and feel it with his fingers. It looks like coins!'

He was proud as a pope to have discovered this little treasure. This finding increased their enthusiasm tenfold and all three worked even more enthusiastically than before. Everyone now wanted to find another treasure.

They didn't feel the hours going by. The end of the afternoon was approaching when the rain appeared again. At first a drizzle, then it intensified as the minutes passed. And always this damn bone-chilling cold. Natasha sneezed several times. It didn't take her much more to stop the search and give up.

'A good hot bath that's what I need. I'm heading back, I can't take it anymore. I'm freezing.'

'You're right, we've already done enough for today. You go ahead. I'll finish up and meet you at the church. At least we'll be sheltered from the rain there.'

Natasha and Gilles put the tools in their respective rucksacks and went back down the hill, following the same path as before.

They passed in front of the castle-farm again, but this time a car was parked in the courtyard.

'It seems to me that Cyril wanted to go there, right?'

'He can go, but it will be without me, the young woman grumbled. I'm exhausted. And anyway, if it's to be scrutinized from head to toe like a curious animal, no thanks.'

'But no, they don't all have to be like that...'

'May heaven hear you.'

'It's crazy. It's not even nine o'clock and it's almost dark. It feels like autumn.'

'Yes, and it's been going on for some years.'

The village seemed deserted. Even though it only had about fifty inhabitants spread over fifteen houses and could not boast any rush-hour traffic in the village square, the place seemed abandoned. There was not a sound to disturb the peace and quiet of the hamlet. Not even a dog barking, nor the slightest mooing or bleating that would remind strangers that they were in the depths of the Moselle countryside.

They went up the stairs and then into the church.

Cyril had asked the mayor of the village that morning to open the shrine to them so that they could visit it. The mayor preferred to give him the keys.

The church was very classical. Rebuilt in the eighteenth century on the foundations of the previous one, it consisted of a bell tower-porch with a pavilion positioned to the west, a rectangular nave itself directly prolonged by the choir and an apse which, in view of the small size of the place, were hardly distinguishable from each other. Three stained glass windows on each side of the side walls allowed a minimum of light to enter. A wooden door at the back separated this part from a tiny sacristy. It was supported from the outside by several buttresses. The church was sober, without embellishment, and more than reasonable in size for the two hundred or so inhabitants of the village at the time, who had paid the entire cost, which led to numerous disputes with the local lord, as the decimators refused to contribute to the costs.

The Mystery of the Lost Crypt

They lit their torches. Gilles' powerful Maglite alone illuminated a large part of the nave. Cracks ran through the vault, mould speckled its original whiteness and spider webs squatted in the corners.

'Ugh, it's musty in here. They must not ventilate often.'

'It is probably only used very occasionally. There is not even a single burnt candle on the candle holder.'

'Oh, look, there's the famous period bench of the squires,' he said, walking towards the choir. 'It has been preserved for two centuries.'

'It must have been renovated since then. I doubt it would have stayed in such a state all this time with the humidity, coolness and temperature differences throughout the seasons. Some of the newer benches are in worse condition. When you see the state of the ceiling...'

Gilles pointed the powerful beam of his torch towards the altar. Made of stone, it was disproportionately large compared to the building itself.

Cyril in turn left the site, having taken great care to tidy up. He did not want to leave anything behind. Bad thoughts came to him. Perhaps wrongly, but given the strange behavior of some of the inhabitants, he was wary and did not want to run the risk of some marauder taking or damaging their equipment.

Unlike his two companions, he cut through the forest as quickly as possible and came upon an orchard where the mist, or perhaps it was low clouds clinging to the hill, covered part of the clearing. It was raining harder and harder. A strong and penetrating drizzle. He was alerted by a cracking sound of branches on his left. He immediately thought of his dog who was still missing and was sure he had heard him earlier in the day. He turned his head towards the noise and two deer leapt from a copse and crossed the orchard less than four meters in front of him. They capered through the air with extraordinary grace and agility and then gradually disappeared into the mist as quickly as they had appeared. He caught a last glimpse of them entering the forest.

Cyril stood still, savoring the magnificent sight that was offered to him and only let out a simple 'Wow'. Still amazed, he continued towards the road and arrived just in front of the castle-farm where he climbed the wooden fence to access the meadow.

He too saw the car parked in the courtyard of the property. He hesitated to go there. It was getting late and he had to meet his friends in the church as agreed. He did not want to make them wait any longer after the hard day's work he had already put them through. Still, he procrastinated.

The temptation was great.

But he abandoned this idea and put it off until the next day, at the risk of finding himself again in front of a closed door. In any case, he was not presentable with his muddy shoes and his wet and dirty trousers. He crossed the gravel driveway leading to the property and continued towards the village.

He, in turn, entered the church to join his friends.

12

London
Wednesday March 12th 2014

Jimmy entered the room alone, his head down, his eyes fixed on his shoes.

'Hello, Jimmy, how are you today?'

He received a simple shrug of the shoulders in response. His father had remained in the waiting room, as he had for the previous five sessions. Until today, Professor John Smith, a child psychiatrist in the English capital, had been unable to find anything. The boy remained silent for the two hours of the consultation, sitting in the chair and playing with his fingers.

Aware that this would take time, the doctor had to change his method. And radically. Few people practiced hypnosis. The idea of being able to be manipulated often put a damper on their enthusiasm. But anyway, this case was different.

However, since it was a child, it was necessary to go slowly. For the boy was about to relive a second time, almost live, the unbearable vision of the murder that had taken place before his eyes. The result could cause an even more violent emotional shock from which the boy would not recover. The mission was therefore extremely delicate.

For this special procedure, the boy's father was exceptionally able to assist him, which reassured Jimmy.

Jimmy lay down on the couch.

Dr. Smith began by explaining in detail the procedure, which immediately reassured them.

'I knew you'd understand, Jimmy. You're a big boy now. Just relax and let go. Try not to think about anything. Clear your head. Focus only on my voice. You only hear my voice. And when I count to three, you will fall into a deep sleep...'

'But I'm not sleepy!' protested Jimmy, opening his eyes.

'Please lie back down and concentrate.'

His father was about to intervene but Smith dissuaded him. Smith started the whole operation again.

'On the count of three you will go into a deep sleep. Listen carefully to my voice. One. Two. Three.'

And just as the psychiatrist had said, Jimmy fell into a deep sleep. His father couldn't believe it. The only time he had ever witnessed such a phenomenon was about ten years ago when he and his wife, who was pregnant with Jimmy, had attended a show by a well-known illusionist. He had always believed that hypnosis was one of the many tricks used by illusionists to enhance their shows.

'Can you still hear me Jimmy?'

'Yes.'

'OK, fine. We'll go back to France on holiday. Do you like holidays?'

'Oh yes, sure!'

'So let's go back to France. To Nice, for example.'

'No, not in Nice. I never want to go back there.'

'Ah, and why is that?'

'[...] I don't know...'

'Yet the weather is nice and warm. And above all there is the sea in Nice. Do you like the sea Jimmy?'

'Yes, I love it. You can swim and play in the sand.'

'I love it too. So let's go for a little walk on the beach. Would you like to?'

A smile came over the boy's face.

The Mystery of the Lost Crypt

Doctor Smith looked at his watch. The hypnosis session had already lasted fifteen minutes. It was time to call it a day.

'Jimmy, I'm going to count to three again and you'll wake up. One. Two. Three.'

The boy opened his eyes and turned to his father.

'When are we going back to the beach, Dad?'

'Soon my little chap, soon,' he smiled.

Jimmy and his father returned the following week.

The first hypnosis session had been very positive and the progress dramatic. They had achieved more in that one session than all the previous ones put together. The boy was already gaining confidence. And he was even eager to do it again. When Smith opened the door, he stumbled into the room, quickly took off his shoes without untying them and lay down on the couch.

'I am ready!'

Smith was taken aback by the boy's reaction and glanced at the father, who shrugged and smiled.

The doctor performed the same ritual.

The aim was to gradually bring Jimmy to the events he had witnessed at the rest area. This second meeting was again a session based on approach and confidence building. A preparation for the next session which, if all went according to plan, would approach the fateful moment.

Jimmy returned with gusto. But his father had briefed him. He carefully placed his trainers at the foot of the couch and calmly lay down.

On three. One, two... and three.

Smith dreaded this moment. He had never practiced this art on a child so young. But it was important not to let his excitement and inexperience in the field show. He took a deep breath, then began.

'You come back from the beach with your parents and your sister and you park your motor home at the rest area for the night. Are you there?'

'Yes. There are lots of other motorhomes in the car park. I met a friend there. We played a bit together and then we had lunch.'

'Very good. Then you went to bed.'

'Yes.'

Jimmy began to fidget on the couch. The first signs of nervousness appeared and increased as the hour drew near.

'So what happened?'

'I fell asleep, I suppose.'

The two adults smiled.

'And so you woke up in the middle of the night. Is that right? Did you look at your watch to see what time it was?'

'...Yes... it was five past four.'

'And what did you do then?'

'I went out. I had to pee.'

'And why did you go out? There is a toilet in the camper van...'

'I didn't want to wake them up.'

'A wise decision. You are really mature for your age. And when you came out, what happened then?'

Jimmy hesitated.

'I went into the bushes to do it. And...'

'And?'

'While I was doing this, a car came and parked next to another one with someone inside.'

The boy's whole body jerked.

His father became concerned and looked at the professor questioningly. He seemed to want to tell him to stop, but Smith ignored his gaze.

It was double or quits.

'Don't worry, you are not alone. Your daddy is beside you and protects you. Nothing will happen to you. Don't be afraid Jimmy.'

These last words soothed the boy, who gradually calmed down.

'Did you see what happened between the two men?'

'No. The lamp post is broken. It is very dark. But he turns on the light, I see him!'

'Who do you see?'

The Mystery of the Lost Crypt

'The killer,' said the boy feverishly.
'Can you describe it to me?'
'It is difficult.'
'I know, but try.'
'He's tall and super-built.'
'Do you see anything else? Any particular detail in his face that would make him more recognizable?'
'He has a mark on his cheek.'
'A scar?'
'Yes.'
'That's good, Jimmy. You're doing great. We're almost finished. One more push. What happens now?'

The boy stiffened and his legs went limp again. He was about to cry. The crucial moment was coming. His father looked at Smith again and motioned for him to leave it at that. Smith replied with a flat, open hand gesture not to worry. Making him endure the murder scene again seemed inconceivable, he had to concentrate on something else. Obviously the crime scene itself would not add anything to the investigation.

'Do you happen to know the make of the car?'
'Yes... a BMW...'

Smith's gaze was caught by the boy's hand.

'Is this the same car you are holding in your hand?'
'Yes...'
'Jimmy, when the car drives off, can you make out the number plate?'
'He makes a sign before leaving... he puts his finger in front of his mouth to tell me to say nothing. He'll find me if I tell you everything! And he will kill me!'
'But no, he won't do anything. He doesn't know you. We're all here to protect you. Don't look at him. We're not interested in him. Concentrate on the car. What do you see?'

He waited for him to calm down again and asked him again.

'I think so. 1 0 0 0 X C 0 6. Yes, that's right.'
'Excellent, Jimmy. You can now let him go.'
'What if he comes back to hurt me and my whole family?'

'Don't worry. With the information you just gave, the police will be able to arrest him and send him to jail. He won't bother you again...' he said, looking at his father.

The boy woke up and went to snuggle up to his father. The next day, a final session was organized to take the pressure off, and this time it was all about good memories. Beach, swimming and friends to give him confidence and make him forget about the car park mishap for good.

All the precious elements gathered were sent to the Nice police station in the following days. The investigation conducted by Le Marseillais could finally begin on the basis of these solid elements.

13

Marimont-lès-Bénestroff
Saturday May 11th 2014

Natasha was startled by her companion's entrance.
Cyril locked the door as soon as he was inside.
'That way no one will come and disturb us!'
'There's really nothing very original about this church,' Gilles commented, a little disappointed by what he saw as he came down from the bell tower with a frightful creak. 'You still have to be careful not to fall through the wooden steps...'
'When it was rebuilt in 1777, this village had no more than one hundred and thirty inhabitants and two hundred at its peak thirty years later. It was already very controversial to rebuild, so they weren't going to build a cathedral either...' replied Cyril. 'It has been rebuilt several times. The first traces of a place of worship date back to the eighth century, when the castle was also built.'
'Indeed, this is understandable. When we know that hundreds of churches, castles or historical monuments will be destroyed in France in the next twenty years because of a lack of money to maintain them, the donors as well as the workers of the time must be turning in their graves.'
'They would do better to reuse them for housing or restaurants. This is a common practice in Anglo-Saxon countries.'
'Well... it's creepy to sleep in a church, next to a cemetery.'

Fifteen rows of wooden pews were arranged on either side of the central aisle leading to the altar. A Virgin Mary stood halfway up on the left and a baroque altarpiece filled the entire back of the nave.

'According to what the village mayor told me, only the floor, the altar and the prayer bench in the first row on the right, the one belonging to the squires, are of the period. The latter would date from the end of the eighteenth century,' Cyril continued. 'By the way, did you know that a very famous abbot officiated here for some years?'

'No, but as I can see that you've done your homework on the subject, you'll soon tell us about it,' said Natasha, while inspecting the place with a little more interest than Gilles.

'Abbé Grégoire.'

'Are you talking about Henri Jean-Baptiste Grégoire, one of the main emblematic figures of the French Revolution?'

'Exactly. He was a curate in his early days. At the time of the reconstruction of the church. He must have been able to convince the then lord of the manor without too much trouble. He was described as having a strong character and a certain presence. Hence his subsequent career in politics.'

'And apart from these three elements, is there anything else from that time?'

— I don't think so... Oh yes, there are two tombs outside, but no one really knows their origins. They look even older than this church. According to the mayor, they are in very bad shape, not far from collapsing.'

'All the more reason to take an interest.'

After a brief visit to the sacristy, which yielded no information, Cyril inspected the altar from every angle. It was what is known as a tomb altar. The table, in this case made of stone, rested on a continuous stone support which could be solid or hollow like a sarcophagus. Various engravings were depicted. Apart from the baroque altarpiece, the altar was the only really interesting part of this church.

'What exactly are you looking for, Cyril?'

'A clue of some kind. In any good novel or film, the hero discovers a secret hiding place or passage. And why not us? He knocked in different places and from the sound of the stone he concluded that there was a void inside.'

'Maybe you shouldn't dream...' Gilles said ironically.

'Don't be fooled. It happens more often than you think,' he added.

Intrigued, he crouched down and looked around. He lifted the carpet that covered the entire area between the altar and the altarpiece with his left hand while the other shined the floor. Marks on the ground intrigued him. He observed them from different angles.

'Look Cyril, they look like grooves. They run in arcs from the stone block.'

'That's right. Like the altar pivots on an axis. Told you. I'm sensing there's something down there.'

Natasha immediately came forward, fascinated by what she had just heard. The three young men stood at the corner of the altar and began to apply pressure. They pushed with all their might but the stone did not budge one iota. Undeterred, they took a breath, relaxed their biceps and tried a second time, but to no avail.

The altar seemed to be sealed.

'It can't be. It weighs a ton at least. There must be an automatic opening mechanism.'

'That's all there is to it! There could also be nothing at all,' commented Natasha. 'These marks on the ground could be something else entirely. But at least we tried...'

But the two boys did not want to leave it at that. They inspected the altar from every angle. Every moulding or protrusion in the stone was carefully inspected. They felt every square inch and systematically exerted a little pressure with a finger or palm in order to trigger some mechanism that would make this huge stone chest turn.

But again nothing would move.

The Mystery of the Lost Crypt

'Then the solution would be to blow it all up with sledgehammers!'

'If you have other ideas as crazy as this one, don't hesitate to keep them to yourself. This altar should be classified as a French heritage site. It must be a thousand years old and a fool like you would like to destroy it to see what might be underneath. Tell me I'm dreaming...'

'But no, it's okay, I was joking. If you can't even joke anymore...'

They had been inspecting the altar for nearly twenty minutes when suddenly Cyril, who had come as close as possible, noticed a gap in an ornamental cross on the side facing the nave. Not the kind of irregular crack caused by time. But a crack that carefully followed the outline of a square cross pattée. The crack was imperceptible to the naked eye beyond a distance of about twenty centimeters. He had almost passed by it without noticing it. But that was without counting on his lynx eyes.

He pulled a scalpel from his briefcase and chiseled all around the cross. With time and the various restorations carried out on the work, the dust had closed the crack almost everywhere. He showed his two companions the discovery he had just made with the help of his powerful torch.

'Come over here. I think I found what we were looking for. Look at this cross. There's a tiny gap around it. It seems to be disjointed from the rest.'

'And now?' asked Gilles

Everyone wanted to believe it, even if the possibility of discovering a secret passage was more of a fantasy.

'It's time for the truth, folks,' said Cyril, who put his hand on the cross and pushed.

At that moment, the latch of the front door of the church was lowered. Someone seemed to want to enter.

The person drummed.

The three young men did not know what to do. They looked at each other, petrified, like thieves caught in the act.

'So what do we do?' whispered Natasha.

Cyril shrugged his shoulders and pouted in response. Gilles turned off his torch by reflex. But it was already too late. It was very dark outside and the beams of light must have been visible through the stained glass windows or the bottom of the door.

Knocking was heard again and then the person addressed the young man by name.

'Mr de Villiers, open the door. I know you are there. I saw you come in earlier.'

He recognized the mayor's voice. It would have been ridiculous to pretend they were not there any longer. Sooner or later they had to leave this place or risk being caught on their way out.

'Put the carpet back in place and clean up a bit in front of the altar. Cyril went to open the door, making sure that his friends had finished their task and already thinking about the excuse he was going to give him for locking the door from the inside. But he had to admit that he had no idea. He turned the key and let the mayor in.'

'But why on earth did you lock yourself in? And in the dark. The switch is at the entrance.'

Embarrassed, he did not know what to say. He looked towards his two companions for inspiration. Natacha had spontaneously taken out her notebook and was reproducing the mouldings and sculptures of the altar. Gilles, for his part, was taking pictures. They had just removed a thorn from his side.

'We just didn't want to be disturbed in our work.'

'Yes, you are right. You have to be quiet to study such a jewel. After all, it is almost twelve centuries old. That's quite something. Especially for such a small village.'

'You can boast of having a beautiful treasure here.'

'As you say. It's an incredible opportunity. And it has been the talk of the town for decades. Some people go so far as to say that kilos of gold are buried in this hill. People's imagination is very fertile when it comes to gold and silver. But the only treasure we have here, and it is a big one, is of course this altar. And nothing else. It has been in existence for over a thousand years and has been through all the great periods of French history. To think that Charlemagne, Hugues Capet and all their descendants touched this stone with their own hands. It's exciting, isn't it?' he said, stroking the stone.

At these words, the young historian felt the effects. For on second thought, the mayor's explanation seemed the most credible, not to say the most sensible. He had mistakenly allowed himself to be fooled by this treasure story. Luckily, the mayor had not noticed the incisions made all around the cross.

The mayor's visit at least focused the task of the three academics on a work they would almost certainly have missed without even contemplating it. The four of them stayed for another hour and then went their separate ways. After closing the church door, double-locked as the mayor had specified, he took back the keys.

They went back to the gite to take the hot bath they had been dreaming of, much to Natacha's benefit, as she was feeling the coolness, humidity and drizzle that had been spitting all day long.

14

Marimont-lès-Bénestroff
Sunday May 12th 2014, 1am

Cyril could not sleep that night. He tossed and turned in his bed to find the best position to fall asleep, but nothing helped. Thoughts plagued his mind. First of all, the disappearance of his dog to which he was attached. He had warned the mayor and the managers who had taken it upon themselves to spread the word to the inhabitants of the village. The second cause of insomnia concerned the church altar. Although the mayor's theory seemed the most reliable, he could not help thinking about the cross he had updated by cutting around it. It must have had a special function to be so disconnected from the rest. Open the altar tray? To move the altar, given the grooves in the floor? He was sure it had some use.

These unanswered questions were becoming unbearable. He wanted to know for sure. He got up and got dressed. Natasha was sleeping peacefully and did not notice anything. Cyril went to knock on his friend's door. There was no reaction. He persisted and after five knocks on the door, Gilles opened it.

'What's going on? Have you seen the time?'
'Get dressed. We're going back to the church.'
'What? Now? You're sick...'
'Don't argue. Put on your clothes and take your torch.'

'[...] Okay, I'm coming,' he says, scowling.

They left the lodge as quietly as possible. Outside, the mist had turned to fog and visibility was much reduced. And still the dampness permeated the clothes.

'How do you plan to get into the church since the mayor has taken over the keys?'

'Don't worry... I actually left the door open.'

'Yet I heard you lock it and even test it afterwards.'

'It's not very complicated. You turn the key once in the right direction and then again in the opposite direction. In the end you get two sounds in a row, but the door stays open. And when you test if your door is closed, instead of pushing, you pull it towards you by shaking the latch several times and the effect remains the same. Elementary my dear Gilles!'

An owl hooted as they stood in front of the church porch. It must have been nesting in one of the two large fir trees. Gilles was startled and looked anxiously at his friend.

'Don't tell me you're afraid?'

'No, but between the proximity of the cemetery, the foggy weather, the time and the screaming animals, it is hard to make it creepier. Besides, I wasn't in the parachute commandos...'

Cyril smiled. He lowered the latch and the door opened with a slight creak. He closed it immediately, blocking it from the inside with a chair. They lowered the intensity of their torch to a minimum so as to betray their presence as little as possible.

The two friends approached the chest. Cyril stood in front of the cross, put his hand on it and applied a gentle push as he had tried to do a few hours before.

Nothing happened.

He tried again, but this time with both hands and pushing as hard as he could.

Still nothing.

They both looked at each other in disappointment.

'I really believed it for a moment...'

'I think the mayor was right after all. These are just legends...' said Gilles, tapping his friend on the shoulder to comfort him. 'Let's go back to sleep.'

'Indeed, I got carried away a bit quickly. I wanted to believe so much. It was too good [...]'

Suddenly, they heard a series of clicks, the characteristic sound of a mechanism being triggered. First the cross sank into the sarcophagus by about fifteen centimeters, then the altar moved with a hellish noise. A rocky creak followed. The two men recoiled in surprise. They were stunned, paralyzed by emotion.

Gilles stepped back so much that he no longer thought about the two steps leading to the altar and fell backwards. Fortunately, it was not serious; he managed to break his fall at the last moment with his hands. He immediately thought of the news item he had just read before falling asleep while reading the latest news on the net. A Korean couple had fallen from the top of a cliff in Etretat while trying to take a selfie of themselves with the well-known arch in the background. A few too many steps backwards to get a better picture and goodbye to the two lovebirds. A silly accident like one that happens every fortnight in the world, with Indians being involved in one in three accidents.

Cyril didn't even notice, so entranced was he by what he saw. Gilles got up immediately and came back to his place. Their pulses quickened.

'Oh dear, Gilles, tell me I'm not dreaming!'

'I was going to ask you the same thing... but if you want, I can slap you in the face and we'll soon be done...'

The altar turned slowly, in the same direction as the grooves they had discovered on the floor during their first visit. The stone crunched. The floor shook. Then it came to rest perpendicular to its original axis less than thirty seconds later, leaving a dark gaping hole from which a cloud of dust escaped.

Cyril waited for the cloud to dissipate and then illuminated the cavity. A staircase about eighty centimeters wide appeared. It descended steeply for several meters. At the bottom he saw a black and white checked floor.

Despite the excitement, Gilles hesitated to commit himself.

'What do we do? Shall we go?' he asked feverishly.

'What do you mean 'we're going'? We've just discovered a passage that no one seems to know exists and you're asking me if we should go? Is this a joke or what? Brave little Gilles, but not reckless... I'm going. If you're scared, wait for me here.'

Stung to the core, he followed him. The steps were narrow and high and the descent dizzying. Cyril was cautious, holding onto the wall with his right hand, sweeping his torch across the steps to see where he was stepping and removing cobwebs as he went. Stone debris littered the steps. The mechanism was undoubtedly very old and had suffered the full weight of the centuries. He therefore took his time. But Gilles did not. He felt it at his back, finally impatient to see what was below. But he didn't have time to tell him to slow down when the latter skidded on one of the steps, fell backwards and went down the stairs on his buttocks, dragging Cyril down with him. The arrival was certainly quicker than expected, but a little rougher.

'Couldn't you do it more gently? But you're a walking disaster, my word!'

'Uh, sorry, I slipped.'

'No, no kidding... nothing broken?'

'A few bruises on my back and posterior, but otherwise it looks fine,' said Gilles as he got up.

They picked up their flashlights, turned up the power to the maximum and then considered the place they had just set foot in a little too suddenly and much more quickly than they had expected.

They found a rectangular room of about seven by five yards divided into two bays. The one near the staircase was barrel-vaulted while the second was cross-vaulted, both of which were made of dry stone. The keystone was relatively low, less than three and a half yards from the ground. They moved forward. On the right side of the wall were a dozen funerary niches arranged in two rows. A good half of these niches were occupied. Skeletons nestled in alcoves. On the left-hand wall was a tiny altar in the center, at the ends of which lay two old candlesticks, a rosary and a leather-crusted pocket Bible with a copper clasp. A processional cross lay against it. An open tabernacle, without a door, of extreme simplicity, stood above and contained a ciborium and a chalice, both of silver blackened by time. Still higher up was a painting, which they attributed to the Virgin Mary in all likelihood. In front of the altar was a wooden prie-Dieu. The black and white checkerboard that Cyril had glimpsed covered the entire floor of the room. The two men moved slowly forward, scanning every part of the room so as not to miss a thing. In the back bay, exactly under the keystone, was a square altar-table supported by four sturdy legs, all made of stone, and surrounded by four thrones, also carved from rock. A wooden chair, identical to those in the nave, was placed against the table. As Cyril walked over to it he found books, one open as if someone had just written in it, a dried-up quill across it and an inkwell beside it. He reached in and blew on the left-hand page to clear away the dust, revealing the written lines. He could clearly read a date in the margin:

20 August 1914

'It is a collection dating from the beginning of the twentieth century.'

Gilles approached and read in turn.

'The war was raging in these parts at that time. If memory serves, the Battle of Morhange began on the nineteenth of August. The first French offensive in Lorraine to take the lead. The results were catastrophic and they were already retreating the next day.'

'I wonder who these memoirs belong to,' said Cyril as he closed the book and inspected the front cover. 'It didn't take him long to find out.'

Memoirs of Abbé Jean Humbert
Book 4

The book was in very good condition. The others, lying on the corner of the monastery table, corresponded to the abbot's other three volumes.

At the back of the crypt, in the left-hand corner, Gilles could make out a bed, the upper part of which was covered with stones from the collapse of the adjoining wall and part of the vault.

Something immediately intrigued him.

He moved forward, pointing to a specific spot with his torch and then widened his eyes when he was close enough to make out the shape.

'Cyril, come and see. I think I've found someone.'

His companion came to his level. The bones of two feet still wrapped in leather sandals were visible. He cleared away some stones and uncovered the shins.

'What if it was this abbot?'

'It looks like it to me. Oh poor thing, he was undoubtedly a victim of the landslide while he was sleeping. Probably as a result of shells falling in the vicinity during the Great War, which weakened the structure. I don't know how old this crypt is, but it must be much older.'

Cyril placed the books in his rucksack after taking a picture of them. As he removed them, he exposed the altar-table and another cross pattee carved in the centre of the stone jumped out at him. The same as the two already spotted, on the altar and the church floor, a few meters above them. He went round the four chairs and saw the same sign engraved on the back of the backrests.

'This symbol comes up frequently,' Gilles remarked. 'At first glance, it looks like the Templar cross.'

'To the Templars? So these elements date from the thirteenth century?'

'Or early fourteenth. Or even beyond. The Order was officially dissolved in 1312, but there is nothing to say that some members did not try to perpetuate their work afterwards. The checkerboard was very common in their commanderies. It was probably added later. The crypt itself must be even older. Hence the bones in the coffins.'

'The what?'

'The enfeus are burial niches. The crypt was later converted into a council chamber, hence the stone table and thrones. Then, at the beginning of the twentieth century, the abbot turned the room into a shelter, probably to take cover from the fire of the fighting outside.'

'But the unfortunate man did not imagine that this room would be returned to its original function, namely as a crypt, to house his remains. One had to be motivated to sleep in this vault!'

'Yes. Or eager to save his skin.'

The two friends went around the room again with feverish eyes like treasure hunters or grave robbers. But they had nothing else to eat. Their discovery was already more than impressive, but they didn't seem to appreciate its importance. Not yet.

'What do we do? Do we inform the mayor?'

'No way. We close the passage and we don't tell anyone. Only to Natasha. Just long enough to read these books and see what's in them. Then I'll talk to Visconti. He will decide. I can't imagine that he would be informed through the press. He would burn me. Especially as he has told me not to talk about it to anyone but him. And now I'm going to impress him with this find! There's no doubt that this time my thesis will be a real golden nugget,' Cyril gloated.

'And he'll get all the credit!'

'Quite possible... but as a disciple of the master, I have a duty to inform him. I don't really have a choice.'

They returned to the nave. But when they emerged from the crypt, a major dilemma awaited them. As much as they had succeeded in triggering the opening mechanism of the trapdoor, somewhat by chance it must be said, they had no idea how to close it.

'There has to be a way to close it again,' grumbled Cyril, who was struggling with the cross in the altar.

But nothing helped.

Gilles illuminated the bottom of the stairs. The white tiles, which had yellowed with age, reflected the light on the wall and revealed a protrusion which neither of them had paid attention to when they descended. But in their defense, their entry had been rather chaotic. A stone was sticking out about fifteen centimeters. He went back down to inspect it more closely. The stone had the same circled cross pattee on its front as on the altar.

A light went on in his brain.

There had to be some way of closing the trapdoor once it was down if people were to meet in peace. Even if he was sure that another closing system existed upstairs at the altar, he would settle for that one. They did not have time to waste hours searching. It was not far from four o'clock in the morning and it was better to leave in the night as quietly as possible. He called Cyril to let him know what he had found.

'I think I've figured out how to close the passage!'

'Well done, but do you know if you'll have time to get back up fast enough? If not, you might get crushed by the altar. Because I doubt very much that those few tons of stone will stop at the slightest reverse pressure.'

'I hadn't taken the time to think about that, but it's a risk we have to take if we want to keep our secret. Be ready to help me when I get to the top of the stairs.'

Gilles took three deep breaths to release the stress and concentrate as much as possible, then applied pressure to the stone. But just as the trap door opened, the mechanism activated immediately. The altar moved much faster than expected. The mechanism had been released, to the great displeasure of the two men. Once the surprise was over, Gilles hurried to climb the steps two by two, using his hands to move faster and to keep his balance as best he could.

The hole was shrinking rapidly.

Far too quickly for his liking.

'Faster,' encouraged Cyril.

Gilles reached the top, his hands touching the floor of the choir. Cyril rushed to him, grabbed his hands and pulled him up as hard as he could. So hard that they both fell backwards. Just in time. The altar returned to its original position in the process.

'That was close... next time we'll try to find another way!'

The two friends lay down for a few seconds, with their backs to the cold floor, to catch their breath and bring their heart rates down to a more reasonable level.

They then put the carpet back in place, cleaned up a bit so as not to leave any visible traces, and returned to the lodge. Gilles was yawning so hard that his jaw dropped.

'I'm going back to bed for a few hours. All these strong emotions have exhausted me. What about you?'

'I'm in great shape ! These discoveries have given me a boost. I'm going to sit in the living room and leaf through these books. I'm far too curious to know what's in them.'

The Mystery of the Lost Crypt

15

Marimont-lès-Bénestroff
Sunday May 12th 2014, 9am

The lack of sleep and the many emotions of the previous night had finally taken their toll on the academic. No sooner had he opened the first volume written by the abbot than he fell asleep in the armchair. It was the lady of the house who woke him up by opening the shutters in the living room. She jumped when she saw him, not expecting to find him there.

'Oh, sorry, I didn't see you!'

'No, don't be sorry, I couldn't get to sleep and came here to read a little so as not to disturb my friend. I think I dozed off a bit," he said, his voice hoarse and his eyelids closed, embarrassed by the sudden brightness in the room. I think a large bowl of coffee will do me a world of good. We've still got a lot of work to do today.'

'So how is your research coming along?'

'Oh yes, beyond our expectations,' he said, before changing his mind. We did find a small leather purse in a low wall of the old castle, but not much else for the moment. Except for items from the three great wars.

'It's not so bad... and this famous tunnel, have you discovered it?'

'... unfortunately not. But we don't lose hope.'

With that, Natasha appeared.

'So you're spending the night away? I'd like to know where you were, you rascal...'

'In the arms of... Morpheus. But here on this sofa. You were snoring too loudly,' he teased.

The manager went off to prepare breakfast. This was the perfect time to tell Natasha about the night's events. He showed her a multitude of photos taken with his mobile phone. She couldn't believe it. She was as excited as they were. But there was a certain frustration in her eyes at once. She wished she could have been with them at the moment of discovery. Cyril reassured her that she would come with them the next time they came to visit, the following weekend.

Breakfast was Pantagruelian. They ate cereals, sweet and savory toast, brioche, all with a large bowl of coffee and a glass of orange juice. They needed this for the intense day of work ahead. The fog seemed to have disappeared, but not the threatening clouds. A shower was always possible. Once they had eaten their meal, they got ready and returned to the excavation site with more enthusiasm than the day before. Their discovery had put a smile on their faces. They couldn't help but glance in the direction of the church as they passed by. They were about to go by the crossroads when someone called out to them on their right. It was the mayor. He looked angry.

'Could I ask what you were up to in the church yesterday?'

The three of them looked at each other, dumbfounded.

'What are you talking about, Mr Mayor?'

'Please follow me.'

He remained silent until they arrived in the church. He looked really furious.

The two men did not give up.

'Do you think he knows?'

His companion shrugged.

The mayor led them to the left to the wall next to the altar and pointed to its base.

'Look at the huge crack. It wasn't there yesterday.'

The Mystery of the Lost Crypt

A gash about two meters long stood out on the immaculate wall. The trio did not know what to say to him. They had a vague idea of where the crack came from, but of course they didn't want to divulge anything.

Cyril launched into a series of explanations, each one more zany than the last, in order to evade the issue.

'I can assure you, Mr. Mayor, that we had nothing to do with it. We only inspected the altar by drawing sketches and taking pictures. Nothing more. All materials work with time. Wood, plaster, stone. Perhaps the floor has moved. An imperceptible earthquake could also have occurred last night, causing this crack. Perhaps we should ask the Central Seismological Bureau in Strasbourg.'

'An earthquake here tonight? Is this a joke or what?' he said in a neutral tone.

'No. In fact, it's quite likely. That's probably why I woke up in the middle of the night. The bed was vibrating slightly. The last seismic tremors in the region were felt in Moselle and throughout Lorraine. Both were of magnitude 4.3 on the Richter scale, says Gilles, consulting a web page on his phone. See for yourselves. Apparently, about ten thousand tremors of less than three magnitudes, barely perceptible, occur every day in the world.'

'And as luck would have it, here... while you were there in the evening.'

'Just a coincidence. You were there for the last hour and we left together. There was no damage and we locked the door on our way out.'

'Yes, it was. I went round again just to see if everything was in order. But I found the door open this morning when I came in... So someone came.'

'Really? We don't have any spare keys and the door doesn't seem to be broken into,' said Gilles, gauging its state.

'I'm going to do a little investigation, because normally only the parish priest and Mother Darcys have a set of keys.'

'Who is this 'Mother Darcys'?' asked Cyril.

'A lady of eighty-six who lives opposite the church, on the corner, at the crossroads. But I doubt that at her age and knowing her habits, she went there last night after nine o'clock... I'm sorry I accused you so quickly.'

'You're welcome. You still haven't heard anything about my missing dog?'

'No. I'm sorry. But I passed the message on at last night's council meeting. Have a nice day,' said the mayor, walking away in annoyance.

Relieved that they had fooled him, they whistled back to the forest. The two friends were apprehensive about his reaction, thinking for a moment that he knew about their wonderful discovery. Or that their suspicious attitude would betray them. But apparently none of this had happened.

As Cyril feared, the courtyard of the castle-farm was empty. The car that had been there the evening before had disappeared. But that was only a temporary setback. He would get another chance during their little getaway next weekend. Between the crypt and the books left by the priest, his discoveries were more than enough and he had no illusions about any additional unpublished information. Luck had already smiled on him enough. And the possibility of the existence of a gallery in the mound would only be the icing on the cake. Nothing more.

The frustration of not being able to meet the owners of the estate was followed by the pleasant surprise of finding the excavation site in the same condition as it had left it the day before. Given the rather unsympathetic attitude of the local fauna, they expected to see some damage caused by a few overly curious or jealous individuals.

This was not the case, much to their relief.

Everyone resumed their task at the place where they had left the day before. The sky was as threatening as ever and Natasha had put on a poncho, protecting her at first from the damp draught that was creeping through the trees on top of the hill and chastising their bodies. The excavation of the site was getting bigger and bigger, revealing the beautiful low walls of the old castle. And always here and there some military remains of the last three Franco-German wars, to Gilles' great delight, who collected them meticulously. These various finds would perhaps one day lead the faculty of Nancy, through its dean, Professor Visconti, to undertake further research on the site, something that had never been done before due to lack of budget.

Lunch was quickly eaten. A ham and butter and pickle sandwich with a packet of crisps and cherry tomatoes. They had refused the bottle of local wine, fearing for good reason that they would not be in optimal condition to work in the afternoon. The whole thing was prepared with the same care by the manager of the gite who seemed to have a soft spot for these three.

At about nine o'clock the light began to fade, made worse by the thick clouds. The weekend was coming to an end and they had to put everything away. They were proud of their work. As they had concentrated mainly on the outer walls of the castle, no other objects from the medieval period were found. But that did not matter. That was not the point.

As Cyril took pictures of the site from all angles, he was again disturbed by the barking of a dog. Once again he was convinced he heard Jack, his golden retriever. This time he had to go and see. He left his friends in the lurch and took off running. The barking was coming from the north, towards the village. The access to the village was more direct on this side, but the steeper slope and dense vegetation made it more difficult to advance. Dead branches, brambles and nettles followed one another and a few curses were uttered when the young man had to fight his way out of a thorny thicket whose thin branches clung to his clothes and threatened to lacerate them. But he didn't give up, and for good reason, the noises became more and more audible as he went on.

He shouted a 'Jack' and was immediately heard. The dog responded with a few barks. The sound seemed close, but at the same time very muffled, cavernous, as if the animal was locked in somewhere or had fallen into a well. Cyril turned round and judged that he was about halfway down the slope. But there were no sheds or caves visible at this point. He was disoriented. He continued to walk forward while calling him, but soon realized that he was too far away and that he had to retrace his steps. He approached another grove and heard his dog's growling more clearly. He made his way through and finally saw a pit. He leaned over it and, with the help of his torch, this time distinguished Jack's figure further back in the dry, his tail chasing around and his moans of joy replacing the calls. But Cyril soon realized that the height of the hole, the front of which was flooded and unaware of the height of the water, was such that it would not allow him to evacuate it alone. He would need help. He tried to call Gilles on his telephone, but the poor network in that area prevented him from reaching him. So he went to look for him, but not without first warning his dog as if he were talking to a person.

'Stay put Jack. Yes, you're a good dog!'

It was heartbreaking to leave his companion, whom he had only just found after two long days. The dog howled to death as soon as he lost sight of his master.

'Don't worry Jack, I'll be back soon,' he shouted.

He scrambled up the slope as fast as he could, tearing his trousers in the brambles and scratching his calf in the process. A trickle of blood escaped from the scrape, but his thoughts were too focused on Jack and how they were going to get him out of this mess to pay any attention. He picked up his companion who was preparing his rucksack and they both left without further ado. Natacha followed them. Apart from some hesitation as to the location of the hole, they were soon on the spot. Jack had not moved. Cyril widened the access to the cavity by breaking the old wooden boards with his heel. They gave way as easily as slabs of thin ice and the debris fell into the water. He broke off a long branch and inserted it into the cavity to judge the height of the water. As he pulled up the stick, it was wet for more than a meter.

'I'm going in,' he said determinedly.

'We don't have much choice anyway,' replied his sidekick. 'You pass him to me as you can, I'll get him the best I can, at worst by his collar, and then I'll help you get come up in the process. That should do it.'

Cyril jumped into the water and was submerged to the hips. Even though he had expected it, it was still a surprise because the water was so cold. In very summery weather, it would have been much more pleasant. Today, he would have done without it. Jack was pawing impatiently on the bank. After a few caresses, it was difficult to see which of the two was happier to find the other, he carried him and then stretched him out at arm's length towards Gilles who pulled him out not without difficulty. Then it was his turn to get out, still with the help of his friend. The rescue operation was over.

The weekend was ending for the better.

Cyril had found his four-legged friend, recovered his car, and above all made great strides in his research by uncovering the first foundations of the castle, which had disappeared a few centuries earlier, and by having the luxury of uncovering a crypt under the church as well as the writings of an abbot. A more than positive result.

Before heading back to Nancy, he sent an SMS to Visconti, his professor and thesis director.

> **Hello Professor. We have found former crypt under the village church. Can we meet tomorrow around 10am after school? Have a nice evening.**
> **Cdly. Cyril de Villiers**

Visconti did not answer the message, but called him directly. The young man was surprised at his speed.

'Hello Cyril. I prefer to talk to you in person, as messages are not my forte. I prefer to decipher hieroglyphics rather than write them. However, I have just read yours and it seems more than interesting!'

'What we have just discovered in this small village is quite extraordinary. The excavations of the old castle on the motte are progressing well. And as we wrote in the text message, we found a secret passage under the altar of the church, which seems to date back to the Carolingian period. There we found the writings of an abbot, four books in all. His last notes stop a few days after the outbreak of the First World War. And all this in just two days.'

'Beautiful. What kind of books?'

'Four of them are testimonies in the abbot's own hand. A personal diary in several volumes. Oh, and I forgot the old codex, which is kept in a beautifully decorated and engraved wooden box, in very good condition, and transcribed in a language unknown to me. At first glance, it looks like Hebrew. However, there is no doubt that it is a Templar codex. The manuscript is called 'Immortalitatis Predictorum Templariorum'.'

There was a silence, and then the dean spoke in a restrained, monotone.

'I look forward to hearing from you and to learning more. Don't forget to bring this codex with you.'

'Well, Professor. See you tomorrow.'

'And above all Cyril, don't mention it to anyone. The same goes for your friends. It's still too early to disclose anything. We must keep it a secret. I'm counting on you.'

'You can count on me, Professor.'

16

Vatican
Sunday May 12th 2014, 7:45pm

Like every night, Luca Armendi was reading a bedtime story to his four-year-old son when he received an alert on his Pager. A rather rudimentary tool in itself these days, but still handy. He wasn't the type to invariably replace old technology with the latest, especially if the former was good. The message came from his duty officer. A 'code 3'. On a scale of up to five. Not an extreme emergency, but his presence was required. He finished the story quicker than expected, kissed his boy on the forehead, then closed the door and announced to his wife, who was lying comfortably in front of the television, that he was going away for a while.

The prefect, the only gendarme with Vatican nationality, lived with his family in the barracks inside the papal city walls, in the same building as the 'bunker', the command center. So he had only three floors to go down. He took the lift, passed through the various security checks, and then entered the sacrosanct security area, a place that would make the secret services of many great nations pale in comparison.

'What's going on, Alfonso'

'I'm sorry to have disturbed you, Commander, but we've just intercepted an interesting message on one of the tapped phones. Here, I have just printed it out in duplicate.'

Armendi took the message handed to him by the gendarme.

'Had he ever had any dealings with this sender?'

'I was just looking around the base. Apparently not,' said the officer after a few minutes of searching.

'Good. Add this number to the list. I'll tell the Grand Chancellor about it. I think this news should be of great interest to him...'

The prefect went back to the 'aquarium' to dial the Order of Malta's fax number, and then put the message he had picked up a few moments earlier on the fax machine after writing an explanatory note. As soon as it was sent, he told the duty officer that he was going back to his flat. But he did not have time to leave the Bunker before the officer called him out.

'Commander, come quickly, this time it's a phone call between the same two numbers.'

'Don't forget to record,' he says, putting the earpiece in place.

At the end of the conversation, he asked the duty officer to transcribe what was said and fax it as soon as possible to the number he gave him.

The prefect of the gendarmerie had been following this case for eleven months at the express request of Cardinal Patronus. Not exclusively, because his schedule and his obligations to the Holy Father did not allow it, but he was supported by one of his subordinates, entirely dedicated to this task. They both worked in direct collaboration with Interpole, the Italian Carabinieri and the French authorities.

The events began in June 2013 with the theft of the Virgin of Philerme, the Order's most precious icon, from the monastery of Cetinje in Montenegro. Since then, a lot of water has flowed under the bridge. There had been a stroke of luck, necessary from time to time to start an investigation, after reading on the Net an article in a daily newspaper in Nice about the murder of a man in a car park overlooking the city. A more than banal case in the region, which was used to settling accounts between rival drug gangs. But by cross-checking with various other information, the carabinieri had managed to find the dead man's identification card and trace his journey the day before his murder and the day of the robbery itself. He had already been convicted of various petty crimes and was known to the Montenegrin authorities. The elements matched the painting theft case in every respect. It remained to discover the murderer and the possible sponsor. For the former, the intervention of a nine-year-old English boy who had witnessed the crime scene could unravel everything. He was completely silent, and only the intervention of a psychologist could help him to make progress. After six months of therapy, the police were able to obtain the number plate of the killer's car, which was arrested the next day after a simple alcohol test at the entrance to Nice. The make of the car matched the elements of the investigation. But for lack of tangible evidence, he could not be taken into custody. This did not prevent Commissioner Piéroni from keeping a close eye on him.

Giacomo Borgia was initialing documents in preparation for the next seminar of the Order's national associations around the world, to be held in Malta at the end of the year, when he was interrupted by the alarm of his fax machine. A page came out. The message was from the Vatican's protected hotline, signed by the Prefect of Gendarmerie himself.

He was amazed at the content of the message.

And by one term in particular.

The Grand Chancellor stroked his chin warily. He stood up and walked towards the library, a huge room adjoining his office, with burr-walnut shelves covering the four sides of the wall to the full height, where only two doors fitted into the decor. The first he had just borrowed, the second communicating with the Grand Master's office. The most beautiful collections of literature and history of civilizations from all over the world, both ancient and contemporary, were represented there, most of which were printed according to the Order's charter. He picked up two very heavy books in aged black leather, with gilt on the page edges and both clasps. Two magnificent copies transcribed at the beginning of the last century, the originals being kept in the Vatican library. In each of these books of more than a thousand pages, an inventory was made of all the commanderies and their respective domains at the date of dissolution of each of the orders, at the beginning of the fourteenth century for the Templars and at the beginning of the nineteenth century for the Hospitallers.

These two books had the particularity of being able to search either in alphabetical order for the town or village housing a commandery, or by administrative division of each country, by region and by department.

At first he searched under the name of Marimont itself, but could not find a single building belonging to either order. He then tried the many names the village had taken over the centuries. No less than a dozen. But he was unsuccessful. He typed the same name into his computer search engine and then clicked on *Maps*. The map of the region appeared on the screen. He zoomed in and compared it with the eighteenth-century Cassini maps at the back of the books.

The result was quite different.

Templar possessions, many of which were taken over by the Hospitallers, abounded in the surrounding area, including an important commandery at Gelucourt, which itself owned a great deal of land in the surrounding villages, particularly in the village of Bourgaltroff, an area adjoining the one at Marimont. There was no mention of the presence of the Templars in Marimont, but this could be plausible given their neighbouring settlements. A census oversight was also possible. Especially at that time.

The Mystery of the Lost Crypt

But this detail intrigued him all the same. He was about to go back into the library when another fax bell rang. Another sheet of paper came out, with the same header as before. The Vatican.

This time it was a short telephone conversation between the same two protagonists, the whole of which had been transcribed. He sat back in his chair. His blood ran cold as he scanned the dialogues, especially one of them.

[The last one looks very old, sheltered in a nicely decorated and engraved wooden box, but in good condition nonetheless, and is transcribed in a language unknown to me. At first glance, it looks like Hebrew. However, there is no doubt that it is a Templar codex. The name of the manuscript seems to be: 'Immortalitatis predictorum Templariorum'.

The Grand Chancellor gasped.

No doubt about it. The main codex mentioned this manuscript.

He made a quick phone call and then headed for the Grand Master's office. He knocked and opened the door. Bertrand de Villaret was in the middle of a telephone conversation. He motioned to him to come closer. When he hung up, Borgia thrust the sheet of paper under his nose.

'Do you remember what I told you about a year ago, a few days after the disappearance of the icon, about the book found in the crypt of the Temple church in Paris and also stolen a few months later?'

'Yes, vaguely. You were telling me that it was referring to other books without which the writings could not be deciphered in their entirety. Just as he finished his sentence, he looked at the fax again and understood the link. So the young man had found one of these famous books?'

'This is also the feeling I have. At least one could assume so. Especially if you couple it with the fact that it is an old Templar hall never listed. You could get a very explosive cocktail.'

'That would be extraordinary. It was a stroke of luck that he should have stumbled across it, while others had searched all their lives and found nothing. And he, with the help of two friends, uncovered a crypt and discovered this document during his very first archaeological dig. Do we know who he is? And his two partners?'

'Not yet, but it won't be long. Prefect Armendi is in charge. We will have his curriculum vitae shortly.'

'It looks like they are going back next weekend.'

'In that case, we will be there too...'

'This small hamlet will suddenly become the center of interest for many people and bubble with activity.'

'Yes, it will be difficult not to be noticed...'

When Borgia sat down at his desk early on that Monday morning with a cup of coffee in hand, the report he had requested from Lucas Armendi was already sitting in the center of the mahogany brown leather desk pad. With 'Cyril de Villiers' written in large letters on the front cover. A biography of several pages related his family origins as well as his studies, his friends and all his years in the army. But the point of detail that instantly jumped out at the Grand Chancellor was his surname.

De Villiers.

This name was well known within the Order of Malta as two former knights bore the same surname. The first was Jean de Villiers, Grand Master from 1289 to 1297. He took part in the battle of St John of Acre two years after his election, alongside the Templars, the Order's all-time enemy, but lost the battle to the formidable army of the young sultan Al-Ashraf Khalil, resulting in the definitive withdrawal of the Frankish positions in the East. They all settled in Cyprus where King Henry II of Lusignan assigned them Limassol, a small and undefended city, where he devoted all his energy and his last years to fortifying it. The second was Philippe de Villiers de l'Isle-Adam, Grand Master of the Order from 1521 to 1534. His many exploits made him rise rapidly through the ranks. Just appointed to the highest position, he took part in the heroic defense of the capital against Suleiman the Magnificent in 1523, but had to surrender six months later, putting an end to their presence on the island. After seven long years of wandering, he settled in Malta, an island assigned to him by Charles V, who conferred sovereignty on them. On his death, the Ottoman sultan, who had always admired his immense qualities, had a panegyric published in all the mosques of his empire in his honor. "*Believers, learn from an infidel how one fulfills his duty to the point of being admired and honored by his enemies.*

Two emblematic figures who each participated in the destiny of this Order. And at the same time a surname destined to achieve great things and participate in great events. Curious, he wanted to know if this young man had a direct family link with one of these two figures. Many of the family trees of the Grand Masters of the Order had been successfully completed. Generally, the registers of the last century in progress were forbidden in the town halls to be distributed and consulted. But not for the Order of Malta, which had its own dedicated genealogy service that updated the data almost in real time. He promptly sent an e-mail enclosing the report to one of the employees of this section in order to check the young man's parentage, notifying the urgency of the request.

Although in recent decades the Order of Malta has been much more open than in its early days, when only the nobility was eligible for knighthood, volunteers from all walks of life and all social classes were now accepted.

However, certain traditions were still firmly established, especially in the upper echelons of the Order.

Borgia took up the report and read it in detail. He concentrated on the young man's entourage and wanted to know the identity of the people who had accompanied him on their weekend trip to the countryside. A whole page was devoted to them. The young woman, named Natasha de Beynac, belonged to a very old noble family, once one of the most powerful in Guyenne, which was one of the four baronies of the Périgord. Borgia typed a few keywords into his computer and started the search. He learned that this family had, among other things, a title of reward from the

Order of the Hospitallers of Saint John of Jerusalem, Rhodes and Malta.

It was a small world...

The second, Gilles Perrin, did not seem to have any connection with any member of the Order, but belonged to a famous family of historians for several generations, his paternal grandfather and great-uncle and his great-grandfather, who was none other than Charles-Edmond Perrin, a great French medievalist. Both of his parents were also illustrious historians who had published numerous works, some of which were systematically related to the history of the Order and which already completed his very rich collection.

After reading the entire report, he got in touch with the small team he had put together the previous year. A new mission was being added.

A top priority.

17

Nancy
Monday May 13th 2014

Cyril waited impatiently outside the closed doors of the lecture theatre for the class to end. The bell rang at ten o'clock sharp. There was a hubbub and the two wooden doors suddenly opened and a tide of people poured out. The students were clearly showing their discontent.
'*The old man looked stressed today!*'
'*I'm surprised, he was so boring... and so was his course!*'
He waited until the tsunami had passed before entering. From the top of the lecture hall, he saw Visconti cleaning the large whiteboard on the back wall. In the cathedral-like silence, the creaking of the steps betrayed his presence with every step he took. The professor turned around and his face lit up at once.
'Ah, Cyril! You are my ray of sunshine. I have to admit that my mind was elsewhere this morning. But I don't think they'll hold it against me. We're all allowed to have moments of absence. In fact, to be honest, it's a bit your fault...'
The young man was careful not to reveal the criticisms of the students he had just heard. He raised his bag in the air as a trophy, despite its weight. He suspected the reason for the temporary wandering of the dean of the faculty of history.
'Here are the objects of the crime! I brought it all back.'

'That's fine. Follow me, we're going back to my office. We'll be much quieter there.'

Visconti walked at such a brisk pace that Cyril, despite his excellent physical condition, found it difficult to keep up with him in the maze of corridors. He was weary of the fact that the cubicle he used as an office was still as untidy as last time, if not worse. The same books were lying around on the chairs and desk - probably picked up by the maid who was trying to clean up what she could - covering every available surface. He could hardly store any more as some of the stacks of books stretched to the ceiling in a most precarious state of stability. Cyril even feared that opening the door would cause a draft strong enough to bring everything down. But it did not. Everything miraculously stayed in place.

He put his bag on the floor and took out the books.

'They weigh their weight. Especially the protected one. Where should I put them?' he asked, scanning the pile of books on the desk.

'Wait, I'll clear the desk for you quickly.'

With a sudden gesture of the arm that was becoming a reflex, not to say an OCD, he made way for the writings to be deposited, much to the annoyance of the young man who was chagrined to see all these books fall to the ground with so little consideration.

'Be careful Cyril, they are fragile...'

Cyril could not believe this last remark. He could not help but object sharply.

'As fragile as these?' he said scathingly, glancing down at the ones the old man had just dropped.

'Oh, the difference is immeasurable. These are unimportant. They are less than a century old. Pale copies without any value whatsoever. I can use them very well next winter to light my fireplace.'

'Yes indeed, if they are less than a century old...'

These explanations hardly convinced Cyril, who still found it difficult to see that works could be treated in this way. Especially coming from a historian, who is also the dean of a faculty...

Visconti quickly swept his eyes over the four books of the abbot's memoirs, which did not seem to interest him, and concentrated on the finely carved wooden box. There was no doubt about its origin and design. A Templar cross inlaid in relief in the wood sat in the middle. He blew away the dust and admired the goldsmith's work done centuries before. A patchwork of thin branches and intertwined vine leaves covered almost the entire box. Only the circle containing the Templar cross was free of it.

'Wonderful!'

The little box had miraculously preserved itself. He opened it and discovered the book inside. The leather had of course aged badly, cracks appeared all over its surface and the pages had yellowed, but the whole was in more than satisfactory condition.

'The cellar must have provided optimal storage conditions all these years. Not too wet and not too dry and at a constant temperature of about 15 degrees. Ideal for a good conservation.'

'Of books and bones. Some niches were occupied. These skeletons must also be several centuries old. It is a real archaeological treasure that has been unearthed.'

But Visconti was already in his bubble and did not listen to the young man's last remark. He was fascinated by this ancient book. He gave the impression that he knew it existed and had been waiting for ages to discover it. And now he had.

'I did some research last night and, strangely enough, there is no mention of any Templar community in any of the manuals. There are some around, but not in this particular place. How can that be?'

'Perhaps it was an oversight in the various censuses taken at the time,' Visconti replied laconically, gazing at the front cover of the old book. Magnificent', he kept repeating.

'Quite possible. Or a very specific reason not to mention it and thus not to attract attention.'

'You have a point Cyril. Because the best way to keep a secret for a long time is to make everyone forget it!'

'Yes, but then it can be forgotten for... eternity. What's the point?'

The Mystery of the Lost Crypt

'In our case, we must not forget one thing. An essential one, in fact. The Templar order, if this is really the origin of your formidable discoveries, was supposed to merge with the Hospitallers. But the dissensions, not to say the hatred that these two orders had for each other, never allowed it. The Order of the Temple was therefore purely and simply dissolved by the Pope and the majority of their property, especially real estate such as the commanderies, distributed to their eternal enemies. It would therefore seem conceivable that they would try to protect their cash assets, such as gold coins and precious stones, in case one day the Order might rise from its ashes like the phoenix, or rather from the ashes of Jacques de Molay, their last master who was burned at the stake. Some believe that the Freemasons are descended from it and other more recent orders claim to have direct line of descent with the Temple. So the aim was to put this treasure on hold so that it could be used by others later... but with the risk, as you have just pointed out, that it will be forgotten for longer than expected and that it will no longer be used for its original purpose.'

'We're getting carried away, but if it turns out there's nothing there at all. Or maybe the so-called treasure has already been recovered by someone. This could explain the birth of the legend that has been running in the village since the dawn of time.'

'What legend are you talking about?'

'The hill is said to hold a great treasure. Some sort of golden bowling alley or something.'

'A golden bowling alley? An original treasure. I doubt very much that the very strict rules imposed on the Templars throughout the day allowed them to indulge in such a game, even if historically it would have been conceivable since this game has existed for much longer. The first traces of the game date back to ancient Egypt, around five thousand years before Christ, and it appeared in our country in the Middle Ages. But this does not mean that there is no hidden treasure. It is just that its representation, in order to make people dream, must be mystical and surprising. Otherwise it loses all connotation. But don't get too excited, Cyril. All archaeologists dream of discovering treasures and few are the chosen ones...'

'Don't worry about me, Professor, I've updated enough over the weekend. I don't expect anything else.'

'You are right. I already have a lot.'

Cyril noticed that Visconti was obsessed with the book in the box. He couldn't take his eyes off it. Such glee was almost embarrassing, especially as his last remark did not fall on deaf ears. **I've already got a lot...**'. Even though he was only his pupil, the credit for the discovery went entirely to him, Natasha and Gilles. But here the teacher seemed to be taking the whole discovery without even integrating it. The young man immediately became more sombre and even began to doubt. Had he been right to reveal everything at once? Shouldn't he have taken the liberty of disclosing the information himself to the parties concerned? Would the three of them be associated the day their discovery was made public? All these questions suddenly nagged at the back of his mind. He could not jump to conclusions at the moment, perhaps he was imagining things, but a certain ambiguity set in.

'What type of ancient writing is it?'

'I would lean towards Syriac, a Semitic language of the Near East and more precisely a dialect of Aramaic from the region of Edessa transformed into a written language since the beginning of the Christian era. Its alphabet derives from Phoenician. And conversely, the Arabic alphabet is linked to Syriac. I was talking about this less than a month ago in class.'

'Yes, that's right,' lied Cyril as he searched the depths of his memory for some snippet of memory from that course.

Visconti put on white gloves and flipped through some pages with extreme delicacy.

'There are three main forms of typography. This one looks like the *Estrangelâ* style.'

'Now that you mention it, it comes back to me. It is characterized by the fact that vowels can be indicated by small signs.'

'I'm glad to see you've learned something from my lecture,' he said wryly.

The professor closed the book and put it back in its protective box. A look of satisfaction came over his face.

'You told me yesterday on the phone that you would go back next weekend. Do you still confirm this?'

There was a blank. The latter did not know what to say.

'Yes... well no. Let's just say that at first we wanted to go back, but we changed our minds right after our conversation. And we decided to postpone our little escapade to a later date,' Cyril answered awkwardly.

'Fine. As you wish. You're right, it's better this way. It's better to take a step back and give yourself time to think about it than to rush headlong into it. As I said on the phone, neither you nor your friends should tell anyone. It's very important to keep it quiet for now. Alerting our community too soon could be disastrous. Just let me know when you go back. Now please leave me. I have work to do.'

This last remark confirmed his suspicions even more. Cyril was very disappointed by the strange impression the professor gave off. The dean's aura seemed to have lost its edge.

Visconti called out to him as the young man walked sheepishly towards the door.

'Wait, Cyril, you forgot your notebooks.'

'You don't even keep them to leaf through?'

'No,' he said without even glancing at it.

'What should I do with it?' he asked in surprise.

'I won't have time to study them. You will do it for me. Read them all and if you find any interesting information, let me know.'

'Well... as you wish.'

'And when you have finished consulting them, we will send them to the diocese of Metz. After all, these notebooks do not seem to have much historical interest at first sight and then they belong to them. Later, perhaps the bishop will return them to the village council if they decide to open the crypt to visitors. They could turn it into an interesting museum, especially for such a small town. Oh, and one last thing, please don't call me on my mobile. I only use it in case of extreme emergency. I can't imagine what a mess it would be if all the students in this faculty started sending me messages like you do...'

This was too much for the academic. The professor's extreme arrogance horrified him. He took the books, put them carefully in his bag and left the office, greeting him coldly, to the total indifference of the dean.

The Mystery of the Lost Crypt

18

Nice
Monday May 13th 2014, 11am

The Grand Master was meticulously pruning the rosebushes on the vast estate, one of his favorite pastimes, when Karl came to him with a telephone.

'It is the Commander, Your Highness.'

He removed the glove from his right hand and picked up the receiver.

'To what do I owe the honor of your call, dear friend?'

His interlocutor told him in great detail the news he had just heard. He was speechless. He asked him to repeat it to make sure he had understood correctly.

'You did it! It's extraordinary [...] Of course. You are absolutely right. Too many people already know about it. Karl is leaving right away to join you. He'll clean up and support you until your mission is accomplished. He is the right man for the job. Don't worry.'

He hung up with a smile on his face.

'I have a new mission for you, Karl. And of the utmost importance. Our future depends on it,' he said, turning to his henchman. 'Take all the gear with you. No one should stand in your way.'

It was three o'clock in the afternoon and Cyril, slumped in one of the two armchairs in his living room, was ruminating in a corner about his disappointment. He still couldn't digest the singularly haughty attitude his thesis master had displayed in the morning. He almost regretted for a moment that he had warned him so early about their formidable and unexpected discoveries. Natasha had tried since her return from university to persuade him to forget about his resentments. But in vain. He could not force himself to forget this episode. In his opinion, Visconti's attitude spoke volumes about his way of being and thinking. Something strong had just happened and the osmosis between the two protagonists would certainly be affected. An air of suspicion was even emerging in the young man's mind.

He stared at his bag, which contained the writings from the beginning of the last century of the abbot who had been stationed in the small village of Marimont. The very ones that his thesis master had purely and simply snubbed. After some hesitation, he decided to take them out and leaf through them. A little reading would at least calm him down and make him forget this morning. He took the first volume, in chronological order of the date of writing, and began to read the pages quickly, diagonally.

Nothing too fancy.

A simple survey of the local population on his arrival in this new area comprising three parishes. This made a total of four hours of reading for nothing very interesting... The most Cyril learned was that the parish priest had done everything he could to get himself transferred there, but without any development as to the reason for this request or this attempt to escape.

He remained hungry.

And he thought that perhaps the Dean had been right to ignore it. The sixth sense of a very experienced man for sure.

Hunger began to tug at his guts. He finished his reading even more quickly than he had started it in order to prepare dinner. An area in which he excelled. His favorite pastime. Left to his own devices during his years with the commandos, he had quickly developed a passion for the culinary arts. Brief stints in the kitchens of renowned chefs between two distant and perilous missions allowed him to evacuate the pressure and get out of this warlike and bestial world. This was not to Natasha's displeasure and she was quite happy to have a chef at home.

Once the succulent meal had been eaten, the dishes washed, the work surface cleaned and the kitchen tidied up as it had been on the first day of his installation - a natural discipline inherited from his military past - he settled back in the armchair to continue his reading, putting his glass of red wine on the pedestal table. Natasha did the same. He began the second book, which was far more shocking than the first and made him very uncomfortable. The clergyman kept an up-to-date list of regular and occasional donors, but above all a black list of villagers who never gave anything, accompanied by comments that were not very glowing and unworthy of his position. He read out the juiciest passages to Natasha, who was devouring an English-language detective novel by his side, wrapped in a fleece blanket. She was equally horrified by the more than derogatory remarks of the cleric. But after three more hours of reading, a little more intense and exciting than the first volume, and the digestion of the feast taking its toll, his eyelids showed signs of weakness and he decided to go to bed. His beloved followed suit.

Karl arrived at the Commander's house at about nine o'clock. He was expected there for dinner. A 'quiet' drive for once. With such an arsenal in the boot, it was better not to attract any attention to himself on the road. Two very quick stops at motorway service areas and a one-hour traffic jam following a collision on the Lyon ring road made for an eight-hour journey. Out of respect for the Commander, he had warned of a possible delay. The two men talked until late in the evening. Their plan had to be fine-tuned. No trace was to be left behind.

And Karl had a lot of experience in this field. Forty-five years old, he was often nicknamed 'The Giant' by the high dignitaries of the order and in particular the Grand Master because of his imposing stature. Almost two meters tall and weighing one hundred and ten kilos. A former member of the BND, the German Federal Intelligence Service, he had been part of the anti-terrorist unit for nearly ten years, dismantling, with the help of his colleagues, a number of terrorist groups close to Al-Qaeda that were planning to commit attacks on German or French territory. He resigned after the terrible attack in the Berlin underground in December 2015, which left twenty dead and a hundred injured. His laxity in monitoring this group was fatal and, no longer in the odor of sanctity, forced him to emigrate to other climes. He found refuge in the south of France via one of his relations.

The next morning, he dropped the Commander off at the faculty and stayed in his car. He had planned ahead and brought several paperbacks to kill time. After a good three hours of waiting, watching the comings and goings behind his tinted windows between two readings, he finally saw his victim appear in the orangey yellow Mini Cooper signaled by the Commander. An unusual color that he had no trouble locating when the time came.

The shadowing could begin.

He had to wait until mid-afternoon to see his prey reappear. He had only been away for ten minutes, just enough time to drink a strong coffee and to relieve himself at the same time at the 'Bistrot des Étudiants', a stone's throw from where he had parked. The young man climbed into his car and drove off. Karl, surprised by such speed, followed him as best he could. After fifteen minutes of rallying through the city, with a few right turns and red lights, the Cooper pulled into an underground car park. The chase was over for the day. He had gathered all the information he needed to complete his mission. He returned to the Commander's home to prepare his equipment. He left in the middle of the night.

It was three in the morning.

The giant parked in a street adjacent to the one he was supposed to go to. To be on the safe side. There wasn't a soul around at this time of night, even in the middle of the university campus. The first end-of-year exams were about to start in most faculties and the students were more focused on revising than on partying. Only one car passed him and turned into the same street. An Italian plate.

Probably tourists... he thought.

Dressed all in black, with a large hood over his head, and aided by the recent regulation to turn off streetlights and commercial signs at this time of day, he went completely unnoticed, unknown to any cameras deployed throughout the city. He turned into the street in question. The automatic gate to the underground car park was closed and could only be operated by remote controls reserved for car park owners. So he went to a small metal door which, luckily, was not locked. As he passed through the porch, the light went on automatically and numerous lamps illuminated the car park as if it were daylight. He had expected this. He immediately spotted the Cooper with its distinctive color in a box. He took an automatic jack out of his suitcase, lifted the front of the car a good thirty centimeters and slid underneath. After five minutes, all the lights in the basement went out. The detection cells saw no activity, so the timer did not go off a second time. He used his torch to set up his device. This was not the first time he had placed explosives under a car, coupled to the starter motor. His trademark was well oiled. The person would have no chance of escaping. Fifteen minutes later, he emerged from the car park. With the satisfaction of a job well done.

Then he returned to the Commander's home.

A car with tinted windows had just parked on the street opposite the entrance to the underground car park of the residence. The couple stayed inside the car. They could not have hoped for a better way to monitor the comings and goings.

They were both Neapolitans, but had never met before joining the Order. She was slim and slender, standing over one meter seventy. Her hair was curly and black with red highlights, her smile and her eyes were devastating. A crazy charm that left no one indifferent. Not really the physique of the job at first sight, but this twenty-five-year-old woman was not to be trifled with. She practiced a martial art and was enrolled in a shooting club. The few men who had dared to be impetuous were quickly put in their place. He was in his thirties, a few centimeters taller than his partner, with black hair slicked to the side and slightly protruding ears. But his large brown eyes gave him a certain appeal to the female population. They had an air of Bonnie and Clyde, so much so that their resemblance to the two American gangsters was almost perfect. But the similarity stopped at the physical.

Because they were not criminals.

They did not wait long before a man entered the underground car park through the small open service door. He was carrying a sports bag with a steady hand. Was it the same man who had been following the young man from the university? But one thing was certain, the suspect car had parked in the adjacent street.

The man emerged from the underground twenty minutes later. He looked relaxed. His bag much lighter. It was a pity that it had started to rain at that moment, forcing the man to put on his hood, preventing them from seeing his face.

'I wonder what he's been up to in such a short time,' says Bonnie. And what's in the bag?

'I have no idea, but it sounds more than suspicious.'

Stay here, I'll follow him.

'You signal me at the slightest movement,' she said to her partner.

Clyde got out of the vehicle and chased the man with the bag who was walking a few dozen meters ahead of him. When the man turned left at the first intersection, Clyde accelerated so as not to lose sight of him for too long. When he turned into the next street, the man had disappeared.

Where could he have gone?

The Mystery of the Lost Crypt

He passed a white van that hid a black car behind it. He saw the man close the trunk and get into the front seat. He continued to walk along the pavement without insisting on looking at it, like a simple passer-by.

The car started up, turned around and drove up the street before disappearing. Clyde turned back.

'It was the car we suspected!'

At these words, Bonnie got out of the car and headed towards the garages, following the same path as the mystery man. The ceiling lights came on instantly thanks to the presence detectors. It wasn't the most discreet thing, but she didn't have much choice. Clyde, on the alert in the car, scanned the alley, ready to alert his partner if the man returned.

Bonnie came out fifteen minutes later.

'I examined the car from every angle and saw nothing. Nothing at all.'

'Are you sure you looked everywhere?'

'Yes, if I tell you. I didn't see anything suspicious. That's odd. The license plate matched, so I couldn't have got the wrong car. I'd rather you check it out yourself, just to be safe. A life may be at stake.'

Clyde went down to the underground car park and came out a few moments later. A second check was in order.

'I can confirm, nothing suspicious,' said Clyde as he sat down in the driver's seat, confident.

Bonnie was relieved to hear this.

The Mystery of the Lost Crypt

19

Nancy
Wednesday May 14th 2014, 7:30am

Like every Wednesday, Gilles went to the university to attend Professor Visconti's class at ten past eight. The last class of the year before the final exams. And Professor Visconti hated being disturbed by latecomers. This last session was all the more important as the dean would be giving his hints about the possible subjects that would be on the exam.

The young man was a little earlier than other mornings. Too eager to hear the latest recommendations. He took his satchel in one hand, put his sandwich in his mouth while waiting to lock the armored door of his flat and then called the lift down to the basement. When the door opened, he was surprised to find the charming young woman who lived one floor up. They had passed each other several times before, but had never engaged in conversation. Politeness and smiles, but nothing more. She had of course caught his eye, but he had never dared to approach her.

This time he took his courage in both hands.

'Would you like to go for a bite to eat tonight? We often bump into each other without talking and it might be time to get to know our neighbours better.'

'I'd love to,' she replied with a cheery smile. 'A bit of relaxation before the finals can only do good.'

'Yes, that's right, I was thinking the same thing, it will help you to relax. By the way, my name is Gilles.'

'Claire. We can be on first-name terms, it's nicer...'

'I couldn't agree more. So Claire, I'll pick you up at about seven. Will that be all right?' he asked her as he stopped in front of her parking space.

'It suits me fine. Is this your car?'

'Yes...'

'Ah, that's funny, what a coincidence [...].'

'Why?'

'No, nothing. A trifle. Have a nice day and see you tonight...' the young woman said, waving as she walked away.

Gilles sat down in the driver's seat. He couldn't believe it. He had just invited the most beautiful and brilliant student on campus. She had accepted immediately. He trembled with joy and took a few minutes to come down from his cloud.

He clipped on his safety belt, put the key in the pocket behind the gearbox and moved his index finger to the 'Start' button.

It was 07:40.

Clyde, who had slipped away for five minutes, returned with two large, long coffees from the McDonald's on the corner when there was a terrible explosion. He immediately dropped them on the pavement, splashing his shoes and trouser bottoms. Dust and smoke mixed in the basement of Gilles' home.

'Shit, what the hell...' shouted Clyde, panicking.

Bonnie jumped out of the car to follow her partner and they both ran towards the building.

A wave of general panic spread through the street. Passers-by ran in all directions, at first shouting that an attack had been made, then turned into simple onlookers, following the scene at a respectable distance. Windows opened in the surrounding buildings to satisfy the curiosity of some and calm the anxiety of others.

Inside, the smoke clouds were getting denser and blacker and escaping through all the existing openings and orifices. The couple entered the underground car park, still through the service door. The air was unbreathable. They placed a handkerchief over their face to breathe through.

Gilles started the engine.

A sudden deafening explosion occurred in the underground. The low ceiling amplified the resonance. A fireball licked the ceiling and spread around, accompanied by a cloud of smoke and concrete dust. A shower of glass fragments and shards of burnt plastic and metal fell violently to the ground.

The young man remained stunned, paralyzed by the explosion, sitting in his driver's seat, one hand clenched on the steering wheel, the index finger still in place in front of the start button. He did not understand what had just happened. He had pressed the button and immediately everything had exploded. His eardrums were temporarily blocked. He remained motionless, his eyes haggard, his vision blurred as if he were underwater, hearing thuds on the surface and shadows passing in front of him.

He finally raised his head above the water when arms pulled him violently out of the vehicle. Two people supported him to walk. A few boxes away, a car was on fire, lying on its side under the blast. The heat was intense, and the dense, toxic fumes made it difficult for them to move forward. Their eyes and throats stung. As they passed the burning vehicle, he had the clarity to notice that it was the same model as his own. A Cooper.

A dozen sprinklers, small sprinkler heads with a heat detection bulb, had just been switched on and were pouring water on the burning vehicle.

Once outside in the open air, the two people who had helped him out vanished. Recovering, he took out his phone and dialled 118, the emergency number for the fire brigade. But it was clear that other people had already called them because at the same time he heard the sirens wailing and getting closer, the fire station being less than a kilometer away. While they were controlling the fire and preventing it from spreading to other cars and even to the building in general, Gilles was already being questioned by the police. He was the only witness at the scene of the accident. Along with the two people who had run away. A little shocked, he told in great detail what he had done from the moment he left his flat until the explosion.

At that moment he remembered Claire's words about his car. He realised with horror what she had meant. That they had the same model and colour car!

A wave of emotion washes over him.

In all likelihood, it was the latter that was burning up in the passenger compartment. He had not made the connection immediately. He didn't have time to turn around and disgorged his entire breakfast onto the pavement, splattering the agent's shoes in the process.

After making sure that the young man was safe and secure, Bonnie and Clyde slipped away, relieved.

As they emerged, the sirens of the fire brigade and police were already blaring in the distance. They quickly returned to their car and left so as not to be caught out. They had a specific mission to fulfill and they had to stick to it.

And going incognito was their priority.

Karl was watching the scene through a pair of binoculars to see the devastating effects of his plan. He had retraced his steps, on foot, leaving his car parked much further away than the first time in case he was followed. Just a professional's precaution. He was gloating, because his plan had worked perfectly. A blast as he liked it. The noise and the consequences were visible.

There was no doubt about it.

The car had exploded on start-up, as expected.

He had connected the bomb under the car directly to the starter cables. It was child's play and left no chance of survival for the person who set the mechanism off.

But he had noticed a couple coming and going. He had no idea they were here, but their quick foray into the underground car park immediately after the blast intrigued him greatly before he left.

From his new position, he did not have a direct view of the entire residence and did not see them leave. But behind his magnifying lenses, he discovered the car into which the individuals rushed to leave the premises.

Something caught his attention.

The car looked strangely like the one he had seen last night. He tried to recall the scene. The Italian number plate confirmed his thoughts. A disturbing coincidence that needed to be investigated.

In the meantime, he could tell the Commander the good news. He picked up his phone and sent a message.

Operation successful, nuisance eradicated.

Visconti was as cheerful and upbeat this morning as he had rarely been in the past year. He looked around the amphitheater at those present and chuckled.

'Ah, I see some people skipped my last class. But too bad for them. They won't have the right to my last prerogatives and my personal point of view on the possible subjects that could fall this year at the test. Knowing that I am rarely wrong...'

A roar of joy could be heard in the lecture hall.

'Let's be calm. I know you're all anxious to hear my verdict, but it'll be at the end of class. Not before. We still have to finish the last chapter.'

He turned on the overhead projector and continued the lecture where he had left off the previous time. Just as the time slot was about to end, a late student ran down the stairs to sit in the third row next to Cyril.

'I'm sorry for the delay,' he said in a deadpan voice to his friend.

'You don't look so good. You're as white as a sheet...' Cyril replied.

'Let's go to the pub after class. I'll tell you all about it. Something crazy happened to me this morning...'

20

Nancy
Wednesday May 14th 2014, 4:30pm

Cyril and Natasha returned home after school, accompanied by Gilles. They had to work out the final parts of their trip for the coming weekend. The detailed account of the morning's events had disturbed them somewhat.

'And if it was you, Gilles, who was targeted by this... attack!'

'Attack? That's a bit rich, isn't it, darling? No one has said anything about an attack yet. It seems to be an accident. Tragic, of course, but just an accident for the moment. You're both getting paranoid,' intervened Natasha.

'Such an explosion does not occur as a result of a small fuel leak or some other almost insignificant problem. The explosion Gilles mentioned is very similar to a car bomb. I've done enough missions in Iraq and Afghanistan to know what I'm talking about. Doesn't the fact that it's the same model of car give you a clue?'

'But who and for what purpose?' asked Gilles, dazed. 'I don't have any enemies. I'm not involved in any drugs or anything else. I'm the perfect boy in every way!'

'I have no idea, but I noticed that a car followed us for a long time when we left the university earlier...'

As he spoke, he walked over to the bay window and looked down at the street below, slightly parting the two large curtains in the middle. He immediately recognized the vehicle he was referring to, parked about a hundred meters from the door of their building. He looked for his binoculars, but saw nothing. The windows were tinted.

'Look over there! This is the car that followed us.'

Natasha and Gilles approached the window and took a look around.

'Are you sure?' asked a puzzled Natasha.

'I'm sure. I'd put my money on it.'

His two companions did not understand the situation.

'But what's this nonsense?' asked Natasha. 'A car bomb, another one that seems to be following us... Are you working for the intelligence service, Gilles? Are you a spy or a double agent? Come on, spit it out!'

'But no, that's nonsense! This whole thing is incomprehensible. Maybe it was this girl who had a double life. She was always so discreet. Nobody saw her. Or maybe it's all just a coincidence...'

'You may be right. But we'll still have to be vigilant in the coming days.'

Gilles ate with them and then returned home at about eleven o'clock. The three of them emptied an excellent magnum of Burgundy wine, a Vacqueyras that went perfectly with the leftover rabbit with thyme that had been reheated. Just to take their minds off things a bit. Once the alcohol fumes had dissipated, Cyril began reading the third volume of the Abbé. He didn't seem very motivated, especially after reading the previous ones, which had not been very interesting. With last weekend's amazing discovery and the incomprehensible reaction of his thesis advisor, the revisions for the end-of-year exams and the unexpected events of the day, he was longing for a little peace and quiet.

The first few pages were as monotonous as ever. Cyril let out a long, weary sigh and his boredom showed. Then came a long, more historical passage about the beginnings of the First World War and the abbot's concerns about his future in the region if such a conflict broke out. Violent fighting was going to take place here, the location being highly strategic with this large hillock standing on it. He hesitated between fleeing or staying put and warding off the bad luck. By the grace of God, perhaps the shells would be deflected and not destroy the church, thus sparing the thousand-year-old altar, the presbytery and even the houses of this hamlet. The abbot had also meticulously detailed over the months the numbers and weapons of the German units stationed in the area. Precise details that would have made their high command pale, but which would have been a godsend if they had fallen into the lap of General de Castelnau, who was in charge of the Second Army stationed on the other side of the border. Perhaps the war would have gone quite differently.

Some passages that Gilles would certainly enjoy. Cyril hastened to send him a text message to make his mouth water and to tell him that he would bring him the tome the next day at the university.

'Is it more interesting than yesterday?' Natasha asked furtively, still immersed in her thriller.

'Mild. No more...'

The stories about the state of the German army's locations went on for many more pages, making the young man's minimal renewed interest in the subject flatten like a soufflé. When at last an interesting passage came along.

Tuesday, 11 July 1914

[...]

To my great regret, I will have to leave my nest. I have no choice. Oberst Ludwig Ernst Von Käbel (equivalent to a colonel in the German army) has just told me. I am sent far away, to Bavaria. In a very quiet place, it seems. It is with great sorrow that I leave this parish, hoping in my heart of hearts to return to it as soon as possible. If I had known earlier, I might have asked him to protect the altar from possible bombing. It is a priceless asset that cannot be

destroyed or damaged. But it's too late', he replied. He didn't have time to deal with that. I tried to force him to change his mind by pointing out that the altar dates from the time of Charlemagne, who is buried in his homeland in Aachen, but he would not listen. We can only pray that it will be spared and rely on God's grace. I am going to prepare the last celebrations and then my things for my departure, which will take place in three days. A page of my life is turning.

Cyril read aloud for Natasha to enjoy. She was quickly caught up in the story.

An extraordinary thing has just happened in the early evening. After the last mass in this church, in the presence of General-Feldmarschall Alfred Von Schlieffen, who had just arrived during the day - which does not augur well - I decided to tidy up and to put away what could be put away. I therefore began to pile up the benches in the left recess of the apse. The latter were of considerable weight, even heavier when one is alone at work. The task was exhausting. The apse, which in the end could be confused with the chancel because this church was so small, was very quickly cluttered, and it became increasingly difficult for me to access it in order to stack the pews on top of each other. With fatigue, I had difficulty coordinating my movements and my steps. I stumbled, the benches collided, hitting the soft wood. Two very old benches did not resist. My muscles became tense with the repeated effort. But at last I could see the end. Only three benches remained, including the one in the front row, sealed, and reserved for the village squire. I took the next pew in the same way as the others, in the middle to distribute the weight better, and lifted it as much as I could to climb the steps separating the nave from the choir. But again I stumbled, my foot hitting the second step, and the bench toppled forward. The wooden plank at the back of the pew, which acted as a kneeler, hit the center of the altar hard and bruised the Celtic cross carved in the stone. At the moment of impact, this stone part sank a few centimeters. I put down the bench and took a closer look at this strange phenomenon. The carved cross formed a square about twenty centimeters wide. I barely had time to study it before the stone returned to its original position. My heart raced. Was there a mystery in this thousand-year-old altar? A cache of treasure? The same treasure that some of the locals regularly spoke of, referring to a legend that dated back to the dawn of time. I wanted to know as soon as possible. I put pressure on the stone and felt it quiver. I gathered the last of my strength - increased tenfold by the adrenaline rush - and intensified my effort until I pushed the cross a good fifteen centimeters. It was then that a mechanism was heard. Frightened at first, then captivated, I took a few steps back. The altar began to rotate slowly towards the apse. I was afraid that the noise would disturb the peace and quiet and attract a German patrol, but it did not. For safety's sake, I hurriedly locked the door. When I returned, the altar had given way to a gaping hole from which an opaque cloud of dust was escaping.

[...]

The young couple could not believe their eyes. Cyril reread the passage a second time so as not to lose a crumb. The priest had indeed uncovered the crypt unexpectedly, just as he and Gilles had done. And his writings seemed to confirm that the human remains buried under the pile of rubble and covered with a woolen cloth belonged in all likelihood to the abbot.

'The First World War seems to have caught up with him. To think that he had discovered everything... and he lost his life in the following days. After Abbé Saunière of Rennes-le-Château, there would have been Abbé Humbert of Marimont,' joked Natasha, all the same sad for the man of the cloth.

The pages that followed until the end of this third booklet were devoted to the description of this discovery. From the counting of the niches that housed the remains to the furniture and decoration of this room which, to his great astonishment, like Cyril and Gilles, seemed to serve as both a necropolis and a meeting room with its table and armchairs arranged in a circle or its black and white chequered floor. But the most intriguing thing to him was the magnificent carved box containing a book, which he thought was very old, written in Latin, but also largely in a language he did not know.

The clock was ticking and it was getting late, but this did not stop Cyril from starting the fourth and final book of the abbot's memoirs.

'That's not the way to pass your exams,' Natasha tackled him as she went to bed.

But his companion pretended not to hear him, too happy to be able to read some interesting passages at last.

21

Nancy
Thursday May 15th 2014, 0:30am

Cyril let out his first yawn, which soon led to others. But he did not give in to the temptation to go and join the arms of Morpheus, or rather those of his sweet and beautiful Natasha. He wanted to read this fourth booklet at all costs and get it over with. Especially as this last book only contained a hundred pages. Even if he didn't learn anything new, he could free his mind without having to think about it again, for fear of having missed something important. He poured himself a strong cup of coffee and started to work on it again.

Thursday, 13 August 1914

[...]
I had made my decision. And I had thought it through. I would stay in this hamlet until this war was over. I have piled up enough food to last me several weeks, which should be more than enough to support me. There are various problems that I will have to solve during this forced stay under... earth. Besides, the idea of staying with all these dead people in these niches gives me the creeps. And sleeping in them even more. Especially in a crypt. I hope that no bird of ill omen will see a sign. If need be, I can always go out again.

I was visited by two French soldiers. How crazy do you have to be to venture so far into the enemy lines? According to the officer, they had come as scouts to report to their army commander on the forces at work. An imminent offensive by the Second Army led by Colonel de Tassigny was being prepared in the region. In Alsace, the French had just suffered a real rout against the Germans. Peace to their souls. I have a feeling that these future battles will be of unprecedented violence. May God preserve them all. I didn't tell them anything about the inventory I took of the forces a few kilometers away. But I told them the safest way to reach the top of the hill in all discretion. I also warned them of the existence of an old underground passageway leading from the medieval castle at the top of the same hill, the last remains of which are still visible in winter. Some villagers think that it is a legend told from generation to generation to make this peaceful village a bit mysterious. Just like the story of a treasure hidden there. Others really believe it, even if no one has really taken the time to look for it yet. The village elder even claims that his grandfather told him this story when he was a child, and that he himself got it from his uncle. It's hard to separate the true from the false. I think that the only real treasures are the altar dating back more than a thousand years and this crypt that I discovered with these old burials and this ancient codex as beautiful as it is enigmatic [...]

This same legend had been told to them by the manager of the gite the previous weekend. A story that had already crossed a century and, if you took into account what the abbot and the old man had said, went back even further. That would put it between the eighteenth and nineteenth centuries. In his research, Cyril had read that Abbé Grégoire had been stationed in this same village shortly before the French Revolution and that he had been very active in encouraging the former lord to enlarge the building that would become the present church. No one ever knew by what subterfuge he succeeded in persuading him to do so, but rumors circulated that the young and penniless abbot had contributed financially to the work. A sudden windfall of money that could not have come from the donations of this modest parish alone.

Cyril put the book down and went to the kitchen to get a glass of water. The shutter had been left open. He went to the window and thought of the car parked down the street. He was curious to see if it was still in the same place. He plunged the room into total darkness and carefully opened the curtain on the right-hand side to slide his binoculars in. To his surprise, the vehicle was still parked there. He remained motionless for about ten minutes, scrutinizing the slightest action or gesture that might betray a presence of some kind inside it. But not a shadow or a glimmer. Not in the street, not in the surrounding buildings, not in the car. Everything was absolutely quiet. What could be more normal given the number of flats for sale or rent. In front of his building, only five signs with telephone numbers of the agencies concerned were fixed to the balcony railings. Two elderly people had left for other places at almost the same time, according to the concierge's indiscretions, two others had gone to a retirement home and a young couple was moving because of a lack of space following the birth of their second child. The concierge had told him everything in great detail. He just hoped that their replacements would be as discreet as their predecessors. He couldn't help but peer into the windows of the building opposite. More out of curiosity than voyeurism. Or perhaps by instinct. The feeling that he had been watched since the beginning of the day was still anchored in him. He slowly scanned the whole building with his binoculars, floor by floor, flat by flat. Not a glimmer of light could be seen. Total darkness reigned on the entire facade, where many shutters were closed. Only the few street lamps offered a pale light. Suddenly his attention was focused on a window opposite his own, one floor up. One of those three windows partly hidden by sales or rental signs. For a moment it seemed to him that the curtain had moved. He concentrated all his attention on the large window, but without success. He told himself that it could only be his imagination playing tricks on him at such a late hour of the night and in such a tired state. That unhealthy curiosity often went hand in hand with the apprehension of being seen and caught at one's own game. This made the imagination more fertile and at the same time gave hope of seeing something came to life. He watched the building for a few more moments, then closed the shutter and returned to continue his reading, slumping into the sofa.

When the couple went to the agency to rent a flat for one month, possibly renewable, the estate agent was surprised by such a request. A hotel would have been more appropriate for such a short period. But on reflection, he agreed, especially after the wad of cash presented before his eyes. The flat was not only ideally located, but also fully furnished, which suited the future tenants.

From the living room window, they could discreetly scan the apartment across the street, one floor below them. This low angle allowed them to have a more global view of the kitchen, the large living room as well as a room that was probably used as an office. And of course the entrance to the building. The day had been quite calm, contrasting with the events of the early morning, fortunately without direct consequences. The young student had come out of the building at about ten o'clock and was immediately chased by their colleague. They could no longer afford any deviation. But to do that, they also had to neutralize the man who had tried to eliminate the young academic. And very quickly. They had obtained information about the killer. They knew what the 'Giant' was capable of. A former German anti-terrorist. An expert. A killing machine. But he did not rush headfirst. Everything was meticulously prepared so as not to leave any clues behind. That's why the police never bothered him.

This morning's unfortunate blunder would soon be made up for.

Tonight Cyril seemed to be struck by insomnia. He was sitting on the couch and still reading without respite. His companion had gone to bed around midnight. Half an hour later Clyde saw him go into the kitchen to pour himself a drink. Then suddenly the light went out and the young man did not reappear in the living room. Clyde was puzzled. He looked around the two rooms with his lens, but saw no one.

'Eva, there's something fishy going on in the flat,' he says to his partner.

'Should we intervene?'

'Wait a minute. I want to be sure...'

'We may be too late...'

He continued to watch the living room meticulously, hoping to see him reappear as he left the kitchen. There was no sign of activity. Yet the two rooms were adjacent to each other with no other way out. He had no choice but to go through the living room to reach the other side. And he was certain that he had not seen him return. After long minutes of waiting, still nothing. He seemed to have disappeared.

'What is he doing in the dark for so long?'

He was about to give Bonnie the signal to intervene when he took one last look at the kitchen. That's when he saw two rounds of binoculars behind the curtain scanning the area. He immediately withdrew from the window so as not to be seen and held the curtain in his hand to stop it from swinging and thus not betraying his presence. Clyde waited a short while and scanned with his naked eye without moving the curtain. The binoculars were still there, but they seemed to be staring at a different place. Then they disappeared, the shutter closed and Cyril reappeared immediately in the living room, continuing his reading.

'False alarm,' said Clyde, relieved. 'On the other hand, we'll have to be careful in the future. He's a clever one...'

Curled up in his armchair, his eyelids heavy, Cyril persisted in his efforts.

The Mystery of the Lost Crypt

Tuesday, 18 August 1914

[...]

I moved into my bunker the day before my official departure. The Germans must have wondered where I had gone. And even more so the Oberst Von Käbel. The rumbling outside leaves no doubt. The table shakes all the time. Even underground I can feel the impact of the shells. War is raging in the region. So the two French soldiers were telling the truth. But unfortunately for them, they were never able to report to their superiors the elements they had in their possession. That was their original purpose in coming here. But it lasted only for a few hours. One of them had come back in the middle of the night, like someone possessed. Almost crazy. He had explained to me as best he could that they had found the entrance to this famous underground. By chance through a rotten wooden board. The legend seems to come alive. Then, in a mental state that was deteriorating rapidly, he explained to me that a door, made of stone, was half-open in a wall. They would both have entered a room where chests were stored at the back. But the lieutenant, who entered first, was soon seized by violent stomach cramps and lost consciousness. That is why his companion came back for help. He was as if possessed, impossible to make him listen to reason. He threw himself on me and tried to strangle me. But a German patrol, alerted by my screams, broke down the door and killed him. So I am the only one today who knows this secret. I wonder what these chests could contain. Was it the treasure of which the legend speaks? Was it the golden skittles? I will wait, holed up in this place, for as long as it takes, doing my own research [...].

Finally, Cyril congratulated himself for staying up so late, because the rest of his reading was worth it. He rushed to his phone to send a message to his friend. Even at two o'clock in the morning, he felt compelled to share it all.

The Mystery of the Lost Crypt

> *The abbot has proof of this. He too speaks of bowling like the manager!*
> *I also have the impression that we are being followed...*
> *Strange... we'll talk about it tomorrow.*

A loud noise woke Karl from his sleep. An alarm was coming from the computer. He jumped out of bed as if he had never fallen asleep and rushed to the small adjoining desk. The screen had lit up together with the alarm and indicated that a text message had just been sent from one of the monitored mobile phones. With a few clicks, he viewed the message and was able to identify both the sender and the recipient. He compiled the data and e-mailed it to the Commander. He did not wait for any response from the latter before taking action. And with good reason. He had carte blanche to act on the spot at any time if the need arose. And the information he had just intercepted last night seemed to be of crucial importance.

He was also keen to make amends for his blunder of the previous day. The commander himself had informed him that a young woman had been killed in a car explosion in an underground car park - no cause had been established by the end of the evening - and that a young man had witnessed the scene a few meters away. This information was confirmed on the radio. His plan had therefore failed. But in order not to arouse any suspicion, he had been ordered not to try anything else in the next few days. His turn was over. Momentarily.

Karl got dressed, took his bag and drove off in his black BMW. As usual, he parked in a street adjacent to his drop-off point and walked the rest of the way. Only one of the three streetlights was lit and none of them were lit in the vicinity of the building in question. Ideal for entering unnoticed. The front door was opened by a small electronic box. All that remained was to find the access code. The Giant looked up and down the street. There was no one in sight. He had a clear shot. He took out his phone and connected it to the box. He launched an application and the numbers scrolled by at an astonishing speed. As fast as the French debt meter that he had seen on a visit to the capital.

After only five seconds, the first number froze. Then every two seconds another until the full five-number code appeared on the screen. He dialed it on the keypad and the door opened as if by magic. The concierge, a charming lady in her sixties, lived on the ground floor. But at about two in the morning, not a soul seemed to be awake. He looked for the young couple's letterbox which would lead him to the floor where they lived. The fourth floor.

He took the stairs around the lift shaft and soon found himself at the door of the flat. Good news awaited him. The door was not armoured. It would be easy for him to open it. He took out a stethoscope from his bag, put it against the door and listened for a few minutes to what was going on inside.

22

Nancy
Thursday May 15th 2014, 1:15am

Nothing.
Not a single suspicious noise inside.
Karl then turned his headlamp towards the lock and, equipped with two nail files, inserted them into the slot and turned them back and forth until they clicked. The trick was done. He carefully pushed the door open, but as he entered he heard muffled grunts.
He had been prepared for the presence of a pet, but had not expected to be confronted with it immediately. He plunged his hand into his jacket and pulled out a pellet which he immediately threw in the direction of the dog. Perfect timing. If the dog had been sleeping in the room, he would have immediately alerted his master by growling or barking.
'Come on, eat it, you mutt!'
The dog did not flinch and continued to growl.
His master had probably taught him not to take food from strangers. But the tempting smell of the meatball in front of his nostrils was tempting. He looked at it several times from the corner of his eye while Karl encouraged him to eat it. Eventually the dog did. Two minutes later he slumped to the ground and snored. The powerful sedative added to the pellet had worked very quickly. Karl was finally able to enter the flat in peace.

A wide corridor faced the hallway and ended at a double glass door. A second one led off to his left into the darkness. As he walked towards the large glass door, his bag bumped into a pedestal table containing a small collection of semi-precious stones. One of them fell from its holder. In this dead silence, the noise seemed to be multiplied. Karl stood still, listening for the slightest sound that might emerge from a room.

The young couple had not wanted to change the old original floor, finding a certain charm in its characteristic creaking. Unlike Karl, who grumbled at almost every step. He examined the room with his headlamp and did not see the object he had been looking for at first sight. On his left appeared a large bookcase where hundreds of books of all sizes were stacked and arranged. Karl looked grim. He had never seen the book he had to retrieve. All he knew was that it had been written in the hand of an abbot. So probably no fancy cover or title on the spine. Something quite simple. He opened the two large glass doors of the cabinet and began his investigations. But after a good fifteen minutes, it was clear that the books were not there. He closed the two doors and went to the other end of the room which led to the kitchen. As he passed the sofa, his lamp stealthily illuminated a dark mass on the floor between the curtains and the sofa. He turned back and went to see what was there. He saw the four books.

Bonnie was recovering, lying on the sofa.

They were both used to getting little sleep, but the all-night shifts they had been putting themselves through for the past two days always took a little more of their sleep quota.

His partner, positioned in front of the living room window, was also struggling against fatigue. His eyelids closed, his head gradually tilted forward until his chin touched his chest and then instantly rose again, only to repeat the process a few seconds later. By the tenth volley, he was asleep for good.

It was 2:30 in the morning.

The Mystery of the Lost Crypt

Bonnie's watch rang. It was her shift. She saw Clyde unresponsive. She smiled and nudged him with her elbow, causing him to jump and almost fall off the chair.

'Go lie down, I'll take over. I'll let you know if there's any suspicious activity. Are they sleeping too?'

'The girl had been there for a long time. But he's only been here an hour. He has been reading all evening.'

But no sooner had he finished his sentence than she saw a powerful beam of light zigzagging through the living room.

The curtain drawn from the window gave a fairly clear view of the people inside. She could make out a tall figure dressed all in black and hooded.

'That build, that walk... no doubt about it, it's the Giant!'

Clyde snatched the binoculars out of her hand and pointed them at the flat.

'What are you looking for, you bastard? We have to get rid of him. I'm going in. You stay at the window and warn me of any suspicious movement.'

He hastily equipped himself, took his gun, put on the silencer and went downstairs. He was about to leave the building when a cyclist passed him by. Staggering across the width of the road, visibly drunk, he finally fell to the pavement, swearing like a trooper as he tried to get up. Clyde put on his balaclava, helped the man back on his bike and then crossed the road into the building opposite. The cyclist didn't notice anything and staggered on. Unlike Karl, Clyde knew the entrance code. The concierge had given it to him when he had pretended to bring parcels regularly to one of the owners of the building whose name he had seen randomly on one of the letterboxes. As he entered, he heard a muffled bang from one of the floors. He immediately questioned his partner and rushed up the stairs.

Across the street, Bonnie watched helplessly as the two men struggled. She saw the burglar take cover behind the wall, watching for his prey. And she was able to give Clyde a live commentary on the scene.

'Hurry up, Pietro. There's a gunfight in the flat. Cyril surprised him. But... wait, the Giant has just come out of the flat now!'

Karl picked up the books, which looked more like ordinary notebooks, and put them in his bag. He was about to go back to the corridor when his bag bumped into the leg of another pedestal table where each trinket was placed in a specific place. Several fell this time with a thud, muffled by the carpet. The front door was less than five meters from his position. He rushed to it without waiting to see if the noise could be heard, reaching for the latch when the light in the hallway came on. A voice was heard.

'Stop! Don't move,' says Cyril.

Karl turned a quarter turn and saw the young man pointing a 44 Magnum at him. A souvenir from his time in the army. The Giant gently reached into his pocket with his left hand, where his silenced weapon was.

'What are you doing here? What are you looking for? Maybe you'll be more articulate when the police get here. Take off your mask so I can see what a bastard burglar looks like.'

Karl did not answer. He remained silent. His hand had reached inside his pocket and was now gripping the butt of his gun. He pulled it out in a fraction of a second and fired it in the direction of the corridor while diving towards the living room to take cover and avoid the bullet that had just expelled in return from the barrel of the Magnum, shredding the wood of the toilet door behind him. He would not have imagined for a second that his opponent's gun was loaded, let alone that he would dare to fire. But the young man's blow seemed to be more of a surprise riposte than an intentional gesture. For his part he had deliberately spared him. His master would never have forgiven him. But the situation was becoming more complicated. Cyril had taken refuge in the bedroom. Natasha, distraught, lay stunned in bed.

The Mystery of the Lost Crypt

'I beg you, let him go, Cyril. It's not worth taking any foolish risks,' she shouted, picking up the receiver and dialing 17.

'Listen to the voice of wisdom. I will not hesitate to kill you if you interfere again. I'm going out. If I see your gun in the corridor, I'll shoot,' Karl replied in hesitant French with a strong Germanic accent.

'You're dreaming, you son of a bitch! I'm gonna make you regret ever coming in here. Just stick your head out and I'll blow it off.'

Karl stuck his head out to see what was going to happen. He saw Cyril doing the same on his side. Cyril fired a second time and the bullet tore through the edge of the wall. Shards of plaster flew by a few centimeters from Karl's head. He had his answer. The young man was not bluffing. Sensing that the situation was getting worse and that his opponent would not seem to let go, he decided to leave the place at once. He slung his bag over his shoulder, took the gun in his right hand and fired a salvo of five shots each spaced a short time apart, but enough to cover his escape and move safely towards the front door.

Cyril protected himself behind the wall of his room and waited for the end of the offensive to retaliate. This time he would give it his all. He still had remnants of his ten years in the commandos and was about to launch the final assault to dislodge his opponent. He glanced in his direction again. Nothing in sight. He walked out of the room, pointing his gun from his outstretched arm, ready to fire at the slightest bit of skin or hair that would stick out from the wall. When he reached the corner of the two corridors, he dashed forward with his gun still at the end of his two outstretched arms, but, oh surprise, saw no one. On his left, in front of the door, lay his dog, lying full length across the passage. He approached it to check its condition. Phew... his dog was breathing quite normally and was even emitting a soft snore. He realized that he had been anesthetized by the burglar.

Cyril had two options. On the right the door to the living room was ajar. On the left, the door to the entrance was ajar. Logic would dictate that he had fled rather than remain locked up and cornered in rooms with no possibility of escape. The footsteps on the stairs confirmed the logic. But he couldn't have gone far yet. Determined to find out more about this individual, he was about to go in after him when a heavy exchange of shots from the stairwell stopped him dead in his tracks. Was he already facing police officers warned by Natasha? They would have done so very quickly, unless, by chance, they were patrolling the area...

Karl had come out with disconcerting ease. He entered the stairwell, aided by his headlamp, and slid down the steps holding onto the banister. He reached the second floor and continued his mad descent when a bullet whistled past his ears, ricocheted off the wall and ended up in the glass of the second floor stairwell, which shattered. He stopped instantly, fired a random shot to scare off his assailant and ran back up the stairs to safety. He thought for a moment. The young man was about to burst in from above and this new individual was blocking his way from below.

He was made like a rat.

Especially as the police would soon be bursting into the building. He had heard the young woman calling them. The whole thing smelled of trouble. He had to find a way out quickly. He looked around with his headlamp. Two doors faced each other. Too long to open. The window caught his attention. He had to be quick, for the two men were closing in on him. He gauged the window, which opened onto an inner courtyard, crushing bits of glass on the floor as he went, and estimated the height. From the second floor, a bad reception could prove fatal for the ankles. But a shelter positioned lower down meant that the fall could be reduced by half. He cleared the last bits of glass from around the frame with the barrel of his gun and climbed onto the ledge. A bullet whizzed by him again, hitting the wooden frame. The stranger had reached his level, protected by the lift. He fought back to gain a few seconds and then jumped. He fell three meters to the roof of the shelter, rolled forward and landed firmly with both feet on the paving stones of the courtyard.

Clyde had seen Karl climb out of the window. He fired, but missed, then hid behind the lift wall to dodge the reply. He heard a clang of sheet metal and then a second, more muffled one. The Giant had just jumped. He ran to the window and saw him running away. He soon realized that he would not be able to catch him again. The first lights were going on all over the flats following the detonations, some would soon be out on the landing or in the street. He too had to get away.

He was about to go back downstairs when he heard someone running down the stairs from the top floor. Probably de Villiers. He had to hurry now, because the latter could mistake him for his burglar, even if they were not of the same build. But black clothes, a balaclava over his head and a gun in his hand would be enough, in the rush and the stress, to be taken for a target. The young man had not hesitated to open fire twice in his flat and would have no qualms about doing it again. Clyde lurked behind the lift and waited for the right moment.

A small stroke of fate would help him.

Really unexpected...

The stairwell timer stopped just as Cyril was about to turn off at his level, plunging them into sudden darkness. He reached out to trip him up. The latter stumbled and went flying. His head hit the bottom of the wall and he lost consciousness. His weapon ended up in a corner. The way was now clear. Clyde lit his torch, made sure the young man was only stunned, picked up the gun and went downstairs.

He was making his way to the front door when an old lady appeared on the ground floor.

She was the concierge.

'What's all the fuss about? What are you doing here?' she said, realizing with fright that she was probably face to face with a burglar.

He stopped at her level and pointed his gun between her eyes.

'Go home, madam, and go back to bed. This is not your concern...'

Panic-stricken, she complied and immediately closed her door without asking for help. Clyde went out into the street and looked around. It was deserted. The man had run off and was probably long gone by now. He crossed the street to find Bonnie when he saw the BMW driving away with the screech of its tires. A shrill noise that split the night, quickly replaced by the sirens of two police cars that were undoubtedly heading here.

It was time to slip away.

He took off his balaclava and crossed the street.

23

Nancy
Thursday May 15th 2014, 9:30am

As agreed, Gilles came to join his friends early in the morning. A police car was parked in front of the building. The police were questioning the concierge in the entrance hall. When he passed by, one of them stared at him and then, recognizing him, asked:

'Here you are, Mr. Perrin!'

— Do we know each other?' asked Gilles, not very responsive.

'We met at the police station when you reported the car explosion in the basement of your home.'

'Oh yes, of course, what was I thinking... Our paths cross again in a short time. Without wanting to seem too curious, did something happen to make you come here in force?'

'A burglar broke into one of the flats in the building last night and shots were even exchanged.'

At the same time the lift doors opened and Cyril walked towards them. He was taking his gun permits to the police.

'Ah, there's our maverick,' joked the Commissioner.

'Are you involved in this story? What happened?' asked Gilles, who was stunned.

'I'll tell you later.'

'Ah, you know each other?'

'Yes, a little,' joked Cyril. 'You could say we're the best of friends...'

The Commissioner remained doubtful, taking note of this new information.

'You think these two cases are related,' said one of his colleagues who had left his ears to the ground.

'Not impossible. One thing is for sure, I don't believe in coincidences. Could the three of us get together as soon as possible?' he asked the two young men.

They both looked at each other in embarrassment. One brief glance had been enough to understand each other.

'No problem at all. We're planning to go away for the weekend, but on our way back on Monday we'll definitely drop by.'

'I am counting on you. This might be the best lead we have.'

Once the two friends were up and about, the commissioner said to his colleagues:

'I have the feeling that they are hiding things from us, those two. The embarrassment was perceptible and their looks eloquent to say the least. Something to look into!'

All three were ready for their second trip to the countryside. The weather was much better than last time and only a few showers were expected throughout the weekend. But it was still cool, the Ice Saints seemed to be a bit late this year.

They arrived at the lodge in the early afternoon. The village seemed as deserted as ever. The manager, who had been informed earlier of their arrival time, had prepared a small snack for them, which they quickly ate. A terrine of rabbits with prunes from a local butcher on homemade country bread, a tabbouleh with grapes and a tomato salad with balsamic vinegar, all topped with a small Alsace Pinot Noir. Quite a hearty snack... very rustic but exquisite. Gilles made himself a large slice of bread and wrapped it in aluminum foil.

'For a snack,' he said to the manager, who smiled back at him.

They took their equipment and headed for the hill. They were anxious to get back to the site and especially anxious to find out what state it was in. Jack, off the leash and always ready to go for a walk, gamboled happily around them, releasing his pheromones whenever he could.

They felt spied upon again as they passed through the main street. Always those curtains shifting, window after window.

'I wouldn't mind ringing the bell to introduce myself. But I doubt the person would dare to show up... says one.'

'Well, probably a little old lady whose only daily activity is that. Can't blame her,' Cyril replied.

The two boys looked at the church with a touch of nostalgia as they thought about the past week and their fantastic discovery. They couldn't wait to go back and share it with Natasha.

'Shall we go back tonight?' asked Gilles.

'Absolutely!' replied the young woman with a smile on her face. 'I can't wait to see this marvel.'

At the crossroads, they continued towards the "new" castle. The house that stood on the corner was abandoned. The wooden shutters were closed and in a sorry state, the façade was falling into disrepair, the roof tiles were missing. The owner had died a few years earlier and the family had never agreed on what to do with the estate. Between selling, renting and taking over for a personal account, the final decision was always postponed and the general state of the house worsened day by day. Cyril scanned the building with a worried look.

'What are you looking at?' asked Natasha.

'Nothing,' he replied, frowning. 'It must be the reflection of the sun's rays through the shutters creating shadows.'

They continued towards the construction site.

They had arrived in Marimont during the night.

After taking the books from the young couple's flat, not without difficulty, Karl had collected the Commander from his home and the two of them had headed for the village Cyril had mentioned in his messages. When they arrived there at about three in the morning, they soon realized that their vehicle would be difficult to hide. About fifteen houses at the most and a small empty car park opposite the town hall. A big German car would not go unnoticed in the village square. It was better not to tempt the devil, especially as his car could very well have been recognized by one of the protagonists when he had fled into the alley. While looking for a hiding place they passed the gite, the only one in the area as suggested by his internet research and the one mentioned by the three friends.

Karl left his car on a forest road less than five hundred meters away, hidden by branches, and returned on foot. He had previously left the Commander at the church where they had spotted a house in a state of near-ruin. The sign of an estate agent hung from one of the windows. This would be an ideal place to watch the comings and goings in the village.

When the Commander forced his way through the back door, he was relieved to find that the house was indeed deserted. He would not have had the heart to sacrifice anyone. And even less to let Karl take care of it. Every piece of furniture was covered with a sheet to protect it from dust. They located the rooms and lay down on the beds. This would allow them to recharge their batteries before the three budding archaeologists arrived. A grueling weekend lay ahead. But they were ready and equipped for any eventuality. Food, a change of clothes, explosives, and of course a whole arsenal of weapons.

Karl had enjoyed himself.

After the failure in Nancy, which he still could not explain, he was going to do everything he could to redeem himself. Conscientious and professional, he could not stand setbacks. He had a reputation to maintain with his masters. And it was not two youngsters who were going to tarnish it.

At about two o'clock, after a late breakfast, they were finally rewarded for their wait. The Commander saw the three folks in the distance and immediately informed the Giant. They were coming towards them. The Giant went upstairs and looked at the village square through the wooden slats of the shutter. He gritted his teeth when he saw Gilles. He aimed the scope of his rifle at his head, but had to force himself not to pull the trigger. He wanted to. One word from the Commander, which of course did not come, would have been enough to make him gloat. He lowered his weapon as they passed the house with a small growl of frustration.

'It's only a postponement, your turn will come soon... Karl whispered.'

But he ducked behind the wall when he saw Cyril turn and look in his direction. Had he spoken too loudly? The windows were tilted forward to let in fresh air and remove as much of the damp and musty smell as possible, the house probably not having been aired for very long. Or was it just a coincidence? He nevertheless remained on the alert, weapon at the ready, watching the young man's reaction. But the latter did not linger.

The Commander, who had also witnessed the scene, let out his breath when they saw them continue on their way. A direct confrontation at that moment would have been catastrophic for the continuation of operations. He needed their talent and their insolent beginner's luck before he could get rid of them...

Clyde and Bonnie had arrived at the lodge shortly before the three young people, thus benefiting from the only indoor covered parking space, which suited them well. They had been lucky enough to be able to book the third and last room a few days before. Their mission being to watch and protect them, it was better for them to be directly in the wolf's den. Their vigilance would be all the easier. They passed themselves off as an Italian couple visiting the region for the weekend. When they came into the dining room at mealtime, Gilles had immediately watched them out of the corner of his eye, looking thoughtful.

Could he recognize them?

Unlikely. The only time they had been in contact was just after the explosion in the underground car parks of his residence, when they helped him out. But they had been careful to put on a hood. But it was better to be on guard. The smallest detail, even if it was insignificant for most people, could attract attention. It was the same for Cyril, even if his encounter with Clyde on the stairs was brief and in the dark. Again, there was no way he could have seen his face. But the information in his file, as reported by the Grand Chancellor, extolled his courage, his coolness, his adaptability and his foresight. All of which had been confirmed the night before. The old academic had learned a lot from his ten years in the army. An experience that he put to good use at the right moments.

For all these reasons, Clyde had decided to stay at the lodge this afternoon and send his accomplice alone to watch the students.

24

Marimont-lès-Bénestroff
Thursday May 15th 2014, 1:30pm

When they arrived at the excavation site, they were pleasantly surprised to find it intact, just as they had left it. A light breeze, milder than the previous week, was blowing over the top of the mound.

This time they would adopt a different strategy.

All three would work together in the same area. This would allow them to dig deeper and check the depth of the walls and foundations. In any case, they would be limited over the whole area of the site as there were oak and beech trees growing there and their roots spread out and prevented any excavation.

The rays of sunshine that passed through the thick foliage gently warmed the small piece of land where the three young people were working, diffusing pleasant scents of moss, mushrooms and dead wood. After the copious meal taken at the gite, all the factors were present for a good digestive nap. Gilles would have liked to lie down on this carpet of soft grass and moss. But his childhood friend did not see it the same way.

Three hours of intensive work went by. And the result was very convincing. The ashlar wall they had been working on since the beginning had preserved itself very well. Here and there, tree roots had crept into the intersection of three blocks, spreading them apart and breaking their alignment. A good meter fifty in height and two meters in width had been cleared. The loose earth had greatly favored them. Gilles sifted through the recovered earth to find ancient fragments of pottery, tools, weapons or coins.

They took a well-deserved break. Natasha took the canteen and took small sips of water, then passed it to Cyril. The place was very quiet and peaceful. The chirping of birds replaced the cicadas of the south of France. Gilles took the opportunity to eat the sandwich prepared at the gite. Then everyone went back to work.

Suddenly the crack of a branch diverted their attention. The three heads popped out of the hole like prairie dogs on their hind legs. Jack, who had been napping peacefully on a pile of leaves, jumped to his feet, ears perked up, nose in action, and gave a muffled growl. This confirmed the suspicious noise.

But they saw no one.

'Probably a deer,' said Natasha, turning around and continuing her task.

'The noise was very distinct. I think a deer would be more delicate.'

'Yes, you are right. More like a deer. The males are bigger and stronger, therefore heavier, and clumsier...'

The two young men, intrigued and hardly believing in the hypothesis of some kind of animal, remained standing for a moment, scanning as far as they could, listening for the slightest noise coming from the surrounding forest. But the undergrowth, which was very dense in places due to the lack of maintenance by the ONF agents[1], whose territory was growing more and more over the years due to the non-replacement of colleagues who had retired and massive budget cuts, offered many hiding places.

'But stop stressing, both of you. I'm telling you it's an animal...' she insisted.

'With what's happened in the last few days, I think we have good reason to be,' Gilles ironically said.

Cyril nodded.

---

1. *National Forest Office*

'A car explodes and a thief breaks into our flat. Just a coincidence? I don't believe it anymore.'

'Correction. A car, identical to Gilles', explodes two garages away as he himself was about to leave. The commissioner confirmed to me that an explosive had been placed in the vehicle and coupled to the starter motor.'

Natasha, who was not aware of this detail, looked at him, stunned and a little offended.

'But you didn't tell me! Which could mean that someone tried to kill him but got into the wrong car?'

'Exactly. It's called attempted murder! Well, for Gilles... because unfortunately the attempt did not fail for everyone. This poor young girl paid the price in spite of herself.'

Gilles swallowed.

'Then in a second step, a man breaks into our flat and the only thing he is interested in are the four notebooks of the abbot. Nothing else. What would a simple burglar be doing with that? Don't you think it's a bit strange? He must have known about it. So many coincidences suggest that... well, for me everything is connected...'

'*Related to* what?'

'To what we are doing. To these excavations... and to the discovery of the crypt, the notebooks. What else?'

'But we are the only ones who know about it!'

'Not quite. I've spoken to the dean of the university, for example.'

'Visconti? Are you saying that he would try to eliminate us? That old fart? No way...'

'He or perhaps others may have spied on us that night in the church. Or someone tapping our mobile phones. I don't know... I don't know for sure, but we'll have to be on our guard for the next few days.'

This discussion gave a chill.

Seeing and hearing nothing more unusual, the two friends were content to continue their work. The hole had grown even larger and the roots of the surrounding trees made the task more and more difficult. The harvesting of ancient evidence continued apace, including numerous coins and pottery fragments. A good quarter of an hour later, when the three neophyte archaeologists had once again been caught up in their task, a voice was heard.

'Ciao!'

Surprise seized them at the sound of the voice. Gilles jumped as he dropped his tools, while Natasha gave a frightened cry. Cyril rushed to his bag, lifted it, dipped his hand in and held the butt of his gun firmly before standing up and checking the person's identity. He had his finger on the trigger, ready to draw and fire back if necessary. But his arm relaxed when he saw the angelic face of the unknown woman. He recognized the Italian woman who had moved into the house with her husband. Natasha immediately understood her companion's intentions and feared for a moment that he would act on them. She knew he was nervous and on edge and it only took one straw to break the camel's back. She was relieved when she saw him take his naked hand out of the backpack, which he put down. The look of distrust towards the stranger did not fade. He remained on the defensive.

'Ah hello!' said Natasha with a large smile to lighten the mood a bit. Have you come to surprise us?

'Mi scuse! I'm sorry if I frightened you. I didn't want to disturb you. I was walking around and remembered what you told us about your dig.'

'No, don't worry, don't worry. Are you alone?'

'Yes... my friend stayed in the room. Tired from the trip... she said while waving her hands.'

Once the three young people had left and the threat of being discovered was over, the Commander gave Karl his instructions.

'You do nothing but watch them! Do you understand? And above all, you inform me of their every move.'

'Well, Master...'

He changed into khaki colored clothes that would allow him to blend in with the landscape, packed his bag and left through the back door. He was careful not to let anyone see him leave this supposedly abandoned house, then followed them, keeping his distance. Discretion had to be the order of the day.

Once there, he chose a choice spot between some bundles of wood and a fir tree whose bushy lower branches fell in a circle around it, forming a natural teepee. He carefully removed some leaves and, equipped with his binoculars, took possession of his new observation post. The hours passed without anything happening. Sitting in his little folding tripod chair, regularly nibbling apples, he watched them working and burying themselves deeper and deeper until they were no longer visible in the middle of the day, putting things aside and taking photos of the progress of the work. His makeshift hiding place was a thick carpet of dead leaves, littered here and there with his cores. At the distance he was at, he had no chance of being heard. At least that's what he thought. Sitting in the same position for more than three hours, his legs began to tingle. He got up to change position and tried to relax his aching muscles in his little one-square-meter den by pacing. With each step, his foot sank until it disappeared into the dry leaves. Just then, a cracking sound of a branch echoed through the forest.

He immediately stopped.

By reflex, he even stopped breathing for a short moment, which was completely ridiculous given the distance he was at. A large dead branch had just given way under the repeated weight of the successive passages. He immediately saw three heads come out of the hole in unison, scanning the surroundings to see where the noise was coming from. The dog had reacted immediately and stood up straight as a post, waiting for an order from his master. Only his ears and nose were fully functional. The two young men remained on the lookout for a long time, so long that he almost cramped up again from standing without moving a single toe. He lost some of his usual phlegm, drops of sweat beading his forehead. But to his great relief, they resumed their work and the dog sat back down and started scratching. Karl, for his part, tidied up his natural refuge, taking care to remove all the branches hidden under the leaves.

Everything had become quiet again since that little incident when, at the stroke of four o'clock, he saw a person approaching the work site casually on his right. He pointed his binoculars and despite the dense vegetation, he quickly recognized her. It was the same woman who had sneaked out of the underground car park shortly after the explosion of the car that should have killed one of the three students, in the company of another man who could very well have been his assailant in the stairwell of Cyril de Villiers' home last night. Dressed all in black, her tight-fitting jacket showed a rather large bulge on the side, at waist level.

Karl immediately thought of a weapon.

He stiffened at the sight and told himself that this was a very good time to get rid of her. A situation made all the more convenient by the fact that she seemed to be alone. He looked back with his binoculars for a long time, but saw no one else. He immediately sent a message to the Commander telling him of the situation. He received a reply immediately.

Green light! But don't touch the young...

Karl gloated when he saw the answer. He would finally be able to take action, which would give him a little relief after all his hours of inactivity.

25

**Marimont-lès-Bénestroff
Friday May 16th 2014, 5pm**

Natasha showed the lanky Italian woman all the work they had already done on their site in such a short time. The latter was impressed. The excavations were greatly facilitated by the wet and rainy weather that had reigned in the region for months, making the soil loose and therefore easy to work. But the downside was the appalling conditions in which they were operating. They were wading through ten centimeters of sticky mud due to a concentration of clay at a certain depth. The three academics felt as if they were wearing lead shoes all the time.

Bonnie did not go down into the pit and just looked down on them. She stayed there for almost two hours. Not that she had any sudden passion for archaeology, which she found tedious and boring. But as soon as she had approached, she had observed on her left, about fifty meters from her position, a silhouette hidden by a mass of opaque brambles. The cracking of a branch heard earlier had attested to a presence and reinforced her suspicion. The whole time she had been with the three young friends, she had kept an eye on the cache, taking care to position herself in front of it for better visibility. Did the person who was hiding there feel that he was being watched in turn? However, since she was in position, no further movement was heard. He seemed to stand still and blend into the landscape like a chameleon. But Bonnie had no doubt. An animal would not have stayed holed up for hours. She was certain of that and sent a message to Clyde to warn him.

Bonnie waited for her partner's signal.

But even before she received it, she detected movement in the cache. The stranger seemed to be slipping out the back. She couldn't wait any longer and decided to take the initiative to follow him or else he would vanish into thin air without being identified. She greeted the three young companions and set off after him. The latter were intrigued by the suddenness of her departure and especially by the direction she was taking. She cut directly through the wood, opposite the path she had come from, making her way through the thick vegetation with difficulty. One eye on the ground so as not to trip over dead branches or roots, and the other concentrated on the position of the runaway.

She had him sporadically in her sights. He seemed to sneak up on her with more ease and dexterity. He could only live in the area to know the place so well. Perhaps he was just a simple onlooker who wanted to keep an eye on the three youngsters and their excavation site. The village mayor or one of his deputies? She wanted to know for sure.

Thanks to a very mild winter and early spring with plenty of water, the forest was a good month ahead of schedule and already in its summer dress. The multitude of shrubs, ferns and brambles that had grown wildly as well as the dead wood rotting on the ground and that could not be removed by the forest rangers due to lack of time and the few means at their disposal, made any progress laborious. Still concentrating as she walked around a thicket of brambles, she tripped over a tree stump and fell flat on her face. The left side of her head hit an old branch covered in moss and partly hidden by dead leaves. A little stunned, she got up unsteadily. She remained motionless to consider the scene. She was totally disoriented, not knowing which way she had come or which way to go. She had to find her fugitive. She tried to bring all her senses back to life despite the pain that was pounding on her temple, blurring her vision, affecting her hearing and especially her balance.

She no longer saw him and had to face the fact that she had lost both his track and even his way. She suddenly felt vulnerable. Without her bearings, she felt a surge of panic. She quickened her pace.

Karl was again holed up, motionless in his hiding place. He had managed the feat of not moving one iota for almost two hours. He could not risk being spotted. And for good reason, the mysterious visitor often looked in his direction. He had spotted her with his binoculars. The first time he had seen her, she was accompanied by a man who did not seem to be there at the moment. He wondered what role they could play in this affair. Her presence could not be a mere coincidence. Was she watching them? Quite possibly. Was she protecting them? Why and for what purpose? But what organization did they belong to? Perhaps a competitor who also wanted to take over future discoveries? He thought for a moment that it would be better to know their motives before acting. But to do so, he had to take the initiative and set a trap for them on his own playing field.

Namely in this forest.

A great adept of commando training, he had successfully completed all his expeditions in the most dangerous and impenetrable forests of the planet. Dropped off alone by helicopter in the middle of each one, with a burlap sack over his head so that he had no visual cues, and without food or water, he had to make the most of all the resources available on the spot to survive. A solid knowledge was essential to overcome such missions.

This place was nothing like the ones he'd been through, but his long experience would serve him well. The camouflage outfit he wore was his first asset. Blending in with his surroundings.

He glanced back surreptitiously from time to time to see her position. He must not lose her if he wanted to lure her into his web. When suddenly he was surprised not to see her. She seemed to have vanished. He waited behind a large tree trunk. But after about thirty seconds, she reappeared. She was holding her head. She must have stumbled. He stood there and waited for her to come to her senses.

She seemed completely baffled.

And luck was with him, for the young woman continued in his direction. All he had to do now was to pick her up, get the useful information, and then get rid of her.

Child's play for Karl.

26

**Marimont-lès-Bénestroff
Friday May 16th 2014**

Clyde didn't waste a minute and went to join Bonnie when he received her message. He had tried to reply, but to no avail. The red exclamation mark to the right of the message indicated a momentary lack of network. The SMS was not delivered. This did not worry him. He knew his colleague to be cautious and to take measured risks. His felt Stetson cap fastened on his head and his low hiking boots gave him the look of a perfect tourist. Ideal for not attracting attention. Even if not many people were likely to see him here. He passed the church, the crossroads and set off in the direction of the castle. He continued to follow the main road and then turned right at the edge of the forest. He walked along the barbed wire fence for a hundred meters before turning off into the woods and starting the gentle climb to the highest point of the hill where the building site was located, as Bonnie had told him in her message. The repeated passes had made a small, loose path. As he struggled with the branches that blocked the path, Clyde heard a short, shrill cry to his left. It was definitely not from an animal.

He then had a bad feeling.

He turned back, quickening his pace, and discreetly drew his gun, his arm stretched along his body. He had put a silencer at the end of the barrel of his Beretta 92. The thick vegetation obstructed his visibility. He was running towards the unknown.

He stopped several times to listen, but only heard the breeze blowing through the branches. So he continued his ascent, walking blindly towards the area where the noise was coming from. It had been drizzling for a few minutes and the top of the mound was soon covered with a thick mist.

Not the weather that was forecasted, obviously...

But the meteorologists could rarely be trusted with all the changes in the climate. Even their powerful calculators were already obsolete.

Suddenly he saw two figures in the distance.

Despite the fading light, he recognized Bonnie and her long brown ponytail. A man was standing behind her, holding her left arm high on her back so that she could not struggle, a sharp blade of a hunting knife pressed to her throat. He stood motionless behind an oak tree and quietly watched the scene, waiting for the right moment. Bonnie looked terrified. The man, who had just released his arm, whispered a few words in her ear while stroking her side. She stiffened a little more and made a pout of disgust. She was trapped and could not defend herself, but only suffer the perversion of this individual. The man quickly stopped the charade and asked her questions. From the look on his face, the answer must not have suited him. Knowing her character only too well, Clyde knew that she had sent the man packing and that he would never get the information he was looking for. He then pressed the sharp edge of the knife even more against her throat, causing the first drops of blood to slide down the blade onto the neck of his victim.

It was high time for Clyde to intervene before it was too late. He took the time to aim and then fired.

The bullet slammed into the trunk at their side, passing within a few centimeters of the colossus' head. The maneuver was certainly risky, but deliberate. A first warning. Nothing more. The Giant felt the bullet graze him. Surprised, he loosened his grip and tried to locate the position of his assailant.

Clyde had just succeeded.

This release allowed Bonnie to pull away. She grabbed the forearm holding the knife with her left hand and elbowed him in the stomach with her right arm. The German colossus bent over and gasped for breath for a moment. He narrowly avoided Bonnie's foot, which was about to strike his head with a circular movement, and then made a judo-fighting sweep with his other leg.

Unbalanced, Bonnie fell backwards, rolled down the slope and came to rest at the foot of a stump several meters away. Clyde took advantage of the fact that the Giant was alone to fire another round. Except that this time he intended to hit him. The second bullet almost hit and shattered the hazel branch just behind Karl, tearing his jacket in the process.

He felt a slight burn.

Nothing too bad. The bullet had only grazed him. Karl now knew where the second thief was. He had to face the fact that he could not fight two enemies armed with pistols with his hunting knife alone. He regretted not having grabbed the woman's weapon earlier. Caught up in his momentum and in too much of a hurry to get information out of her, he had given it no further thought. So he took off. The thick coat of greenery would make his escape easier.

Bonnie was on the ground and trying to get up, but could not. Lying on her back, she was held up by her belt, which had been caught on a dead branch. By the time she grabbed her weapon and drew it, the colossus had already fled. Clyde came up to her level, not without difficulty, on this climb made slippery by the drizzle.

He wasted far too much time.

'Don't worry about me. Get that bastard!'

Seeing that his colleague was fine, he continued his run. But the assailant had already gained a good lead. After a few minutes of frantic running, Clyde came out of the forest and stopped. In front of him were sown fields as far as the eye could see. And less than a hundred yards away was another island of greenery, much smaller than the one he had just climbed out of. For Clyde, it was impossible that the man had had time to cross the field and take refuge there. He had a head start, but not that much either. Which meant that he was still somewhere in this forest. Clyde therefore turned back in the hope of flushing him out. Always on his guard, he moved forward cautiously, scanning every parcel of land that could potentially be a hiding place. He wondered what Bonnie was doing and hoped that the giant had not set another trap to finish her off for good. At the thought, his pulse quickened. He hastened his pace when suddenly he heard the steady rustle of crushed leaves a few yards ahead.

Someone seemed to be walking towards him.

He stretched out his arm, gun in hand, both hands on the stock, and walked around an old oak tree. Determined, with his finger on the trigger, he was ready to fire when he came face to face with a gun pointed at him.

The adrenalin went up a notch.

The head appeared. Bonnie's.

Relieved, they immediately let their guard down. Clyde put his index finger to his lips, telling her not to make any more noise, and then he listened. Only the sound of a dog barking could be heard, in the direction of the work site. Nothing else. They realized with frustration that they had lost track of the attacker.

'It was the same guy who planted the bomb in the garage in Nancy,' commented Bonnie.

'And the same one that was in the flat and in the stairwell,' said Clyde. 'AKA the Giant! I have no idea where it came from, but it seems that other people are interested in the find of our three budding archaeologists. We'll have to be careful. We don't let them out of our sight. We're watching them day and night,' he added. 'And from now on we're not going to disperse. We stay together!'

'And what do we do with the other one? Do we continue the hunt?'

'No, too dangerous and obviously he seems to be in his element in this forest. I am convinced that sooner or later we will find him again on our way. This time it's up to us to be attentive and reactive.'

They returned to the students, first passing through the colossus' hideout in search of any clues that might help identify him. This was done discreetly, so as not to arouse their attention.

But the place was absolutely untouched.

Karl had once again erred on the side of pride.

He was furious, even though he had had no trouble losing the man. The same man who had tried to chase him down the stairwell. There was no longer any doubt about it. But the worst part of all this was undoubtedly the fact that he had not obtained any information from the woman. He still didn't know who they were working for and especially why they were there.

It was time for the three friends to pack up. The day had once again been rich in discoveries and the excavation site was sufficiently advanced to stop at this stage. The objective had already been achieved. Cyril had more than enough to add to his thesis, especially with the discovery of the crypt and its opening mechanism, which he would not fail to mention in his thesis.

Totally unconcerned, they had no idea that a battle was going on around them, let alone that they were the sinews of this war, even though both boys had serious doubts.

The Mystery of the Lost Crypt

27

Saint John of Acre (Kingdom of Jerusalem) April 5th 1291

The sun had only been up for three short hours when a leaden blanket fell over the city, despite the light sea breeze waving the banners hoisted on the tops of the towers. It burned every bit of bare skin, forcing the newly arrived western soldiers and merchants, who were not inclined to this extreme climate, to hide in the shade or to wrap themselves from head to toe.

Amaury de Beynac had arrived just a month ago from his native Perigord, where he had been received at the commandery of Sergeac, the most important in the region, less than a year earlier. The Order, which was fighting in the East to hold on to its last Frankish positions and keep alive the hope of a future reconquest, was in great need of soldiers. His initiation had lasted the time of a pregnancy before he was given his white mantle flanked by the red cross pattée during an official ceremony that was quickly dispatched. Not yet seasoned and totally inexperienced in combat, he was immediately sent with thirty-four other brother knights and as many sergeants to Saint John of Acre, the current headquarters of the Order. They had embarked in Marseilles with food, weapons and horses for a crossing of the Mediterranean that had proved to be very turbulent.

A decisive battle was about to begin.

The young Sultan Al-Ashraf Khalil, whose sole aim was to reconquer all the Eastern territories still in the possession of the Crusaders, had broken the ten-year truce agreed a year earlier between Henry II, King of Cyprus and Jerusalem, and his late father Qalâ'ûn after the latter had taken Tripoli, using as a pretext the massacre of Muslim peasants and merchants in Acre by drunken Italian pirates.

Beynac and his brothers-in-arms were soon to be thrown into the deep end and would learn the techniques of warfare on the job, as the Mamelukes attacked and replicated those of their new, older and far more experienced brothers-in-arms.

He had not yet become accustomed to this harsh climate. This was probably due to his complete knight's outfit, which weighed more than twenty kilos. He was always wearing an undergarment consisting of a linen shirt and braids. On top of this was a heavy chain mail made up of thousands of intertwined and riveted rings and itself made up of four separate parts, followed by a white surcoat sewn with a red cross on the front and back held to the body by a belt. Mesh gloves, a helmet and a shield completed the protection of the knight's body. Finally, each Templar received a sword, a lance, a mace and three knives.

With all this heavy gear on, he was sweating profusely. When he was not on guard on the ramparts, he was training with the other novices in the handling of the sword. Whole hours of uninterrupted and exhausting instruction in the stifling heat, where their muscles and lucidity were put to the test against a vigorous and experienced master of arms. He taught them to dodge solo or grouped attacks and to counter immediately. Effective techniques coupled with indispensable resistance exercises. The enemy assaults would last for hours and they had to hold out both physically and psychologically until the end if they wanted to have any hope.

Perched on one of the two towers flanking the Saint-Lazare gate to the north of the city in the Montmusart suburb, an area allocated to the Templars and Hospitallers at the time of the great council which had seen the representatives of each order share the defense of the city, he had been scanning the horizon ever since the changing of the guard, just after the first prayer. The bright light reverberating off the sand quickly tired his eyes, which were continually bothered by drops of sweat, and it was very difficult for him to stay focused. The temptation was great to close them for good and take a nap. But one of his companions had informed him that the punishment would be terrible for anyone caught dozing.

The excitement of the city he had experienced on his arrival had since faded. Between the arrival of soldiers, weapons and ammunition and the departure of merchants and wealthy inhabitants, only the port was experiencing a revival of activity. There were few districts where the scent of spices and cooked local products still filled the air. As a security measure, all the city gates remained closed and only opened four times a day for half an hour to let the few Arab merchants who still dared to venture out into the area through.

The day before, a scout had returned, telling the Council the terrible news they all feared. Al-Ashraf's Egyptian army was advancing rapidly and other Muslim armies were joining its ranks along the way, including his cousin Al-Muzaffar's Syrian troops and their many catapults. The knight of Acre ventured a figure of one hundred thousand foot soldiers and nearly thirty thousand horsemen and pointed out that the column of soldiers and equipment stretched over several dozen kilometers. This made all the members of the Council of Acre blush without exception. A city defended by less than twenty thousand soldiers, some of whom were simple villagers who had decided to take up arms to protect their property.

But for the moment, everything was still peaceful. An almost ominous calm that certainly did not bode well. The latest reports from the riders were unequivocal.

'The calm before the storm..., one of his comrades-in-arms had whispered to him when he was relieved.'

Sitting in the shadow of a wall, his helmet on the ground, his eyes stared at the horizon without respite except for the time needed to quench his thirst. The last spy had just taken refuge behind the ramparts this very morning. No one knew where this unusual army was now, but it was not far away. His vision was beginning to blur and fatigue was making itself felt. It was getting close to the sexton prayer and his stomach was crying out with a loud gurgling sound. Beynac was about to be relieved of his turn on guard duty. A knight appeared on the tower, ready to take his place. He picked up his helmet and took one last look at the mountains surrounding the great dry plain before handing over.

Something in the distance caught his attention.

At first Beynac thought it was just a gust of wind blowing sand and dust, as was often the case, or perhaps his eyes were playing tricks on him because he had been concentrating so long. But as the seconds passed and the horizon grew darker, he soon realised that the plume of dust was not caused by the winds but by the passage of a never-ending cohort.

The great reunified army was fast approaching.

He ordered the sergeant at the bottom of the tower to hurry and tell the Grand Master, who returned less than twenty minutes later with Marshal Pierre de Sevry, Commander Thibaut Gaudin and the Grand Master of the Hospitaller Order, Jean de Villiers. The hairs on the backs of the four men bristled as they saw the picture taking shape before their eyes.

Their disillusionment was immense. Even in their worst nightmares, they could never have imagined such a picture. It was no longer just the horizon that was darkening, but the whole valley and the surrounding mountains, like a wave engulfing everything in its path.

'Even if the battle is clearly unbalanced, we will fight to the death with the help of God Almighty. For all our brothers in arms who have already fallen in the last two centuries and who have given their lives in the Holy Land in the name of our Lord, we will not give up! Let us prepare for a great and beautiful battle. Our presence on this soil will depend on its outcome,' Guillaume de Beaujeu said proudly as he descended from the tower, putting on a brave face to keep the flame alive.

By evening, Al-Ashraf's army had taken up positions all around the city. It was certainly the largest army ever assembled. In the end, the number of soldiers was almost double the figure given by the scout. No less than sixty thousand horsemen and one hundred and sixty thousand infantrymen were camped all over the plain of Acre. Hundreds of fireplaces lit up the entire valley between the tents. The spectacle was almost breathtaking. But more worrying was the number of catapults, mangonels and ballistas lined up one by one at regular intervals along the entire front line. It took them barely two days to fully reassemble two gigantic and formidable catapults, brought back in pieces in dozens of carts and pulled by hundreds of oxen each. Placed opposite the main towers of the surrounding wall at about two hundred paces, the *Victorious* one faced the Saint-Lazare gate while the *Furious* one was dedicated to the Saint-Nicolas gate.

The next day, at dawn, Beynac witnessed the first salvo of stone throwing. A shower of stones and rocks fell on the town and its ramparts. With a load of around three hundred pounds, the *Victory* hit the bottom of the tower where he was stationed, shaking the ramparts over a hundred meters and tearing a good dozen stones from the wall. The *Furieuse* and the two hundred mangonels mostly reached the first houses, passing beyond the two lines of ramparts and causing general panic among the inhabitants who took refuge deeper in the city. This was the enemy's aim. To sow chaos and fear among the soldiers and the population where the first wounded were found.

Beynac, dazed by the impact of the huge catapult, called the Grand Master back to show him the damage.

'Al-Ashraf's strategy is subtle and highly effective. Create confusion and then terrorize the population into surrendering immediately,' said Guillaume de Beaujeu, leaning forward to assess the cavity left by the huge block of stone. 'Spies have told me that it can fire a dozen times a day. At this rate, and by concentrating the shots only in certain places, knowing that all the other catapults take half the time to be reloaded, the wall will give way in just a few days.'

'So it's a waste of time trying to fix it...'

'We will see when the walls are more damaged.'

'But what can we do? We cannot sit back and watch our walls and buildings being destroyed without reacting.'

'Of course not. We are the pious Knights Templar. You must not forget that, young brother. We have never failed in the face of adversity. We will fight to the death if necessary, for that is the will of God. Tonight I will give orders to several of our brothers. You two will be among them. Your first mission in the Holy Land! We will mount a counter-offensive and try to put their war machines out of action. Keep it quiet. Our action must be as secret as possible so that the effect of surprise is total.'

'Do you know when the second salvo will be launched?'

'It should not be long now.'

Less than ten minutes later, the Grand Master witnessed the second shower of rocks, most of which fell on the houses, once again causing commotion and panic among the pilgrims.

'When will they sound the charge?'

'Not yet. They will try to breach and demolish the towers first. Stay on guard and pray that none of these stones fall on us. That's all we can do for now... You'll be notified in due course of the ongoing operation.'

Four days after the beginning of hostilities, on the 15th of April, the Templars organized a night operation to set fire to the great catapult, the *Victorious,* which bore its name by wreaking such havoc in its area. No less than three hundred Templars and Teutons rode out of the city under a full moon and very quickly neutralized the watchmen of the Hamâ contingent camped around the Porte Saint-Lazare. But the situation was quickly reversed in favor of the Mamelukes when the horsemen's horses got their hooves tangled in the ropes of the tents, allowing the besiegers to organize themselves and counter the attack. The knights of Acre were forced to retreat and fell back urgently into the city. Those who were not so lucky, about twenty of them, were beheaded and displayed for the Westerners to see on a horse that rode back and forth along the walls.

Beynac regurgitated his meal as he witnessed this sinister scene. His companion on watch, as well as all the other soldiers posted along the ramparts, ranted and raved like rabid beasts. This tactic had only succeeded in increasing the hatred and thirst for vengeance of the soldiers of God.

A second outing, this time orchestrated by the Order of Hospitallers, which was offended at not having been associated with the first, was aborted a few days later.

Meanwhile, the catapults continued their undermining work as predicted by Guillaume de Beaujeu, in perfect sync.

In order to kill time and to ward off future enemy attacks, the young knights practiced their swords and defense techniques in the temple citadel at the far end of the city between two rounds of guard duty. Under the Mediterranean sun, bodies were put to the test. The arms of Beynac and his companions burned with fatigue under the weight of their swords wielded during hours of consecutive training. But they were not allowed to weaken. They had to grit their teeth and hold on beyond fatigue. They knew that the days after, the real fighting would last for hours, even days, with no chance to rest. So they had to prepare themselves as best they could.

Physically and mentally.

Only the prayers of Sext and None allowed them to relax their exhausted limbs. And although their faith was unshakeable, they had never been so eager to go to prayer. Between two rounds of instruction, they wolfed down a stump of bread, a piece of cheese and an onion, washed down with a poor Italian rosé wine diluted with water. Hardly enough to eat to recover from all the effort.

The Mystery of the Lost Crypt

28

Marimont-lès-Bénestroff
Friday May 16th 2014, 11:45pm

Small wispy clouds escaped from their mouths into the icy night air. The beautiful starry sky had caused the temperature to drop dramatically to near zero. There were patches of fog in places. Not unusual for the time of year as the Holy Ice period had just ended.

Natasha was so eager to see the opening of the crypt and the amazing discovery her two companions had made the previous week that she walked ten meters ahead of them, speeding up her pace. She waited for them near the church door, behind the big fir tree, urging them to hurry and stamping her feet to warm up. They hadn't had time to get the key from the village mayor during the day and were taking the risk of finding themselves in front of a closed door. Cyril put his hand on the handle, looked at Natasha as if to ward off fate and then lowered it.

The door opened.

They smiled briefly in satisfaction.

Gilles turned round and glanced briefly at the village square, just to make sure they were not attracting anyone's attention, before entering the holy place last, lighting his headlamp as his friends had just done. He took a chair and wedged it behind the door again, still without a key. They were impatient.

Both for the young woman and for her companions, eager to relive the same sensations as last week.

Cyril approached the altar at a snail's pace, also frantically scanning around for an unlikely presence. But even knowing what to expect, his heart was beating as hard as the first time. Natasha, for her part, scrutinized her companion's every move. He knelt down and with both hands applied pressure to the stone cross in the center of the altar, facing forward. Meanwhile, Gilles had folded part of the large carpet in the way of the opening mechanism. Two seconds later, a loud noise was heard, the cross sank and then the sacred table swung around, causing the floor and the pews to shake. The three young men moved closer and closer to the altar as it moved away. The altar finally stopped perpendicular to its initial position, revealing the first steps of a staircase that seemed to descend into the depths of the earth. Natasha did not dare to take the first step. Stiffness and this gaping darkness took over. She left it to Cyril to lead the way.

Curious, but not reckless.

'It's great. I feel like I'm in a Benjamin Gates or Indiana Jones adventure movie,' joked the young woman.

'I have a soft spot for Lara Croft...' Gilles continued.

'In that case, she'd need a belt and two big guns hanging on either side... she already has all the other assets,' Cyril hilariously exaggerated.

Natasha marveled as the room revealed its secrets in the light of their torches. Even though she had seen the few shots her companion had taken from his mobile phone beforehand, admiring the room live, with her own eyes, was nothing like it.

She lived the moment as intensely as her friends.

Once downstairs, and having found nothing more ingenious than to block the entrance door with a wooden chair, they decided to close the access to the crypt by pushing in the prominent stone at the bottom of the stairs. The altar gradually returned to its original position, rattling the ceiling of the crypt and releasing dust and stone debris in the process. All three of them protected the top of their heads and put a handkerchief in front of their noses to avoid breathing in the dirt.

'Brrr, I feel like I'm being buried alive. I hope you're sure of yourselves and that this old mechanism doesn't act up when we want to get out,' she said anxiously. 'Because no one will come looking for us here...'

'Well... let's just say that for the moment we've managed to close the access to the crypt, but we haven't yet tested its reopening from that point...' Gilles swallowed.

'What?' she exclaimed in panic. 'Is this a joke?'

— Well, no...' he said sheepishly, turning to his friend to come to his rescue.

'Let's stop the bickering, girls, and calm down right now. There's no reason why it shouldn't work. The passageway has opened three times without any difficulty.'

'Except the first time...'

At these words, Natasha glared at Cyril.

Karl finished eating an apple, leaning against the corner of the wall, pushing the curtain aside slightly with his free hand. His gaze remained fixed on the church, always attentive to the slightest movement.

He was champing at the bit. His successive failures were piling up and were beginning to seriously undermine his morale.

He was eager to regain control of the situation.

But acting out of anger and rushing in would do no good. It was precisely for this reason that he was momentarily left to rest, to allow him to regain his mind and discernment in order to start again on the right foot.

This was the decision of the Commander.

Suddenly a shadow appeared in front of the church. Then two others followed. Karl had no trouble identifying them.

It was exactly midnight. The clock struck twelve.

They entered the church. He immediately went to wake up his master who was dozing in the next room.

Dressed all in black, he sneaked out of the house a few minutes later, crossed the road and then walked around the building to stand in front of the front door, listening for what was going on inside. But after many minutes of listening, it was clear that there was total silence. Had they already gone out? He looked through the keyhole, but saw no light inside.

But where the hell are they?

He lowered the latch. No effect.

The door did not open.

Strange... the door is locked. Either they have the key or Karl really needs some rest!

He made a second attempt by placing both hands on the latch and pushing a little harder. He found that the door offered less resistance. If the door had been locked, it would not have moved one iota. He deduced that something was blocking it from the inside. He took another look through the keyhole and decided to force it open. He breathed in deeply, lowered the latch once more with both hands and gave the door a hard shove. The door gave way at the first attempt with a resounding crack. He massaged his shoulder, which the years had made sensitive to pain. He was no longer twenty. It was in these precise moments that he remembered it best. He entered, lit his torch and saw the debris of a chair scattered around the entrance. He closed the door, intact despite the violence of the shock, and moved towards the heart.

There was indeed no one there.

The first detail quickly intrigued him.

An unusual amount of dust was dancing in front of the light beam of his torch. The air had just been seriously stirred. That was certain. He walked around the altar, swept the floor with his torch and discovered a long rolled-up carpet. As he tried to make the connection between the two elements, he noticed fine curved grooves in the tiles running from the altar to the edge of the carpet. They formed a perfect quarter circle. He ran his finger along one of the grooves and a thin film of dust enveloped it. The explanation seemed luminous. Only the displacement of the altar, from which the marks originated, could cause such grooves. So they had indeed found the entrance to the crypt, as Cyril had mentioned in one of his messages.

The altar is therefore the entrance to this famous crypt, he deduced. *And they probably went down there.*

All he had to do now was to discover the mechanism that would allow the altar to rotate. For this, the three students would help him. The commander decided to hide in a corner until they reappeared.

Patience was the key word here.

But now he had to find a good hiding place.

He took stock of the premises and considered the various possibilities open to him. Facing the narthex, there was a door on his right which opened onto an old wooden staircase with high, steep steps which gave access to the gallery. He could see the organ, its pipes and woodwork protruding from the balustrade. He soon noticed that the railing was not solid, but made of thin slats spaced about fifteen centimeters apart. It was impossible to hide there without being seen. He continued scanning the place and stopped at the confessional in the opposite corner.

It was the ideal hideout.

None of them would come and flush him out.

So the waiting could begin.

After half an hour, his eyes were already getting tired. The lack of sleep was taking its toll. Age was helping once again. He finally gave in and dozed off, sitting on the clergyman's chair, his head resting against the wooden wall of the confessional.

When he woke up with a start, disoriented as he was, the voting booth was vibrating and a loud, rocky, prolonged screech filled the church. A ruckus to wake the dead. The darkness did not allow him to see what was going on, but he easily deduced the source of the noise. The maneuver lasted about fifteen seconds and then calm returned. Then a glow emerged from the ground, breaking on the vault. A haloed head was gradually emerging from the ground. It was like an apparition. It was Cyril's friend with his headlamp. The other two followed with less grace and poise, their respective torches showing early signs of weakness.

The Commander was finally rewarded for his wait.

All his senses were now in action. He did not miss a moment of the spectacle, but their voices only reached him through the shutters of the voting booth. They seemed to be looking for something when suddenly one of them called out to his friends:

'I have found it. Come on over here!'

The two companions joined Gilles. The Commander saw the hole in the center of the altar gradually close and the cross carved in the rock reappear. The powerful monolith had once again found its original place.

He smiled.

When they wanted to leave, Cyril discovered, along with his companions, the splinters of wood scattered in the entrance.

'Someone broke in,' he whispered.

Instinctively, they searched every corner of the church with their torches, when Natasha looked at the confessions box.

The Commander immediately put the curtain back in place. He could only see the shadow of the light beam increase, quickly joined by a second one. They were getting closer.

Of course, there was no way out.

Suddenly the curtain of the penitents' box opened. A dazzling light quickly swept through the interior. He wedged himself into the back of the seat so as not to be seen through the small, curtained window.

'Empty... said a man's voice.'

He recognized Cyril's voice.

The curtain fell again.

'Look next door... said a woman's voice.'

The footsteps approached the main lodge.

This time he was made like a rat.

In a short while, the door to the confessional would open and he would be unmasked. He wouldn't know what story to make up to explain his presence. He closed his eyes when a third voice was heard further back.

'Cyril, there's a noise outside!'

They joined their friend and then slipped away.

The Commander closed his eyes and breathed several times in relief. Another second and his sick old heart would have given out. He could not have hoped for a better way out of this predicament without the need for Karl's more brutal intervention. He waited a few moments for calm to return and then walked towards the altar.

That night, Clyde took over.

With his ear to the bedroom door, he had heard the three young men - discretion did not seem to be their forte - leave in the middle of the night. He in turn left the house to follow them forgetting the instructions he had given to Bonnie. That they would stay together to watch them. But he didn't want to wake her up. She was sleeping so soundly.

He could let them take off thanks to his pair of night vision binoculars. But he didn't have to go very far.

He saw them rush like thieves into the church. The main entrance door was the only access to the building. He had noticed this while scouting earlier in the day at the same time that Bonnie was busy watching them. So there was no need to stick to their heels. He would just wait for them to come out. It didn't take him long to find the right place, between two houses. The top of a buried water tank right in front of the church offered a perfectly clear view. But he didn't expect it to be so cold and hurried back to the lodge to get a warmer jacket, especially if he had to stand still and wait. He had no desire to catch a bad cold.

He waited there without seeing anyone. At most, a few cats passed by and ran away at the sight of Clyde, probably frightened by his night binoculars.

Worried that no one was still coming out, he decided to approach. He crossed the square quickly, climbed the stairs and froze when he heard voices inside. It was them, one of them whispering to his friends that the door had been broken into. Reassured, he was about to hide behind the tree to the left of the entrance when he crushed a dead branch that cracked under his step. He was in place in a flash and the door opened. The trio exited the church as quietly as they had come, skirted the building and made their way back to the lodge through the cemetery at the back and finally through the fields.

But Clyde's job was not over yet. Their mission was more than just being a bodyguard. It went far beyond that. After making sure they had returned to the lodge, he went back to the church. He would take advantage of this moment of calm and solitude to unravel the mystery that had been held back for so long. Borgia was waiting for answers. The secret would be of no use if they did not discover how they had gained access to the crypt.

29

**Marimont-lès-Bénestroff
Saturday May 17th 2014, 0:30am**

The Commander approached the altar and examined the stone cross from every angle. With an expert eye, he noticed that the edge of the cross was chiseled and that there was a clear gap between it and the rest. He walked around the block and looked at the opposite side. Another cross, identical to the first in size and location, lay in its center. He stroked the cross with the palm of his hand as if to soak up the centuries of history and then dusted the surface. An acronym appeared distinctly in the middle. He scratched the grooves with a small blade and uncovered a monogram well known to historians. His heart raced, his hands shook and adrenaline tingled in his limbs with excitement.

The letters K, R, L and S could be clearly seen forming the word 'KaRoLuS'. Charlemagne, the Frankish emperor Charles the First, known in Latin as Karolus Magnus, 'Charles the Great', literally and very awkwardly translated into French as 'Charlesmagne'. The central lozenge formed the three vowels together, corresponding respectively to A, O and U.

The Commander remembered it all the more because he had studied it personally a few decades earlier as part of his research. But more importantly, it was the acronym mentioned in the codex!

He had indeed carried out research, but as curious as it may seem, no book or ancient document mentioned the presence of an altar dating from the Carolingian era. Whether this is a legend or a historical fact can only be confirmed by carbon dating. But one of the sentences in the codex was unambiguous and fully justified the popular rumor.

On the stone of the first Emperor of the West lies the cross that will open the Holy Door'.

All the elements of the sentence matched. The stone corresponded to the altar. The monogram engraved in the middle of the cross was that of Charlemagne, considered the first emperor of the West. A cross carved on each side of the altar was present and finally the 'Holy Door' was the stairway to the crypt revealed by the three scholars.

He smiled as he recalled the whole nights spent inside the cathedral of Aachen where the emperor was buried, looking for the stone mentioned in the codex as well as a possible hidden passage in the surroundings. Despite a battery of sophisticated electronic devices, he naturally came up empty. The same thing happened in Metz and Thionville, two cities where Charlemagne regularly lived. But how could he have imagined that this unrecorded stone could be found in this tiny hamlet on the Lorraine plateau, where hardly anyone knew of its existence?

He took out his notes and read them again. He placed both palms together on the stone, as specified in the codex, and pushed.

The Mystery of the Lost Crypt

But nothing happened.

The cross did not move one iota.

He applied more pressure with the same result. The commander pouted, annoyed by this failure. How had these insolent young men opened the trap door? Reclining in the confessional, he had not been able to see exactly how they had closed the trap door. But he had gone through the last volume of Abbé Humbert's book the day before, while Karl had been in charge of the surveillance.

He got up, walked around to position himself again in front of the twin cross, knelt down and did the same thing. Under the pressure of his two palms, the stone slowly sank and the same crash began. The same one that had awakened him from his sleep a few moments before.

A moment of jubilation.

He saw the altar rotate and give way to a gaping cavity. He brought his torch closer and discovered a staircase. His heart throbbed with excitement. He stood for a few seconds with his mouth agape before stepping onto it. He was trembling as he had been the day he had first discovered it. At his advanced age, he never expected to experience such a moment again. The same excitement as forty years ago when he had uncovered the tomb of an Egyptian king and its fabulous treasure, which brought him worldwide fame. All in all, relative. He quickly fell back into anonymity a few years later. The two codices had finally given some spice to his life after a long period in the desert. This umpteenth discovery, probably the last of his career, would certainly put him back in the spotlight and make him enter the pantheon of the greatest in his profession.

When he reached the bottom of the steps, he discovered the extraordinary crypt, its two keystones, the black and white checkered floor, the recesses where bones lay here and there, the monastery table and the chairs positioned all around as if someone had just prepared the room for an imminent meeting. And in the background, the scree covering part of the bed, split down the middle by the weight of the stones.

He was finally approaching his ultimate quest, his Grail, after so many years of research and study. A tear of emotion rolled down his cheek. Flashes came spontaneously to his mind. Images replaced the words in the codex, the treasure he had possessed for almost a year, to which was added the new one, freshly acquired, and from which he managed to detach himself, studying it night and day.

The puzzle was slowly falling into place, the elements fitting together perfectly.

His curiosity led him to inspect the place before looking for the possible passage mentioned in the old book. The characteristic two-tone tiles left no doubt as to their origin. It was indeed a Templar hall. The table and chairs confirmed this. This crypt had been refurbished as a meeting room around the 13th century. Even if the archives did not mention any direct commandery in this village, others were present in the vicinity within a radius of fifteen kilometers. This made this secret room all the more important.

'Why hide such a room if not for a very specific reason? So the treasure is here, somewhere in this mound, as the Templar Amaury de Beynac mentioned in the codex. Open yourself to me, my beautiful one, so that I may contemplate you and admire your long golden dress, set with diamonds and precious stones...' he continued, scanning the walls, as if possessed.

He stopped at the niches. In one of them he saw bones partially covered with a dark, dusty, age-weary cloth, probably a monk's habit, with a scabbard sticking out of it. He grabbed it and pulled it towards him without the slightest qualms. He had not expected such a weight and simply dragged it across the back of the niche without being able to lift it. The cassock tore to shreds and the bones dislocated without further ado. He pulled out the weapon with both hands. It must have weighed between ten and fifteen kilos. The silver disc-shaped pommel was also unequivocal, confirming his certainty. A beautiful red Templar cross was engraved on it. The leather wrapped around the fuse had certainly aged, but was still in its entirety. He took it out of its scabbard and exposed a silver blade with wide, parallel cutting edges to the light. The strong side of the blade had a wide gutter followed by a central ridge along the entire length of the weak side. The point was rounded to form an effective sword. It was a beautiful sword in excellent condition.

'I've got a special place for you, you'll make the rest of my collection pale in comparison,' he whispered to her as he looked at her.

He put it on the table and continued his exploration. The entrance to the tunnel could only be on the wall facing the cells, towards the castle. He saw the small altar with a candlestick at each end and a rosary and Bible in the center. A processional cross was leaning against it. An open tabernacle stood above and contained a ciborium and chalice. Above this was a painting, probably of the Virgin Mary, and in front of the altar a wooden prie-Dieu. All these elements were extremely sober, without embellishment. The Commander examined the entire surface of the wall, looking for straight, sufficiently deep cracks and the slightest roughness that might betray the opening of a passage. But his torch, which was too dimly lit, coupled with eyes weakened by age, did not allow him to work under optimal conditions.

No matter. It was only a postponement.

He would return tomorrow with more material, but also with the riddle extracted from the codex that he had managed to decipher and that he no longer had in mind.

He had reached his goal. He was now convinced of it.

Clyde climbed the steps two at a time and stood in front of the front door. He heard the thud of stone crunching against stone as he placed his hand on the latch to enter the building and felt vibrations on the floor. Then the silence and stillness of the night returned.

He cautiously entered the holy place. A strong musty smell caught his nostrils. He always felt a twinge of sadness when a place of prayer was no longer used or was used too little. This was the case with this church, which was open to the faithful less than once a year. The stoup at the entrance was empty. He made a quick genuflection, signed himself, then inspected the premises. When he reached the choir level, he stopped his circular tour and remained frozen at the level of the high altar. He was surprised to see it positioned orthogonally to its normal axis. A very unusual position, especially for such a small church. He then remembered the message from the scholar intercepted by the Vatican special services which reported the updated crypt entrance. He approached and discovered a pit. He stopped in front of the staircase and saw a faint glow coming and going in the background and muffled voices.

He wondered who might be there. Certainly none of the three young men, as he had seen them return to the lodge.

Could it have been villagers who had spied on them?

Clyde wanted to know for sure. He put his right foot on the first step and engaged his other foot when he saw the wall supporting the staircase light up immediately. The circle of light was getting smaller as the brightness was getting finer. This meant that the person was getting closer to the wall and therefore to the stairs. He was in danger of coming face to face with this person. Clyde backed away from the choir and moved with velvet steps. He could already hear behind him the first step of the staircase echoing under a heavy step. He directed his flight towards the front door. He surreptitiously relit his torch and spotted an old wooden door in the right-hand corner of the church. He ran to it.

'*The door to the gallery and the organ*,' he thought.

He slid in and folded it down immediately, taking care to leave a slight gap. He did not climb the wooden steps. It was too late. Too old and too noisy. It was better not to be noticed. The view from this place was perfect. He could keep an eye out and perhaps examine the way the trap door closed.

A figure gradually made its way up the crypt stairs. Clyde could not recognize it. Not enough light. The person who appeared at the top of the stairs seemed to be of relatively advanced age. More than sixty according to him. The slow gait and stooped posture left no doubt about it. Who could he be? He was carrying an object. Very long and thin, but also obviously very heavy. At this distance, Clyde was leaning towards a long sword in its scabbard.

He pointed his high-definition camera integrated into his night vision binoculars at the stranger and took a few shots. When he returned to the lodge, he would e-mail them to the Vatican Gendarmerie Service, headed by Prefect Luca Armendi. Perhaps they could help him identify him via the Interpol database. The zoom confirmed his initial hypothesis. It was indeed a scabbard extended by a sword hilt. Who could this man be? An occasional grave robber? Possible but too unlikely given the past events. He had a feeling that he would see him again. The man walked around the altar, bent down, and seemed to apply pressure. A few seconds later, the floor began to shake again and the altar returned to its original position. He also replaced the carpet. Then he went down the three steps of the choir and headed out through the central aisle of the nave.

The man disappeared into the night.

Clyde decided to follow him.

He opened the door and looked through. Across the street, the staircase and the village square were deserted. He stood there for a few seconds, but saw no one.

Suddenly he heard footsteps on gravel to his left. There was no other way out. The man must have gone along the building and was slipping out the back. Clyde went out in his turn and took the small concrete path on the right. At the corner he stopped and glanced around briefly.

Still no one.

He walked along the wing of the church and the first graves of the small cemetery situated in a U-shape around the nave. He slowed down and stopped at the next corner.

Clyde saw a shadow about ten meters ahead of him, passing through a wrought-iron gate and up a flight of stairs. Then suddenly the man grumbled and let out an expletive. He had just slipped on the wet grass and was lying in the ditch. His jacket was wet and covered in mud. Clyde moved closer to the low wall and saw the man hobble across the road and squeeze through the two high wooden gates of the yard, which he promptly closed.

The unknown seemed to live in this village. This in itself did not seem to represent a threat. He was an opportunist who had just plundered the village's heritage.

Disturbed, Clyde went back into the church again. He placed another chair against the door. So as not to be disturbed, he looked around the confessional, the balcony where the organ was located and the sacristy.

This time he was indeed alone.

He approached the stone altar.

30

**Saint John of Acre
May 15th 1291**

The various siege devices had been relentlessly destroying the city's fortifications for a good month. The pace had even increased in recent days, raising fears of an imminent first offensive by the belligerents. The city's craftsmen assigned to the repairs were filling in the gaping holes caused by the projectiles with wooden beams and planks as best they could, but were struggling to keep up. Everyone seemed overwhelmed. Repairing the walls had become impossible.

On the morning of the fifteenth of May, as Beynac lay on his straw mattress to rest for two hours after his night's watch, the whole city was awakened with a start. A terrifying noise was heard and the whole city vibrated. The few remaining inhabitants ran out into the streets in panic. The first rumors suggested an earthquake. But it was not. The Perigordian knight put on his uniform and went without delay to the Porte Saint-Lazare to inquire about these explosions. The explanations of the knights on guard at that moment were terrible to hear. Several concomitant explosions had occurred at the height of the outer enclosure, leaving gaping holes at the base of certain towers.

The turning point of the siege was taking place.

While the Mamelukes continued their undermining work on the surface, several thousand slaves had dug galleries from the camps to under the main towers and laid mines. When they were triggered, whole sections of wall, including that of the New Tower, collapsed into the ditches, filling them in partially. This was a double boon for the Sultan's army. The breaching of the New Tower, the most strategic point in the city's defense, was quickly filled with a wooden tower, but this proved to be of little use.

The Frankish situation was very bad.

However, the fury and courage of the brave knights of the various orders did not waver, even though losses were multiplying. They would fight to the death. To make matters worse for the people still present, the raging sea prevented any boats from leaving the port. And those who had already left were forced to return to take refuge there.

The day after the destruction of part of the New Tower, Al-Ashraf launched the biggest offensive since the beginning of the siege, allowing the Mamelukes to seize the tower without much resistance. Templars and Hospitallers, united for the first time in two centuries and forgetting their untimely quarrels, heroically repulsed the attackers a first time despite the bombardment of wildfire and the rain of arrows. The Marshal of the Hospital, Matthew de Clermont, was the main architect of this charge. His courage and valor increased tenfold over his fellow soldiers. But the bravery of these dozens of knights, including the two Grand Masters, could not resist indefinitely the succession of Mamelukes waves breaking before the Porte Saint Antoine. With the bulk of the attacks taking place there, Beynac was urgently assigned to the gate and had the honour of fighting alongside the two Grand Masters. This increased his courage and strength tenfold.

The fighting had been raging for hours in the suffocating heat. Behind their helmets, the air was unbreathable and the sweat that beaded made it difficult to see. Added to this heat were the stench of thousands of rotting bodies in the ditches and around the gaps where the Mamelukes hordes were trying to infiltrate. Fresh blood, burnt oil, the acrid fumes of burning buildings and the nauseating stench of sweat, bile, excrement, urine and burnt flesh all combined to stir the most hardened stomach.

He had stepped back slightly from the battlefield between attacks by enemy squads and raised the visor of his helmet. He opened his mouth wide like a carp in search of oxygen and swallowed great gulps of slightly less stale air. Sweat trickled down his temples. He tore a large piece of cloth from the ground and mopped his forehead to calm the sweat. A man approached and offered him a large goatskin canteen. Dehydrated, he snatched it out of his hands before the man could offer him any.

'Give me, my throat and mouth are as dry as the damn desert.'

Despite the fatigue, the muscles in his shoulders and arms stiffened, he lifted the large pouch above his head to quench his thirst and let the liquid flow into his mouth. The man rolled his eyes but said nothing and waited impatiently for the knight's reaction. When the stream hit his throat and then his stomach, he had the unpleasant sensation that an opponent was thrusting a flaming arrow into him. What he had taken for water was a strong local alcohol, undrinkable to the uninitiated. His eyes became inflamed. Even the rising tears seemed to be soaked in alcohol. He swallowed several gulps to put on a brave face for the other knights who were waiting their turn. His eyes popped out of his sockets and he sweated even harder than before. He tried as best he could to stifle the coughing fit that was coming on. He passed the goatskin to his neighbor without taking any more gulps and then returned to the two masters who were relentlessly fighting the enemy hordes.

The bodies of both sides piled up in the moat at the threshold of the gaping hole in the wall, offering the attackers the possibility of crossing it at the end of the day like a natural bridge covered with wooden planks to consolidate access to the battlefield. The number of Frankish fighters then melted like snow in the sun.

The end seemed near.

When the young knight returned to fight at the Porte Saint-Antoine, the Grand Master of the Temple, Guillaume de Beaujeu, ordered him to stop fighting and wait for him at the Temple Commandery. He had imagined for him a very different future than perishing at the foot of these walls.

And to accomplish this, he had to make sure that he stayed alive.

Beynac could not disobey this order, but it was a real heartbreak for him to have to stop the fight and let the Grand Master and all his brothers in arms continue the battle without him. At the time he took it as a punishment. Was he not a good soldier of God worthy of fighting with them? He kept repeating the same sentence: "*I have an even more important mission to entrust to you, blessed brother. Much more important than the defense of Acre.*"

Why him? He was young, full of enthusiasm and hope and had only just arrived. William of Beaujeu barely knew him. What mission could be more important than fighting to keep one of the last Frankish bastions in the Holy Land? Two centuries of effort to maintain a Christian presence and dominance in the Holy Land would be wasted if this last stronghold was taken.

He waited, pensive and anxious, alone in the great council chamber, sitting on one of the twelve chairs around the large monastery table where a clay jug filled with fresh water was placed. He swallowed a good glassful after having first cleaned his face and hands. It took him several sips to rinse his mouth and throat of dust, soot and dried blood.

A good hour had passed when a commotion, followed by a bewildering din, was heard on the stairs. Asleep, Beynac jumped out of his chair and drew his sword from its sheath, ready to defend his life dearly.

In the name of God and the Blessed Virgin.

The noise intensified, a sign that the belligerents were getting closer and closer.

He heard screams.

Probably the cries of pain of the villagers who were paying with their lives, having had no possibility to flee before.

He cocked his sword, ready to slay the first person who came through the door. He told himself that he was probably living his last moments.

With his heart ready to explode, the door opened.

A sergeant of the Order appeared first, surprised to see a knight threatening him with his weapon.

'Our Grand Master is seriously injured.'

Beynac swept his arm across the large table to lay the Grand Master's bloodied body. Hit by an arrow under the armpit which had perforated a lung, he had been evacuated on a stretcher and brought back to the commandery. The doctor arrived at once.

Clearly aware of his personal fate and the final outcome, Guillaume de Beaujeu asked to be left alone with the young knight in order to tell him of his last wish and the future he had in mind.

Shortly afterwards, it was Jean de Villiers' turn to be seriously wounded by a wildfire explosion on the top of the enclosure gate, spraying the flaming oil, thus spraying all those around, including the Grand Master of the Hospital, causing them deep burns. The latter was immediately evacuated on a ship to Cyprus with the last knights of the order and a hundred inhabitants who had not been able to evacuate before.

The successive Mamelukes waves were inexhaustible. It was clear that there was no hope. The olifants sounded the retreat of the troops throughout the city. The last knights of the various orders present at the St. Anthony gate, as well as all the other defenders of the city positioned at the other gates and towers and some ten thousand inhabitants who had not been able to flee before because of the bad weather, all withdrew to the Templar citadel located at the extreme south-western tip of the city of Acre, on the sea.

As a result of this retreat, the city was completely abandoned to looting and exactions of all kinds. No one was spared. Men had their throats slit, women and children were sold as slaves. And to speed things up, Al-Ashraf ordered the city to be burnt down.

The Grand Master of the Temple, Guillaume de Beaujeu, succumbed to his wounds a few hours later, but not without having first entrusted Beynac with the plans for the future that he had drawn up for him. Thibaud Gaudin, then Grand Commander, took charge of the military operations with Pierre de Sevry, both of whom remained with a handful of knights. He urgently embarked on one of the last ships of the Order still in port. The one carrying the rest of the treasure. Most of it had already left the city a few months earlier, when the first bastions had fallen into the hands of the Mamelukes, and been taken to the Temple in Paris.

Direction the island of Cyprus.

31

Marimont-lès-Bénestroff
Saturday May 17th 2014, 1:15am

Back from his nocturnal escapade, the Commander decided not to say anything to Karl. He did not forget that the latter had belonged to the Teutonic Order before coming to France and did not know if he had definitively broken the ties with this organization or not. The two orders were simply friends, nothing more. It was better to remain on guard, especially at such a crucial moment. If, as he thought, part of the Templars' treasure was here, somewhere in the meanders of the galleries of this mound, there was no doubt that it would arouse the covetousness of all horizons. And even more so from orders still in existence and claiming some kind of affiliation with the original order. Fortunately, few people were really aware of the current situation, assuming of course that the information had not circulated beyond the circle of young men. Which he did not doubt.

He took the codex and his notes and immediately set to work. The first sentence was thus, in retrospect, disconcertingly clear. *'On the stone of the first Emperor of the West lies the cross that will open the Holy Door'.*

The access to the crypt had been solved.

Even if the authenticity of the altar was not formal and was based more on the persistence of a belief, it was clear that the first half of the sentence corresponded to reality.

This was a good omen for the future.

'In the tomb of the pious knight lies the key to the vault where the treasure of our brothers is kept'.

On reading these words, the Commander remembered the enfeus on the wall near the staircase. He therefore assumed that the aforementioned knight lived in one of these mortuary niches. And if so, the key must be there. He took his phone and looked at the pictures he had taken on the spot. Only a few niches were occupied. He zoomed in on each of them to maximize the resolution. The image was incomparably sharp for such a small camera.

But problem.

All of them, without exception, seemed to contain ecclesiastical burials. The characteristic thick fabric, even if eroded, was clearly visible.

The old man frowned.

His body had been betraying him for some time, his joint pains were not letting him rest, but fortunately he still had his wits about him. He felt that he was close to his goal. All he needed was a little extra effort. He looked at the photo, then at the room he was in, his eyes lost. He was pensive. He was looking for a common thread in all this. What if the knight was buried elsewhere? In the small cemetery, for example.

A hypothesis to be taken into account while other places likely to welcome the remains of such a valiant knight paraded before his eyes. When his eyes fixed on the scabbard on the bed, recovered precisely in one of these enfeus. Then on the pommel.

It was a Templar cross.

The colours had faded, but the red of the cross pattée still stood out against the white of the pommel.

Everything lit up.

He remembered the history lesson on the Order of the Temple. And more particularly the last chapter which concerned the end of this order and its repercussions on its members. When the order was dissolved by the Pope on March 22nd 1312 with the bull 'Vox in excelso', the property was largely returned to the Order of the Hospital and the dignitaries either returned to civilian life or were incorporated into other religious orders. This must have been the case here, especially as the village did not officially have a Templar commandery. Logic dictated that any knights would have to pose as monks in order to make the deception perfect.

— *Hence the term 'pious knight' in the codex*, thought the Commander.

So he knew what he had to do.

Go back to that crypt as soon as possible and find the key mentioned in the book. It must undoubtedly be in the tomb. His perseverance encouraged him to go there immediately. It was better to strike while the iron was hot. Especially as the three clever youngsters could very well stumble upon it and steal it before he did.

But his reason ordered him to rest for a few hours.

The best remedy is often rest. The next day was likely to be long. His former ardor and the excitement of the digging allowed him to spend several sleepless nights in a row without feeling the slightest sign of fatigue. But those days were over. The years had passed and limited his movements a little more every day, his hip hurting him.

He slumped on the bed, turned off the veiled bedside lamp to dim it and fell asleep almost immediately.

Exploiting the absence of the Commander, Karl had taken the opportunity to make a phone call to the stranger. The discussion was brief, but the orders were precise and direct.

His mission suddenly took a different turn.

A further step had to be taken.

He had been standing all night behind the curtain of the window of one of the upstairs rooms which afforded the best view of the square and the church. When the 'old man', as he called him whenever he spoke of him, had come out of the church earlier, he had seen a shadow creeping through the darkness of the night, up the steps and into the sacred place. Thanks to his binoculars, he had seen who it was. The second thief had finally shown himself.

It was high time to get rid of him.

He put on a black parka, placed his balaclava in the pocket, retrieved his handgun, making sure the magazine was full, and screwed the silencer on the end, along with his binoculars.

As he passed the room, he saw the Commander lying on the bed with a low snore. He passed on his way, delighted not to have to explain or justify himself, and went out of the building through the back and into the church through the same gate at the back of the little cemetery that the old man had used earlier. As he approached the choir he saw a gaping hole in front of the altar from which a light source was shining, betraying a new presence. He descended the steps with a light step, his weapon pointed forward so as not to be surprised.

Standing still, facing the altar, Clyde thought back to what he had seen earlier and perceived from the conversations in the room next to the lodge. He hoped he had not misunderstood and hesitantly applied a first pressure with his hand and then a second more confident one. The force exerted on the raised cross saw the old stone slip on the first attempt. Like all those who had gone before him, his throat tightened and the palpitations of his heart quickened. He lit his torch and took his turn in the abyss of the church. His fascination was similar to that of his predecessors. And for him in particular, since he belonged to a thousand-year-old parallel order founded at the same time and still active. He used his mobile phone to take pictures and send them to the Grand Chancellor to confirm what the students had said about the existence of the crypt and the possible consequences. He

The Mystery of the Lost Crypt

validated the sending of the message. Pointing his torch at the staircase, he recoiled.

A man was standing at the bottom of the steps.

He was pointing a gun.

'You?' he scoffed. 'I should have bet, your colleague is not with you? Too bad, because I like her. That's for later...' said Karl in a calm voice.

Clyde couldn't make out the face, hidden by the night vision binoculars, and he recognized the voice even less. But he could guess his identity without any difficulty, remembering their previous exchanges.

'Who are you? And what do you want?' he asked.

'Probably the same as you. Finding that famous treasure. Except in your case, the adventure ends here. And what better place to rest in peace than in this crypt. I must admit I've been looking forward to this moment since Nancy,' he said sarcastically.

Clyde had no time to react. A sharp pain pierced his chest. The explosion was barely perceptible.

He slumped to the checkered floor, dropping his phone as it slid under a chair. His agony lasted only a few seconds before he breathed his last, his eyes open in amazement.

'That's a good thing done!' said Karl, sheathing his gun in his jacket.

In the subdued atmosphere of the living room where the three companions continued their evening, lying on the sofas, discussions about the crypt were going on. Natasha still couldn't believe it and was still overwhelmed with emotion. Cyril had immortalized the place from every angle with his mobile phone, which amounted to almost a hundred shots. When he returned, he would perhaps show them to Visconti. He had no doubt that the dean of the university would be very impressed by these photos, but the professor's change of attitude intrigued him.

Gilles asked Cyril about their discovery when the door to the living room suddenly creaked. The three of them were startled, not expecting anyone to come in at such an ungodly hour.

It was Bonnie.

She looked worried.

'Have you been here long?'

'Er, a good hour or so,' replied Cyril, surprised by the Italian's presence. 'Why?'

Worry gripped her. She didn't answer anything, immersed in her thoughts. Clyde's only instructions were to keep an eye on the three young men. He should have been home long ago if he had just followed the instructions. This was obviously not the case.

She left the room just as abruptly.

'She was weird, wasn't she?'

'That's the least we can say... her boyfriend dumped her?' answered Gilles.

'Well, on that note, I think it's high time we went to bed,' said Cyril, winking at his friend.

'Yes, you are right. We'll continue this discussion later today.'

'Go upstairs, darling, I'll be there in a moment. I'm going to take a breath of fresh air with Gilles.'

32

Marimont-lès-Bénestroff
Saturday May 17th 2014, 2:30am

The commander woke up with a start, large drops of sweat beading on his forehead. He looked at his watch.

He had lain on that bed barely an hour earlier and then nothingness. It hadn't taken him long to fall asleep. He had once read a study on the average time to fall asleep. Less than ten minutes on average. That evening, it had taken him no more than thirty seconds, certainly... only a short hour of rest, very restorative. He got up with some difficulty and went to the adjoining room.

Karl, lying on his back, still dressed, his shoes parallel to the bedside table and his jacket hanging on the back of the chair, was also visibly dozing.

The praise he received did not seem very justified. This sniper had already failed twice. He was beginning to doubt his abilities and his motives. He would be sure to refer to the Grand Master when this whole affair was over.

In the meantime, the old man felt better without him.

He returned to the room he had taken possession of, sat down on the bed and opened his notebook where he had been scribbling notes and read the second riddle. *In the tomb of the pious knight lies the key to the vault that houses the treasure of our brothers.*

He closed his eyes, concentrated, and visualized the different niches in his head. He went through them one by one. He did not see anything that looked like a key. He continued his reflection. He must have forgotten something. Suddenly he opened his eyes, stunned, as if he had just had an apparition. He looked at the chair next to the bed, which he pointed to with his torch. A look of satisfaction came over his face.

He immediately grabbed the object, put on his jacket and went back into the crypt without further ado. The fog had thickened again. He was surprised when he entered the church and approached the altar. The entrance to the crypt was gaping.

Strange, I was the last one to leave and I remember closing the passage, he thought. *Would the young people be there again?*

No light seemed to be emanating from the crypt, but as a precaution the old man took his gun from his jacket and began the descent cautiously, the light of his torch fixed on his step so as not to miss any. At the bottom of the stairs, grimacing, he turned up the intensity of his torch and scanned the entire room.

He could only see that the place was abandoned.

He then took out of his backpack a neon light that would illuminate the entire crypt and placed it on the table. It was now imperative to solve the riddle. He took out his notebook, sat down on one of the chairs and reread his notes.

He looked up and scanned the wall in front of him. As he had noticed a few hours earlier, not all the enfeus were occupied. He looked at them all for the umpteenth time when his eyes were struck by one of them.

The third in the bottom row.

He crouched down to better examine the entire cavity and his surprise was complete. Unlike those occupied by relics of the time, this one had a completely different character. He was astonished to see brown hiking boots and then a modern outfit on the inert body of a man.

He didn't remember seeing this body earlier in the evening. He looked again at the photos on his mobile phone. The body had indeed not been there two hours earlier. The blood in the burial niche had not even coagulated yet, which confirmed that it had just been placed there.

How was this possible?

On his guard, he scanned the whole room once more, by simple reflex, and then illuminated the back of the tomb to try to discern the person who was there. But the features of the partially hidden face were unknown to him.

Who could have killed this man? He immediately eliminated the three academics, who in his opinion were incapable of such an action. Could it be that Karl had taken advantage of his sleep to go there and have a bad encounter? Possibly. The giant could very well have acted during this interlude. Suddenly Karl's last message of the day before came to mind. He had mentioned the presence of an unknown young woman on the site of the excavations. He had already spotted her once in Nancy with the assailant. So it was possible that the dead man lying there was her partner. But it did not matter who he was. There was another, much more important thing that concerned him now.

Karl seemed to know about the existence of this crypt.

And he no longer trusted him!

Cyril and Gilles had gone out to get some fresh air and have a last cigarette. It was damp and cool. In his short-sleeved polo shirt, Gilles' hair stood on end as soon as he passed the porch. They were surprised to see the Italian woman sitting on the low wall, arms crossed, thinking.

'It's chilly...' Gilles mumbled, letting out vaporous clouds like the bellows of a locomotive.

But the attractive Italian did not react, lost in her thoughts. She was worried sick about Clyde. She imagined all the darkest scenarios. And rightly so, especially after the previous day's incidents in the forest.

'Isn't your friend with you?'

'No. And that's the problem. He should have been home long ago. I hope nothing has happened to him...'

'I can't imagine what could have happened to him in this place...' replied Gilles.

Cyril glared at him with a frown, telling him to take it easy with his remarks.

Bonnie was careful not to recount the events of the previous day.

'If it makes you feel better, we can go for a walk around the village and the edge of the forest,' Cyril suggested.

Bonnie thought about it and then accepted the proposal. She knew that if something had happened to her colleague, she would be next in line. So it was better not to be alone. She had been made aware of his military past and assistance from him could only be appreciated.

They each went back to their rooms to get a jacket. On the way back, Bonnie gave Cyril a gun.

'You probably know how to use it, don't you?' she said, handing him a Glock semi-automatic pistol.

'Erm... yes. But is that really necessary? Or maybe I missed an episode...'

'I promise to explain everything to you, but later,' said the Transalpine woman.

The two young men looked at each other, dumbfounded.

'What's this crazy talk about? Did you see that stuff! Is she part of the mafia or what?' whispered Gilles to his friend.

'I don't know, but I trust her...'

They walked up the lane on both sides of the road, sifting through ditches and groves with their powerful torches.

CLEAR.

They then entered the church. The wooden debris of the chair still lay on the floor. Bonnie, who had entered last, paid no attention to it, absorbed by a bad feeling, imagining she would discover the body of her friend lying in his blood. The beams of the three lamps ran through the nave in a disorganized ballet. Gilles looked into the confessional, Bonnie went up to the small platform where the organ was located. Not a cat, and certainly not a dead body. Then Cyril froze his lamp on the high altar and was petrified to see it open.

'Look Gilles, the access to the crypt is open. It was locked. I'm sure of it.'

'I confirm. I can still see you pushing the stone.'

The two friends looked at each other in amazement.

'But then who opened the trap door?'

It could only be the woman's friend, Cyril thought. Hence his prolonged absence. He must have surprised them when they came out and understood the opening mechanism. Which could also explain the wooden debris of the chair at the entrance. It all added up. He was eager to know more about the presence of this unusual couple. Were they grave robbers? Were they people sent by Visconti, the Dean of the Faculty, to watch over them? So far, he was the only person who had been informed. And after the incidents of the past week, anything was possible. The beautiful Italian woman had promised to explain everything to him. Whatever the case, he had to be more and more wary of all these people.

Bonnie was relieved that Clyde was in the crypt. She rushed in, eager to see him again, but also to see the crypt with her own eyes.

The two academics followed suit. Cyril did not have time to tell her to watch her head. The Italian woman hit the slab head-on and then, dizzy, her foot in the air, tipped backwards. Her skull hit the sharp edge of a step which cut the back of her scalp, then she tumbled like a rag doll, unconscious.

The Commander was racking his brains for the next part of the riddle. He had already solved the first two sentences, aided by the trio of scholars, namely how to get into the crypt and the key to the vault. The place was monastically silent. Worse. A cold, heavy silence for the old man. The still warm body hidden in one of the vaults was surely a factor. He tried to ignore it and concentrated on his task.

But the effort was short-lived. A door slammed shut, voices followed, then hurried footsteps on the tiles.

Still in his thoughts, he was caught off guard. He did not know how to react to this unexpected event. He turned off his lamp and prayed that it was only Karl. The situation would be much easier to handle. But from the voices, there were several of them up there. The sound of footsteps on the staircase could already be heard and the beams of the torches ran down the steps. They were approaching without any scenario coming to mind.

No exit this time, let alone a confessional.

He would have to improvise.

His second instinct was to put his right hand in his jacket pocket and wrap the butt of his gun around it, ready to use it if the conditions demanded it. Then he waited to see the faces appear. What followed was more than unexpected. A scream, a thud, and he saw a motionless body fall to the bottom of the stairs. The commander approached and looked at the person lying on the ground.

A woman.

But at once other footsteps sped down the stairs to the aid of the unfortunate girl. He took a step back, his hand still firmly on his pistol, and flicked the switch on the neon light on the wooden table. Two people appeared in the amber glow of the crypt.

The surprise was total on both sides.

33

Paris
January 1307

Amaury de Beynac had returned from Cyprus two years earlier, as had most of the other Templars scattered throughout the kingdom's many commanderies. Only a small number of them had remained on the island, as the idea of raising a new crusade was still on the agenda in the West. He had been assigned to the Temple enclosure in Paris, the head office of the order in France and above all its bank. He worked on the first floor of the Grande Tour.

The winter was harsh this year. Having spent a few years in the East, Beynac had forgotten the combined effects of wind, snow and freezing temperatures and had become accustomed to mild winters and warm summers. He had to get used to it, and quickly, because he knew that he would not be returning to Cyprus any time soon. But he could not complain. He had a place of choice. A fire was lit in the hearth in the centre of the room where he worked, warming this tower of almost forty meters high and twenty meters wide. A privilege in this immense castle 'safe' that looked more like a prison with its bars on the windows. A four-storey vaulted keep, with a cellar and an attic, flanked in its corners by four round, long and oppressive turrets, one of which housed the spiral staircase. There was also a well, a mill, an oven and a chapel. A tower that could therefore live in total autarky if it were ever besieged.

The situation of the Templars had changed considerably since the loss of their Frankish positions in the Holy Land and their exodus to Cyprus. So much so that the question of their raison d'être arose, as their initial purpose was to protect pilgrims going to Jerusalem. As Christians were no longer admitted, the legitimacy of the Order's existence was at stake. For a time, the Order was protected from the French king Philip the Fair by the bull issued by Pope Boniface VIII in 1302, which affirmed the superiority of pontifical law over royal power. Clement V, a French pope, was elected in June 1305 and eased all tensions between the papacy and the French king.

Jacques de Molay, narrowly elected Grand Master in 1293 in Cyprus, suddenly burst into the room.

'Assembly in five minutes in the main hall with the Marshal and the Masters of Province. You too, Brother Jean!'

The young knight, surprised to be invited to such a meeting, dried the quill and closed the inkwell, putting the codex he was writing in the drawer of his desk which he locked. He kept this key permanently attached to a cord around his neck. This book was far more important to him than all the gold in the chest.

All the protagonists went to the main hall.

The Grand Master's face hardened.

'There are many rumors about us,' he began. 'Is it jealousy or quite rightly? Probably both, in my opinion. It is said that King Philip, at this very moment, is amassing all sorts of evidence to bring us to justice. He condemns the deviation from our primary goal, which is to defend the pilgrims, for the purposes of enrichment and ignoble practices.'

'That traitor! We all know around this table that he ordered the attack on Anagni, which led to the death of Boniface VIII. He devalued the currency, impoverished his people by raising taxes, confiscated the property of Lombard and Jewish merchants and came to beg our financial aid for immeasurable sums so that he could wage war. You even welcomed him here so that he could escape the public lynching following the Parisians' revolt against rising rents. And he would turn against us without the slightest scruple? He deserves nothing but death this mangy dog. To hell with him,' spat Ymbert Blanc, Master of the Auvergne province.

'Did Our Holiness know about these rumors?'

'Bertrand de Got is entirely in the pay of this felon! He was elected thanks to the king by reconciling him with the church and cancelling everything that our Holy Father Boniface VIII had put in place to remove him,' Blanc continued. 'He will do whatever the King tells him to do. We must not expect any help in return from him. Quite the contrary.'

Raymond de Barber, the Marshal appointed by de Molay upon his election, took offense at these harsh words for the new pontiff. Two opposing camps clashed verbally and chaos ensued. Beynac, seated at the back of the room, watched the scene in amazement.

The Grand Master intervened with his fist on the table.

'Calm down brothers! Let us not get carried away. I have gathered you here to tell you of my decisions regarding the future of our venerable Order. Not to quarrel. And under no circumstances will I tolerate deliberate attacks on our most Holy Father...'

'The facts do not indeed plead in our favor. The last attempt to reconquer our strongholds in the East was aborted,' said Marshal Baudoin de Landrin, looking kindly on the Grand Master, to whom the failure of the crusade was largely attributed as much as to himself. 'As the sovereigns are all over-indebted, as we well know, there is very little chance that the Pope will manage to organize a new one in the next few years!'

'Why not merge with our Hospitaller brothers, as our Holiness Nicholas IV had already suggested in the year of grace 1294,' asked Martin de Lou, treasurer of the order.

'This has indeed been the wish of the Holy See for about ten years. I have discussed this on many occasions with successive popes as well as with William and Foulques de Villaret, our Hospitaller brothers. It appears that the situation is not as simple as that. Personally, I had always refused. But the situation has changed somewhat...'

The debates continued well into the night, interspersed with the prayers of Vespers and Matins.

'I am aware that our order has grown enormously and is also a formidable military power of more than fifteen thousand seasoned soldiers. I have also been fighting since my accession to the head of the order to bring all our lost souls back to the right path. And God knows there are some. But if everyone turns against us, out of jealousy, envy or fear, we will be forced to radically change our objectives. Brother John here has been commissioned since the fall of Acre to tell the story of our order, and I have entrusted him with an even more important task for some years now. As you know, I have journeyed all over Europe for two years. I have also commissioned a group of about ten of our valiant brothers to continue the work of exploring new uninhabited or indigenous lands that we started fifty years ago in collaboration with our Viking friends. They embarked in Sweden and went to the virgin lands of the West. The Swedish people had already been trading there for almost two centuries. The silver ore that arrives in the port of La Rochelle comes from deposits in these distant lands. I propose that a camp be set up there as soon as possible.'

'What would we do in such remote places?'

'Chased out of the East, reviled in Europe, we could found a new society that would develop and prosper in peace, far from the tumult and the vindictiveness of the rulers. Swedes, English, Irish and even French would be ready to settle there, and we would help them in their tasks.'

'And what is this task you have given to Brother John?'

'You will know in due course. But if the king is looking to bail out our assets, we'll make sure he gets nothing. Or only crumbs to feed him.'

34

**Marimont-lès-Bénestroff
Saturday May 17th 2014, 2:30am**

'Professor Visconti!' said Cyril, dumbfounded.

'Ah, Cyril! Surprised, aren't you? You're just in time,' he stammered. 'I thought you could use all the help I could get and I couldn't resist. I tried to warn you, but you didn't answer. And now we meet in the middle of the night. Unbelievable, isn't it?'

A long blank followed and the old man's cheeks flushed. He saw them looking at each other out of the corner of his eye. They were doubtful. The two academics did not seem to agree with this far-fetched explanation.

'You must have dialed the wrong number, because I didn't get any calls from you...'

Lying on the floor, Bonnie let out a moan. She was gradually coming to. The shock had been violent, as the swelling on her forehead could already testify. Her hair was sticky, soaked in blood. But fortunately, the wound on the top of her head was not deep. It was only then that Cyril and Gilles turned their attention back to her and gently helped her to sit up.

Meanwhile, Visconti looked on without flinching, more concerned with trying to get out of it with another spin than with being of any help.

After a few minutes the Italian got up, staggering, the pain visible on her tense features. She applied a handkerchief to the lesion to stop the bleeding and then turned pale, a shiver of terror running down her spine at the sight of the shoes. The brown pair looked familiar. She approached with her lamp and shone it on the grave with a trembling hand. Her blood froze.

She let out a shrill cry as she slid to the ground and then turned to Visconti helplessly.

'Oh my God, what have you done? You killed him...' she said in a plaintive voice, horrified and incredulous that this old man could have done such a thing.

'No, I didn't do it! I assure you,' he defended himself vigorously, feeling threatened by the two boys' eyes. 'I am not a murderer. Why would I do it? It's all nonsense. The body was already there when I came down. Let's see.'

Bonnie dropped her makeshift bandage, grabbed the body's feet and started pulling it out!

'Help me!' she pleaded, turning back to the boys.

Immediately, both of them ran over and took charge of taking the body out and laying it gently on the ground. A thick trail of blood covered the stone on which it had lain. Cyril felt the carotid artery and brought his ear to Clyde's mouth.

Bonnie watched the scene, tears streaming freely down her face.

Cyril took a few moments and then exclaimed:

'I have a pulse. He's breathing, but very weakly...'

Bonnie breathed out in relief before saying:

'You have to call for help, right away!'

'Stop! No one is to be called... it is categorically ruled out that anyone will learn about this crypt,' Visconti said angrily.

'Are you kidding, Professor? This man's life is at stake. He needs urgent attention. Every second that passes could be fatal.'

'I said no!' thundered the professor.

'But the old man is completely senile,' Gilles told his colleague. 'A man's life is at stake and he's talking to us from that arched rat hole!'

The Mystery of the Lost Crypt

'No one is going to stop us from calling the ambulance,' Bonnie said as she picked up her phone and dialed the emergency number.

Visconti was taken aback. He hesitated, then stammered out 'put the phone down now or...' and no one took him seriously. But the dial tone indicated that there was no signal. She headed for the stairs to call from outside when the teacher intervened firmly.

'All right, the joke's over,' he said, pulling his gun from his pocket and pointing it at Bonnie. 'Nobody leaves the premises! You all stay here. Don't make me use this gun.'

The two young men's eyes widened. This night seemed to be full of surprises.

'What exactly do you intend to do, Professor?' asked Cyril, both surprised and offended that the historian he revered was pointing a gun at them.

This vision seemed totally surreal to him. He saw him again in the amphitheater of the faculty of Nancy, only a few days ago, making a fool of himself in front of all the students with his overhead projector problem. Today that same person was standing in front of them holding them at gunpoint. Unlike the high-tech tools, he seemed perfectly at ease in handling this object.

Cyril looked at Gilles to convince himself that he was not dreaming, which he confirmed, then turned to Visconti.

'Are you losing your mind?'

'I have spent too many years deciphering the codex of the Temple Church in Paris. And now three little budding archaeologists have found, by the greatest of coincidences, the second codex, the very one that made it possible to decipher the first one, like Champollion's Rosetta Stone, written in the hand of the last Grand Master of the order himself, Jacques de Molay. I am in the home stretch and no one will stand in my way.'

'You must think you're not cut out for this job,' Gilles ironized. 'You've been looking for years in a vacuum. It took us less than a weekend and we found it! And it wasn't luck...'

'I see... such a discovery would put you back in the media spotlight and, above all, would give you back the notoriety you have lacked for more than 30 years. You would finish on a high note. An exit through the front door. That's all you're looking for, isn't it? If that's the only reason, you can keep OUR discovery,' Cyril added with a tone of disgust.

'Shut up, you cheeky kids, or I'll shut you up like this. Of course it was pure chance. Nothing more. Contrary to what you think, I don't care about fame anymore. I passed that point a long time ago. You would have learned very quickly that, in this business, you are forgotten even more quickly than you were raised on your pedestal. It's not the crypt that interests me, that one I would have gladly left to you. But since you want to play this little game, let's see if you are as clever as that. Come over here. Come on!' he said, throwing his notebook on the table.

The determination in his eyes was clear.

Bonnie could not bring herself to let her companion die. She had to find a way to neutralize this man at all costs. And by any means necessary.

They both approached, intrigued. Gilles took the notebook and leafed through it.

'What is this gibberish?' he shouted.

'This is the enigma we will have to solve to find the Templar treasure hidden in the bowels of this castle mound. And time is of the essence if you do not want this man to die...'

Cyril realized that the teacher was not joking and fully appreciated what was at stake. He snatched the notes from his friend's hands and began to read.

'*On the stone of the first Emperor of the West lies the cross that will open the Holy Door,*' he read aloud.

'That's the cross on the altar that enabled the trapdoor to be opened,' commented Gilles.

'*In the tomb of the pious knight lies the key to the vault where the treasure of our brothers is kept*'.

Cyril turned mechanically towards the enfeus, followed by Gilles. Visconti looked at them, curious as to the answer the two neophytes would give.

'According to the ancient text, one of these niches would therefore house the remains of a knight where a key would have been deposited.'

They scrupulously checked each niche one by one, taking care not to move the bones.

'I can only see shreds of cloth,' Gilles noted with disappointment, delicately picking up the fragments of cloth with an old stick he had found on the spot. 'Yet the sentence seems clear to me. The key will be found in the knight's tomb.'

'Or maybe the tomb is somewhere else...'

'In the small cemetery behind the church?'

'Quite possible. There are two very old tombs at the bottom, the origin of which nobody seems to know.'

'But then, why send us here? Because even if we get our hands on this key, I don't see any door or lock where we can insert it,' said Gilles, scanning the entire room.

'It all depends on whether the text refers to a real key or to another object acting as a key... don't forget that the sentence refers to a knight.'

'Good point. In those days the sword of the knight of the temple was either placed on the tombstone or its outline was traced on it and then chiseled out so that the engraving would persist over the centuries. Here they would have had no choice but to leave it in the niche with the body.'

But the two academics had not spotted any weapons during their methodical inspection of the premises. One fact intrigued Cyril. He approached one of the graves and noticed the bones and fragments scattered around, unlike the others.

'Someone seems to have beaten us to the punch.'

Bonnie stood back by the stairs and hatched a plan to try and neutralize Visconti as quickly as possible. She was scrutinizing his every move and was on the lookout. But for the moment the professor had not given her even one small opportunity to turn her back and was still keeping an eye on the beautiful Italian.

'Is this what you're looking for?' said Visconti, not very proudly, brandishing the iron blade he had previously retrieved from the burial ground. 'Finally, I must admit that you are asking the right questions and are not as novice as I thought.'

'I suppose you got it from that alcove,' said Cyril curtly.

'Yes, it did. And with such a heavy weight, I can tell you that it gave me a hard time with these back and forth movements.'

'What? You desecrated this ancestral tomb without the slightest scruple. If someone had ever told me, I would never have believed it. You're no more respectful than any of these site robbers. It's downright unworthy of an archaeologist of your reputation!'

The professor's face reddened. He turned to Gilles, exasperated by the young man's arrogance. It was time for him to teach him a little lesson. He approached him, who at the same time took a few steps back. The latter understood that he had gone too far this time. Visconti raised his arm and pointed the weapon.

Gilles was stunned, thinking that his last hour had come. He looked incredulously at Cyril who shrugged his shoulders in helplessness.

'I warned you, young impertinent one,s' Visconti inveighed forcefully.'

The professor was unrecognizable.

His attitude when the discovery was announced and his actions in the days that followed had already aroused some suspicion in Cyril. But here the dean had gone to a whole new dimension. He was armed, a man was lying on the ground, who he had probably wounded himself, and he did not hesitate to threaten them with death.

Cyril was stunned.

The opportunity finally presented itself.

The Italian took the opportunity to rush at the old man without hesitating for a second. The latter, far too busy settling accounts with the academics, had left her unguarded, thus opening an unexpected window of opportunity. But in too much of a hurry, she hit her thigh on the corner of the wooden table, knocking over the neon sign on top. Unbalanced, she nevertheless managed to stay on her two feet by leaning on Cyril.

Alerted by the noise, Visconti turned around and was surprised to see the woman running towards him.

The Mystery of the Lost Crypt

35

Nice
Saturday May 17th 2014, 5am

Piéroni had done a titanic job on the case he had been following for a year already. But he was aware that without the boy's precious help, the investigation would still be at a standstill. A search in the national registration file had enabled him to confirm the boy's statements about the make of the vehicle. A BMW 7 Series Limousine. Its owner lived not far from there, in the hinterland, only ten kilometers away. After further investigation, Piéroni learned that the estate was officially the French headquarters of the Order of the Hospitallers of Jerusalem.

He spent much of the day researching the subject, trying to understand the various ramifications of this ancient order. According to the website, the order was a direct descendant of the Hospitallers, which were founded around the eleventh century to care for pilgrims traveling to Jerusalem. It quickly became a military order and ruled the region for almost two hundred years in competition with the Templars. United for the first time at the battle of St. John of Acre in 1291, their joint defeat against the huge Mamluk army of Al Ashraf Khalil put an end to the Frankish presence in the Holy Land and condemned them to expatriate to the island of Cyprus and then Rhodes in 1310 where, after inheriting the Templars' property, they prospered for another two hundred years before obtaining sovereignty over the island of Malta from Charles V in 1530. Having become rich and powerful, with their naval fleet ruling the whole Mediterranean, the order was dissolved by Napoleon in 1798, who was in great need of funds to finance his Egyptian campaign. From then on, the Hospitallers dispersed throughout Europe. A branch was welcomed in St. Petersburg by the Russian Tsar Paul 1st. After a few years of wandering, a second branch was established in Italy, in Rome. It was the latter that the Vatican recognized in 1953 without any possible discussion as the order incardinated in the Holy See. From a purely historical point of view, however, there is some ambiguity. Many considered that the Order had been definitively dissolved, each one differing on the exact date of this dissolution, thus creating even more uncertainties.

Once the case was closed and the prosecutor had given his consent to search the residence, there was no obstacle left for Piéroni to intervene at the headquarters of the order. Accompanied by several colleagues, he went early one morning to the heights of Nice.

The three police cars arrived at the estate in front of a magnificent wrought-iron castle gate in the baroque style, which stood out at the entrance to the property.

It was of course closed.

The building was not visible from the road, hidden almost entirely by a cypress forest. Piéroni hesitated as to how to proceed. The ideal was often the effect of surprise. The enclosure was certainly high, but it could be crossed. Ringing the bell and waiting for the gate to be opened would give the occupants a good ten minutes to take the lead, as would concealing certain compromising documents or even failing them outright.

So they opted for the first option. With a little luck, the surveillance cameras scattered around the property would not spot them until the last moment.

Several policemen, including the Marseillais, climbed over the wall, helped by their colleagues who were giving them a lift. Not very supple or athletic, with a nice belly maintained over the years with beer and good food, they had to work together to propel him into the air before he fell heavily on the other side, surprised by the strength of his colleagues. This incident caused general hilarity.

'One car stays behind,' said Piéroni, glaring at the two guys who had helped him. 'The rest of you will join us as soon as we can open the gate.'

The agents moved quickly along the path. The sun had not yet risen and the night was still resisting, but as the minutes ticked by, the beginnings of light could already be seen to the east.

'I hope they don't have any bloody big dogs chasing us...' worried Piéroni.

When they got close to the house, they split up. The commissioner, accompanied by three of his henchmen, would take care of the main entrance while their colleagues would surround the building to prevent any attempt at escape.

It was five o'clock sharp. Everyone was in place.

Piéroni rang.

An alarm went off and a beep sounded through the loudspeakers, startling the tenants.

Someone was obviously trespassing on the estate.

The man ran into the office, pressed the button to turn off the thundering alarm and glanced at the monitors of the various security cameras. The one at the entrance gate left no doubt. Men with armbands on their arms were sneaking through the pine grove towards the building. Others were waiting outside in their vehicles.

He left the office just as hastily.

'The police, Grand Prior!'

'At this time of day, it's certainly not for breakfast or a social visit,' says the latter, dressing quickly. 'Just give me a few minutes to collect a few documents from my office.'

The butler tracked intruders directly on his touchscreen tablet. An application linked it to the entire security system. He connected the Grand Prior's watch so that he too could follow the progress of the police in real time. As soon as a thermal camera detected the slightest movement or any source of heat, the image was immediately projected onto the various connected screens.

A handy little piece of technology...

The Grand Prior did not have to wait long. The image from the camera at the main entrance appeared on his watch and showed two policemen on the stoop. Then other cameras spat out their images in bursts.

The commandery was surrounded.

The Grand Prior smiled.

All this deployment of force would in no way prevent him from slipping away and escaping from them. But for that, he had to hurry. His watch emitted an alarm more pronounced than the previous ones and startled him. This time it was the interior cameras. The one in the entrance hall. The police had obviously already entered the house. He was caught off guard. He had told his butler to let them stay outside as long as possible. Their insistence had, it seems, worn down his patience.

Now he had to move as quickly as possible.

The Grand Prior went to his desk to retrieve a large briefcase from the back of his chair and some other documents. He bent over the desk to retrieve the book from the opposite corner, but it slipped from his grasp in the rush. The heavy manuscript fell flat on the oak floor with a resounding crash. He stood still as if time was suspended, waiting. But it was already too late.

The picture of the grand staircase appeared on his watch. He saw a man with an orange armband on his arm and a gun in his hand going up the stairs two by two, followed by a woman.

He instinctively glanced towards the door with concern. He had only a handful of seconds before the policeman crossed the porch of his office. He could hear the hurried footsteps clattering on the marble and then on the wooden floor of the first level.

His pulse quickened and his face tightened.

No one responded to his first request. A classic of the genre. Piéroni expected this and immediately insisted, drumming vigorously on the large wooden door.

'Police! Open up, quickly, or we'll break down this splendid door," he shouted, pointing his gun at the lock.'

The door opened as if by magic. The man who appeared was calm and unimpressed by the crowd of officers. From the way he was dressed and the way he spoke, the police knew at once that they were dealing with a butler. Piéroni rushed inside the mansion, brandishing the search warrant which he stuck in front of his nose. He had to step back to read what it said.

'Are there any other people here besides you?'

'No, I am alone. My master is on a trip.'

As if by chance, thought the Commissioner.

He ordered his colleagues to start the search. He huffed in annoyance when he saw the inordinate size of the residence. He already knew that they would spend a good part of the day there.

To the left was a huge staircase leading to the upper floors. The Commissioner looked up and asked the butler what was there.

'Mainly rooms.'

'And what else?'

At the same time a brief bang alerted everyone. The noise was coming from upstairs. It sounded like a gunshot.

'And what is this? A mouse trap in the attic?' shouted Piéroni as he rushed up the stairs, followed by his colleague.

When he arrived on the next floor, he found himself on a large mezzanine which opened onto two perpendicular corridors. He signaled to his colleague to take the one on the left. He crossed the loggia and walked briskly in the opposite direction.

He was moving forward when he heard a sound, this time duller and longer. He stopped and concentrated on identifying its origin. The impression was that a piece of furniture had been moved. Or something similar.

He followed the sound, which lasted for a few seconds, then faded away, only to resume at once with the same rhythm. Arriving at the place where the noise seemed to come from, he glanced briefly at the doorway and, seeing no one, entered the room, his arm extended with a weapon pointed forward. He had not forgotten that one of the people they were looking for was a murderer.

So it was better to take every precaution.

36

Marimont-lès-Bénestroff
Saturday May 17th 2014, 3am

Bonnie grabbed both of Visconti's hands and they both went over. She surprised herself with this outburst of uncontrollable energy. The professor fell heavily on his back, the weight of his assailant on his chest. As his hand touched the ground, a shot went off just before he dropped the weapon. The bullet pierced the old straw mattress on which the abbot had been lying for a century under the rubble.

Visconti gasped, unable to react or get up. A few decades earlier, he would have been back on his feet immediately. Now his body and reflexes betrayed him. Disoriented by the fall, he groped for his weapon with his right hand, but felt nothing. He turned his head and did not see it either. The light source on the table was too dimly lit in this part of the room.

Without that weapon, the roles were reversed now and he suspected they were not going to let him go. Especially not after what had just happened. There was no turning back.

Panic took hold of him.

He got up on all fours and frantically searched for his weapon. But it seemed to have vanished. It was impossible to get his hands on it again.

'Is this what you're looking for?' said a female voice.

The Mystery of the Lost Crypt

Visconti turned and saw the Italian woman brandishing her weapon.

This time all hope was lost.

She would call for help in the next few minutes to try to save her friend and the gendarmes. He would spend his last days in prison. His name would be tarnished, his honor and fame swept away. And what will his dear and loving wife think.

He wouldn't even dare to look her in the eye.

'My greed got the better of me. I don't know what came over me. I beg your forgiveness,' said the Dean of Faculty as he struggled to his feet.

Cyril almost felt sorry for the old man.

Was it a futile attempt at bribing?

He hesitated to answer. But he kept quiet. He could not ignore what had just happened. His tutor had gone too far. In word, but especially in deed. A man was between life and death and that didn't seem to bother him, his mind being taken up with this treasure hunt alone, which for the moment was still only a legend. The riddle proved nothing and brought no certainty as to the possible contents of the treasure and its presence.

As for Gilles, he only dreamed of punching him in the face with a well-placed punch as a form of revenge.

Still panting with emotion from her tussle with the historian, Bonnie asked Cyril to go back upstairs as soon as possible and call for help. She preferred to stay with Gilles to keep an eye on this old fool who seemed capable of anything. Clyde remained unconscious but his sporadic moaning was a good sign.

Cyril grabbed his torch and rushed up the stairs. Every minute counted now in trying to save Clyde.

When he reached the top, he stopped abruptly.

He was paralyzed.

A man stood before him, pointing a gun.

A Glock with a silencer.

With a sharp gesture of his armed hand, the latter told Cyril to turn around and go back down. He complied without flinching, the man on his heels. The other three were surprised to see him reappear so suddenly.

'Is there a problem? The call isn't going through? It's not working, is it?'

At the same time, they saw a man appear behind him. As Cyril reached the last step, the man pushed him slightly and wrapped his free arm around his throat, putting his gun to his head.

Bonnie instinctively pointed at him. She had no trouble recognizing the individual. He was none other than her attacker from the day before. The same one who had attacked her in the forest and the bomber in Gilles' house.

'You bastard!' Bonnie shouted.

'Well, what language! But let's see who's there. What a surprise. The whole family...' said Karl with a demented look. 'Put that down immediately or I'll blow your protégé's head off,' he added, pressing the barrel of the gun harder against Cyril's temple.

Bonnie didn't move. Her brain was in turmoil.

What to do?

She was once again trapped. If she put down her weapon as the bastard in front of her asked, all hope of saving her friend would be lost. Not to mention her primary mission, which was why she was in this mess.

Protecting Cyril.

She thought about the options available to her. The choice was a difficult one.

'I won't say it a third time. Don't make me pull the trigger and blow his brains out. While I understand that the walls of this room could use a little sprucing up...'

This time Visconti intervened.

'Wait, Karl!'

Bonnie had no room for error with this shot. Nerves on edge, clutching her gun, her indecision shone through. There would be only one attempt. The retaliation would be immediate, heavy with consequences.

Her hand began to shake.

'Please, drop your weapon,' Gilles begged her. 'If you don't, everything will end in a bloodbath. That's all we'll have gained from this story.'

'I fear that in any case it will come to this. This madman will not let us go. He was the one who booby-trapped the car in the car park of your residence. Fortunately for you, he got the wrong car and it was this poor girl who suffered the consequences. He also tried to eliminate me yesterday in the forest after I had visited you. Nothing seems to stop him. I wouldn't be surprised if he had also seriously injured my friend. We're just getting a bit of a break from his clumsiness and greed.'

'In that case, shoot!' shouted Cyril. 'A bullet in the head and that's it, it's all over. I trust you.'

'Don't listen to him,' said Visconti in turn. 'He won't back down from anything or anyone. He is a robot programmed to do his job. You are no match for him. Come on, be reasonable, give me the gun. I promise you no harm will come to you.'

She looked her target straight in the eye.

Karl smiled at this announcement. He shifted to stand a little further back behind Cyril. It was better to take all precautions. A cornered animal was capable of anything.

But he was getting tired of all this talk.

He became impatient.

This was not a good sign for anyone.

37

Nice
Saturday May 17th 2014, 5:15am

The footsteps on the tiles were getting closer and closer.
The Grand Prior had to leave as soon as possible.
And so much for the book that fell to the ground. He had no time to retrieve it. He pressed a button and a back door opened slowly. He had always complained that the mechanism was far too slow. He rushed to it and immediately clicked it shut. Just in time.
When he reached the bottom of the stairs, he hurriedly typed a few words to his butler advising him to put the work in a safe place before making his escape. After five minutes of brisk walking on a false uphill slope, he opened a door that led to the back of the estate. Normally, the view over the small wooded valley was superb. With the azure blue of the Mediterranean Sea in the distance as a bonus. He sat down in a small electric golf cart parked in front of the gate and disappeared into the morning mist.

Piéroni entered a spacious office.

A patchwork of books cluttered the shelves.

What a disappointment. He could have sworn that the noise was coming from here.

But at the back of the room, on the right, a brief movement caught his attention. It was as if part of the bookcase had just shifted. A slight clicking sound completed the scene. He immediately thought of the door closing mechanism.

There was no doubt about it.

He scanned the walls, which were all lined with shelves all over. But no door was visible. He then left the room and continued to see where the rest of the corridor led when he met his colleague coming in the opposite direction who assured him that he had not met anyone.

Piéroni returned to the office, more determined than ever. His intuition was rarely wrong.

There is a back door in these walls, he thought. *Now I just have to figure out how to open it...*

He put his gun away and began the search. He inspected the shelves carefully, also searching under the shelves, and manipulated the books at ground level in order to eventually find the mechanism that would trigger the opening of a secret passage. He found nothing in this part of the library.

He prayed that it wasn't a remote control that was the trigger. He was going to continue with the wall opposite, but first he decided to use the desk in the middle of the room. He pressed every button on the landline phone and the keys on the computer keyboard. At a guess.

Still nothing.

He crouched down and felt under the worktop and the blanks when suddenly his hand caught a protrusion. A small box acting as a switch in the right-hand corner.

As he pressed the push-button, the same characteristic sound was heard. He turned around and found a section of bookcase, about sixty centimeters wide and a hundred and fifty centimeters high, swiveling. Bingo! He had just found it.

He rushed in. A spiral staircase made of stone plunged in front of him. He took his torch from his belt and began the descent. The steps were so high and close together that he almost slipped several times, but each time he caught himself by holding on to the rope attached to the central pillar.

The descent seemed interminable. He felt as if he were going into the underworld. He considered that the arrival must be well below the level of the entrance. Strong smells of stale and mouldy air filled his nostrils, reminding him of his grandparents' cellar. Finally, the last step. Before him stood an old wooden door. He turned the round iron latch and opened it. A longitudinal vaulted tunnel in perfect condition presented itself to him.

Piéroni ran into it. With a bit of luck, he would catch up with the person who had run off almost in front of him. But the false flat soon got the better of him. He gasped loudly and ended up exhaling like a bull in rut. It was at times like this that he regretted smoking two packets of cigarettes for over twenty years. A new door appeared at the end of the tunnel.

A crisp, fresh air blew into his face as he opened the door. A release. On the ground, two long fresh skid marks on the stones. The fugitive must have sped off in a small motorized vehicle. He listened carefully, but only heard birds chirping and the soft sound of morning cicadas. He could be far away. The chase was over.

He contacted the police car in front of the residence and asked them to patrol the area to try to apprehend the fleeing individual. He had no idea where the gravel path led, but they would lose nothing by trying.

He was exhausted and lit two cigarettes in quick succession to recover from his sudden physical effort. Climbing, running. It had been a long time since he had done so much physical activity. A nightmare day...

He climbed the mound that covered the tunnel exit and saw the residence in the distance, which he quietly reached through the dew-covered lawn.

As he walked, he wondered who had run away. Was it the owner of the place? Jean de Rosières, a well-known and very influential businessman in the region and national representative of an ancient order. But if so, why would he run away like a thief? Or was it the man he was looking for, the car park murderer identified by the young Englishman? Which seemed more likely according to the butler.

Some questions to the latter were necessary.

Back in the house, Piéroni returned to the study on the floor where it all began. There he surprised the butler who was busy around the table.

'If you want to run away, you have to press the switch on the left of the drawer,' Piéroni ironically said.

The butler had not heard him come and was startled.

'And... why should I run away?'

— Probably for the same reason as the one who used this secret passage to escape.

'I don't know what you are talking about...'

'I would have expected no less from you. I would have been surprised if you hadn't...'

While he was still staring at the butler from the doorway of the office, something intrigued him. The Commissioner could not say what it was, yet he felt that objects had been moved. He concentrated on remembering when he had come to this very room half an hour before. He looked down at the floor and remembered the book at the foot of the table.

'What did you do with the book?'

He sensed the astonishment of the butler, who was visibly uncomfortable. But the latter quickly recovered.

'What book are you talking about?'

'You don't seem to be very cooperative. Where did you hide the damn book,' he asked without much conviction.

And rightly so, for the man did not answer.

But this silence was even more eloquent.

So did the sweat that glistened on his forehead.

Piéroni entered and surveyed the room once again, looking for the book he had only glimpsed briefly. It was a book with worn brown leather and looked very old. He immediately had flashes of one of his favorite films 'The Name of the Rose' with Sean Connery playing a Franciscan monk, William of Baskerville, investigating mysterious deaths in a Benedictine abbey. The book glimpsed briefly on the floor looked exactly like the ones the monks were trying to save. He loved this film.

He opened the drawers one by one. The four small side compartments contained nothing of the sort. Finally, he tried the central drawer, which was larger.

The latter put up resistance. It was locked.

Piéroni had no doubt.

He was sure that the man standing in front of the desk when he came in had just hidden the book there. He could see it on his face. His embarrassment betrayed him.

'The key please...' he asked her, holding out his arm, palm open to receive the precious sesame.

The butler was no more cooperative than before, which annoyed the Commissioner.

'It's time to cooperate if you don't want to be charged with everything.'

'And on what grounds, please?'

'Accessory to murder... among others...'

'This is a joke! And whose murder?'

'Ivica Godic, a Montenegrin, was found murdered in his car with a bullet in the head in a car park in the hills above Nice. He had stolen a painting two days earlier from a monastery in his country, a painting that has still not been found. And not just any painting. The icon of the Hospitaller order. The Virgin of Philerme. An Order that is a competitor to yours, according to my research, each of you claiming direct descent from the Order. So everything seems to be connected. The car identified as the killer's is in the name of the owner of this estate. Hence our presence here. CQFD.'

The man swallowed.

'Never heard of this Godic... and regarding the official descent of the Order, everyone has their own arguments.'

'The notable difference is that the Vatican officially recognizes the other order and not this one...'

'Again, not everything seems as clear-cut as you claim.'

'That may be so. But they have made their choice.'

While talking, Piéroni noticed a mark in the trouser pocket of the local employee. Before the latter could even suspect anything and react, Piéroni plunged his hand in and pulled out the precious object.

'Oh, look, a key... how surprising...'

The man remained petrified. Piéroni's speed of execution had left him without the slightest reaction. He tried to protest by mumbling a few words, but the superintendent paid no attention to them, obsessed as he was with the possible contents of the drawer.

He inserted it into the lock of the drawer.

Then unlocked it.

'What luck, tell me, it was the right one...' said Piéroni caustically.

Sliding it towards him, he discovered, without much surprise, the coveted object. He took it, placed it gently on the desk pad and then walked around the desk to face the man so as to keep an eye on his movements. The book was much smaller than he had imagined.

Piéroni handled the grimoire with care. He opened it and was almost disappointed by its contents. He had expected a patchwork of colors, drawings and exceptional calligraphy. But the truth was quite different. A book of an almost excessive banality, without embellishment or fuss, the text continuous and regular and above all in a language that was totally unknown to him.

He remained doubtful as to the possible relevance of this book to his investigation. There was no mention of an ancient book stolen from his knowledge, only a painting. But the fact that the butler had tried to hide it quickly showed its importance.

The butler remained impassive.

To Piéroni, he seemed to be a mere executor, which did not absolve him of suspicion. He had tried to gain time to open the front door, had allowed a stranger to escape and had hidden the book and the key. These obstacles to the work of the police were minimal. Not enough to take them into custody. But it at least proved that he was making a difference.

He closed the book and continued to rummage in the drawer. Beneath the book he had just taken out lay a package about forty centimeters by fifty and five centimeters thick, crudely wrapped in kraft paper and tied up. It took up almost the entire surface of the drawer, as if it had been designed for that purpose. He found it very difficult to pick it up, not even having room to slip a finger in and lift it.

He chose a more radical solution.

He took out the whole drawer, forcing it a little at the end, and turned it over to retrieve the package. For great ills, great remedies. He opened the wrapping paper at the top and gently slid out the contents.

The surprise was total.

Far beyond his expectations.

'I think it's my lucky day,' he says with a smile. 'I know some people who will be happy...'

The Mystery of the Lost Crypt

38

**Marimont-lès-Bénestroff
Saturday May 17th 2014, 3:15**

His face tightened and the determination in his eyes left Bonnie in no doubt. The fate of her partner weighed in the balance. She slowly lowered her arm and placed the weapon on the table, totally disappointed.

Visconti rushed to get it back.

The wind had changed again.

Karl's little grin was eloquent. He had succeeded without too much difficulty in wearing down his opponent with the trump card he had at his disposal. He moved the weapon away from his hostage's head and pushed him violently forward. Cyril had the reflex to catch himself at the edge of the table so as not to burst his eyebrow.

'There, everyone is present now. We can concentrate on the next step,' said the old man.

'And my friend?' protested Bonnie.

Visconti and Karl did not even react.

'And the next person who tries anything, I'll blow his brains out,' added Karl, who took the opportunity to close the passage by pressing against the stone at the foot of the stairs. 'Put your phones on the table.'

The three of them did so.

Visconti handed Cyril his notebook.

'I've told you before, the sooner we solve the riddle, the better chance this man has of getting out. But the minutes are ticking away, so I advise you both to get on with it without further delay. Surprise me, young man,' he said, glowering at Gilles, who looked down.

Cyril reread the passage where they had left off a few moments earlier. *In the tomb of the pious knight lies the key to the vault that holds the treasure of our brothers.*

'So we assume that this sword is a key. We must now discover the entrance to a passageway to this alleged treasure room,' Cyril summarized, before reading aloud the following sentence. '*Only a hermit will be allowed to go to the Holy Mountain and worship the Mother of God, who will open the door to darkness with a knock.*'

'It's getting complicated,' grumbled the university dean.

'So much so that I don't understand it anymore,' sighed Cyril.

Cyril, Gilles and Visconti scrutinized the walls of the room. Bonnie remained at her companion's bedside, holding his hand. Karl stood back and watched their every move, gun at the ready.

'So we're supposed to find a slot to insert the blade?'

'At first sight. Hopefully not the part that collapsed,' Cyril replied worriedly.

He picked up the torch he had dropped when Karl had pushed him violently towards the table and inspected every gap between the stones. Unlike the other two who were looking for the notch that would hold the sword, he concentrated on the door itself. He remembered the cross on the altar which he had cleared easily enough by scraping the outline with his knife blade. But unlike the passage under the altar which had been reopened a hundred years ago by the abbot, there was a strong presumption that the door they were looking for had never been opened for more than six centuries since the abbot's writings made no mention of it. The gaps would therefore be much less clear, not to say invisible.

Despite the halogen lamp on the table, the light in the room was still weak. The decrepitude of the mortar offered many possibilities, forcing Visconti and Gilles to regularly pass the sword to each other for testing. But after several dozen minutes of research, it was clear that none of these tests were conclusive. Gilles reread the corresponding riddle. The solution could only be found in the sentence.

'What does a hermit have to do with this story,' said Gilles incredulously.

'Perhaps he was the guardian of the place. A hospitable man who passed on his secret to another chosen one before his death in order to perpetuate the tradition. The same one who kept the key. Namely the sword,' Cyril continued. Perhaps he lived in seclusion like a hermit.

'OK, good explanation. So the fact that the sword was found in one of the niches would mean that the skeleton belonged to the last guardian of this secret. That's all very well, but it doesn't get us any further,' replied Giles, examining the niche in question. 'I don't see any slot that could accommodate a blade, either at the bottom of this niche or around its edges'.

'The mountain' would refer to the mound that encloses the room and the 'door of darkness' to a passageway leading to it. A corridor or a well...'

'So the room would be under our feet,' Gilles wondered, contemplating the black and white tiles.

'Everything is possible. This church, like all the others, was built on a promontory. There is therefore room to build superimposed rooms.'

Bonnie's concern was growing, as her partner's condition was becoming more than a little worrying. His pulse was dangerously low.

'We're going to lose him. Hurry up, I beg you...'

At these words, Karl laughed, alone in the darkness. This did not fail to arouse almost general indignation.

Gilles was repeating the sentence over and over again as his gaze probed every inch of the room when he came to rest on the tabernacle on the wall.

He approached it. The Eucharistic box was surmounted by a picture of a face.

'Does anyone know who that is?' he asked, pointing to him.

Visconti joined him and opened the two wooden and glass doors that protected the painting.

'A representation of the Madonna of Philerme. The most precious possession for the knights of the Order of St. John of Jerusalem. The original was on display in the Museum of Art and History in Cetinje before it was stolen last year and separated from its two relics, a piece of the Holy Cross and the relic of the hand of St. John the Baptist, both of which remained in the monastery,' said Bonnie, pulling the rug out from under the professor.

The latter felt offended.

'And what exactly is its history?'

Bonnie was about to continue, but this time Visconti outpaced her.

'It is an icon of Byzantine origin which, according to the beliefs of the inhabitants of Rhodes, was painted by Saint Luke in Jerusalem and brought back to the island around the year 1000 after having previously passed through the monastery of Saint John the Baptist in Trullo in Constantinople. It is named after the sanctuary on Mount Phileremos where this miraculous icon was placed and whose fame extended to the whole of the Aegean Sea. The chapel is dedicated to Our Lady following her appearance to a man who was attempting to commit suicide on a Friday, the thirteenth of October, which became a day of commemoration. The Hospitallers, who found the icon in this chapel of Our Lady of Philerme, appropriated it and it followed them on their journeys throughout Europe, from Malta to Russia, from Denmark to Kiev, passing through Berlin, Belgrade, and finally to Montenegro. In the end, the icon made quite a journey. She survived many battles in Rhodes and Malta, storms in the Mediterranean Sea, the Bolshevik revolution, the Nazi invasion, several fires and many other events.'

'You said that the virgin of Philerme takes her name from Mount Phileremos...' said Gilles slowly. 'Phileremos...'

His eyes widened.

'I think I've got it!' he shouted.

He read the riddle again.

'Only a hermit will be allowed to go to the Holy Mountain and venerate the Mother of God, who will open the door of darkness by striking with her sword... the Mother of God... Mount Phileremos...'

'Stop making us wait. You're going to tell us once and for all what you've found,' Cyril said impatiently.

'In ancient Greek, Phileremos comes from 'Philos', the friend, and 'Eremos', a deserted place. So the term literally means 'one who loves solitude'. This refers to the hermit. *Only a hermit will be allowed to go to the Holy Mountain and worship the Mother of God, who will open the door of darkness for him with a knock.* He also speaks of the Mother of God, or in other words, the Virgin of Philerme! The text thus refers directly to the icon represented here.'

'Excellent deduction, young man. I confess I didn't think of it at the time,' said Visconti dryly.

'No kidding...' he replied, glowering at him.

The three of them approached the tabernacle sealed to the wall where the icon of Our Lady was enthroned in its center.

'This replica of the same size seems very faithful to the original. It is magnificent. Even more beautiful than the copy in the Basilica of Santa Maria degli Angeli in Assisi, Umbria. Perhaps even one of the most beautiful copies I have ever seen... but time and storage conditions have not spared it, look at this crack,' said Visconti.

'On the contrary. This crack is perfectly normal,' Cyril corrected, bringing his torch closer to illuminate the area. 'Whoever made this copy knew exactly what they were doing. Such a perfect cut is not the result of natural decay...'

He picked up the sword on the table and approached the icon.

'But what are you doing Cyril,' asked Visconti.

The Mystery of the Lost Crypt

39

Nice
Saturday May 17th 2014, 5:30

He immediately recognized what he had uncovered.
'This is the famous Virgin of Philerme. I've read that this painting is over a thousand years old, two thousand according to the legend, and it seems to be in surprisingly good condition. Although...' said Piéroni in dismay as he turned the painting over and saw that the protective canvas on the back had been cut away. 'You dared to vandalize this jewel?'
'Do I have to remind you captain that I am only a butler here. I never said that I condone the slightest action of the owner of the premises. And I take even less responsibility for them.'
'Of course. But I was not addressing you in particular. I was addressing all the people living under this roof and who are part of this order by extension. And would its new and short-lived owner have said, by any chance, what he hoped to find there?'
'I am by no means in the confession of the gods.'
'Domestic employees often have wandering ears... it's one of their main qualities, also perpetuated through the ages. You might have overheard a conversation...'
He shook his head to deny it.
The officer soon realized that he would have nothing to gain from his testimony. There was no point in insisting. Even if he

was convinced that he must have known something, he would remain as silent as a grave.

'Where is the owner, Jean de Rosières, anyway?'

'I've already told you. On a business trip. Or rather a humanitarian trip, as part of his duties within the order.'

'Where exactly?'

'Abroad. In South America, I think.'

'When he returns from his trip to the end of the world, tell him to pay us a courtesy call...'

'I will be sure to tell him.'

When Piéroni had emptied the contents of the drawer, a very thick envelope had slipped behind the desk. He picked it up and discovered two small initials written on the back of the envelope at the binding.

I and G

He did not have long to think.

Ivica Godic.

He opened the envelope and discovered a bundle of two hundred and five hundred euro notes. There must have been several tens of thousands of euros at the very least. He continued to search. He found a diary and an address book. He turned on the computer, but a password was required to log on. He would leave it to one of his colleagues, a computer specialist, who would have no trouble cracking the code. He put the whole thing in a large box that was lying around the office.

The police spent the whole morning searching the residence and then left at midday. They did not find any weapons on the premises. Nor the famous BMW. Piéroni left two of his men in hiding to monitor the comings and goings. His intuition told him that the fugitive was none other than the owner of the premises himself. And that he would certainly not belong in making his appearance again.

Back in Nice at the police station, Piéroni consulted the diary and the address book. One detail struck him immediately. The diary did not show any trips abroad. So it seemed that the butler at the residence had fooled him. This did not surprise him too much. But the noose was tightening. At the same time, his colleague had just decrypted the computer's password and he was able to consult the e-mail.

One email address came up frequently.

That of a certain George Visconti.

In one of them appeared his official signature. Apparently the dean of the faculty of history in Nancy. Piéroni typed the name into the search engine of his own computer. The results back confirmed the data. This older man also appeared to be a historian and archaeologist. Dozens of articles had been written about his discoveries over the decades. The first thing he clicked on was his biography on the free encyclopedia Wikipedia. His main discoveries were listed there. But what interested the police officer most was the mention of his membership of the OHJ order. He even seemed to be a high dignitary of the Priory of France.

And the headquarters was none other than the residence searched earlier in the day in the hinterland of Nice.

The Marseillais also sought information about the painting he had retrieved from the drawer. Among other things, he learned that this icon of the Virgin Mary had followed the original Order founded in the eleventh century to Malta, its last official home before it was dissolved by Napoleon. But then everything became complicated. The break-up of the original order into several branches.

'If I read correctly, after its dissolution, the order split into several groups. One, now called the Order of Malta, has its headquarters in Rome and is the only one recognized by the Vatican. Another has gone through Russia, the former Yugoslavia, has had a merger between different American and English branches, etc. In short, it's hard to understand. But in the end, they all seem to claim their affiliation to the primary order.'

'Wait, not so fast. I don't understand,' said his colleague. 'So they stole their own painting somehow? That's completely... stupid...'

'It's true that the story sounds twisted. Perhaps to try to appropriate it permanently, since it seems to belong to all the orders claiming to be direct descendants of the ancestral order. Or maybe this painting is hiding something else,' said Piéroni, turning the painting over and scanning it to see if he could find anything.

He saw a dozen sigils engraved towards the bottom of the board.

'Maybe that's what they were looking for,' he said, showing his colleague his discovery.

'They could probably have studied it on request, couldn't they?'

'Possibly, but then everyone would have known about their search. And of their possible findings... but we must not forget that the canvas that protected the back of the painting was always intact. And that these initials were therefore not visible...'

'And what are these hieroglyphs supposed to represent?'

'Well, my dear Watson, only the person who engraved them should know... or else brilliant historians... this painting is a thousand years old, maybe two thousand. So let's find out when these letters were added and by whom... and in any case it's not our problem. In the meantime, it was stolen from the art museum in Cetinje by a guy who was murdered here in Nice and it all leads back to this house. And the only thing to remember in all this is that the bastard is still at large. On the other hand, we're going to pay a little visit to this historian, this Professor Visconti. I have a feeling he'll be able to tell us more...'

40

Marimont-lès-Bénestroff
Saturday May 17th 2014, 3:30

'The phrase says *'the Mother of God who, by striking with her sword, will open the door of darkness to him'*. This is now very clear. And this notch would be nothing other than the lock we are looking for!'

As the old man looked on in amazement, Cyril brought the blade up to the lower part of the frame and gently pushed it in. Nothing disturbed his progress, least of all the spider's web that blocked the entrance. The past centuries seemed to have had no ill effect. The blade slid almost like butter.

Gilles and the professor held their breath, waiting feverishly for what was to come. They had the feeling that time had stopped and were living the scene in slow motion, too impatient to see what would happen next. Cyril seemed to reach the bottom, but the blade was still sticking out about ten centimeters.

But then, nothing happened!

No mechanism clicked and no door or hatch opened. The disappointment was enormous. The momentum was lost.

'So that's it? We must have missed something... it's not possible to end like this,' said Gilles, totally disappointed.

Cyril considered the frame.

The wood was slightly depressed on both sides of the cut. And these slightly rounded moldings corresponded to the shape of the two quillons that made up the sword's hilt.

'Wait a minute, I don't think I've completely finished my maneuver...'

Cyril pressed with all his strength, one hand on the handle and the other on the pommel, until the entire blade disappeared. The two pins did indeed act as a stop and were placed precisely in the moldings of the frame.

A click was heard, rekindling the flame of hope for Gilles and the professor. The adrenaline was pulsating in the crypt. Visconti was exultant. Even Karl seemed to be suddenly caught up in the game, eager to find out what happened next.

Another clatter. A part of the wall, the size of a door, sank very slightly into the wall on the right of the tabernacle. Cyril reached for it and pushed with all his might, leaving a gaping hole of impenetrable blackness.

A pungent smell came from the crypt, making Cyril recoil. Two rats scurried into the crypt, causing a stir in Bonnie and Visconti, who hated these rodents.

'I present to you '*The Door of Darkness*'...' exclaimed Gilles in ecstasy before the passage like all the others.

Only Bonnie seemed indifferent by this find. She was much more concerned about her companion's condition.

All the available torches converged on the same spot, illuminating a vaulted stone tunnel, about a meter wide and almost two meters high, which was riddled with spider webs.

'We're getting closer and closer to the end,' Visconti gloated.

'Let's say that we are getting closer and closer to the room. No one can say whether the treasure is still there. Or even if it ever existed...' replied Cyril.

The professor paid no attention to the young man's words. Two golden Louis d'Or shone in his eyes. His greed and avarice shone through his whole being.

Karl, still positioned near the staircase, was watching the scene from afar, ready to intervene if necessary. He was waiting for the right moment to accomplish his new mission. The one he was dictated on the phone the day before. After his various setbacks, he had just learned an essential thing. That patience was the mother of wisdom. And he would wait patiently for as long as it took to take his revenge.

'Come on Cyril, read on,' Visconti shouted as if suddenly possessed by the devil, pointing his gun at Clyde. 'What are you waiting for? For this wretch to die?'

One of the rats scurried under the bed.

'So what do you think?' he said impatiently.

'Just like you, I'm still in the euphoria of the previous discovery.'

'So let's go into this tunnel and think about it as we walk. I can't wait to find out what's in there.'

Cyril retrieved the sword.

'You never know, it might come in handy...'

'Very good. You are already adopting the right attitudes. I am proud of you. Keep it up. You will go far.'

This remark left Cyril cold. He was a little confused about his mentor's very ambiguous position. What would become of them all after the discovery or otherwise of the Treasure Room? Even after what he had just seen, he saw him as incapable of harming anyone. Let alone be able to kill.

Unlike the colossus, who didn't seem to be doing anything sentimental.

'Let's all go! Go on,' Karl said to Bonnie, surprised by this decision as much as the other three.

'But we can't leave him here alone,' she replied.

'And why is that? Your friend is not likely to go away in his state...' Karl ironically asked. It's all over for him anyway.

He grabbed Bonnie's ponytail, who let out a cry of pain, and pulled her up to force her to her feet, then pushed her towards the others.

'I just said we'd all go together. If anyone has a problem with that, tell me right away and I'll take care of it,' he said, brandishing his gun.

He stepped forward and pointed his gun at Clyde.

'No, not that,' shouted the Italian.

Visconti in turn protested.

'Karl, no! Let's just find the treasure.'

In vain.

The shot went off.

He hit Clyde a second time in the chest.

'Now we won't have to worry about him,' Karl said in a calm voice.

Bonnie watched in disbelief. She put both hands to her mouth, terrified. Then she burst into tears. She threw herself on the ground over Clyde's lifeless body. This time he was not breathing. She stroked his face, sobbing.

The coolness and indifference with which Karl had just killed Clyde petrified Cyril and Gilles, who could not believe what they had just seen.

Even Visconti didn't dare say anything.

Bonnie turned her head towards the colossus. Hatred was now in her eyes. She was capable of anything.

But Karl guessed her intentions. He now pointed his gun at her in anticipation of any lightning retaliation.

'Well, there you go, all you have to do is join him,' he laughed, pretending for the first time that he was pulling the trigger.

Cyril remained on the alert, ready to intervene. In view of past events, there was no longer any doubt that the Italian would be next on the list. He had to act. He had to try a maneuver, even a desperate one, because in any case, they would all die sooner or later. He slipped a word to Gilles. He would take care of Karl while his friend neutralized the old man who also had a weapon.

'Farewell my beautiful one!' said Karl.

Cyril shouted a thunderous 'no' to divert Karl's attention and leapt towards him holding the sword in both hands. He struck him with all his might in the chest, but with the flat of the blade. In surprise, a shot went off, grazing the top of Bonnie's skull by only a few inches.

The sword fell to the ground under the violence of the blow and its excessive weight.

The German colossus fell backwards, breathless.

His weapon fell far behind, at the level of the stairs, and was lost to view in the darkness.

At the same moment, Gilles turned and swept his torch violently across Visconti's forearm, who also lost his weapon and his balance. The weapon twirled in the air before falling back and breaking on a protruding stone. The firing pin came loose from the rest of the weapon. The old man's body toppled backwards and he hit his head on one of the stones that littered the back of the room.

They were both out of action.

The opportunity had to be seized.

And quickly.

Cyril had no desire to fight this force of nature. His chances would be too slim.

Since the crypt hatch was closed, there was only one way for them to get out quickly.

Enter the underground.

'Come on,' said Cyril.

Bonnie did not react. She was in shock.

'Come on, quickly,' insisted Cyril.

He took her hand and forced her into the tunnel.

She followed like a rag doll.

'Gilles, help me quickly, we have to close this door,' he said, handing the torch to Bonnie.

They both tried, but could not move the stone door one millimeter. Something seemed to block it. But what was it?

'What do we do now Cyril?'

'I don't know... the sword!'

'What about the sword?'

'We need to get her back. She's the one who has to stop that damn door from closing.'

Gilles immediately went back inside the room, Visconti and Karl, stunned, still on the ground, were slowly emerging. He picked it up not far from Karl, measuring his movements while watching the colossus, then joined them. He put the sword against the wall and helped Cyril close the heavy door. They managed to close it just before Karl could counterbalance it on the other side. A click was heard. The door was locked again.

'And since we have the key to this door, they won't run after us. At least not from this side,' he said, pointing to the sword.

'Well done. Just hope there's a way out, otherwise we'll be caught in our trap. That door doesn't seem to open from our side,' replied his companion, illuminating the outline.

'There must be an opening system, but that is not our priority. We have to tell the police.'

'We no longer have our phones...'

'Gee, are we silly... they were on the table... We'll have to crash at someone's place. No choice. In the meantime, let's try to find the exit.'

The three of them sank into the bowels of the mound.

41

**Marimont-lès-Bénestroff
Saturday May 17th 2014, 5:30**

Karl did not see it coming.
The young man had put all his rage and ardor into it and had hit him in the chest. Fortunately for him, it was with the flat of the blade and not the edge that would have settled his account. He sat up painfully, gasping for breath, trying to regain his composure.
When he was back on his feet, he realized that he had not suffered any other attack, and with good reason, as he looked around, he saw only Visconti, also lying on the ground, and of course the lifeless body between them. All the others had disappeared. It took him a moment to realize what was happening when his attention was drawn to the stone door of the passageway which was slowly closing.
He frantically felt the ground with both hands for his weapon, which he could not find. He got up and ran towards the passage to prevent his obstruction. Just as his shoulder hit the stone, a click was heard. The door did not move one iota.
He was too late.
He struck a blow with his raging fist.
'Ach, verdamt nochmal!' he swore.
His anger rekindled, he reached for his weapon before he could even deal with Visconti, who was struggling to get up. The old

man had hit a stone when he fell and was bleeding a little from the back of his head.

'Where are they?' asked the latter.

'Enter through the underground...'

'The sword must be reinserted into the slot.'

'The only small problem is that I can't see the sword anymore. They must have taken it with them.'

'We must find them, Karl! And before they tell everything. Otherwise we are finished and the treasure will go to other hands. The Great Master will not forgive us for such a mistake. Do you hear?'

'We don't know where this tunnel leads...'

'It's no big deal. We need a little more finesse and composure,' he said, looking Karl straight in the eye to make it clear that rushing in like a bull was not the best way to go. 'We're going to play strategy so we don't miss them. They don't have phones anymore, he said when he saw them on the table, and they'll have to go back to the village and the lodge to call for help and join their friend!'

Karl smiled broadly. They had a new means of pressure at their disposal. He had not thought of that.

'Let's go out again!'

Visconti pushed in the cross at the bottom of the stairs and the altar moved.

'A mechanism that is almost 700 years old and works like it did on the first day. It's fantastic,' he enthused.

After having put everything back in order to leave no trace, including the carpet, they left the church. It was after half past four in the morning and in less than two hours the first light of day would be breaking through and some of the inhabitants would be getting busy. So the hunt had to be short and efficient.

But reality caught up with them at once. The persistent fog had thickened considerably, which dampened their spirits. With the reduced visibility, the manhunt was going to be more difficult than expected. Karl decided to position himself behind the low wall of the church. A strategic position to have a view of the

The Mystery of the Lost Crypt

crossroads and the square of this small village. A place not to be missed. Visconti, for his part, went further down to the outskirts of the gite.

He would pick them off in any case, even if they escaped the colossus' sharp claws.

The wait began.

Both were in place, night vision binoculars screwed to their heads, ready to intervene at the slightest suspicious movement.

Cyril entered the underground first, closely followed by Bonnie. Gilles, on the alert, closed the gap, making sure that no one was following them.

The former soldier used the long sword to clear the cobwebs that blocked the path, weaving clouds of impenetrable curtains. It was damp and the walls were oozing.

Bonnie, still in shock from her friend's execution, followed suit mechanically. Her inexpressive eyes and pallid complexion were chilling.

After descending a staircase cut into the rock, they had just completed a horizontal gallery almost fifty meters long.

'There, if I've got my bearings right, we must have gone under the road and we're going to start climbing the hill,' said Cyril. 'This tunnel must have served as a secret passage between the church and the old castle.'

'The only problem is that the old castle no longer exists. The foundations are completely filled in. You saw it on the building site. The access must have been sealed off a long time ago,' replied Gilles. So we have no way out...

'The manager of the gite spoke of an exit more than two kilometers from the castle. We can still hope that the tunnel is still intact and passable.'

Another ten meters or so and they came to a staircase. Cyril shone a light on it. It seemed endless. They did not see the end of it. The steps were narrow and made very slippery by centuries of water infiltration, forming stalactites between the cobblestones of the vault, but also limestone concretions on the floor, turning it into an ice rink in places. Droplets that did not fall directly to the ground dripped down the wall and ended up in a small groove at the junction with the ground where it was drained away.

'Clever sewer system,' commented Gilles. 'I wonder where it comes out.'

'It is probably a system for collecting water which is then stored somewhere in a well, allowing the tenants of the castle to be provided with water in all circumstances, even in the event of a siege.'

The trio attacked the hellish climb with Cyril still at the head, holding the Italian's clenched hand. They advanced cautiously. Much too slowly for Gilles' taste, who sighed for a long time, just to make Cyril understand that he should speed up.

This was a great disservice to him.

At the fifteenth step only, his foot lapped on a limestone slab. He fell, barely managed to put his elbows forward to protect his face and avoid shattering his nose or teeth, then tumbled down the stairs, trying in vain to hold on to the steps to stop the fall. Here again it was better not to insist if he wanted to keep all his nails whole.

But more fear than harm in the end.

Luckily, he had not fallen from a great height and got up without difficulty, at most a few bruises that were not serious.

'Take your time now...' Cyril prodded him.

Gilles muttered a few incomprehensible words and then joined them. Everyone was able to move on. They reached a first landing where an old iron gate with crenellations and rivets appeared on their left, slightly ajar. Cyril shone his torch through a crosspiece to see what lay behind it, but saw only a tangle of roots and a mound of scree in between.

The stone vault at this point did not seem to have withstood the test of time, let alone the three great wars that had taken place in this region.

'This opening is not natural. I can see why the staircase was strewn with cobblestones and debris.'

'Do you think it leads to the outside?'

'Do you feel that little cold draft? I'm willing to bet that an exit is not far away. Besides, all this vegetation is a good sign. It's worth a try.'

Cyril slipped into the excavation and disappeared.

'Is it feasible?'

'Yes, follow me. We should be able to do this.'

They struggled to make their way through the roots. Every time they touched one of them, an avalanche of earth and dust fell like a curtain of rain. They emerged from the forest of buried roots and dusted their heads to remove the residue. They ended their journey in a natural cave which the two men swept with their torches to measure its size and nature.

'This place looks familiar...' whispered Cyril.

'Not to me...'

'I get it. This is where I found Jack!'

'Now that you mention it, I recognize this place too. To think that we were less than ten meters from the underground. It's crazy...'

'The three of us will have to get wet. We won't have a choice, unfortunately,' says Cyril.

'After what just happened to us, a little bit of water isn't going to stop me,' said Bonnie.

It was her first words since the death of her friend.

The two boys entered the sticky, icy water. The water level quickly rose to the top of their thighs and then stabilized.

'The only thing that puts me off is the bugs.'

'Don't think about it. In five minutes we'll all be out.'

When they reached the hole, Gilles crossed his fingers and stood ready to receive Cyril's foot in his clasped hands. Bonnie was lighting them from a distance with the two torches. Cyril put one foot in his friend's hands and the second on his shoulder, holding the top of his head so as not to lose his balance.

'Are you ready?'

'Yes.'

'1, 2, 3... go!'

Gilles pushed the foot upwards with all his might, propelling Cyril almost halfway out of the cavity. The strength of Cyril's arms did the rest.

Then it was the Italian's turn. She found it very difficult to find her balance. The first attempt was a failure. Her foot slipped on Gilles' wet hands and he managed to hold her back just before she fell full length into the water. The second attempt was successful, Cyril grabbed her by the arms and pulled her out. It was only a formality for Gilles who, despite his imposing physique, had kept the agility and flexibility of his years as a gymnast. With the help of his friend and a sturdy root that served as a rope, he pulled himself out of the quagmire.

'That's a good thing done. Now we have to find a phone! Let's dim our torches so we don't attract attention, because they're probably on the prowl,' Cyril remarked. 'I doubt very much if they've given up the game...'

'The weather is with us. With all this fog, we'll be able to get through as unnoticed as possible,' replied Bonnie.

They went down the hill, trying as best they could not to slip despite the omnipresent moss and the exuberant vegetation due to the extreme humidity that had been raging for months in the region. It was difficult to move through, almost as much as in a tropical forest, without the machetes. They had to keep forking through dead trees, fallen branches and all sorts of unwanted vegetation.

They finally reached the bottom of the hill, not far from the crossroads and the central square of the hamlet. Bonnie was shivering. All three of them were wet from the waist down and the low temperatures made it feel even worse. She sneezed helplessly.

In this majestic silence, the noise resounded even louder. They looked at each other, stunned, aware that they might have just blown their joker. They waited for a few moments, still hidden in the bushes, to see if there would be any reaction. But nothing like that.

They snuck across the road and decided to go through a garden between two houses which led to the water tank. The very spot that Clyde had used as an observation point a few hours earlier. They stopped there, their senses alert, but nothing disturbed the peace of the place.

'It's awfully quiet around here, I don't really feel it...' Gilles pointed out.

'Yes, you're right, let's be on our guard. I wouldn't be surprised if that German colossus came along. And this time he won't do us any favors. Especially not you, Eva,' said Cyril, looking at the beautiful and slender Italian.

This thought changed everything. Cyril had not thought of it earlier. Too many things were happening that night.

They had to separate.

The Mystery of the Lost Crypt

42

**Paris,
Spring 1307**

At the first light of dawn, the main gate of the temple enclosure opened. A covered wagon pulled by two oxen emerged, followed by two riders.

It was the last convoy to leave.

Located outside the new city walls built a hundred years earlier by Philippe Auguste, this area of Paris was almost uninhabited. This was a beneficial isolation that allowed people to come and go in complete discretion. All the more so as at this hour, no one was still working in the fields. There was not a soul in sight.

Beynac had taken his place at the front of the cart, sitting next to a sergeant who held the reins. In order not to attract attention on their journey, they pretended to be merchants and had exchanged their Templar garb for more rudimentary clothing. They were not to show any sign of belonging to the order. This was the rule stipulated by Jacques de Molay. Only their swords were hidden under the tarpaulin, within reach if the need arose. Highway thieves were everywhere and robbed merchants and travelers at every turn. They had to be on their guard.

Heading east, beyond the kingdom of France.

The first two days went smoothly. The convoy took the trade routes along the Marne and arrived in the vicinity of Meaux on the first evening. They stayed on the outskirts, in a small hamlet, always with the aim of remaining as discreet as possible. They reached Château-Thierry on the second evening. They travelled about fifty kilometers a day, which allowed the animals to recuperate and not accumulate any fatigue. Each evening they managed to ask a farmer for board and lodging in return for a fee, and set up their straw mattresses in the barns to keep their wagons safe and within sight.

It couldn't be left unattended.

Beynac was never at ease, always on the alert, day and night, attentive to the slightest noise, his right hand close to his dagger.

It was on the third day that things went wrong.

Halfway to Epernay, the final stage of the day, towards Dormans, as they were traveling along a bumpy forest road gullied by the heavy rains of the previous weeks, the front-right wheel of the cart hit a large stone and broke cleanly. Beynac was thrown to the side of the road, taken by surprise and not having had the reflex to hold on to the frame of the cart. He got up without difficulty and noted with satisfaction that the six boxes had remained in place despite the jolts. Too cumbersome and heavy, they had not seen fit to bring a spare wheel. One of the two riders had to turn back and find a cartwright in Dormans to repair or buy a new wheel.

The round trip alone was estimated to take a good hour, not including the time it would take to repair.

The place was dark and the vegetation dense. The absence of sunlight that day only accentuated this gloom. This large forest area was very little frequented, travelers having the choice of bypassing it. The whole of the east of the kingdom of France and the Duchy of Lorraine was still very wooded despite the severe deforestation that had begun two centuries earlier. The four Templars hoped to be sheltered from the storm that was looming in the distance, aware also that the place breathed danger and the risk of ambush.

Beynac distributed the swords to his two companions. All three remained on guard.

'I have a bad feeling about this forest,' he said to the sergeant.

No sooner had he finished his sentence than a horde of brigands leapt out of the undergrowth, screaming with swords and daggers. This did not impress the Templars, who were already ready to fight back. The three of them remained grouped back to back, forming a triangle so that they could see all their opponents and none of them could take them on.

From the way they held their rudimentary weapons, Beynac soon realized that they were dealing with poor fighters. Only one of them seemed more expert than the others. Probably their leader. He was standing right in front of him.

Their eyes met and never left each other.

Beynac would attack him first.

The rain intensified at the same time, making the forest even darker. A few flashes of lightning stealthily illuminated the scene and the faces of their rivals.

He took his sword in both hands and twirled it in the air in a circular movement to leave the first brigands who were approaching him on the sides at a distance and rushed at his target in one bound. The power of his first strike disarmed the latter, surprised by the suddenness of the attack. The second salvo was fatal. The knight aimed directly at the neck and separated the head from the body in a split second. This macabre sight immediately calmed the ardor of the other members of the gang who, as Beynac had predicted, immediately fled and disappeared into the forest as quickly as they had appeared. The final toll was two dead and three wounded among the belligerents. Not a scratch on the Templars.

'We won't be seeing them again soon,' laughed the sergeant, still exhilarated by the brief hand-to-hand combat.

'Let's be on our guard all the same. One must always be wary of a wounded beast...' replied Beynac, far from being reassured by their victory.

The sound of the brigands fleeing through the branches and foliage quickly faded away, muffled by the stormy rain and its heavy drops falling on the vegetation.

The rider returned an hour later with a new wheel, bringing with him a bright sun. The rays pierced the thick foliage, allowing their storm-soaked clothes to dry and giving them a gentle sensation of warmth.

This terrain meant that they had to be constantly on their guard, but the end of the day was calm. No further ambushes were found to hinder their progress. The initial objective of Epernay was not reached and they camped in the middle of the forest in a small clearing which they shared with other merchants coming in the opposite direction who were delighted by their presence. Watchtowers were set up in pairs and changed every two hours. But the group of robbers did not show up again.

The next day they went to Châlons-en-Champagne, whose duchy had recently been attached to the French crown following the marriage of the king and countess of Champagne.

The Templar presence there was significant and the temptation to take shelter in their commandery attractive, especially after the events of the previous day. But they had to respect the orders of the Grand Master. They found refuge in the outbuildings of an isolated but busy inn in the countryside. The town of Châlons had experienced a tremendous economic and cultural boom a hundred and fifty years earlier thanks to the Cistercians and Templars, notably thanks to the textile production whose cloth industry was renowned throughout the Mediterranean basin. This prosperity inevitably attracted people.

All kinds of people.

Settled in the barn on the comfortable straw beds they had made for themselves, the four Templars dropped off, worn out by the exhausting day of repeatedly unloading the wagon after the heavy rain of the previous day. Beynac often dreamed in his sleep of the few months he had spent in Acre and of the terrible battle in which he had taken part. He saw himself fighting alongside the great masters of the two orders, impressed by their fighting spirit and their ability to motivate the other knights, even in the most desperate cases. He also relived all those long days of initiation before the final battle where Brother Amaury, one of the oldest

The Mystery of the Lost Crypt

and most experienced knights, trained the young recruits who had just arrived in recent months. Training sessions which, at the end, gave way to real-life situations where gross errors were not forgiven and could lead to serious injuries to those who did not follow the instructor's orders. Beynac had experienced this bitterly when he found himself with a dagger on his throat, the deliberate cut of which caused a trickle of warm blood to flow. He still had a slight scar, but above all the moral trauma of having found himself in such a situation.

He felt it so strongly that he woke up.

When he opened his eyes, he was unpleasantly surprised to find that a blade was indeed pressed to his throat. The dream was taking shape. The full moon and the many gaps in the barn were enough for Beynac to make out the silhouette of his attacker leaning over him. Before his assailant had time to strike the fatal blow, he held his forearm firmly and struck him violently on the temple with his other hand.

His assailant let go and fell heavily to the ground.

Beynac got up, followed by two of his companions, alerted by the noise. They had sunk deeper into the straw pile for warmth and comfort. While the man still lay stunned on the ground, unable to get up, others approached ready to fight. Disarmed of his sword, perhaps taken by the brigand, the knight managed to grab a nearby pitchfork and narrowly dodged the first attack by stabbing the sharp points into the flank of the attacker, who screamed in pain. At the same time another was attacking on his right. He had just enough time to turn around to see the blade coming towards him. In a tremendous reflex, he avoided the sword which scraped him, tearing his shirt, and sent the end of the fork into the jaw of his opponent. A sinister cracking sound came from it. The intensity of the pain caused the man to lose consciousness.

His two companions also knocked out a few thieves. The rest of the troop fled, seeing that their opponents were far too formidable for them. Once the situation calmed down, lanterns were lit. Beynac recognized one of the brigands who had tried to ambush them in the forest outside Epernay. They had followed them here and waited patiently for the right moment for a new attempt. Unfortunately for them they had just been routed a second time.

With one notable difference.

After checking the identity of each stiff, the Templars saw one of their number, the sergeant who had driven the cart since they left, motionless, his straw reddened, his shirt bloody, his eyes wide open and his mouth gaping. Slightly behind his companions, the unfortunate man had probably been slaughtered in his sleep, without being able to defend himself. He was buried discreetly the next day on the outskirts of the village cemetery and the convoy set off again with a heavy heart.

They arrived in the vicinity of Metz five days later. Nothing and no one interfered with the rest of their journey.

They only had about two days of travel left to reach their goal.

For the first time in nine days, they spent the night inside the city walls, at the home of the Duke of Lorraine Thiébaud II who had succeeded his father Ferry III in 1303.

The meeting between the Duke and Jacques de Molay a few years earlier, when his father was still in office, had led to the sealing of a pact.

43

Marimont-lès-Bénestroff
Saturday May 17th 2014, 3:45

The teacher was getting impatient, hiding behind some bushes.
He had a clear view of the entire front of the lodge. Anyone who came close would inevitably pass into his field of vision. But his rheumatism did not like the damp cold, and in his uncomfortable position his limbs gradually became numb.
He changed his plan and decided to wait for them inside.
The academics' car was parked in front of the garage door, just to the left of the main entrance. The driver's side door was unlocked. A good thing for the university dean, who had never broken into a car lock before. It would have been a mere formality for Karl if he had had to do it. He opened it, removed the plastic cover under the steering wheel and then ripped out all the cables. This was an action that anyone could do.
Satisfied, he listened behind the front door.
All seemed quiet inside.
Luck smiled on him once again. The front door was not locked. He opened it carefully and slipped inside. His first move was to turn off the two small accent lights in the hallway and the living room so that he could use only his binoculars at night and thus have more room to maneuver in case of an unexpected visit.

He walked around the ground floor rooms, down a corridor and came to a closed door. He did not have to guess long. There were loud snores coming from it. He hesitated to enter. An idea came to him. He opened the door, reached in and retrieved the key from the lock inside the room. Karl would probably have gotten rid of them. He preferred to lock them up.

This done, he continued upstairs.

Karl had been standing still behind the parapet of the church for a good half hour. He had previously taken care of a few details before taking up his position. On the edge of the square was an EDF electric box. He fired a shot with his silencer at the lock, which shattered and then cut several cables. He killed two birds with one stone. No more landline telephony and no more network for mobile phones, because the box also controlled the mobile antenna located behind the mound, about two kilometers away, which grouped together all the operators present in the area. The hamlet was now cut off from the world for some time. Just long enough to carry out their mission.

A sneeze echoed through the hamlet.

Perhaps the sound had escaped from a resident's window. But a few moments later, through the pea soup, he saw furtive movements on the road in the distance. A sneeze, three shadows.

'It can only be them. So they would have found a way out. Interesting....,' he whispered.

He warned Visconti by walkie-talkie to be ready. Without a telephone network, it was at times like these that old technology took over.

He followed them as far as the town hall when suddenly two figures turned back and the third continued in the opposite direction.

They seemed to change their strategy and split up. From the size of their bodies, he estimated that the woman and the taller

Gilles had stayed together and were retracing their steps. Cyril, on the other hand, seemed to be heading for the lodge.

Annoying for the future. But far from insurmountable. Visconti was ready to intercept anyone who came along. After all, only Cyril really mattered. The riddle was almost solved now that the tunnel had been discovered. All that remained was to find the strong room. All he needed was the young man to see their quest through to the end. He seemed to have a sharper mind than his friends, even though he was the one who had opened the famous door.

The other two were no longer of any use to them.

He had to do it as soon as possible.

He knew the end of this adventure long ago if the treasure was discovered.

But only on this last condition.

He reported the situation to the professor by radio and then went to meet them.

Cyril had a bad feeling.

He was convinced that the big nut and Visconti were going to go after Natasha in order to get leverage on him. Perhaps she was already in their hands.

Shivers run down his spine.

He was careful not to take the road back to the gîte. He went around the first two buildings next to the town hall through the field that surrounded them.

On the other side, he moved closer to the road to decide what to do next. The lodge was only a hundred meters away as the crow flies, yet it was impossible for him to travel that distance if he wanted to continue to stay under cover. The next street lamp was positioned in such a way that it flooded the whole area with a dim light. He therefore also had to go around the last two houses from behind to get as close as possible. This was no mean feat, as the two vast properties stretched far apart and were separated by a multitude of plots of farmland all bounded by barbed wire.

The sharp little razor blades of the fences clung to his clothes, cutting into his flesh. He shackled them without undermining himself. He continued, driven by his will, and thinking of only one thing. Natasha.

He found himself at the eastern entrance to the village, hidden by a thick row of cedar trees, and crossed the road to reach the gite by the garden and the pool. All the shutters on the ground floor were closed. No light came through the slats of the wooden shutters. It was impossible for Cyril to look inside.

He then walked along the house.

The front door was ajar...

That's never a good sign, he thought.

Inside, it was completely dark. However, both the lamp on the pedestal table in the entrance hall and the one in the living room had to be left on at all times. This was the manager's rule. A rule that could not be broken. She was strict on this subject, even maniacal.

He picked up the telephone, the base of which was fixed to the wall in the entrance hallway. He had to call the emergency services without delay. He dialed seventeen and pressed the green button.

No tone.

These were all worrying elements.

His heartbeat quickened after what he had just experienced. Cyril was prepared for the worst. He had proof that the colossus was capable of anything. Even killing in cold blood.

He lit his torch and inspected the living room first.

Desert.

The same went for the kitchen and bathroom.

The owners of the place were staying in the room at the end of the corridor. He approached it and put his ear to the door. But there was no sound.

He hesitated to enter the room.

Had they been eliminated or were they sleeping peacefully? Considering the latter, he would be hard pressed to justify himself. He listened for a moment, then changed his mind and went upstairs. The wooden steps creaked with every step he took, but the creaking was muffled by the thick felt covering the rise.

He went straight to his room.

His pulse raced as soon as he faced the door.

He opened it slowly and stupefaction seized him.

Gilles and Bonnie retraced their steps with the task of finding a telephone. This would be no easy task. Especially since there had been no public phone box for a long time.

They tried the first house adjacent to the reservoir. The gate to the rear was locked with a padlock. All the shutters were closed and the dilapidated state of the terrace left no doubt. It was uninhabited. But it was not abandoned. A red light was flashing on a box, probably an alarm system.

'A country house,' Bonnie concludes. 'You can't get in. The house is as secure as a bunker.'

They moved on to the next one.

'At least here we are sure to find someone. She spies on us behind her curtains every time we pass,' Gilles whispered.

'Indeed, I had the same impression when I passed yesterday. But that doesn't mean that she will open up to us. Maybe she's quite old.'

They were careful to stay at the back of the house so as not to expose themselves. They climbed onto the terrace which overlooked the garden. Some of the shutters were open, probably to spy on what was going on around them, and a faint light shone through the glass of one door. Gilles slowly climbed the stairs and knocked.

No reaction.

He insisted on containing his gesture so as not to alert their pursuers.

No one reacted.

He was about to strike again when they heard a noise behind the laurel hedge that separated them from the road. Someone was walking on gravel. The sound was getting closer. Cyril was at the lodge, so it could only be Visconti or his henchman. But the rapid pace of the individual left no doubt. They leaned towards the latter. It wouldn't take them long to catch up.

Gilles frantically scanned the place for a solution. Perched on the terrace in front of a closed door, there was no way out. They had only a few seconds left to get out, which barely gave them time to go back down the flight of stairs. No more.

Bonnie, frightened, sobs clenching her throat, begged the owner to let them in, scratching the glass with her fingernails.

'Please, open the door for us, I beg you. They will kill us... let us in... per favore...'

44

Marimont-lès-Bénestroff
Saturday May 17th 2014, 3:45

Karl walked around the square to the left to catch them if they crossed the road. He walked along a hedge of laurel trees three meters high and just as wide. The many gravels thrown up on the pavement crackled under the rubber soles of his rangers.

He heard thumping noises coming from the house.

He quickened his pace.

Another two meters and he would reach the end of this natural fence. He could certainly have the two fugitives in his sights. He pointed the weapon forward, holding it with both hands in preparation to pick them off and give them no chance.

When he reached the end of the hedge, he swerved away from it, jumping up and sweeping his weapon through the darkness.

No one.

The hedge continued perpendicular to the first one for a good twenty meters more. He had not expected it. It ran almost the entire perimeter of the property.

He ran along it.

Suddenly drops beaded on his forehead.

He paid no attention to the cracking of the branch he had just stepped on. At the end he found himself on the edge of a vegetable garden. He looked around, but still saw no one. There was no sign of movement. They could not have gone so far in such a short time without his seeing them passing through the gardens. So they were still around, but probably very well hidden.

'*Where are you my little lambs...,*' he whispered.

When, in the midst of the laurels, branches stirred.

He approached slowly, gun in hand.

'Get out of there,' he said. 'Hurry up!'

He gave them the same order a second time.

Then a cat leapt furiously from the hedge, spitting, pursued by a second cat who was chasing it. Karl, frightened, recoiled and came close to pulling the trigger.

'Damn thing!' he growled, seized by the animal's heart-rending cry

He went round the property but got no more results. He had to face the fact that they had managed to get away faster than he thought.

He was approaching the adjoining house when the sound of glass breaking on the ground was heard.

Natasha stood between the bed and the window, dressed in a short, almost transparent nightie. The bedside lamp behind her gave a glimpse of her sensual forms which, in other circumstances, might have been more than a little disturbing.

She was shaking all over her body.

An arm was wrapped around her neck.

Another was holding a gun to her head. Behind Visconti.

The same demented smile on his lips.

'Here we're meeting again,' he says, jubilant.

Cyril was seething on the bedroom porch, fists and jaw clenched. The gun he had brought with him was in his travel bag less than two meters away, slightly to his left. For the moment it was impossible for him to retrieve it. He was enraged. And at the same time he was worried about his girl.

'What the hell! What's wrong with you? You're as crazy as that other brute. Drop it or I swear I'll get you this time.'

'Here comes the student who rebels. If you want her to stay alive, I advise you to behave yourself. Otherwise...'

At that very moment Cyril dreamed of gutting him, strangling him, killing him. But Natasha's life was priceless and he had seen with his own eyes what the German was capable of doing and he would stop at nothing. For the time being, he had to keep a low profile, contain himself and be patient. But when his time came, he would not let his chance pass.

The teacher pushed Natasha onto the bed.

'Get dressed! We're going for a little walk. It seems to me that we have more to do.'

Natasha was lost.

'What's going on?' she whispered in fear to Cyril.

'The lure of fame and gain. He and his henchman are looking for the famous treasure that the manageress was talking about, which is said to be hidden somewhere on the hill. A subterranean path has been found leading from the crypt from an old codex that he has translated. A series of riddles that would lead to the treasure.'

'I would never have thought that this old fart would ever be involved in something like this. And to threaten one of his students, a lecturer? I mean, it's madness! What does he want from us?'

Cyril sat helplessly on the bed while she hastily dressed. He looked at her, forgetting for a moment Visconti's presence, and whispered:

'Help them find their bloody treasure. If it exists. And for that, they seem capable of the worst. The other lunatic executed Eva's husband in cold blood.'

'What, killed? Oh my God, but that's not possible... not for a legend? But that's insane...'

'Indeed, all this is beyond comprehension. It is at moments like this that you discover the true nature of people. But frankly I would never have imagined that from Visconti. He was hiding his game well, the old monkey!'

'I'm scared, Cyril...' she said, still in shock at the news of Clyde's death.

'Don't worry Natasha, I'm here,' Cyril whispered reassuringly.

'And where did Gilles go?'

'By now, Karl has probably got rid of him...' replied the professor.

The young couple's eyes were filled with fear and horror.

'Well, enough chit-chat, let's go! We still have work to do. And no tricks. I'll keep an eye on your girlfriend, and if anything goes wrong, I won't hesitate...'

'And I suppose that when the work is done, we'll both go too?'

'Shut up and move on!'

The three of them left the room.

A private jet was flying over the Alsace plain towards Lorraine. It had left Rome's Leonardo da Vinci airport an hour earlier and was due to arrive at Metz airport in a quarter of an hour thanks to the favorable winds and the top speed of the Falcon 900LX. A helicopter would be waiting to take them to their final destination.

Alerted by Bonnie as she was going on a reconnaissance trip with the two boys to find Clyde, Borgia had immediately gone to the airport where the two Falcon pilots were waiting for him, engines on, accompanied by two Vatican carabinieri put at his disposal by the prefect Luca Armendi.

Sitting comfortably in his beige leather armchair, a steaming cup of coffee on the table in front of him, Borgia was pensive. The news reported by his team members in the last few hours was not good. The discovery of the crypt seemed to interest others. The latest report also mentioned the suspicious absence of one of the members. And after the attack on Bonnie in the last few hours, this was definitely not a good sign.

He had therefore decided to go there personally.

His phone vibrated.

The Mystery of the Lost Crypt

It was the Grand Master.

Borgia had not expected to hear him so soon. But he had asked to be kept informed of everything and at the minute. So he should not blame himself.

'I just read your message. You have a knack for waking me up in the middle of the night... you shouldn't get used to it either. What's going on?'

'Everything is speeding up, Bertrand. I think we're getting close. But it seems that there are incidents on site. It won't be as easy as I thought. My team is gradually losing control. That's why I'm going there to support them, helped by two policemen.'

'I'm counting on you to keep it quiet.'

'Yes I know, don't worry. According to Luca's sources, in two hours the French police will search the residence of the Hospitallers of Jerusalem in the hinterland of Nice.'

'For what purpose?'

'There are at least two reasons for this, both of which converge on the icon of the Virgin of Philerme. The first concerns the murder of the person who stole it, and the French police are suspicious of a man who lives there. And the second concerns the possible presence of the painting in this residence.'

'I hope they find it. And that's the end of this bastard order.'

'Eva sent me a photo of their attacker. I immediately sent it to Armendi. I'm waiting for his reply. But it's not impossible that it's the same guy. I'll keep you posted.'

As soon as they landed, the three men climbed into the helicopter, whose rotor was already in motion. The pilot told Borgia that the transfer to their destination would take less than ten minutes. The Order's and the Vatican's connections allowed Borgia to have a stealthy French air force helicopter immediately at his disposal, undetectable on radar and above all ultra-quiet. With this dense fog, the machine could drop its occupants a few dozen meters from a person without the latter noticing. Quite impressive.

Borgia was eager to intervene.

The Mystery of the Lost Crypt

45

**Marimont-lès-Bénestroff
Saturday May 17th 2014, 4am**

The noise that Karl heard very clearly came from inside the house.

No doubt about it.

He turned back and approached it, climbed the few steps that led to a terrace and stood in front of the partially glazed door. The curtain behind the glass door was curiously pleated to the left. This opening allowed him to peer into the house.

One detail caught his eye. On the floor, traces of earth were starting from the door and moving away towards... it was then that he saw shards of glass strewn across the wet tiles as well as scattered flowers. He quickly understood the scene that had taken place a few seconds before. The person who had spied him had not had time to put the curtain back in place in the rush and then in the darkness had knocked over the vase. Further on, other muddy marks were visible. Obviously the two fugitives had taken refuge in this house.

All he had to do was to dislodge them.

Moreover, no break-in was visible and the door was locked. Someone had obviously let them in.

He stayed a few more minutes to observe, but no human presence was apparent. All was quiet. He peered through the hole again and examined the muddy tracks. They went in two different directions. One went out into a corridor while the second went to the right. He saw the reflection of a familiar face in the large mirror on the wall. That of Gilles who was hiding behind the wall, to the right of the door in a recess, ready to welcome him with what seemed to be a poker that he held firmly in his hands.

He considered the door and then took two steps back and looked around the house when, on his left, a large cat nonchalantly approached the door leading to the basement. The cat pawed at it, rubbed against it, and then managed to open the door a little before slipping through.

Karl climbed down from the terrace and rushed into the garage, slamming the door in his tracks. He had underestimated his weight. He bit his lip. They must have heard him. There was no time to lose now. He climbed the stairs to the ground floor two at a time like a madman.

And so much for the surprise effect.

At the top of the stairs he opened the door, but had no time to react. He found himself at the bottom of the stairs, stunned, head down, feet up, a sharp pain lacerating his skull. He had no idea how he got there. His last memory was of opening the door to the ground floor of the house and then nothing.

When he opened his eyes, he saw an old woman on the stairs, two steps above him, shouting at him and hitting him in the shoes with a broom. He got to his feet and narrowly avoided the broom which was about to crash into his head. He picked up his weapon and hurried back up the stairs, passing by the valiant octogenarian without even bothering. He had better things to do than go after her.

He went out into the square in a rage, but they had already disappeared. He set off again in the direction of the lodge.

Cyril and Natasha came out of the room, closely followed by the professor, all three carrying torches.

'Where are we going?' asked Cyril.

'I don't know where you came out of the tunnel but the easiest way is to go back to the crypt and start again. Right where you left us after opening the tunnel.'

Cyril quickly took stock of the situation. Returning from the crypt meant reopening the passage by inserting the sword into the slot. This also meant that they had to be in possession of the sword. Which was no longer the case. He had placed it against the wall of the underground passage in order to have both hands free to close the tunnel door, then had forgotten it on the spot.

But the professor didn't seem to remember this detail. Or not yet. This would allow Cyril to gain time and come up with another plan.

On the stairs, he pretended to tie his shoes in the middle of the descent. He knelt down and asked Natasha to go ahead.

'What are you doing?' murmured Visconti threateningly.

'My laces have opened!'

'Hurry up...'

Natasha passed him.

Visconti followed, not wanting to leave too much distance. As the professor passed, Cyril grabbed his foot and tried to throw him off balance.

But Visconti did not fall into the trap.

He stopped just in time to avoid being knocked off balance by Cyril's hand, which was still firmly gripping his ankle, and struck him in the back of the head with his rifle butt. The latter let go of him immediately.

'I felt you coming, Cyril. I may not be fully alert at my age, but I'm not senile yet... my advice to you and your girlfriend is not to do it again. Karl will have far less patience than I have. And I wouldn't want him to ruin a beautiful face like this,' he said, shining a light in Natasha's face.

They left the house.

Karl came to join them.

'So then?'

'They won't bother us anymore,' stammered the colossus.

Cyril saw a hint of hesitation in his eyes. Something was wrong. He winked at Natasha, who was about to burst into tears at the German's words. She understood the message instantly.

'Good. Then we can continue in peace. If our friends here are willing to make a final effort...'

Bonnie and the old lady who had opened the door in a hurry had taken refuge in the kitchen, out of sight of the balcony. As for Gilles, he had taken refuge behind the wall to the right of the door in a recess that opened onto the living room. He had managed to grab the poker from the fireplace at the last moment before it too fell to the ground. He was ready to use it if the colossus came into the house. He would spring up and strike him in the face to immobilize him. He would not see the blow go off.

He glanced sporadically in the direction of the door and each time the specter of Karl was present.

But what is he doing? He seems indecisive, thought Gilles.

And to his surprise, the shadow moved away.

He heard footsteps on the stairs leading to the garden.

Then nothing.

He was leaving again.

Gilles was relieved. They could finally have a moment's respite and make that phone call.

'I think he's gone,' he whispered.

But a noise soon came up from the basement.

The two pairs of eyes met, terrified.

'Where is the stairwell?' asked Gilles of the old woman.

'Over there,' she replied, pointing to the place.

'And your front door, is it locked?'

'Never. It does not open from the outside...'

'Well, you two stay hidden here. When I tell you, Eva, we'll be out of the house in no time.'

'Yes, go away. I'll take care of that scoundrel myself,' said the unimpressed old lady. 'You'll see what I'm made of!'

The Mystery of the Lost Crypt

Still carrying the poker, Gilles walked towards the cellar door. The sound of footsteps was getting dangerously close when he saw the handle drop. He put all his momentum into his leg which hit the door with all its weight.

The colossus toppled backwards and tumbled down the stairs.

Gilles did not even try to find out if his opponent was out of action or not. He gave the signal to Bonnie and both of them fled through the main gate to the village square, leaving the old woman to her fate.

But where to go?

They stopped on the pavement.

'Which way?' asked Bonnie in panic.

'Frankly, I don't know a damn thing about it,' Gilles replied in a disappointed tone.

'If we go back to the lodge, we might run into the old man. And besides, we'll be out in the open by the road.'

'That's right.'

The seconds ticked away without any inspiration. Worse, they could already see themselves caught by Karl, thus signing their death warrant.

'There is only one solution then,' she says brightly.

'Which one?'

'We go back to the water-filled cavity that overlooked the tunnel. We are the only ones who know its location. He won't look for us there.'

'Excellent idea. Let's hurry up.'

They ran towards the forest, to the same spot from which they had emerged with Cyril earlier at the bottom of the knoll, on the edge of a ruined house. They rushed through the undergrowth, with Bonnie leading the way. Gilles glanced behind him to see whether or not their killer had caught them.

Just as he wanted to turn and follow the Italian woman, the giant's build appeared in the pale light of the street lamp at the junction of the two roads.

'Stop!' whispered Gilles.

The Mystery of the Lost Crypt

They both stood still, lurking in the tall wet grass, watching for his reaction. A dog barked at the same moment, probably roused by all the comings and goings of the night around the square, forcing Karl to leave the place more quickly than expected. He went in the opposite direction, towards the lodge.

'Wait Eva, we can't leave Cyril and Natasha to deal with these two sick people. We have to do something. We can't just leave them.'

'I understand you very well Gilles, but it is a huge risk. We have no idea what happened to him. Maybe he managed to get rid of the old man.'

'Even if that were the case, he would still have to avoid the other lunatic. And in that case we could be of great help to him. There is strength in numbers.'

'I'm still convinced that coming back to the hostel would be like walking into the lion's den. We'll be of more help to him if we stay apart. If he avoided them, he'll know where to find us. And if not, they won't hurt him. The professor still needs him to find his treasure and they're bound to come back into the tunnel where we'll be waiting for them.'

Gilles took one last hesitant look towards the village square.

'I hope we are making the right choice...'

46

**Marimont-lès-Bénestroff
Saturday May 17th 2014, 4am**

'Where are we going?' asked Karl, his face tense with anger, his features drawn with hatred.
'We return to the crypt. To find the treasure, you have to solve the riddles in order. You have to start from the last one solved, i.e. the tunnel door.'
Cyril said nothing, but immediately thought of the sword. To retrieve it, they would have no choice but to go through the cave where they had emerged. It was almost daybreak. They had to gain as much time as possible.
The four of them headed for the church, Visconti in the lead, Karl keeping a close eye on the lovebirds. He had let himself be surprised twice. The next one was going to get it.
Inside the building, Visconti himself opened the crypt. He looked so proud that for a moment one might have thought that he was the author of the discovery, whereas it was the young man standing behind him who was responsible...
Natasha did not miss the opportunity to remind him.
'You really did a great job, Cyril.'
The professor looked at her with disdain. What more could he say but admit the truth?

Even his henchman knew about it. So he could not convince anyone in this place.

The four of them went underground. The professor had left the lamp on the table, which he quickly turned on.

Clyde was still there, lying lifeless on the floor, partly hidden by the shadow of the table and the darkness of the enfeus. A pool of coagulated blood could be seen on the floor, covering the tiles. Karl and the professor did not even pay attention to it any more.

Natasha, horrified, stifled a scream and then looked away before snuggling into Cyril's arms, sobbing. This was her first encounter with death. And not just any death. A murder. An execution even!

'Here we are,' said Visconti, placing himself in front of the tabernacle and the painting of the Virgin of Philerme. 'All that remains is to insert the sword. It's up to you, Cyril.'

The young man did not react.

'Come on, don't make us wait any longer.'

Save time. As much time as possible. That was all that mattered at the moment. Perhaps it would be useless, but he risked nothing by trying.

'The young man stammered.'

'What's that?' the teacher snapped.

'To open it, we need the sword.'

'Of course you need the sword. I understood you correctly, Cyril. Do you think I'm stupid? Goddamn it, I feel like I'm losing my patience!

'[...] in the slot?'

Visconti was seething.

Karl grabbed Natasha by the hair and put his gun to her head again. She felt the warm breath of the colossus on the back of her neck and his deep breathing.

'I wouldn't try being too clever if I were you... unless you want me to take care of her.'

Cyril did not dither any further. The look and the tone of his voice spoke for themselves.

'To tell you the truth, I left it on the other side of that door, in the tunnel, when we fled. We're going to have to go around and get it back. There's no other choice.'

'I warned you,' Karl said angrily, putting his gun even harder to the young woman's head.

Natasha screamed. She moaned in terror.

'No, stop it! I assure you it's the truth. You can see that I don't have it with me and that it's not in this room! It's on the other side of this door.'

'Can we open the door on the underground side?'

'No idea.'

Karl went after Natasha again, but Cyril immediately retaliated by pointing to the palm of his hand as a stop sign.

'We didn't have time to look. We were in a hurry to get away. I don't know, I tell you...'

Visconti looked at the young man and then at Karl.

'You two go and get it. I'll stay here with her. I advise you not to do anything, Cyril, otherwise your friend will suffer the same fate as the other. Hurry, the fog is slowly lifting and dawn is already breaking.'

Even if the idea of being separated from her for a moment was unbearable, he still preferred to leave Natasha alone with the professor than in the hands of the German, despite his threatening tone. He was convinced that he would not take action. Greedy for treasure and recognition, of course, but not to the point of turning into a killer. And he would stay with the other murderer.

They came out of the church and headed for the hill. The village was still sleeping peacefully, indifferent to the comings and goings of the night.

Visconti closed the passage so that no one could sneak in.

At night and in the fog, Gilles and Bonnie had a hard time finding the entrance to the cave, which was hidden from view by the numerous bushes. But they managed to find it.

'Well, unfortunately I have no choice but to dive back in...'
'My trousers never really dried anyway. So, wet for wet, I don't mind.'
The young man jumped first.
'I'd forgotten how bad it smells. I thought I'd never have to go back,' Gilles grumbled.
He helped Bonnie down by encircling her at knee level and slowly sliding her down his body to prevent her from becoming unbalanced and falling full length into the water. When her feet touched the bottom of the cavity, Gilles' arms touched the breasts of the beautiful Italian woman.
'It's OK, Gilles, you can let go now. I won't fall off again... Gilles?'
'Oh sorry. So sorry,' he apologized, confused by her appetizing form.
They emerged from the foul-smelling pool and made their way down the tunnel, past the tangled roots that sprinkled them with soil once more.
Gilles was about to start when he stopped dead in his tracks.
'What is it?' asked Bonnie.
'The sword...'
'And?'
'We left it in the tunnel. I have to go and get it. It is absolutely necessary. This discovery belongs to us and it is out of the question that it falls into the hands of the other two madmen.'
'The treasure is really not the priority at the moment.'
'Of course not, but I have memorized the rest of the riddle and this sword should again serve as a key to the rest. There's no doubt about it. It could even become a bargaining chip. Start climbing, Eva, I'll join you. Wait for me at the first intersection, if there is one...'
'Hurry up. They'll be coming this way if they get Cyril.'
They both went in opposite directions.
Never separate.
What Clyde always told her.

The Mystery of the Lost Crypt

And until now, something had always happened to them when they had split up.

Bonnie felt insecure, alone in the underground. She took her time climbing the stairs. The back of her head still bore the scars of her fall. Gilles advanced in the horizontal part and then climbed the few steps to stand in front of the door leading to the crypt.

Borgia had specifically asked the pilots during the flight to land as close to the village as possible. This they did. They had spotted on their radar screen a field at the foot of the hill on the north side, with a dirt road running through it. It was an ideal place to land.

They had left Rome less than two hours ago under a starry sky and a mild summer's day, and now found themselves in the middle of the French countryside in a dense fog and a temperature approaching zero degrees. He stepped out of the helicopter with the two carabinieri. He could hardly hear the wheels turning. He hadn't paid much attention at the airport, but there was no noticeable swirl of wind. Stealth. This machine really lived up to its name.

On his right stood the dark hillock and its dense forest, largely obscured by the fog. Ahead of him, about a hundred meters away, he saw a residence with a shed in its extension. He signaled to his two companions to head for it. He took out his semi-automatic Glock and cocked it. In case of need. They reached the edge of the road when one of the two policemen signaled to stop.

They crouched in the tall, wet grass.

Muffled noises at the bottom of the forest intrigued them. Faint beams of light zigzagged through the woods.

The policeman took out thermal binoculars from his bag and scanned the whole area. His colleague did the same.

'What do you see?' Borgia asked them in Italian.

'Due persone. Uno tiene un'arma,' replied one.

Borgia took his phone out of his pocket and logged on to an application. A rough map of the area appeared on the screen with two dots flashing, indicating the position of the team members through the microchip each was wearing. The initials gave the real-time position of each member. A blue dot meant the person was stationary, a green one meant they were moving, while a red one meant real problems. A little jewel of technology bought by the Vatican from NASA.

An hour earlier, on the plane, the audible alert on his phone had told Borgia that the dot assigned to Clyde had suddenly turned red. A fault in the chip? He knew from the start that this operation could be risky. That was why he had selected the most seasoned and experienced of them. But it was clear that those opposite were just as, if not more so. This red dot was worrying.

Eva is up there..., he thought, looking up at the hill.

Borgia gave the order to continue and the three men went into the woods after them.

47

Duchy of Lorraine
Spring 1307

The three Templars arrived at their destination after sunset. The fortress was perched on top of a large, bare mound overlooking the town of Moresperch and the surrounding area. This late hour was just the right time to go as unnoticed as possible by the inhabitants.

Beynac gave the soldier on guard duty the letter which had been given to him by the Grand Master before they left. It was signed by the Duke of Lorraine Ferry III and his son who had succeeded him in 1303 and whose meeting with Jacques de Molay had led to an agreement between the three men. After a few minutes the large entrance door opened and the portcullis was raised. The three men were received by the lord of the castle, a former general of Duke Ferry III who had been ennobled.

'Please follow me. The Earl of Moresperch invites you to his supper,' said a servant, addressing Beynac, who asked his two companions to guard the cart.

'Can you bring my friends some food and wine? It has been a long journey and bellies are hungry,' he asked her on the dungeon stairs leading to the dining room, making a point of using the term friend and not brother as was customary among the Templars.

The Mystery of the Lost Crypt

Only he, the Grand Master of the Temple, the two dukes of Lorraine, father and son, and the lord of the castle knew about the affair for which they had come here. Not even his brothers in arms knew the end of the story. And above all, no one else was to discover their true identity.

Beynac entered the room and was immediately surprised by the opulence of the place, contrasting with the austerity of the Temple Tower and even other castles in France. Various massive pieces of furniture, in the Gothic style, decorated the room. A sideboard and a credenza on one side, two large chests on the opposite side and a dresser between two windows. In the center stood a huge monastery table seating about twenty, where usually a board with trestles was set up, with a magnificent cathedra at the end occupied by the chatelain. The two side walls were covered with brightly colored tapestries depicting hunting scenes, which not only decorated the room but also made it more comfortable by keeping it warm.

The Count got up and went to meet Beynac

'Welcome to our home, you and your companions. You can stay here as long as you like.'

'We are very grateful to you, my lord, and we will be faithful and loyal to you, rest assured.'

The knight sat down and ate the numerous dishes of roasted meat, game and poultry, accompanied by legumes and fresh bread. A real feast that he did not deprive himself of and which he had not had the right to eat since he joined the order. So much so that he stunned the whole table. Only the Count was amused, for only he knew his true identity. His two companions received the same treatment. Much more than enough.

They were given a home in the castle. The count preferred to keep these brave warriors under his roof.

The three men's main concern over the next few days was to put their cargo in a safe place until a permanent cache could be built.

It didn't take them long to find it.

The day after their arrival, they went to the church to celebrate he different times of prayer according to the duties of every Templar. They had decided not to deviate from this essential rule, even if they had to blend in so as not to arouse any suspicion of them.

They quickly became friends with the Abbot, who was delighted to converse with fervent and learned believers. They also learned of the existence of a crypt left abandoned under the building and accessible through a trapdoor located just behind the altar, under the straw mattress in the middle of the choir.

'Who knows about this crypt?' asked the knight.

'No one but me. I am the only one who walks on this choir. It has no particular interest or function, except perhaps to provide shelter in case of attack. I have only been down there once, and that was a long time ago. The only thing of value in this church is the altar. It is said to have been donated by Charlemagne himself when he visited the region in 805.'

The ideal place that Beynac was looking for had just materialized.

The three Templars spent their days training the count's soldiers in the use of the sword and their nights, when the abbot was asleep, in repairing the crypt where they stored the six boxes. He discreetly ordered black and white tiles from a Venetian merchant, which were delivered one night. Three months later the room was finished. The walls were reinforced, the vaults and arches were bricked up, the enfeus were neatly rebuilt and the tiles were laid. In addition, a mechanism for accessing the crypt via the existing staircase had been skillfully added, positioning the altar just above it, incorporating a complex system that Beynac had already had the opportunity to install in Cyprus in the company of other brothers.

Satisfied, the count had another project to submit to them, this one titanic. Nothing less than the construction of an underground passage under the castle.

It would pass through the bowels of the mound in two opposite directions. The first tunnel would lead to the church below and the second would lead a good kilometer further on.

Beynac was not happy about this complex undertaking. It forced him to find a way to deal with the cargo stored in the crypt. For sooner or later it would be necessary to reveal its existence. But he had time before him. Especially since the death of the old abbot a few days earlier had taken with it the secret of the existence of the underground room.

They set to work at the end of September with the help of several trusted people.

The ground was sufficiently loose and construction was well underway. The soldiers were in charge of digging while the three Templars cleared away the surplus and built the interior, from the floor to the vault. By mid-October, a hundred meters of gallery had already been dug. At this rate and barring any setbacks, this first part would be finished before the summer.

On the evening of October 20, the count wanted to talk with Beynac and his companions before supper.

With a serious look on his face, he told them the bad news.

'Your Grand Master and one hundred and forty Templars were arrested in the temple of Paris by Guillaume de Nogaret on Friday morning, the thirteenth, with the same number of arrests throughout the kingdom, there is talk of at least six hundred Templars in the hands of the seneschals and bailiffs.'

'Did they defend themselves?' asked Beynac.

'No. There was no resistance. Everything went smoothly. But some of them still managed to escape.'

All three men were shocked.

'What will happen to them?'

'They will most likely be imprisoned while awaiting trial. Jacques de Molay and some other high dignitaries will be locked up in the castle of Gisors.'

'Their trial? But what are we accused of?'

'Philip the Fair is said to have accumulated evidence from former Templars excluded from the order who would have testified to a lack of charity, which is difficult to contest given the wealth accumulated in a few decades, depraved behavior and heretical practices! Guillaume de Nogaret is said to have had a first-rate repentant in the person of Esquieu de Floyran, who is at the origin of all these rumors. But you know as well as I do that the King of France has long had the intention of getting rid of your order in order to pocket all its wealth and thus cancel its debts. He has the support of the Pope in his quest, although the Pope probably has no choice, and he has overruled the conclusions of Molay's request to Clement V for a papal investigation.'

'They will torture them into saying what they want to hear. No more order.'

'I can only advise you to be very vigilant. They will not spare anyone.'

'We will carry out our mission to the end as Jacques de Molay has asked me to do. Even if in his heart, as upright and honest as he is, he thinks he can counteract all these false allegations, this perfidious king will do everything to condemn him.'

'Don't worry, I'll keep you regularly informed.'

The three Templars redoubled their efforts to complete the first section as soon as possible. The count's project was a timely one. These new galleries dug into the mound were proving to be a godsend.

The Mystery of the Lost Crypt

48

Marimont-lès-Bénestroff
Saturday May 17th 2014, 4:15

Clyde remembered going down into the crypt shortly before someone joined him. He recognized the man with the thick German accent. The same man who had attacked Eva in the forest. He had pulled out a gun and then the gun had gone off. He couldn't react. His memories stopped there. Afterwards, he couldn't say how long it had been, his body had twitched a second time. Had he been dreaming? Or was he still dreaming? If so, he was anxious to wake up. For this nightmare was becoming all too real...

He opened his eyes.

Finally, the end of this horrible dream.

A stone vault made of small cobblestones presented itself to his eyes. He was still in the crypt.

Two sharp burns were tearing at his chest and lower abdomen. He stood up and inspected his body and, as he pushed aside his jacket, discovered two red holes in his shirt. His body was pierced by bullets, but he felt nothing. Yet with such wounds he should be dead.

There was something wrong with this story.

Was this a new dream?

He suddenly felt cold and shivered. Mist came out of his mouth. Yet the temperature in this crypt was temperate, around fourteen degrees.

Something was very wrong.

His stream of thought was interrupted by a hellish noise that burst his eardrums. The altar began to move. Someone was coming. At last four people came down into the room. He recognized them all. The young couple from the lodge that he and his colleague had been assigned to protect, the old man who, after investigation, turned out to be a historian and archaeologist, professor and dean of the University of Nancy, and finally the man with the strong Germanic accent. His attacker.

The latter two each held a weapon in their hands.

All his muscles tensed and his whole body stiffened at the sight. He took his gun and pointed it at them, shouting:

'Stay where you are! Drop your guns or I'll shoot.'

But nobody seemed to pay any attention to him. It was as if no one could see or hear him. He reached for Karl's gun, but his hand slipped through without being able to grasp it. He tried again, but without success. The colossus advanced and pierced his body from side to side.

Anxiety gripped him as he began to realize the unthinkable.

He seemed to be a ghost.

He turned around and saw the body lying in front of the enfeus, slightly in the dark. He approached it and discovered with horror the identity of the person, stunned.

He saw his face, livid, lifeless.

Instinctively, he put his hand on his chest, his gaze assessing the impacts on the body lying down and ending up where his hand was covering. He raised his head, stunned.

He was well and truly dead.

Yet it all seemed so real. He had the same feelings as before. Anxiety, fear, anger... just about everything... except the pain.

He began to shiver again.

The Mystery of the Lost Crypt

During his lifetime, he had heard testimonies from people who had near-death experiences of bright light, tunnels, feelings of infinite love, peace, tranquility and warmth.

None of this is happening right now.

What if this condition was directly related to his tumultuous past? Was he preparing to go to hell instead of heaven?

Nostalgia overcame him. Memories came flooding back. He remembered all those last years spent working for the Order of Malta. He had trained as a nurse's aide and had been caring for the neediest in a hospice of the Order's foundation in Rome. This was undoubtedly the best time of his life. He had just come out of prison and wanted to draw a definitive line under his mafia past of violence and debauchery. He was looking for a new path. A path that would be in complete contrast to the previous one. Calmer, more spiritual and above all more attentive to others. The prison chaplain had a lot to do with this. After having bullied and abused his fellow men to the point of death, he now wanted to be of service to the community to help them. During the ten long years he had spent behind bars - he had originally been sentenced to twenty years for murder, but had been given a reprieve for good behavior thanks in part to the priest's report. He had spent all his days and nights learning about Christian doctrine, talking to the prison chaplain and reading all the sacred texts of the Old and New Testaments, including the four Gospels, the Acts of the Apostles, the Epistles and the Book of Revelation.

The chaplain put him in touch with the Order of Malta. Initially a volunteer, but tested during the first months, he fully embraced the principles of the Order and its motto "Tuitio Fidei et Obsequium Pauperum" - to bear witness, to protect the faith and to serve the poor and the sick. After fifteen years of loyal service, he had risen through the ranks to become a Professed Knight. When Borgia had created his small team, he had naturally thought of him. Clyde, who had drawn a line under his former life, had at first refused his proposal, not wanting to return to his old demons. He had been afraid to take the plunge again. But the Grand Chancellor was a persuasive man. He was a sort of mentor to

Borgia, by his side since the beginning of his adventure. He owed him a lot and could not refuse his request.

Lost in his thoughts, Clyde did not notice Cyril and Karl leaving. He would have liked so much to help the poor young woman to free herself from the yoke of the old man, but he could not. He was now a mere actor, powerless, useless.

And what had become of Eva? Had she suffered the same fate as him?

While he was asking himself a thousand questions, something unexpected happened. Beams of light shot out of the tabernacle and then took the form of a halo of light that grew larger and brighter. He had never seen anything like this before, except perhaps in a film. But never in real life. Even if he was no longer sure in which world he was located...

A feeling of fullness suddenly enveloped him. He was no longer afraid and felt protected by this enlightenment.

Perhaps God had finally changed his mind and was sending him to heaven instead of hell? That was the best news he could get at that moment. In any case, he seemed to be experiencing the same manifestations of IME as he had read about here and there. Feelings of peace and tranquility. A bright light. It all fit together.

But the most extraordinary thing was yet to come.

Out of this intense halo of light suddenly appeared a woman with an angelic smile. She seemed to be hovering in the air. He recognized her immediately by her red and emerald green scarf, haloed by an intense white light. He had had the great honor of accompanying Borgia and other prominent members of the Order on a ceremonial trip to Montenegro on the thirteenth of October the previous year. He was able to admire the original icon in the Museum of Art and History in Cetinje.

Our Lady of Philerme in person.

According to beliefs and traditions, she had appeared twice. The first event took place on the island of Rhodes, at Lalysos on Mount Philerimos. Our Lady appeared to a desperate man who was planning to commit suicide in the ruins of an ancient Phoenician temple dedicated to Phaeton, the divinity of the sun, one of the seven sons of Helios. She convinced him to renounce his act and to enter into penance. He built a chapel there and placed a miraculous icon there, apparently from the Monastery of St. John the Baptist in Constantinople and painted, according to belief, by St. Luke in Jerusalem. This act was the beginning of the veneration of the Madonna of Philerme by the islanders at first and then by the Knights of the Order on their arrival on the island. The second apparition took place during the siege of 1480 on the island of Rhodes, when the Virgin and St. John the Baptist both appeared on the breach of a wall and routed the invaders. Two new chapels were then added to the original sanctuary in favor of the Knights through the intercession of the Virgin and John the Baptist.

Clyde knew this story by heart.

Was he witnessing a third miraculous apparition of the Virgin? Or was it the dream of every knight of the Order who vows infinite devotion to her? He could not say. In any case, he was fascinated by this vision.

For the first time since he had passed into the afterlife, he felt good. A feeling of completeness came over him. If this was death, then he accepted his fate with joy.

He was standing between Natasha and Visconti who, like him, found it difficult to understand what was happening to them and wondered if they too were dreaming.

When the Madonna of Philerme disappeared and the intense light faded, Clyde was sucked into her body, which was still lying on the ground. He could not fight against this force.

His inert flesh claimed his soul.

Then he opened his eyes again.

The Mystery of the Lost Crypt

49

Marimont-lès-Bénestroff
Saturday May 17th 2014, 4:30

Gilles found himself at the end of the underground passageway leading to the crypt. The sword was there, resting against the wall on the right, where his friend had left it earlier.

He hesitated to approach. Not more than half a meter of rock separated him from the crypt room. He wondered if anyone was there at the moment, apart from the unfortunate Italian who had been coldly shot. Perhaps Cyril was a prisoner there again. This thought filled him with sadness. He began to regret the discovery of this crypt which had become nothing but trouble. If only his friend had listened to him. All this would not have happened if he had not revealed everything to the old man. But who would have thought for a second that they were throwing themselves into the lion's den...

He took the opportunity to inspect the outline of the door, but did not see any cuts the width of the blade. It seemed impossible to access the room from inside the tunnel. This time it was a one-way trip. This in itself was not a problem, since the breach through which they had passed made it possible to emerge without problems. But there had to be another way out. He took the blade and then retraced his steps at a steady pace. Arriving at the bottom of the endless staircase, he saw a faint glow at the top.

The slope from the bottom looked vertiginous. Bonnie climbed the steps one by one with extreme caution and was so concentrated that she did not even notice the halo of light that illuminated her.

He started to climb to reach her.

Halfway across, Gilles heard the distinctive sound of a huge splash from the gap. Something or someone had obviously fallen into the water. He stopped dead in his tracks, balancing unsteadily on two steps, and listened. A second identical sound followed. Then nothing more. He climbed the few steps separating him from the breach, extinguished his torch, then scanned in the direction of the flooded cavity. Through the tangle of roots he saw two faint beams swirling in the natural gallery.

They would soon come in his direction.

It could have been Cyril and Natasha also seeking refuge. But it could also be Visconti and his bull-dog, or anyone else at this point. He did not hesitate for a second. They had previously agreed on a course of action and so decided to join Eva who was waiting for him further up and would wait for the confirmation signal.

He relit his torch and continued his ascent, climbing the steps as fast as he could, panting like a bull and using the sword as an ice axe. He was only a few steps from the end when he was put in the spotlight. The strangers had just entered the tunnel.

He heard someone shouting and immediately recognized his voice. It was the same as always. That German colossus. A bang sounded and the first bullet whistled a few centimeters from his head and ricocheted off the roof. Gilles bent down and redoubled his efforts by climbing the last few steps two by two. In this narrow gallery, it was a real stroke of luck not to have been hit. He would certainly not get a second one.

He reached the penultimate step and was making a dash for safety when his foot lapped at a limestone concretion. He flattened himself on the ground and tried to hold on with his hands, but the wetness and the flatness of the ground gave him no opportunity. The weight of his body was dragging him down.

There was no hope. It was all over for him.

Gilles felt himself sliding backwards when a saving hand reached out in front of him. He grabbed it and in a last effort managed to pull himself up onto the platform just as a second shot rang out. The bullet bounced off the last ridge and tore off a piece of stone. The bullet ricocheted and hit Gilles in the calf, who let out a cry of pain.

But Bonnie had certainly saved the day.

Visconti sat facing the tabernacle and the wall containing the stone trapdoor. His weapon lay prominently on the table beside his right hand. Natasha stood on his left, slightly back from the table, silent as a mouse. She hadn't said a word since the two of them had been alone. She was impatiently waiting for Cyril to return. She would have liked to know Visconti's motives for going to such extremes, but given the circumstances, she preferred not to add fuel to the fire. Generally impulsive, it was better to keep a low profile for the time being.

In a claustral silence, the professor read the next riddle and tried to decipher it. But it seemed far more complicated than the previous ones. He, too, wanted Cyril to be there as soon as possible. He couldn't do it without his young, sharp mind.

Lost in his thoughts, a halo of light on the wall in front of him suddenly caught his attention. The source seemed to come from the icon. The Madonna of Philerme glowed more and more as the seconds passed. So much so that the light eventually flooded the whole room as if it were daylight. At first dazzling, the light became almost blinding, but still warm and soothing.

Natasha and Visconti were both stunned by this phenomenon and remained petrified, unable to react. They were as if hypnotized by the light, which faded a few seconds later and disappeared as quickly as it had appeared.

'What was this phenomenon?' asked a troubled Visconti.

'I don't know anything about it. It's the first time I've ever seen anything like that. I don't know where it came from or what or who it was for, but it was fabulous.'

The professor found it difficult to regain his senses and concentrate on his work. Too many questions haunted him now. He looked at his weapon on the table. He wondered what he was doing with it. What was the origin of all this escalating violence? He no longer recognized himself. A feeling of guilt invaded him. Assailed by doubt, lost since this strange and inexplicable event, he looked at Natasha.

The young woman seemed to be upset too. Her lips trembled, her body was so tense and her eyes stared at the enfeus.

'Get over it, my dear. Even if I grant you that the situation is not commonplace, it must be a natural phenomenon,' he ironically reassured himself. But what are you looking at?

She did not react to his question. He picked up his gun and was about to turn around to see what was troubling her so much when he felt a sharp pain on the top of his head.

Then the blackout.

Cyril was still hoping to hold back time. He knew exactly where the cavity was, but he kept zigzagging, taking advantage of the tangles of dead tree trunks and branches, as well as the bramble thickets.

Karl was following him closely, cursing in German at every return of a branch that whipped across his face. He suspected that this was intentional on the part of the young man and would not fail to take revenge when the time came. When they reached the halfway point of the hill, the two men went deeper into a thicket.

Cyril lit up the floor, revealing the cavity. He was careful not to tell the colossus how much water was there. He was ordered to go first. He crouched down and grabbed two large roots plunging into the pit. He landed softly in the pool and waited for the colossus. This might be the best opportunity he had to try and neutralize him. If he followed suit, he would have to do without his weapon to hold on to the roots. But he did not expect what would happen next.

With the torch in one hand and the weapon in the other, Karl decided to jump directly into the cavity and was in turn surprised by the height of the water. He landed by bending his knees slightly to keep his balance.

He let out another swear word and gave Cyril an evil look. He came up to him and hit him hard in the face with the butt of the gun. The young man staggered, but took the blow. A trickle of blood gushed from the corner of his lip. Cyril wiped it away with the back of his sleeve and checked that his jaw was intact. He had expected this kind of reaction. But no matter where the consequences of his actions would lead him, he would not deviate one iota from his original intention.

'Don't ever do that again,' Karl threatened.

With a brief gesture of his armed hand, he signaled to him to go first.

They went into the depths of the hillside.

Cyril was moving in conquered territory.

The Mystery of the Lost Crypt

50

Marimont-lès-Bénestroff
Saturday May 17th 2014, 4:45

When he opened his eyes, Clyde felt as if he had been there before. He looked at the stone arch above him with a sense of déjà vu. Was it death? Had he been dreaming this whole crazy story? That would undoubtedly be the most plausible hypothesis. Lying on the ground, unresponsive, he remembered the bright, warm light from which the Virgin had emerged.

He felt divinely comfortable there.

Thinking about it, the scene became surreal, it could only be the fruit of his imagination. He then remembered the bloodstains on his jumper. Without further ado, he sat up and pulled his jacket aside with both hands.

They were always there, the same orifices.

His sweatshirt was stained with blood, the two stains having come together to form one. He slid his hand in, but felt no wounds, not the slightest swelling in his lower abdomen or chest from bullet penetration. He lifted his suit and found two scars that were barely perceptible to the touch. Unthinkable of course that bullet wounds could have healed so quickly.

Baffled, he searched for a rational explanation for all this. He stood up and looked at the ground. The body had evaporated.

He seemed to have regained his physical body. The thesis of death suddenly seemed very uncertain. Hesitating, he moved his hand closer to the enfeus, and it came up against the wall. It all seemed inconceivable. Emotion gripped him.

He picked up his torch and walked towards the table.

Natasha saw him and stared at him as if he had come down from another planet. He approached and was about to speak when the old man put his hand on his weapon. Clyde didn't give him time to turn around and hit him on the top of the head with the torch, knocking him out cold. Then he tied him to the chair with the means at hand.

'Am I dreaming?' asked Clyde naively.

'I've been asking myself the same question for a while now,' Natasha replied, with a wary look on her face.

She shook her head from side to side as if to chase away the thoughts that beset her, it seemed so unlikely, she finally added

'I have just witnessed two quite incredible phenomena.'

'Which is? Specify!'

'Just a few minutes ago, a very bright white light appeared from this painting,' Natasha pointed to the tabernacle.

'Ditto. And the woman, did you see her too?'

'What woman?'

'The Virgin, well, the Virgin of Philerme. The one represented in the painting you are showing me.'

'No, neither I nor the professor saw it. Only a very strong light. Are you telling me that the Virgin appeared to you?'

'I guess...'

'Well, that would explain the second phenomenon then.'

'Which one?'

'Your resurrection...' smiled Natasha.

'Ahhh, I've been shot in the leg,' shouted Gilles.

'We have to get out of here. Get up, I'll help you walk. Lean on my shoulder.'

Gilles winced as he got to his feet. The pain was sharp. But Bonnie was right. They had to get away as soon as possible. Karl must have heard him scream and knew that he had hit the nail on the head. The young man gritted his teeth and supported himself on Bonnie to move forward. The gallery went on for about ten meters in a false uphill direction before coming to a fork in the road. Bonnie shone the light to the left. The access seemed difficult, partly blocked by scree. The diminished young man would certainly not be able to squeeze through. On their right, a long, endless tunnel with a gentle downward slope would give them a chance to escape their attacker. They entered it. The width of the tunnel was just enough for two people to walk side by side. This was a godsend for Gilles, who could rest on the beautiful Italian woman.

'Can you do it?' asked Bonnie.

'I don't think I have much choice. I don't want to end my life in this damp gallery.'

He let out an expletive.

'This leg is killing me. But with this madman on our tail, the motivation is there... too bad I don't have the sword anymore, I could at least use it as a walking stick.'

'That's what might save us for a moment. In my opinion, this is what they were looking for, so that they could resume the puzzles chronologically. That's all they're interested in in the first place.'

'Everything'... that's easy to say. They don't want to leave any trace and they also want our skin.'

They continued down the gallery, hobbling along. Bonnie glanced back from time to time to see if they were being followed or not. For the moment everything was quiet. But they were aware that things could get out of hand very quickly. They were completely exposed in this long straight line and occupying the whole width, they would need another miracle not to be hit by a projectile.

This seemed rather unlikely!

Bonnie shone the light in front of her. In the distance she could see a low wall across the gallery. The very weak beam of the torch did not allow her to understand exactly what was waiting for them there. But she had a bad feeling.

She immediately thought of a dead end.

'Are you thinking the same thing as me?'

'I didn't dare to tell you about it, but I only hope one thing. That we are wrong in our judgement...'

Fear overcame them. They turned around together, almost hitting their heads. Their pulse quickened. And their fear was unfortunately well founded. A pale glow was gradually eating away at the deep, intense darkness of the tunnel.

'Damn... so the sword wasn't his only goal. I think we made the wrong choice by entering here. Dead end or back door, we're done for,' exclaimed Giles, already imagining what was waiting for them.

Despite the pain in his leg, Gilles quickened his pace.

Borgia regularly glanced at his smartphone. Bonnie kept moving, unlike Clyde who remained motionless when the latter suddenly turned green again. He was relieved, reassured that there must have been a connection problem.

Everyone stayed in the race.

They began the toughest part of the climb when the carabinieri stopped their progress.

'osa sta succedendo?'[1] asked Borgia.

'Se ne sono andati!'[2] replied a carabiniere.

'E 'impossibile!'

The policemen tried in vain to spot them, but even their thermal glasses were hopelessly blind. A moment of panic gripped the trio. They could not have disappeared so suddenly. There had to be a cavity in the mound where they had probably gone in. All that remained was to find it...

---

1. *What's going on ?*
2. *They have disappeared !*

Borgia motioned for them to continue and head in the direction of the last place they had seen them. There he did not have long to look. A large clump of mulberry trees choked with young hazel trees blocked any progress up the hillside, providing natural protection for the tunnel entrance. He scanned the entrance to this copse with his torch. He stopped at some high lying grass and followed the trail to the entrance where bramble branches had been pushed aside. This confirmed to him that people had made their way through, not without difficulty in view of the thorny thicket.

He snapped his fingers to call out to the two carabinieri who advanced. A gaping, dark hole was revealed.

The Grand Chancellor knelt down and glanced cautiously to the bottom. He could see nothing.

Immediately after, a shot rang out.

There was not a second to lose.

Then a second shot.

The two policemen went ahead to help Borgia down into the pit and, above all, to prevent him from getting soaked. They placed him on the dry surface like a prince on his throne, which he was not far from being given the importance of his responsibilities in the order.

The shots alarmed Borgia. All the more so as there was absolute silence afterwards. This did not augur well.

Like all those who had gone before him, he squeezed his way through a shaped stone wall and emerged in the middle of the staircase.

He heard another gunshot.

And another one.

The blasts came from above.

Karl was ranting. His bald head was covered with dirt and he had the unpleasant impression that a colony of insects was using it as a landing strip.

Cyril entered the gallery and saw a faint glow illuminating the top of the tunnel. Someone was coming up. He resisted the urge to point his torch, not wanting to attract Karl's attention. It could only be Gilles or Eva. He immediately recognized his friend's build as he hurried up the last few steps. Cyril slowed down, pretended to turn his attention to the right, thus obstructing his opponent's field of vision.

Too late.

Karl was suspicious and soon realized his subterfuge. He pushed Cyril and saw the person at the top of the stairs. He had no doubt about his identity. He had also recognized him.

He pointed his gun and fired a first shot without hesitation.

Missed.

The bullet ricocheted off the arched wall only a few units from the runner's head, causing a small spark on the stone as it passed.

Cyril had no time to react.

The gun spat out a second bullet.

This time it seemed to hit him right in the face. The young man let out a cry of pain that left no doubt. He disappeared from his field of vision. A thunderous noise filled the underground. Something tumbled down the steps. He pointed to his torch and saw the sword.

Cyril watched helplessly, unable to do anything to save his friend, and prayed that he would have escaped without too much harm. But what he had seen had given him hope. Gilles was not alone. A helping hand had pulled him out of this predicament. Eva was still with him.

Karl smiled.

The coveted object came to him. Without any particular effort. He did not expect so much. He slowed down the object by blocking it firmly with his sole.

The joke had gone on long enough. He wanted to get it over with once and for all before he went back to the Commander. He ordered Cyril not to try anything, or he would go after his friend, still trapped in the crypt.

'Hurry up and don't mess around this time,' he said, brandishing his weapon and pushing him back with his other hand, which held both the torch and the sword.

The Mystery of the Lost Crypt

51

Paris
March 1314

Some of their Templar brothers had been imprisoned for over six years. Among them was Jacques de Molay and other great dignitaries. A number of the captives had succumbed to their injuries as a result of the relentless torture. The interrogations had been orchestrated by Guillaume Humbert, the king's confessor and above all Grand Inquisitor of France. Those who had broken down and confessed against their will were allowed to live. Among the main sins confessed were the denial of the Holy Cross and of Christ, sodomy and the worship of Baphomet. But those among them, about fifty Templars, who had already denied their confessions under torture in 1310, were therefore considered relapsed and thus perished at the stake. All the interrogations were officially concluded on May 26th 1311. The following year, the Council of Vienna decided the fate of the order with the papal bull 'Vox in excelso' ordering the dissolution of the Temple order, the bull 'Ad providam' deciding that all property would be transferred to the order of the Hospital and finally the last bull 'Considerantes dudum' dealing with the fate of the men, namely an annuity for the innocent or repentant and the death penalty for all those who had denied or recanted.

Only the fate of the four high dignitaries, including the Grand Master, remained in question, with the decision resting with the Pope. The latter appointed a pontifical commission at the end of 1313 to decide their fate. On this occasion the four Templars renewed their confessions. They set the date of the sentence for March 18th 1314.

Beynac had decided to go to Paris to attend the verdict, despite the possible consequences of such a decision. Over time, he had grown a few wrinkles, shaved his beard and let his hair grow, but when he had lived in the temple enclosure a few years earlier, he had made a habit of going outside the enclosure, mixing with the population and the merchants. He also mingled with the king's relatives in the company of the order's high dignitaries. He therefore covered the risk of being recognized. However, for the Grand Master, the Templar was ready to brave the danger.

He set off alone on horseback a good week before, slept in passing inns, and reached the capital without having suffered a single skirmish this time. He settled in the Benedictine abbey of Saint-Germain-des-Prés, west of Paris, outside the city walls. He remained cloistered there for two days and only came out to join the square in front of Notre-Dame on the fateful day. Hiding under a black blanket, he entered the city through the Porte de Buci and proceeded through the Rue St Germain towards the Ile de la Cité, which he reached by the Petit Pont located in front of the Hôtel-Dieu. Having lived in the country for several years, he had almost forgotten the stench emanating from Paris, the most populous city in Europe. Rubbish was thrown on the streets and the gutters in the center carried the rubbish to the Seine. Only the main streets were paved, the others being left to the pigs and the mud. These were veritable open sewers that were only cleaned during epidemics or when the king passed through. An effort was required of the inhabitants, who also dumped their filth into wells built for this purpose, thus contaminating the water table, but it was in vain.

The closer he got to the island, the bigger the crowd became. Although the reputation of the Templars had been somewhat flayed, vilified and sullied by this trial, the Grand Master of an order that had ruled the world for almost two centuries was still as popular as ever. The thirst for curiosity brought in the world from all over the kingdom and beyond. No high dignitaries from the Hospitallers were present. The agreement to merge the two orders, proposed by the Pope, had been categorically refused by Jacques de Molay.

Beynac made his way through the compact crowd, sometimes forcing his way through and playing with his shoulders to get as close as possible to the podium, raising the hackles of some onlookers in the process. But his imposing stature and his monk's habit silenced them. He stopped less than twenty meters behind a man of equal stature and remained in his shadow. Soldiers surrounded the platform to prevent the crowd from attacking the condemned directly. He could not and would not come any closer, at the risk of being recognized by the King of France's solicitors, appointed to form the papal commission along with three cardinals. He had been in contact with all of them before and this was another reason to be on his guard.

At two o'clock the four Templars appeared. The Grand Master, Jacques de Molay, arrived first, closely followed by Geoffroy de Charnay, preceptor of Normandy, Hugues de Pairaud, visitor to France, and Geoffroy de Goneville, preceptor of Poitou-Aquitaine. Chained hand and foot, wearing the same tunic soiled by the years, the cross covered with dirt, they climbed the wooden steps of the platform with difficulty under the roar and the booing of the crowd. Seven years of imprisonment and torture had diminished them greatly. Their cheeks, temples and eye sockets hollowed out, their forearms and calves emaciated, there was little left of the valiant knights they had been. Despite their emaciated bodies, they held their heads high, probably hoping that the years they had spent in prison would be enough for them.

As the charges were read out, their jaws tightened. The hubbub in the square intensified with each charge, and insults and death threats were heard when the charge of sodomy was brought up.

Adored ten years ago, hated today.

Philip the Fair, standing at the end of the platform on the royal throne, was gloating. His Machiavellian plan had worked perfectly and in a few minutes the order would cease to exist with the breath of its last influential members.

A drum roll was heard.

The sentence was about to be pronounced.

Beynac's heart fluttered.

Life imprisonment for the four convicts'.

Beynac's body shuddered at this announcement.

The crowd was exultant. Some, like the woman next to him, were shouting "Burn!" at the top of their lungs, their faces disfigured by hatred.

The Templar case seemed to be settled!

Upon hearing this announcement, which was considered senseless and unacceptable, Jacques de Molay and Geoffroy de Charnay immediately retracted their statements and loudly proclaimed their innocence and that of the order, unlike their fellow students who accepted their fate. This sudden declaration surprised everyone, the cardinals in the first place, and they considered this new testimony as a lie following the first confessions made before the judges of the inquisition. Thus their fate was sealed and they were both considered relapsed.

Philip the Fair smiled - he expected no less from them - and rose from his throne. He condemned the two Templars to the stake, not caring about the opinion of the cardinals present.

The crowd went wild. A thunder of applause, shouts and insults resounded.

This irrevocable announcement of a death sentence came as a shock to Beynac. He closed his eyes, clasped his hands together, hidden by the long, loose sleeves of his robe, and prayed. All he could hear was his heart pounding and no external noise. Not for a moment had he imagined that he would see Jacques de Molay for the last time today. In a few hours he and Charnay would be burned alive, thanks to this king of France.

He did not dare to believe it.

He was interrupted in his meditation by the jostling and comments of the crowd. **They are going to be burned at the other end of the city, on the Isle of Jews! Let's go. The show is about to start!** '. Beynac was carried along by the flow of the crowd. He followed mechanically, looking haggard, totally overwhelmed by events, powerless. He did not understand the reaction of the people, who were so changeable and above all so easily influenced.

He had imagined many scenarios, but certainly not this one.

As the western end of the 'Ile de la Cité' was reserved for the Palais, the king's residence, the crowds were amassed on both banks of the Seine. The 'Ile aux Juifs' belonged to the abbey of Saint-Germain-des-Prés, the same abbey where Beynac had taken up residence. He was therefore entitled to go to the very place where the sentence had been carried out and to approach the Grand Master one last time.

The pyre was set up.

The king dominated the scene from his Palace.

The two convicts were brought in late in the day. The sky was dark and full of threatening clouds. When the two Templars were tied to their posts, thunder rumbled in the distance. Some onlookers saw this as a bad omen and signed themselves with the cross. The euphoria and intoxication of the crowd had disappeared. All was quiet, except for the rolls of thunder that startled many believers with each crack.

The king feared only one thing at that moment, that the storm was approaching and that it would pour down. The execution of the sentence would have to be postponed, and many would see this as a sign from the Almighty, allowing the Pope to interfere and put pressure on him to overturn the hasty verdict. The stake had to be lit at all costs. And Philip the Fair was favored by heaven that evening. The storm passed the outskirts of the capital and then slid eastwards. Nothing could stand in the way of the festivities.

Beynac stood less than ten meters from the stake. Jacques de Molay and Geoffroy de Charnay were each tied to a post. In a final request, they asked to face Notre-Dame, which the king granted. He immediately regretted this. Jacques de Molay then took the floor to proclaim his innocence once again.

'It is only just,' he cried, 'that on such a terrible day and in the last moments of my life, I should uncover the iniquity of the lie and make the truth triumph. I declare to the face of heaven and earth, though to my eternal shame, that I have committed the greatest of crimes... that of having accused myself of an Order which I now recognize as Innocent! I only passed the declaration required of me to suspend the excessive pains of torture and to bend those who made me suffer them. I know the torments inflicted on all the knights who had the courage to revoke such a confession; but the awful spectacle presented to me is not capable of making me confirm a first lie by a second one on such an infamous condition, I willingly renounce life, which is already only too hateful to me! And what would be the use of prolonging sad days that I owe only to calumny?'

Then the executioner lit the fire all around the pyre, as far away from the two men as possible so that their torment would last as long as possible. The flames licked at the Templars' feet and rose around them in an impenetrable wall.

The Grand Master spoke one last time.

'Pope Clement! King Philip! Within a year, I summon you to appear before the tribunal of God to receive your just punishment! Cursed! Cursed! Cursed to the thirteenth generation of your races!'

At these words, the glass held by Philip the Fair shattered under the pressure of his fingers, inflicting slight cuts.

'May this scoundrel burn in hell...' he shouted as a valet wrapped his bloody hand in a cloth.

When the flames reached them, both of them sang a hymn, thus forcing the admiration of a crowd suddenly resistant to the cruelty of the sentence, driven by the unfailing courage of these two tortured men. Emotions ran high on the two quays of the Seine. Weeping and murmurs were heard. A hint of guilt and shame could be detected in the pout of the French king, who had suddenly become mute, lost in thought, with a serious expression on his face. Some of them even asked the king for mercy so that they could be released. The same people who had been scolding them a few minutes earlier on the square in front of Notre-Dame. Then the chants died down.

The two Templars had just died with immeasurable dignity, without having uttered the slightest moan despite their suffering, imploring their innocence to God.

The crowd dispersed in silence.

Beynac had hidden his eyes as soon as they were transformed into living torches, hearing only their incantations. He too left, not wanting to witness the burning of the Templars. The next day he learned that some nuns had recovered the charred bones and ashes.

For the Pope and the King of France, the chapter of the Templars was well and truly closed. But this total victory over the order had left a bitter taste in the mouth of the latter. He recovered only a few crumbs of the much hoped-for treasure and bequeathed the commanderies to the Hospitallers of Saint John of Jerusalem, as written in the papal bull *Ad providam Christi vicarii*. He kept only the Temple Tower.

But for Beynac, this was only the beginning.

The Mystery of the Lost Crypt

52

**Marimont-lès-Bénestroff
Saturday May 17th 2014, 5am**

'Sorry?'

'I can assure you that you were quite dead a short time ago and now you are back among the living. The professor will be able to confirm this when he wakes up.'

Clyde had to face the fact that everything he had just experienced was not a figment of his imagination. He tried to put his thoughts in order.

'I remember being hit by the first bullet. But not the second. I must have been unconscious already. But I have the sensation of having felt my body twitch.'

'According to Cyril, the man shot you in cold blood with a second bullet to the chest.'

Clyde was petrified at the thought that he had just come back from the dead, and was finally aware of how lucky he was to have escaped.

'I saw myself lying on the floor, thinking I was dreaming. I saw the four of you descend into the crypt. I tried to disarm them, but I was feeling the emptiness, passing through the bodies each time. I must admit that it was a rather frustrating situation... I didn't notice it, but it seemed to me that I was levitating, I had this impression of lightness, as if my feet were no longer touching the ground. Then there was this dazzling light emanating from the painting and the Virgin appeared to me with her magnificent smile.'

'And that's it? She didn't... say anything?'

'*Do your work, Pietro*'... nothing else. Then it disappeared. Then I was sucked into my own body and there I woke up. My wounds have completely healed. It's incredible...'

'I would even say more... it is a miracle...'

'It seems to be one, indeed! he said, equally perplexed.'

Visconti regained consciousness and was confused by the position he was in. He was still sitting in the chair, but his hands were tied behind his back. He twisted around trying to get out of his bonds but could not.

That's when he saw the Italian.

'You! But how is that possible?'

'You have to ask the Virgin of Philerme...'

Visconti did not dare to make the connection with the intense light that had burst forth from the painting a few minutes earlier.

'This is even more extraordinary than the treasure itself. It is a real miracle that the Madonna has accomplished. Quickly, untie me, I must study this painting,' said the exalted dean. 'Come on, what do you fear from an unarmed old man like me. I beg you, take these bonds off me.'

His attempt to coax them again failed. Neither of them would fall for it. No one could trust him again. Especially not after what had just happened.

'What do we do?' asked Natasha worriedly.

'Better to wait here. It will be safer. Reinforcements will arrive soon...'

'Did you call the gendarmes?'

'No, not at all. I have received specific orders from the Grand Chancellor of the Order of Malta. He will be here soon.'

Visconti's eyes widened at this announcement.

'The Grand Chancellor of what?'

The wall was getting closer and with it the worry of being trapped. The bloody trouser bottoms were sticking to Gilles' right leg. No doubt the intense physical effort was not helping. His jaw was clenched and the pain in his calf was getting worse.

Bonnie glanced back again with concern. The halo of light was becoming more and more distinct and was positioned horizontally, indicating that he had just climbed the stairs and that they would be in their sights shortly and be targeted again. Walking side by side as they were, they would need more than a miracle to escape the bullets this time.

Fortunately for them, the wall that obstructed the gallery was a mere optical illusion. Two low walls were placed two meters apart, one behind the other, making it look like a uniform wall from a distance.

'Ingenious architects of yesteryear, whispered Gilles. A double partition allowing escape without being hit by crossbow bolts or musket balls. A firewall protecting the fugitives from certain death in the event of retaliation in a straight and narrow gallery. It's a good idea!'

The two fugitives turned around one last time. Their executioner could appear at any second. They looked at each other. They had the same idea in mind. They visualized the location of the first low wall, less than five meters from them, and then turned off their torches, which would give them another two or three seconds to take cover.

Less than two meters.

A dim light suddenly illuminated the section they were in, allowing them to find their bearings just in time. Gilles had stretched his left arm forward to anticipate the impact with the wall. He touched it with his hand and went around it just before a bullet ricocheted off the same spot.

They protected themselves behind the second low wall. A second bullet also bounced off it. They heard a howl of frustration and rage. The colossus was beside himself.

'We're pissing him off just fine. I hope he doesn't take it out on Cyril just out of annoyance.'

When they turned the lamp back on, they could both see that the gallery continued beyond as far as the eye could see, probably with the same defense strategy a little further on. Gilles could go no further. His leg hurt like hell and Bonnie was not strong enough to support him. They had to find another solution. He scanned the floor and the walls and discovered a real archaeological treasure. A gift from heaven. A crossbow lay against the wall, along with a quiver full of bolts.

'We could always use it...' he said, grabbing the crossbow.

Unfortunately for him, the rope had not withstood the centuries. It disintegrated at the first vibration.

He lifted the quiver, which was largely lying in the drainage channel. But as with the rope, the leather had not stood the test of time either. The bottom of the case immediately fell to the ground, taking with it all the bolts which fell to the ground, most of them breaking into several pieces. Only one, obviously positioned in the opposite direction to the others, remained half intact. The point was sharp enough to cause damage if the need arose to use it as a hand weapon.

At last, at the top of the stairs, the tunnel continued horizontally, this time on a slope. Droplets of blood stained the ground at regular intervals, like Little Thumb sowing his pebbles to find his way back.

All you had to do was follow to find them.

These spots, of the same size all along the path, suggested that Gilles seemed only partially affected. One was reassured, the other even more annoyed.

They came to an intersection.

With his prisoner on his right, Karl instinctively looked to his left. The gallery quickly led to a staircase cluttered with fallen rocks. There was still a gap where a medium-sized person could squeeze through.

He scanned the ground.

The bloodstains continued to the right. He shone a light on the gallery and saw his two fugitives walking away. A wall seemed to block their path. Surely a dead end. He smiled. They were as good as rats and could no longer escape him.

He pushed Cyril back so that he would not try anything by putting him at a good distance from him, then stretched out his arm and fired. The first bullet bounced off the wall to the left of the young man. The second bullet did not have time to hit its target, for both suddenly disappeared, as if they had passed through the wall.

He was stunned. He hesitated to pursue them.

It was hard to know what was waiting for him behind that wall. His patience gone, Karl froze with rage. He tightened his grip on the pommel of the sword. The muscles in his arm tightened and the veins bulged. He glared demonically at Cyril. Impulsive, he could have seen himself smashing that sword over his head. The latter sensed this and instinctively stepped back a good meter, leaving a reasonable distance to dodge any attack.

But reason took over. They still needed him. Karl was lucid enough to remember that.

But his nerves were on edge.

Having recovered what they had come for, there was no point in pursuing them. They went back to where they had come from.

This time, the teacher had to be reached as soon as possible.

The transalpine trio started up the stairs when a halo of light illuminated the gallery from above.

Two men appeared.

Even in this gloomy atmosphere, he immediately recognized the right-wing man. He had been studying his file again on the plane to France. The photo he saw was unmistakable. Cyril de Villiers.

'Halt, or we open fire,' shouted Borgia in very good French.

The Mystery of the Lost Crypt

But his order did not have the desired effect. The other man fired several times in their direction.

They immediately replied.

One of the two policemen collapsed, hit in the chest. Borgia dived behind the inert body of the policeman. The other carabiniere, superficially wounded in the arm, went back down to take cover just in front of the wrought iron gate.

'Stop or I'll kill him,' shouted the Giant, positioning himself behind the young man and pointing his gun at him.

Borgia knew he wasn't bluffing.

'Tiro di arresto,' cria Borgia.

The rifleman stopped firing as the Grand Chancellor had just ordered, but kept him at gunpoint.

Then they both witnessed a fight.

The man who had threatened them was suddenly disarmed.

53

Marimont-lès-Bénestroff
Saturday May 17th 2014, 5:15

Cyril was being used as a human shield for the second time that night. He had to react and neutralize this maniac once and for all. And only then would he worry about freeing Natasha. He didn't know who was down there, but given their reactions, they could only be on his side.

At least he hoped so.

Cyril took advantage of the moment when the colossus fired to grab his armed hand and strike him with a violent elbow in the ribs. The latter, far from suspecting such a maneuver, bent in two, allowing the young man to place a knee blow in his face which threw him backwards.

In surprise, the colossus dropped the weapon in his right hand and the sword and torch in his other hand and fell heavily to the ground.

Cyril saw the weapon spinning through the air and tried to catch it in mid-air. But only too late did he realize that he was on the edge of the plunging staircase and put his foot on the edge of the first step. He managed to catch the weapon, but was thrown off balance and toppled into the void.

He could not hold on to anything and at first thought only of breaking his fall by raising his arms.

And so much for the weapon, which he instinctively released.

He rolled down the stairs, protecting his head and neck but unable to stop his fall at any point. About halfway down, he was stopped by the body of the Italian carabiniere lying on the ground and had a torch pointed at his face as a welcoming committee.

Karl quickly recovered his senses and saw the young man lose his balance and disappear into the darkness. He grabbed the lamp and looked around. Only the sword lay near the precipice. But there was no trace of his weapon.

A thud was then heard. His prisoner was tumbling down the stairs. Then at the same time a metallic sound.

His pistol was obviously following the same route.

Without his weapon, Karl could not fight.

He grabbed the sword and retreated. He had to leave as soon as possible, because from that moment on, faced with armed people, he became the hunted animal! He ran like a bull in the ring through the gallery, straight to the place where his two fugitives had disappeared as if by magic.

This was his only opportunity.

Only the few puddles on the rocky, uneven floor of the tunnel betrayed his presence. Running at a good pace, he quickly reached that wall built across the path. He slowed down a few meters beforehand. All seemed quiet.

Were they both still there?

He would soon find out.

He glanced back quickly. No one was in sight. He had a good head start on them if they came after him. He then got the gist of the story as he moved forward. Very clever, those ramparts across the gallery.

He stepped forward cautiously, sword in hand, to keep any possible attacker at bay. Even his Herculean strength would not be enough to fight with one hand. He stuck to the right wall in

The Mystery of the Lost Crypt

order to have a maximum view to see if anyone was hiding behind the low wall.

No one.

He did the opposite at the next low wall.

He took a step forward and probed the darkened corner with his sword. The place seemed deserted.

Where could they have gone?

Gilles and Bonnie remained hidden behind the second low wall, ready to ambush anyone who wandered near.

Silence had returned after the last shots. No one seemed to be heading towards them for the moment. But the calm was very short-lived, interrupted by a heavy exchange of gunfire.

But none of these bullets ricocheted off the walls.

The battle was being waged on another front.

'Who could it be?' asked Gilles, surprised but happy with this new twist. The gendarmes?

'Maybe Cyril did call them.'

They thought for a moment.

'But yes, of course, I think I know,' replied Bonnie, cheered up by the thought. 'Giacomo Borgia!'

'Erm... and who is that?'

'The Grand Chancellor of the Order of Malta. I warned him that the situation was getting out of hand when we went looking for Pietro. And here he is. He came all the way from Rome. I'm part of it too.'

'I don't understand what you're telling me, Eva...'

'When this is over, you will know everything. I promise.'

As she spoke, Gilles' attention was caught by a strange sound that intensified.

'Listen. Someone is coming,' he whispered.

They both kept their eyes open. The footsteps were becoming more and more audible. Someone was running in their direction.

'You are right. '

Gilles pulled himself up behind the first low wall and glanced towards the gallery. The figure approaching in long strides left no doubt as to his identity.

'Oh shit, here he comes again! He can't forget us for a moment.'

'Is he alone?'

'Yes.'

'So your friend is no longer with... I hope he managed to escape,' she said in a serious tone.

'In the meantime, we will have to deal with his case.'

'Without a weapon it will be difficult.'

'We still have the half crossbow bolt we retrieved from the quiver! '

'Against bullets, it's not much...' Bonnie worried.

'But I don't see a weapon... just the sword actually.'

Bonnie turned off her torch.

They both stuck behind the second low wall, the young woman in the corner, Gilles at her side, his makeshift weapon in his right hand raised ready to strike the colossus. The adrenaline momentarily masked the pain that throbbed along his leg.

The footsteps and splashing stopped.

It was very close.

They heard the sword crunch against the stone.

Their pulse quickened.

Gilles cocked his trembling arm.

The tension rose again.

Then the tip of the sword appeared before his eyes.

He followed it with his eyes as it moved ahead of him.

Gilles was ready.

But just as they were about to face each other, more footsteps were heard in the distance. There seemed to be several of them. There was no doubt about it.

The blade then disappeared.

They heard the colossus turn back, most likely assessing the situation behind his back.

It must have been the perpetrators of the shots exchanged with this madman who were now pursuing him. Gilles hoped that Cyril was in their presence or under cover.

He took advantage of this moment to attack.

It was a golden opportunity to take the lead that might not happen again.

He went around the wall and struck a first sharp blow in the shoulder. He put all his energy and ardor into it. The point, however blunt and rusty, of the bolt sank halfway into the flesh. The colossus immediately let go and the sword fell heavily to the ground. As Gilles pulled out his makeshift weapon, blood spilled. He must have hit a large vein, because a geyser of blood spurted out. But the colossus did not flinch. The young man rushed at his attacker to try to strike him a fatal blow to the neck. The latter narrowly avoided the bloody arrow, then with a swing of his arms, sent Gilles against the low wall who slid to the ground. The colossus threw himself on him and tried to strangle him with his wounded hand. Blood ran down his arm, but this did not prevent him from putting pressure on Gilles' neck.

Bonnie dropped her torch and lunged at the Giant's back, also trying to strangle him to get him to let go. One of the members of the group that was closing in on them shone his torch. The colossus, seeing that he couldn't cope with all these people, reluctantly let go and gave a big kick to get rid of Bonnie who crashed against the back wall. Then he dashed into the unexplored part of the gallery.

Borgia was relieved to see Cyril.

'Pleased to meet you, Mr. de Villiers.'

'Do we know each other?' Cyril asked in surprise, his hand on his head trying to suppress the dizziness that his fall had caused.

'Not yet, but it will be soon. I would have liked to do it under different circumstances, but unfortunately we do not have all the parameters under control. I am Giacomo Borgia, Grand Chancellor of the Order of Malta.'

'What does the Order of Malta have to do with this?'

'It is a very long story. What is certain is that at least two of your ancestors did great things for our order.'

Cyril looked at him, dazed.

'Enough talk, I'll explain everything later. We have to deal with the other neurotic. '

The Italian policeman checked his colleague's pulse.

'Dead!'

'Riposa in pace,' said Borgia, signing. 'Where is Eva?'

'With my friend who is injured. They are in danger. We have to help them,' said Cyril, picking up the gun of the killed carabinieri.

Sensing Borgia's reluctance to do so, he reassured him.

'I know how to use it!'

The new trio set off.

They arrived at the top of the steps well before the young man and did not wait for him. They went straight to the intersection of the two galleries. Immediately they heard a metallic noise that echoed in the long gallery. They entered. Cyril, younger and more athletic, quickly made up for his delay.

Borgia made sure that he stayed behind.

The policeman was at the forefront.

54

**Moresperg
1314**

He had been back at the castle for three weeks and was struggling to sleep. Every night the same images came back to haunt him. That of Grand Master Jacques de Molay, consumed by the flames and exhorting him to achieve the task he had entrusted to him. Each time he woke up with a start, covered in sweat.

With the help of his two companions, he continued to excavate the mound relentlessly while doing other work for the squire. This way he could think of something else. This part of the underground was much rougher than the previous one. The deeper they went, the harder the rock was to work. They cut the steps directly into the stone. Only about fifteen were chiseled. They were only at the beginning. The staircase would be endless. Months passed without anything interfering with the peaceful life in the castle. The choice of location seemed, in retrospect, to be very wise.

As the Grand Master had prophesied on the stake, both King Philip the Fair and Pope Clement had succumbed before the end of the year. The latter as early as April, while the king expired at the end of November. It remained to be seen whether his three sons, on acceding to the throne, would die within the next twelve years, ending the direct line of the Capetians. If so, his curse would prove to be accurate and forever marked with the seal of God.

Beynac was entering his thirty-fifth year, but still looked surprisingly young in contrast to his two companions, only four years older, whose faces, eaten away by an already greying beard and features hardened by the elements, betrayed their age. Their paths within the order had been diametrically opposed. His two comrades had participated in illustrious battles before and after the final fall of Acre. But above all they had taken part in the last crusade organized by Jacques de Molay to try to reconquer the land of the East for the umpteenth time, while Beynac, meanwhile, had remained in Paris, sitting at his desk from morning to night. Few had survived these bitter battles and those who had returned were marked for life by these successive defeats. Both mentally and physically.

The knight's youthful appearance did not go unnoticed by women. The squire's two young daughters, in their twenties, never failed to make eyes at him as soon as they met. He did not care at first. In his heart he remained a Templar despite the official dissolution of the order, with all its constraints. But he had also heard that many of his former companions had returned to civilian life and started families, and had thus renounced the vows they had taken at the time of their induction. Not being insensitive to the charms of the two young ladies himself, his conscience ended up playing tricks on him and came to nag at him day and night, putting aside his nightmares for a while.

Like every evening, after dinner, Beynac went to church for Compline. The autumnal chill was falling fast at the end of October, and an icy breeze blowing from the north accentuated this effect even more that evening. He decided to go back to his room to retrieve his coat given to him by the Earl as a thank you for completing the first underground passage. As he made his way up the narrow spiral staircase, he heard footsteps coming in the opposite direction. Despite the dimness of the place, with candles burning only on the upper floor, he immediately recognized the figure of the overlord's youngest daughter, Odile, illuminated by a candlestick she held at face level. Her blond hair fluttered in the wind and draughts. Her green eyes captivated him at every glance.

Any encounter on the stairs required an effort on both sides. Like the gallant man he was, the Templar Knight was ready to go back down to the lower landing to let her pass, but the latter did not give him the opportunity. She forced her way through, brushing against him as much as she could. He immediately had a sudden movement of retreat placing his back against the central core of the staircase, bumping his lumbar in an iron clamp holding the rope handrail. He took the shock without the slightest sound, so as not to let anything show, but the pain ran down his spine. The narrowness of the steps in the center was such that he was balanced on only a few centimeters of stone. Any deviation would be fatal. He threw his arms back, encircling the rounded stone on either side to hold on and keep some semblance of stability. Deprived of his arms, hands behind his back, the young woman took advantage of the situation and disregarded the conventions and pressed against him. He was trapped and could not do anything without risking falling backwards. Intoxicated by the dizzying scent of lavender water, his heart capsized. He felt Odile's chest rubbing against him. His legs wobbled and he held on to Odile's presence, still clinging to him. Then she surreptitiously brought her full lips to his.

She ran away as soon as the kiss was placed, giggling like a young teenager. He remained motionless for several seconds. This was a first for Beynac. Having joined the order at a very young age, he had never had the opportunity to taste this intoxicating pleasure. Now he had, and the sensation delighted him. He came back to reality. In an extraordinary reflex, he managed to hold on to the rope just before he went down the stairs. He hurriedly retrieved his cloak and went down to the village, his mind still hazy from what had just happened. Odile stared at him out of the corner of her eye for the duration of the mass, a naughty smile on the corner of her lip. He had never felt as uncomfortable as he did that evening and did not dare to look in her direction.

He tried to avoid her for the next few days, but this was impossible. The girl became more and more insistent. A game of hide-and-seek began between the two of them. Lost, his mind tortured by his past, he decided at first to seek advice from the abbot, without revealing his true identity, which would undoubtedly have biased the priest's judgment. The priest had no satisfactory solution to suggest to him. He had to talk to his two companions. Especially as rumors were circulating in the village about them. They had to be silenced as soon as possible.

He decided to gather them in the crypt the next night. It had changed a lot since they arrived. They had completely restored it from floor to ceiling. Black and white tiles, masonry vaults, renovated enfeus. The bones of the previous abbot had been placed there and he had probably done the same with the confrere he had replaced. They had also added a table and chairs. Even if this improvised meeting room in the middle of a necropolis seemed inappropriate, no one would disturb them or hear their discussions. For the time being, the crates remained stored at the back of the room, in a corner, covered with a simple burlap sheet.

They made sure that the abbot was lying down before entering the church. They went around the wooden altarpiece that housed the tabernacle at the back of the choir as if to go into the sacristy and moved the large rush mat on the floor, revealing a trapdoor. By opening it with a small iron utensil that Beynac had specially designed to prevent anyone from opening it, a wooden ladder gave them access to the crypt.

'Does the abbot know about the crypt?'

'There are only three of us for the moment and soon the count,' replied Beynac. 'It was he who took the initiative for the underground passage linking the castle to the church. He doesn't know about the existence of this crypt but he will one day, when the work is finished.'

'Who knows. The fellow might have passed away before we'll finish and before he'd even told anyone...'

The Mystery of the Lost Crypt

'I'd be in favor of strengthening the opening system. A wooden trap door is so quick to open,' said the first mate, looking at the crates. 'And their contents so easily stolen...'

His two friends still didn't know what was in them, although they had their own ideas.

'It's hard to figure out how,' Beynac reflected, stroking his chin with his right hand.

'The system itself is fairly simple to set up. It is the implementation that can be time-consuming depending on the type of materials you have to deal with. In this case stone. It will inevitably take a little longer. In Cyprus I worked on a device of this type, it was a back door that opened when a book in the library was operated.'

'Very good. I was thinking of using the altar. The Count told me that the Emperor Charlemagne himself left it to us during a visit to the region. We would close the current trap door and put the entrance right under the altar by placing a stone staircase.'

'This type of mechanism is extremely large. Ideally, it should always be concealed so that no one has access to it.'

'In that case, we would use the whole part of the crypt between the altar and the current trapdoor and the staircase could lean against a wall that would close off access to the mechanism's chamber,' replied Beynac after a few minutes of reflection.

'Great idea brother!'

Beynac was surprised by the last word. It had been more than seven years since he had been named this way. It was the ideal transition to the main topic of the day.

'We have been so busy since we came here with the construction of these two underground tunnels that we have never had the opportunity to talk in person about our future as Templars. As you know, our order was dissolved by his holiness. All the members who managed to escape and even those found not guilty either joined the Hospitaller order or abandoned their habit altogether, some to start a family.'

'We know all that very well, Amaury. What are you getting at?' asked Jean.

'There's nothing holding you back here. So you are free to do what you want. Stay here or settle elsewhere, return to your respective families. I can't hold you back. No one can hold you back anymore.'

The long silence that followed was edifying.

'You don't have to make a decision in the minute. As I have just explained to you, you can do what you want when you want. It is your personal choice. I want you to know that I will abide by your decision without any ulterior motive or judgment. I myself am in the process of thinking about my future...'

'Have you already made a decision?'

They quickly understood what Beynac was getting at.

'My faith and devotion to our God remain intact. But nothing binds us to our oath and its drastic rules. And then a radical change in our habits would immediately silence the rumors about us.'

'We are not blind. Lady Odile has been circling around you for months. As you yourself said, everyone is now free to make their own choice without the inquisitive eyes of their companions. We have understood and accepted this long ago. We will stick to your decision.'

'I think I'll settle here, start a family, while continuing the mission the Grand Master has given me!'

55

**Marimont-lès-Bénestroff
Saturday May 17th 2014, 5:30**

Karl was heading into the unknown.
He had no idea what was waiting for him further on.
There was complete uncertainty at each low wall that was again flanked across the gallery every hundred meters. Did the tunnel continue behind? Was it a dead end? Had the gallery collapsed as a result of natural landslides or as a consequence of the various major wars in the past?
All these questions were nagging at him. For if this were the case, he would soon be caught and trapped. He no longer had a weapon, unlike his pursuers, and to attempt a final direct hand-to-hand fight would be suicide.
As he passed a fourth defensive wall, he glanced back quickly, confirming his thoughts. At least two shadows were moving at the previous low wall. He was only a hundred meters ahead now. One of the reasons was his wound, which he had had to treat quickly to stop the bleeding.
He started again.
The gallery, which could not be straighter, continued on an almost imperceptible downward slope. But enough to allow water to trickle down into the deep gullies dug on either side of the central path.

The question was where all this water ended up.

The low walls followed one after the other. Karl counted a good ten of them. That is to say a little more than a kilometer already covered.

But one detail intrigued him.

He estimated that he had travelled well over a hundred meters since he had passed the last low wall.

Was the end of the tunnel near?

He stopped his frantic run.

He had expected everything but what was in front of his eyes.

A new staircase descended.

He didn't know how far he could go, as the third step was already flooded... So he was at a dead end.

The heavy rains of the past weeks and months were certainly responsible for this.

He turned his head. A halo of light appeared.

They were approaching.

Karl had to make a choice.

Let yourself be taken in... or take a chance.

He thought no more about it and went down the first steps when he heard a voice shouting 'Halt! '.

Then a bang.

But he was already out of reach.

He had no time to procrastinate.

Karl entered gradually. He had water now up to the hip. The water was still and incredibly attractive, crystal clear. But so cold.

He filled his lungs with air and dove in.

Cyril found Gilles still lying on the ground when they reached him, struggling to take deep breaths of oxygen. Bonnie appeared in turn, holding the back of her head which had hit the wall slightly.

'He's running away. He is unarmed and injured, she says.'

'In avanti,' said Borgia.

The Mystery of the Lost Crypt

The policeman immediately set off in pursuit of the fugitive. Cyril followed him before Borgia could say a word.

'Your friend is really incorrigible! It must be in his genes since his ancestors...' he said to Gilles.

'I would be very curious to hear all this, because at the moment it's doesn't really make sense.'

Borgia asked Bonnie where Pietro was. The Italian's face immediately frowned. So did Gilles'.

'In the crypt. He was killed by that bastard, executed at point-blank range when he had already seriously wounded him, she told him with wet eyes and rage in her heart.'

'His chip seemed to say the opposite earlier.'

'I can confirm what Eva said. Your friend was as cold as the ground I'm lying on right now. He is dead and has been for some time.'

Borgia remained perplexed. His eyes were riveted to his screen. The dot representing Clyde changed from blue to green and back again. According to his application, he was still alive. There had been no system malfunction so far. He was eager to get to the crypt. But first he had to wait for the return of the two hunters who had gone after the Giant.

With the help of Clyde's photo and Interpol's data, Borgia had also learnt a great deal about the fugitive's profile.

The man's name was Karl von Feuchtwangen.

Born in Bavaria in 1972 to a Danish mother and a German father, the Giant, as he was nicknamed, was a former member of the German Federal Intelligence Service specializing in the anti-terrorist branch. With the help of his colleagues, he had dismantled a number of terrorist groups close to Al Qaeda that were planning to carry out attacks on German and French territory. He resigned, or rather was forced to resign, after the terrible attack in the Berlin metro in December 2015, which left twenty dead and a hundred injured. His laxity in monitoring this group had been fatal and, no longer in the odor of sanctity, he had migrated to other climes. He found refuge in the south of France through his numerous contacts. But the most important piece of information in the file for Borgia concerned his personal details. His descendants were all long-time members of the Teutonic Order. This family of Franconian nobility had bequeathed two illustrious representatives to the order. Konrad von Feuchtwangen was the thirteenth Grand Master of the Order, from 1291 to 1296, who had taken part in the Battle of St. John of Acre, the last Crusader stronghold in the Kingdom of Jerusalem, whose defeat by the Muslims forced him to move his headquarters to Venice. The second was Siegfried von Feuchtwangen, who led the order shortly afterwards, from 1303 to 1311. During his reign, he transferred the headquarters from Venice to the fortress of Marienburg in Poland, concerned for their existence following the persecution of the Templars.

Borgia noticed that Karl was apparently still a member of the Teutonic Order. Yet he was currently working for the Hospitaller Order of Jerusalem. There seemed to be no proven link between the two orders. If there was, his multiple informants would have told him.

Did the Teutonic Order know anything about the possible Templar treasure? Did they have any additional information that would allow them to cross-check the information of the Order of St. John? Everything suggested that Karl had infiltrated the order and was acting as an informant for the Teutonic Order.

His capture would surely answer all these questions.

While waiting for Cyril and the Carabiniere to return, Borgia took the opportunity to organize the rescue operation to treat Gilles and repatriate the Carabiniere's body. A brand new hospital belonging to the Order of Malta France had recently opened in the suburbs of Nancy. Borgia could not have hoped for a better way of keeping the matter quiet.

An ambulance was on its way.

Gilles was freezing. The temperature in the tunnel must not have been more than ten degrees Celsius and the multiple passages in the stagnant water of the cavity had wetted his clothes and contributed to his current state of near-hypothermia. It was high time he got out.

Still pondering why, the Giant was there, Borgia heard someone approaching from the back of the gallery. He alerted Gilles and Eva.

All three remained on guard.

Borgia held the butt of his Beretta firmly.

Cyril was still running behind the Italian policeman when they saw the man standing still in the distance. According to his calculations, they had already covered a good kilometer in this underground passage. The carabiniere ordered the fugitive not to move, which he obviously did not. The first bullet went off and ricocheted off the wall. Breathless, they arrived at the place where the colossus had just disappeared almost before their eyes. Before them lay a staircase, submerged from the third step. At the bottom, less than three meters from them and in water disturbed by the stirring of the sediments as it passed, they saw a glow whose intensity was gradually diminishing. The colossus' legs disappeared.

All they could retrieve from him was his black cap floating on the surface, lost while submerging.

'He plunged without knowing what awaits him further,' Cyril said to the Italian.

'Wait until he reappears.'

The best thing to do would have been to wait for him to turn around for lack of air and to pick him up then. But if he managed to emerge further away by finding an exit, then he would escape them for good.

A decision had to be taken quickly.

Cyril didn't want to give him such an opportunity and so he decided to dive in to try and catch him.

The young man took off his jacket and shoes.

He told himself that he had had a good idea the day he had chosen to buy a waterproof headlamp, despite the taunts of his friends. Today, it was finally of use to him.

The water was very cold. Not more than eight to ten degrees. But he didn't hesitate long to get in. Every second counted. He immersed himself up to his chest, breathed in and out three times, then took a bigger gulp of air and disappeared into the water. His heart rate increased rapidly.

Under normal conditions, without stress and in calm, temperate water, he was able to hold his breath for four to five minutes. This was already exceptional. Here the conditions were different. Not only was the water cold, but he was breathless from all the effort he had put into this hellish chase and could hardly catch his breath.

Two parameters that totally changed the situation.

For him, but also for his opponent, who was injured.

Cyril quickly reached the bottom of the staircase, using the imperfections in the vault. The submerged tunnel turned at an angle to the left. Visibility was exceptional in the crystal clear water. Small red shreds were rapidly dispersing in the water, a sign that Karl was indeed injured. He was only five or six meters ahead at the most and was making great strides with both arms and legs, torch in hand. After much effort, Cyril came even closer, greatly helped by the fact that the colossus had stopped swimming. Only three more meters and a hand-to-hand fight was about to begin between the two men.

But Cyril suddenly stopped in his turn.

56

Marimont-lès-Bénestroff
Saturday May 17th 2014, 5:45

Intrigued by the sudden brightness, Karl glanced back and saw with frustration that his pursuers were still at it.

But the disappointment was short-lived, as only the academic seemed mad enough to give chase underwater. It was time to end the manhunt for him.

He swam a few breaststroke and was working out different scenarios when he passed under a wooden arch. The supporting beams, weakened by the high pressure of the vault and the fact that it had been immersed in water for decades or even centuries, were threatening the gallery. He glanced around again and saw that Cyril was rapidly approaching him. This young man seemed to be very resourceful and was as comfortable underwater as he was on land. He had to act.

He pulled with all his strength on one of the two wooden props, pressing his feet against the wall for support. The beam did not resist the German's Herculean strength.

In poor condition, it broke in two.

Everything collapsed like a house of cards.

Surprised himself by the ability with which he had just broken it, Karl did not have time to free his left foot, which remained stuck under the rock and earth.

He couldn't get out of the way.

The Mystery of the Lost Crypt

He struggled like a madman, but nothing helped.

The trap had just closed on him!

The energy expended in extracting himself had significantly reduced his air supply. An endless stream of bubbles was escaping from his mouth. There was not much time left before his lungs were completely empty. He had to get out of this predicament quickly, otherwise he would drown.

Another important fact was that the submerged part of the underground was now in total darkness. He was no longer in possession of the torch which he had dropped during the landslide and which had been swallowed up by the stones. The darkness that enveloped him like a shroud aroused his apprehensions.

He was underwater, blind, with his foot caught between rocks, and soon the air would run out.

But Karl was not a man to give up without trying. He felt around for something that could be used to pry him free from the rocks. He felt nothing on his right, but managed to grab a piece of wood on his left. Hopefully it was strong enough to be of some use. He pushed it forward to try to topple the rocks. But nothing happened. He tried a second time without more success. In a last gasp, he pressed the makeshift lever with all his might, wedging his free foot against a large stone. The pile moved, dislodged, causing a second screech which finally allowed him to free his foot. He had managed to extricate himself. But it was not over yet. The last breath of air he breathed out burned his lungs, immediately extinguished by the long gulp of water that poured in. Panic overcame him.

He took a second swallow.

He had to face the fact that he would not have enough breath to cover the remaining distance.

His lungs filled with water for the third time. He would soon lose consciousness. In desperation, he blindly felt the arch around him.

No result.

Cyril saw the colossus struggling with the beam and understood his intention. In just a fraction of a second, everything collapsed before him.

The shockwave took him back several meters and slammed him against the wall leading to the steps. Running out of air and with the water completely opaque, he turned back.

When he surfaced, he saw that the water level had risen as a result of the landslide. The whole staircase was under water and even several meters of the gallery. The Italian policeman who was waiting for him had not been able to avoid this tsunami and his feet were soaked.

'What happened?' asked the surprised Italian with a strong accent from his native country.

'A collapse... Cannot go through...'

'What about the man?'

'Probably dead.'

Cold and blue-lipped, Cyril put on his jacket and shoes. They left immediately to join the rest of the group.

The return journey seemed interminable.

When they finally passed the last low wall, they were met by Borgia who held them at gunpoint with his Beretta, which he lowered as soon as he recognized them.

'Dove si trova?' he asked the carabiniere.

'Mancante...' replied the latter in disappointment.

'About two kilometers away, we came across a new staircase that was completely flooded. He didn't hesitate for a second and tried his luck by diving down. I followed him, but he was foolish enough to get caught in his own trap.'

'You took a very big risk. You too could have been left behind.'

'After all he did, we couldn't let him escape...'

They all emerged from the bowels of the mound and went under the three tall trees. A light breeze blew through the leaves, scattering here and there patches of mist.

The ambulance arrived shortly afterwards.

The Mystery of the Lost Crypt

But the traditional blue six-pointed star with the staff of Asclepius in its center, with a snake coiled around it, the Star of Life, was here replaced by a white eight-pointed cross in a red shield with 'Ordre de Malte France' inscribed next to it instead of the traditional 'Samu' acronym. This did not fail to arouse curiosity.

'Where did they come from?' laughed Gilles.

'I've warned them,' Borgia replied calmly. 'You will be in good hands, believe me.'

Gilles immediately turned to Cyril, as if to ask his opinion. The latter reassured him by nodding and whispering:

'I think we can trust him...'

'You can tell me about the rest of the puzzle. I can't wait for the epilogue...'

The ambulance left with Gilles and a lifeless body.

Now they had one last problem to solve.

And not the least.

Visconti, armed, held Natasha in the crypt.

Cyril knew how to get in, but it was impossible to get in by surprise. They had no idea how the old man would react if he felt trapped.

Only negotiation could work.

'Aren't you going to call the gendarmes?'

'No. We're dealing with each other for now,' the Grand Commander replied curtly. 'We're not supposed to be here without the approval of the French authorities. I don't want to create any diplomatic incident. If anyone asks, just ignore them.'

'But there is another dead person in the crypt!'

Borgia consulted his phone again.

'He is part of my team. From the Order of Malta. He paces around there and seems as alive as you and I...'

'You are mistaken, I assure you. I don't know who it is, but not your friend, that's for sure!'

'I have always applied the principle of believing only what I see. Like Saint Thomas.'

'And what will you do with Professor Visconti?'

The Mystery of the Lost Crypt

'I can't tell you that. It's an internal matter. A stealth helicopter is sitting at the foot of the hill waiting for us. We'll all be leaving for Rome when it's over.'

'What do you mean 'all'?'

'Let's deal with your friend first, if you don't mind. It's more urgent. I'll tell you all about it later.'

'This must be the fourth time in a few hours that I have heard this sentence. I'm beginning to despair. But you are right, Natasha's fate is more important than anything else.'

They entered the church and Cyril revealed the trapdoor opening to the Grand Chancellor.

As always, a thunderous noise echoed through the church and the floor vibrated. And all had the same fascination in their eyes. Borgia was no exception.

The altar froze at right angles to its original position, and then there was complete silence.

A very worrying silence.

They went down in a line.

Cyril staggered at the vision before him.

Clyde was pacing back and forth across the black and white checkered floor. Phone in hand, he was trying to find a network in every nook and cranny of the crypt. He was unsuccessful. He put it away in his pocket. He leaned against the wall of the crypt, drowning in his thoughts.

A flood of questions overwhelmed him.

And first of all the fate of Eva. He hadn't heard from her for several hours now. What had become of her? Killed by the same bastard? She had warned Borgia who had replied that he would come with reinforcements. Was he here on the spot? What if no one came for them? Not many people knew the entrance to this crypt. In fact, on second thought, only the two young men, apart from the two people present with him, knew about the opening and closing system of the stairs leading to the crypt. If anything were to happen to them, no one would know they were here and would not come looking for them.

All these questions remained unanswered for the time being.

He stared coldly at Visconti, who turned his head away under the insistent gaze. The Dean of Faculty was ashamed and properly shaken by the pallid complexion of the Italian who had returned from the dead. The whole story gave him the shivers every time he thought about it.

But the short moment of meditation was interrupted by a deafening noise. A wave of panic swept over him. He had never before witnessed the opening of the trapdoor directly. And just like the others before him, he thought of an earthquake, before Natasha reassured him. For a while.

'Someone is coming,' she whispered.

The professor felt a surge of hope.

He smiled, which Clyde saw, worried in his turn. Karl was back. He was bound to be surprised to see the Italian alive and well, despite the two bullets he had received in the body, which would not prevent him from killing him a second time, that was certain.

Footsteps followed.

Clyde took up a position behind the professor to protect himself, weapon in hand. He asked Natasha to take refuge in the back of the crypt, in the most remote corner that remained in darkness.

His heartbeat increased.

The first man appeared, pistol in hand.

With their suspicious and surprised looks, neither Clyde nor Visconti seemed to know him.

Then a second one.

57

Marimont-lès-Bénestroff
Saturday May 17th 2014, 5:45

Karl's eyes rolled back.
But he continued to feel the vault. It was his only and last hope. Only a few more seconds and he would be finished. He would end his life here, in this flooded and dark gallery, ignored by all like a hermit at the bottom of a cave.
Like many people, he had read and heard that the film of his life in pictures was flashing before his eyes just before he died. And so it happened. Flashes of the most important moments of his life followed one another frantically. Everything came back to him. His bright childhood in a manor house in the northwest of Germany near the Dutch border to the dark and harsh teenage years in the boarding school where he had been placed with his brother by their father after the tragic death of their mother, the vision of her hanging in the cellar as well as that of his brother a few years later, entering an Airbus A320 bound for Sydney on a one-way trip and never to be seen again. But despite all the hardships he endured during the first twenty years of his life, he clung to life and forged a shell of ron.
This time his end seemed inevitable.
There was no point in fighting any more.

The Mystery of the Lost Crypt

Suddenly his left hand broke through the stone wall into the open air.

In a last instinct of survival, he managed to pull himself up to the spot. The landslide and the tangle of stones had created a cavity large enough for the colossus to get his head above water. A providential pocket of air. Numb from lack of oxygen, shaken by violent spasms, and regurgitating all the water he had swallowed, he had also managed to rest his two feet on a large stone, allowing him to calmly regain the upper hand.

Immersed in the cold water for many minutes now, his limbs were gradually becoming numb. He could no longer feel the tips of his toes. Hypothermia was now threatening him. He had to try to get out as soon as possible. As soon as his breathing became normal again, armed only with his will, he dove back in and continued blindly on his way.

He had taken part in many commando courses around the world, one of which was reputed to be the most difficult, that of the famous British SAS, and he was no stranger to this kind of situation. He had passed the SERE - Survival, Evasion, Resistance and Extraction - tests with flying colors and had achieved exceptional results, placing him among the best results ever achieved, but he would never have been able to join these elite troops because of his German nationality, recruitment being open exclusively to British or Commonwealth forces staff.

Using the vault to progress, he covered, as he had sensed, the same distance before coming upon a new staircase going up and just like the previous one, at right angles to the main gallery. He followed the steps and then miraculously sprang out of the water.

Exhausted, cold, but safe!

Freed from this water prison, he was not yet completely free. In the deep night that surrounded him, he still had to validate his definitive exit ticket or else he would end up buried alive in this gallery, to the delight of vermin, rats and other rodents.

After having partially undressed to wring out his clothes, Karl rubbed his limbs vigorously for a few minutes in an attempt to warm himself up. A short-lived sensation.

The first sneeze came without warning.

The noise increased tenfold. He instinctively stood still, putting all his senses on alert even though there was little chance of being heard. A wall of water and stones separated him from his pursuers.

So there is no reason to worry.

He advanced cautiously in the gallery until he came face to face with a low wall. He was in the same configuration as before. He passed five more when he tripped over a step and fell forward onto what looked like a staircase. He stood up and looked up to see a very faint glow in the total darkness. He climbed up and felt the surface before him. Damp, rotten, worm-eaten wood was the door. He struck a huge blow with his last remaining strength. The boards gave way without resistance, his arm piercing the passage. He didn't hesitate to throw a few more punches, not only to make a hole big enough to get out more easily, but also to let off steam after all the frustration he had suffered. He got out and fell to his knees, sucking in the air greedily. Hard and insensitive as he was, he could not forget that he had just come close to death.

He appreciated this moment of freedom all the more.

Outside, the dense fog that was still present completely obscured the first light of day. This was not to his displeasure. Transi by the damp cold and his wet clothes, the colossus set off in the opposite direction towards the village.

He had just lost another round.

But not the game.

Clyde's face broke into a broad smile as he recognized the Grand Chancellor and lit up at the sight of his teammate.

'Nice to see you all,' Clyde exploded with joy.

'E 'un miracolo,' Bonnie shouted when she saw him.

'You can see that he is not dead! I told you that from the start. My electronic toy never lies.'

At Borgia's words, Bonnie rushed into her partner's arms.

The Mystery of the Lost Crypt

'Come è possibile?' she sobbed.

That was the question on everyone's mind. How could this be?

'E'una lunga storia...' Clyde replied, his eyes misty.

Indeed, his story was atypical, to say the least.

Still in disbelief, Cyril naturally moved towards Natasha who came out of her hiding place. They too were relieved that everything ended well. He was angry at himself for having involved her in this senseless story and would never have forgiven himself if anything had happened to her.

'Where is Gilles?'

'Don't worry. He's fine. Just a few scratches. He was taken care of by an ambulance of the Order of Malta. We'll meet him tomorrow in Nancy on the way back.'

'And the other crazy guy?'

'Where he is, he won't bother us anymore...'

Cyril glared at the teacher with contempt.

'And what will be done with him?'

'We will of course hand him over to the French police. The list of charges is rather long.'

'It's a shame to end up like this... especially for a treasure that, if it turns out, doesn't even exist!'

Clyde untied the old man from his chair. He had tightened the ties so much that the rope had cut deep into the skin of his wrists and his hands had turned purple. The old man complained about this to general indifference.

Clyde turned his attention away for a moment and followed Borgia's gaze as he approached Cyril. Then the old man, in a desperate attempt, lunged at him and tried to grab his gun. A brief tussle ensued when a shot rang out in the crypt.

In the confusion, no one knew who had been hit.

But grimacing with pain, Visconti collapsed to the ground.

The bullet had perforated his lung.

A trickle of blood flowed from his mouth.

'I didn't mean to... He turned the gun on himself and put pressure on my finger!' said Clyde as he turned to the Grand Chancellor, stunned by what he had just witnessed.

They all approached the old man, who muttered a few words with difficulty:

'I'm... sorry... Cyril... I don't know... what came over me... I dedicated half of my life... to trying to find the Templar treasure... and like many I hit a brick wall ... I'm sad to leave... so close to my goal...'

He paused to catch his breath and swallowed, the blood running down his chin.

'Don't speak any more, save your last strength, help will come,' replied the young man, softened by these words.

'I have one last... favor... to ask you...'

'Which one Professor?'

'Find that treasure!' he shouted with a final effort.

His head tilted back and then remained motionless forever.

Cyril closed his eyes.

'But what's the matter with him?' he asked, somewhat confused.

'Perhaps he felt remorse and preferred to end his life rather than be brought to justice and watch his own downfall. After such a career, this illustrious historian and archaeologist must have had too much self-respect to bear the possible mockery and 'what they will say' of his colleagues, Borgia replied.'

'It's a bad way to end. After all he has accomplished. All this for a so-called treasure,' Cyril finished, saddened by the fate of his tutor, who had taught him so much. 'I have a favor to ask of you, Mr. Borgia. To lie about him to the police and to keep quiet about all the evil that was done last night.'

'How can you still have empathy for this old man who would have sacrificed you for his quest?'

'He would never have done it. I'm sure he wouldn't. Probably the other madman, but not him. There was good in him.'

'I'll give you that. We'll skip this final, inglorious episode and tell them that he was killed by his henchman. Everything points to him. And then he's not here to dispute our version.'

'Thank you.'

'Thank you Cyril for all you have done. We are very grateful to you. And while we're on the subject of favors, I also have one to ask of you.'

'If you promise to tell me one day what you told me in the underground.'

'I promise you that. I will invite the three of you to the Order's headquarters in Rome, in the presence of our Grand Master, whom you will meet. He is already very eager to come to know you. And you will hear everything in detail.'

'We gladly accept the invitation,' said Cyril, who was already chomping at the bit. 'Rome is one of the most beautiful playgrounds for budding archaeologists like us. But in the meantime, how can I help you?'

'So, Cyril, do you feel up to finishing this fabulous quest? I don't know if it's going to get us anywhere, but it would be a shame to stop before we get to the bottom of it. And from the feedback I've had, you've done beautifully so far. The puzzle is almost completely solved.'

'It will be a pleasure. We might as well strike while the iron is hot. I would have liked Gilles to be there. And then I cannot refuse the last wish of the deceased. Just give me time to change, because I'm soaked to the skin and cold. Time to get to the lodge and back.'

'Well, we are waiting for you. Be discreet and make sure that no one follows you into the church. It would be embarrassing if someone discovered the entrance to the crypt.'

'I'm coming with you!' protested Natasha.

'Stay here. You're exhausted. I won't be long.'

58

Marimont-lès-Bénestroff
Saturday May 17th 2014, 6am

Cyril hurried back to the lodge and exchanged his dirty, wet clothes for clean, dry ones. The house was as quiet as he had left it a few hours earlier.

He closed the door behind him, took off his muddy shoes and stomped down the corridor to the owners' room. He was shaking. He didn't know if it was the consequences of his time in the water and his soaked clothes or the idea of being confronted by two stiffs in a bed. He wanted to know for sure. Something about the German had seemed suspicious when he had announced that he had got rid of the couple.

His nose tickled. The sneeze that followed was so spontaneous and unpredictable that he scared himself. The first effects of a cold were probably being felt, if not for all the dust and other moulds inhaled in the meantime. The noise echoed throughout the house, enough to wake the dead! He stopped and listened. He heard them grumbling to his relief, 'What are *they doing up on a Saturday at six in the morning? ... It's all right, it's nothing, go back to sleep darling...*'.

He had his answer. A deep sense of relief came over him. Enough people had been injured and killed without adding to the toll. He went upstairs to change and came back down less than five minutes later, with one difference, this time he had his gun with him.

Still reeling from the incidents of the night, he agreed that it was better to take precautions.

The miserable weather was a godsend. Cyril didn't pass anyone on the way back to the church. There was not a soul in sight. One wondered whether every living thing in the village had not fallen under the scythe of the Teutonic colossus.

He hurried up the steps and crept inside. From above he heard Borgia rave about the discovery of the crypt. Worried and wary glances greeted him at the bottom of the stairs, which were soon dispelled.

Although he was still dealing with the sudden death of the dean, the treasure hunt was still on his mind. He was impatient, ready to continue to the delight of Borgia.

Karl brooded over his successive failures on the way back to the house he had taken possession of with Visconti on his arrival in the village. An accumulation of frustration was suffocating him. The task was becoming more difficult. The enemy was more numerous, reinforcements had joined them, and above all they were all armed, which changed the situation, even if he had managed to disable one of them in the underground. They had heard them speaking in Italian. They were probably part of the same team as the couple who had been playing cat-and-mouse with him for a few weeks and whose man he had just coldly shot in the crypt. But a question nagged at him.

What had become of Visconti?

He had left him in charge of the young woman as a hostage. It was difficult to know how things would develop on their side, they had to wonder what he was doing all this time. In the crypt, the chances of achieving his goal were slim, perhaps it was already too late.

Were they still there?

Those who were supporting the three young academics must have had the same objective in mind. And the old man, alone, would be no match for this armada. Would he even have the desire or the necessary guts? Karl doubted it. In any case, he had received very precise orders. He had to get rid of them once the riddle was solved and the treasure was in his possession.

A race against time was underway.

He came out of the forest at the northern end to have the least distance to cover in the open. He passed behind the farmhouse which was opposite the church, crossed the road and arrived directly at his squat where he could finally change and restock his weapons. And it's fair to say that this time he wouldn't be shy about taking the heavy artillery. He grabbed an assault rifle, an AK-47, which he slung over his back, a Gsg Tooled Up machine pistol with a small flashlight under the barrel which he attached to his thigh, and a Beretta 92FS chrome semi-automatic pistol which he kept in his hand.

Dressed all in black, he was ready to fight.

This time his strategy would be quite different.

His pursuers probably thought him dead. He was therefore no longer considered a threat and he was free to do as he pleased. Haste was a poor guide. He had learned that the hard way last night. He would wait patiently for the best moment to fall upon them. He looked towards the church. Visibility was gradually improving in spite of the fog that was still latent. The dawn was breaking, but it was struggling to illuminate the new day.

No one in sight.

None of the villagers had ventured outside yet, not even a car had passed through the village, even though it was frequently used during the week. A real blessing.

Thirty minutes passed when suddenly a shadow crept into the building. Karl would have recognized him under any circumstances. That youngster who had already given him so much trouble was obliterated in his memory.

Cyril.

He would make a point of making him his priority.

Cyril joined the small group in the crypt. They had moved the professor's body to the back and covered it with an old blanket they had found there. He couldn't help but glance at it and felt a twinge of sadness. At the same time, Borgia received a message on his phone. This surprised many people. Strangely enough, his phone seemed to be receiving a signal in the underground, especially since it had been cut off in the whole village.

It came from the Vatican's operational command center. The Grand Chancellor had just been informed that the French police had found the Virgin of Philerme in the hinterland of Nice at the headquarters of the rival order.

Without doubt the best news of the day.

The real treasure had just been found. The other one, the one for which they were there and which was perhaps a fabrication, would only be the icing on the cake if it was proven. This unexpected news cheered up the three members of the order.

'Let's pick up where you left off if you don't mind, Cyril.'

He retrieved the old man's scribbled notes from the table and reread everything from the beginning, explaining to Borgia the various clues that had led them so far. He inserted the sword again in the slot under the table, freeing the access to the tunnel.

The lure of a possible treasure was a thrill for everyone involved. Borgia was no exception to this rule. He seemed to be caught up in the same frenzy as the dean before him. This worried Cyril even more, who gave him a look of apprehension and suspicion. Even if the ambulance that had picked up Gilles had the Order of Malta's coat of arms on each side - which he knew from having seen it in the streets of Nancy and on the internet during his research - and Borgia had a red border with an eight-pointed white cross on his jacket, he could not be reassured as to their real origin. What if all this was just another decoy to fool him and lead them to this possible treasure? He had to remain on his guard. The weapon hidden in his jacket would be his safe-conduct if things got out of hand again.

'What is the next riddle?' asked Borgia.

Cyril's eyes widened as he read the sentence.

'It's really gibberish, it doesn't mean anything...'

'Indeed, I can confirm that at first reading, the beginning seems totally incomprehensible. Can you read it again, please,' he answered.

'From a royal cubit of the Blessed Virgin of St. Luke, Pisano will guide the perfect being beyond the fateful day brought to our Order and last beloved Grand Master. Only his dagger will be able to sink into the mother rock and open the door to the Holy Room, whose breath of God will bring the final punishment to every infidel'.'

Cyril recited it to himself.

Again and again.

He had to admit that he was totally stumped on this last riddle. Certainly the most important if it led to the treasure chamber, but without question the most difficult of all. As he let his gaze wander over the discomfited faces around him, he noticed that he was obviously not the only one in this case. He regretted the absence of Gilles, who had managed to resolve the situation during the previous enigma, and the death of Visconti, who would have been of precious help in this area.

'Let's go step by step, analyzing each part of the sentence,' suggested Borgia. 'First of all, let's try to find out what this royal cubit represents. I have an idea in mind, but it needs to be validated.'

'Why don't we just look up the answer on the internet?'

'I tried, but unfortunately no network seems to be available.'

'Yet you used it,' Cyril questioned him, very suspiciously.

'It's a secure direct line to the Vatican Gendarmerie's operations center. But it's just a phone, nothing else...'

'In this case, try to call someone from your order or from the Vatican! They can help us from a distance.'

'The situation is much more complex than you can imagine. As in all organizations in this world, there are many conflicts of interest within our order. For the time being, no one but us here should know about it. Not even our Grand Master. As for the Vatican, this does not concern them,' he said, a little embarrassed by the presence of the Carabiniere. 'Not yet, I would say. There has been a certain animosity between the Holy See and us for some months, the outcome of which is still very uncertain. There will always be time to talk about it if our research is successful. This future discovery could perhaps tip the balance in our favor...'

'I understand completely... in that case we'll make do with what we have... our brains... and to return to our main subject, this notion of 'royal cubit' is the only one for which I would have an explanation, Cyril replied.'

'We'll start with that,' Borgia reassured him. 'Tell us your idea.'

'The royal cubit comes from the Egyptians. In the time of the Pharaohs, their architects used it as the main measure for building temples and pyramids. It was a digital system that was divided into fingers, palms, equivalent to four fingers, hands, equivalent to five fingers, small yoke, measuring three palms, and large yoke, measuring three and a half palms.'

'Very good. And the royal cubit?'

'It is worth seven palms, or twenty-eight fingers.'

'It's all wonderful, but we're not much further ahead,' the Grand Chancellor was already beginning to get irritated, a sign that he had absolutely no control over the situation.

'Let's say fifty-three centimeters on average. With a variation of more or less one centimeter depending on whether you are before or after the famous reform...'

'All right. I don't think that this difference of one or two centimeters is crucial for the future, but... you can always keep this information in the corner of your mind just in case.'

One could tell from his answers the true nature of Borgia, the man of leadership and decision making that Clyde and Bonnie were used to. Only Cyril, who didn't know him, took a dim view of this exaggerated arrogance. What did he have to gain in this affair in the end? If not to put his life and that of his companions in danger. He then had a thought for his friend Gilles. Was it wise to let him go alone in this ambulance with an eight-pointed cross that came from nowhere? He suddenly felt remorse. After all these adventures, he could no longer trust anyone, except of course his companion.

'So let's start with that. A royal cubit is equal to about fifty-three centimeters. The Blessed Virgin of St. Luke is of course the Virgin of Philerme, the Order of Malta's first icon,' continued Borgia. The picture is said to have been painted by St Luke the Evangelist himself. The most extraordinary thing is that its face would reflect as closely as possible the face of the Blessed Virgin during her mortal life. Precisely this painting, present here in the crypt and which was the passage of the previous enigma.'

'And whose appearance I witnessed. It was she who brought me back to life,' Clyde hastened to add.

At these words, the four Transalpine men made the sign of the cross.

'A miracolo! We will have to inform the Holy Father as soon as we return. This would be the third miracle.'

'Why would a Templar refer to a relic of the Hospitaller order? They've always been antagonistic as far as I know, right?'

'Not quite. For more than two centuries they were, but Popes Nicholas IV, Celestine V and Boniface VIII, in office at the end of the thirteenth century, made repeated attempts to bring the two orders together. Perhaps they felt the wind turning in the East. But without success. Yet the two orders had fought side by side during the battle of St. John of Acre in 1291 and had subsequently grown closer during their exile in Cyprus. Negotiations on a merger had even begun between them, but a majority of the dignitaries of the Order of the Temple refused to accept the explanations of their Grand Master Jacques de Molay and rejected this possible merger. This was a great disservice to them, for the Order was subsequently attacked by the King of France, its members imprisoned and tortured, and then dissolved by the Pope. The other consequence of the dissolution was the passage of all de facto Templar commanderies into the fold of the Hospitallers following a papal bull. The author of this codex may have recognized his errors and joined the order to avoid the same punishment as his brothers. In order for the spirit and assets of the order to survive, it was imperative that some of its members officially broke away from the Temple and joined other organizations across Europe so that it could one day rise from its ashes. Or perhaps he did so with full knowledge of the facts, since he had been in contact with the Hospitallers since their captivity in Cyprus.'

'Seen from this angle, everything would be explained.'

59

Marimont-lès-Bénestroff
Saturday May 17th 2014, 6:15

'And Pisano, who is he? Another member of one of the two orders?' asked Cyril.

'Leonardo Pisano, a famous Italian mathematician who is better known in France as Leonardo of Pisa, but above all Leonardo Fibonacci! He lived between the twelfth and thirteenth centuries.'

'The Fibonacci sequence!' exclaimed Natasha, proud to be able to participate in the debates and to do her bits.

Everyone turned to the young woman, surprised by her sudden intervention.

'It's a sequence of whole numbers in which each one is the sum of the two preceding ones,' Natasha continued, listing about ten terms in the sequence.

0 1 1 2 3 5 8 13 21 34 55 89 144

'And what would be the point of this sequel?' asked Cyril.

Fibonacci published the 'liber abaci' in 1202, in which he explained the Indo-Arabic numbering system that is now used almost worldwide. In the third section, he presents mathematical problems and formulas such as the famous arithmetic sequence, which bears his name, in which he describes the growth of a rabbit population. I won't go into the details, but the bottom line is that each term of this sequence is equal to the sum of the two previous terms. We put 0 and 1 by default and then we get the other terms of the sequence. Zero plus one equals one, one plus one equals two, one plus two equals three, two plus three equals five, three and five equals eight and so on...'

'Okay, we understand the principle, but I wonder what we're going to use it for here...' Cyril asked himself.

'All I can say is that this sequence is directly associated with the golden ratio.'

'What the hell is this,' exclaimed Clyde, who was beginning to lose his footing during the lecture given by the young woman.

'This number has many nicknames, the young woman continued. The number of creation, the number of universal harmony, the number of God, the Creator, the divine proportion, the golden section, the golden proportion. But it is best known as the 'golden ratio' since the twentieth century. Doesn't that remind you of your mathematics classes? It is represented today by the Greek letter phi in honor of the Greek sculptor Phidias who lived, if memory serves, in the fifth century BC. As she spoke, she drew the Greek letter with her finger.'

$$\varphi$$

And continued her explanation.

'It has been used since the dawn of time in many fields. The first traces come from the Temple of Andros in the Bahamian Sea. This golden number, which is worth 1.618 in round figures, was used for the construction of the Parthenon in Athens. Painters such as Nicolas Poussin, Michelangelo, Raphael and Leonardo da Vinci have used this golden ratio in their works such as the Mona Lisa and the Vitruvian Man. Or more recently 'The Sacrament of the Last Supper' by Salvador Dali. It can even be found in nature. This number simply gives the perfect harmony of a form or a construction.'

'And? '

'And each number in the Fibonacci sequence divided by its preceding number tends towards this golden number.'

'Glad to hear it. And so?'

'Well... and so nothing. I'm telling you this in case you need it,' she replied sheepishly and a little offended that no one seemed to understand.

'Thank you for this mine of information, Miss,' Borgia interjected, rubbing his jaw as he thought about what Natasha had just said, she was pleased that someone was showing an interest in her words. 'We'll see if we can use this data. Any idea or suggestion is good to take, my friends.'

'To finish on this subject that seems to fascinate you, the letter phi is perhaps engraved somewhere on a stone, showing the location of another door or anything else related to the room you are looking for...' Natasha ended.

'I must admit I hadn't thought of that. I was lost in your mathematical explanations...' replied Cyril.

'So let us also bear in mind that this Greek symbol may play a role in our future research. Let us now look at the rest of the riddle. Pisano will guide the perfect being beyond the fateful day brought to our Order and last Beloved Grand Master'. The 'last' would certainly refer to Jacques de Molay, the last Grand Master of the Order of the Temple. He had been elected on the twenty-seventh of April 1292 following the early death of Thibaud Gaudin - whose Marshal he was throughout his term of office - who had been elected just six months earlier in October 1291 in Cyprus, where the last Knights Templar and Hospitallers had retreated following the fall of their stronghold at St. John of Acre and the loss of the last Frankish positions in the East. He was arrested in October 1307 along with all the other Templars throughout France on the same day following a missive sent by King Philip the Fair and signed by Pope Clement, whom he had under his thumb. Financially desperate and unable to repay the colossal debt he had incurred with the Order, which had become the world's leading bank, he used the behavioral abuses and above all the heretical practices of the members of the Order as an excuse to seize all the movable and immovable property. Unfortunately for him, he did not get his hands on the treasure of gold coins and precious stones that had been accumulated over nearly two centuries in the East and West. De Molay and all his brothers paid a high price, but despite all the abuse and torture they suffered, they never revealed their secret. He died at the stake on the 18th of March 1314 on the Ile de la Cité in Paris.'

'So 'the fateful day' could correspond to this date. The day of Jacques de Molay's death and therefore of the order itself. Or the eighteenth. But eighteen what?' asked Cyril.

No one answered him this time.

Everyone was focused and thinking.

The minutes were ticking away when Natasha suddenly raised her finger, like the student she still was, letting out a few smiles around her.

'Eureka!'

Karl went through the back of the church and broke into the sacristy. The weight of years had taken its toll and the worm-eaten wooden door had not withstood the assault of the crowbar for long. The work was clean and smooth, barely audible. He entered the choir behind the great tabernacle of the high altar and then approached the access hatch to the crypt. A halo of light came out of it, making the atmosphere in the church almost mystical, the dust suspended in the air forming a real curtain.

He approached as closely as possible and glanced down. A man was standing guard, gun in hand. He had never seen him before. Probably one of the three strangers he had dealt with in the underground. He quickly withdrew his head from the trapdoor opening just as the man turned his head in his direction. Had he seen him? It would seem not. The colossus strained his ear, but not a word came out. He concluded that the guard was alone.

This was a blessing for him.

The simplest and least dangerous way was to lure it out of its lair.

'We are all ears, Natasha.'

'If I remember correctly, the previous riddle was about a royal cubit. Which was about fifty-two centimeters, right Cyril?'

'Yes, it is. Now I see what you are getting at. If we take into account the date of the eighteenth and this measurement, we would then get about nine meters. But... nine from where?'

Everyone looked at each other again, wary.

The carabiniere, who had stayed back at the bottom of the stairs, did not seem to understand a word of what was being said, given his perplexed look.

Clyde suggested rereading the whole riddle, which Cyril undertook as he remained the guarantor of Professor Visconti's notebook. He stopped immediately at the beginning of the sentence. From a royal cubit of the Blessed Virgin of St Luke'.

'It seems to me that the starting point is here. A royal cubit behind the icon of the Virgin of Philerme would represent the hidden stone door, Clyde argued, mimicking the fifty centimeters thickness of his hands.'

'This would suggest that it would take nine meters from the start of the underground. It's as childish as that!' Borgia summarized as he went in without waiting.

The other four followed suit, all surprised by the Grand Chancellor's swiftness. Borgia suddenly stopped at the spot where he calculated the supposed opening would be. It was about a third of the way down the horizontal section between the two staircases leading to the crypt on one side and up the mound on the other. The place had not suffered any apparent damage and was in a perfect state of preservation, unlike the rest.

'So it should be around here if I've counted the nine meters correctly,' he said as he examined the walls with his torch.

'I confirm,' says the academic.

'What does the rest of the riddle say?'

'Only his dagger will be able to sink into the mother rock and open the door to the Holy Room, whose breath of God will bring the final punishment to all infidels,' read Cyril.

'His dagger'? Damn, we missed that one. You two go back into the crypt and see if you can get your hands on it,' Borgia ordered, pointing at Clyde and Bonnie. 'Meanwhile, the three of us will search for the opening. '

'So we have to look for an even smaller slot than the one found on the icon's frame. A notch in a stone or in the mortar, horizontal or vertical,' added Cyril.

The prospecting began.

The Grand Chancellor looked on one side, Cyril and Natasha on the other. The artificial rays of the torches and the irregularities in the wall made the task difficult. Time had taken its toll. The mortar was cracking in many places. It was like looking for a needle in a haystack, because they all looked the same...

The search would prove to be long and arduous.

The accumulated fatigue and the sleepless night made it difficult to concentrate and the eyelids of the participants were heavy.

Clyde and Bonnie returned to the crypt as Borgia had ordered. They had to find the dagger that would allow them to open the passage to the treasure room. When they got there, they immediately noticed that the carabiniere who had been on guard until then had disappeared.

60

**Marimont-lès-Bénestroff
Saturday May 17th 2014, 6:30**

Leaning against the wall opposite the staircase leading to the choir, the Carabiniere could hear the voices of Borgia and Cyril echoing in the gallery.

A metallic noise resounded in the church.

A sound similar to a coin that falls on a tile floor and spins around until it stops on one of its two sides. Then silence.

Intrigued, the Italian policeman went up to have a look.

Only his head and his left forearm holding his Maglite emerged from the darkness. He methodically inspected the interior of the church despite the darkness, but saw nothing unusual. He was about to go back downstairs when he heard the same noise behind the altarpiece again. This time he climbed the last few steps of the staircase and moved towards the source, his gun pointed forward.

'C'è qualcuno?'

The appeal was in vain.

The policeman moved forward when, as he was about to go around the altarpiece, a hand from nowhere grabbed his cocked arm and turned him around, putting his back to the wall. He found himself face to face with a gun fitted with a silencer. He could not retaliate. On command, he immediately dropped his Beretta. His assailant snatched the torch from him and took a few steps back, keeping the pressure of the weapon on his forehead. He did not even have time to show his astonishment at recognizing the face of the man who was threatening him when a faint bang was heard. A bullet lodged in his forehead, the Italian policeman slumped to the folded carpet.

And that's three, the murderer thought.

Clyde and Bonnie took a quick look around the dimly lit corners of the crypt. They were alone. Where could their colleague have gone? There was only silence, interspersed with occasional snatches of muffled voices from the underground. The couple didn't bother any further and assumed that he had gone upstairs to relieve himself or have a cigarette. They had more important things to do at the moment. They searched the burial niches from top to bottom, taking great care not to damage the occupied ones. Respect remained the priority. Especially with the experience Clyde had just had. He now knew that the Madonna of Philerme was watching.

When he reached the grave where he himself had been laid a few hours before, he suddenly recoiled in fear. Stains of his own blood were visible on the floor and the entrance to the tomb. Memories of those moments came back to him like powerful flashes that hit his face. He remembered his presence in the crypt. The German colossus pulling the trigger. Then the burning in his stomach. He was floating in the air, as if levitating. He saw Bonnie crying, the three young men stunned, the colossus and that old man. And then that bright light. Someone appeared and spoke to him. He felt so good. When his inert body on the ground seemed to draw him in, he finally woke up. The pain was gone, no trace of the wounds in his stomach or head.

Bonnie gently approached him to rouse him from his torpor. He took a deep breath and exchanged a look of approval with his teammate. Everything was fine.

But not a single dagger in sight.

The Mystery of the Lost Crypt

Their disappointment was growing.

— Dobbiamo continuare a cercare! he said in a dry tone that surprised his teammate.

Keep searching, again and again.

They both knew that Borgia would be very demanding and that he would not be satisfied with such a failure. Possession of the weapon seemed crucial to the continuation of the puzzle. So they searched frantically in all the smallest recesses of the crypt, but nothing resembled the coveted object. There was only one place left. The entire scree-covered corner of the room. This was their last chance.

The two neon lights of the massive lamp on the table were directed there and they placed their two torches in the lower mortuary niches to provide the best possible illumination of this dark corner. They cleared away the stones one by one and the tattered burial cloth of the buried priest was quickly exposed. At last Clyde lifted the last stone. At the level of the skeleton's skull, he saw that it was split along its entire length. The falling stones had probably hit him in his sleep, killing him instantly.

They lifted what was left of the weathered woollen cloth here and there, but nothing. Inspired, Clyde made a second, slightly less respectful inspection than the first and detected a metallic sound as he stirred the fabric of the right sleeve. He slipped his hand in and pulled out a dagger in as good condition as the sword. In this dry air of constant temperature, the preservation of metal objects was unparalleled.

Bonnie's features lit up.

With patience and perseverance, they had finally managed to get their hands on the object and had to hurry back to the Grand Chancellor. They were heading for the underground when a voice called out to them:

'Halt!'

Both of them turned around, shaken by the sharp voice. Their bodies tensed and their eyes showed disbelief, amazement and horror at the unexpected presence of this man.

'Non è possibile...' said a petrified Clyde.

Bonnie was speechless, on the verge of tears, refusing to believe what she was seeing. Her wobbly legs could no longer support her under the violence of the emotional shock. She staggered and had to hold onto the table to keep from falling.

In front of them, his gun at the ready, stood the German colossus, his eyes reddened, his jaw set, his teeth clenched. Determination pierced his eyes. His thirst for vengeance shone through his whole being.

But the incomprehension was shared.

'You! I did not dream, I killed you. But then who did I kill before? Your twin brother?'

'The question can be returned to you.'

'I must admit I was lucky. I don't know how you managed to get away with two bullets in your body, but I promise you I won't miss you a second time!'

He pointed his gun at him with his finger on the trigger.

Bonnie was terrified. She put her hands in front of her eyes.

Two loud bangs sounded.

She shuddered.

Borgia meticulously analyzed the wall, inch by inch. The smallest cut in the rock or mortar was tested. But each time the blade of the automatic switchblade only went in a centimeter or two at the most.

As the search in the tunnel continued without any convincing results, Cyril suddenly stopped searching and reached out, concentrating on the voices coming from the crypt. A familiar sound had briefly diverted his attention.

'I'll be back,' he said.

The closer he got to the room, the more audible and recognizable the voices became. He had a bad feeling, but didn't dare to believe it. Was it a nightmare? The voice he thought he recognized belonged to a dead man. Could it be that he had escaped? Many inexplicable things were happening tonight. He approached the stone door and peered into the crypt. What he saw confirmed his suspicions. He was not dreaming. It was indeed the German colossus who was facing the Italian couple in the flesh, threatening them with his weapon.

Everything went very fast.

The assailant seemed determined to finish quickly.

Lurking in the shadows of the tunnel and partly hidden by the stone door, Cyril stood ready to intervene, weapon in hand.

He saw the menacing behemoth aiming at Clyde at point blank range. He heard only one word come out of his mouth: 'Goodbye'.

There was no time to hesitate.

He took the initiative and imposed himself just before his opponent fired. The colossus was thrown backwards under the power of Cyril's calibre, letting a bullet escape towards the vault which ricocheted and was lost in the pile of stones. The young man had fired just right, hitting him in the heart. A scarlet bloodstain quickly formed around the lifeless body. As he killed the man, memories of the past flooded back with the same uneasy feeling. Six years had passed since his last mission, when he had shot Taliban.

'This time it's definitely over with him, Cyril said wearily as he entered the crypt to the bewildered and relieved looks of the two Italians, still shaken by this incredible apparition.'

'I'm going to stay here anyway, you never know what else might happen in this place...' Clyde replied, handing him the dagger he had found a few moments earlier.

He picked up the German Colossus' weapon and sat down on a chair. He needed to recover a little from all these emotions.

Bonnie stayed with her partner in the room.

When they heard the two shots, Natasha and Borgia stiffened.

'No! It can't happen again... it will never end,' she whispered with tears in her eyes, terrified. 'I hope nothing has happened to them,' she continued with clasped hands.

The wait became unbearable.

Borgia beckoned her to be quiet and drew her against the wall when at last Cyril reappeared.

The tension subsided, but the nerves remained sore after so many successive emotions. Natasha's face showed occasional red patches on her forehead, a sign of extreme fatigue.

'What happened?' asked Borgia immediately.

'The other madman I thought had drowned managed to get out! It's crazy, he's not human, that guy! But I intervened just before he shot your friends, I iced him once and for all. I hope so... at this point we're not sure of anything. Eva and Pietro stayed with him in the crypt. In case Our Lady decides to give him a second chance too...'

'Well done Cyril. But I doubt very much that she will help such murderers... they are burning in hell!'

'So now we can finally get on with the job with more peace of mind.'

'It's hard to concentrate with all these adventures...'

Indeed, something didn't seem to add up in their calculations. They had examined the walls carefully, but none of the cracks seemed to match their expectations.

They were obviously going about it the wrong way.

61

Marimont-lès-Bénestroff
Saturday May 17th 2014, 6:45

They had to start all over again.
They were bound to have missed a key element.
Borgia took the notebook and shone his torch on it.
'With a royal cubit of the Blessed Virgin of St. Luke, Pisano will guide the perfect being beyond the fateful day brought to our Order and last Beloved Grand Master.' We must have been wrong somewhere...' the Italian muttered. 'Either in our calculations, or perhaps we made the wrong choice of date. Which one did we use before?'
'We started on the eighteenth day of his death and converted it to the royal cubit.'
'This solution seems consistent with the text.'
'Yes, indeed. But we left out some important details,' Natasha added.
'Which ones?' replied the men in chorus.
'The riddle first mentions Pisano. We did not take this into account... then the phrase 'beyond the fateful day brought to our Order'. Again we did not pay attention.'
'Quite right. Carried away by our thirst for discovery and our impatience, we rushed headlong into it. So let's take it from the top...'

The two young men looked at each other. The same thought crossed their minds. Whose fault was it?

The three of them returned to the crypt, with Clyde and Bonnie looking on in amazement.

'Hai trovato qualcosa?' asked Clyde.

'No, we haven't found anything. It even seems that we were wrong in our judgement...' Cyril replied, his voice betraying his weariness and the extreme fatigue accumulated since the beginning of this crazy all-nighter.

He was only hoping for one thing now, to get it over with as quickly as possible. This treasure story was seriously starting to weigh on his shoulders. The motivation was gone.

The lifeless body of the colossus lay on the black and white checkered floor. Natasha immediately turned her head away as she entered the room. Professor Visconti's had already traumatized her enough not to add another. She walked over to the table with her back to the corpses.

'Where is Vittorio?' asked a worried Borgia.

'We don't know,' said Bonnie. 'Out for some fresh air or a cigarette. Should we go check?'

'I asked him to stay here. And with that nutty here, something must have happened. Yes, he may be injured, he may need help. Go ahead, but take care of yourselves. There has been enough death for one day.'

Bonnie took the colossus's gun from his thigh and followed Clyde, who was already climbing.

'So you were saying, Natasha, and rightly so, that several clues have not been taken into account. Let's start again from the beginning, it will be easier. As for the beginning of the sentence, we must be right. The stone door is the equivalent of a royal cubit thick, which puts us well behind the Blessed Virgin of St Luke here,' he said, pointing to the painting.

Cyril nodded.

'Pisano will guide the perfect being beyond the fateful day brought to our Order and last Beloved Grand Master. This is where it gets complicated, apparently. Well, on the face of it, the identities of Pisano and the last Grand Master are not in doubt. They are Leonardo of Pisa, better known as Leonardo Fibonacci, and Jacques de Molay. Is everyone in agreement on this point?'

'That's what makes the most sense to me too,' Cyril replied, and Natasha nodded in agreement.

'This would leave the famous 'fateful day'. Either the date was wrong or the unit of conversion was wrong. The date of his death was the eighteenth of March, the day we have retained as the last day of the order.'

'Is there a date for the official dissolution of the Order by the Vatican or the King of France?'

'Yes, on the twenty-second of March thirteen hundred and twelve, Pope Clement V issued the bull Vox In Excelso ordering the dissolution of the Temple. The goods were granted to the Hospitaller order by the papal bull Ad Providam of the second of May and the fate of the Templars was sealed by the Considerantes Dudum of the sixth of May. There are plenty of dates.'

'We could also remember this date of the twenty-second! Do you see any other important dates?'

As the silence of reflection continued, Borgia had an epiphany.

'And why not the date of the arrest of the Templars? The famous Friday the thirteenth!'

The number immediately ricocheted to Natasha.

'Thirteen! Like the number in the Fibonacci sequence!' she said, listing all the components of the sequence and stopping on the last one.

'Hence the presence of his name in the riddle,' Cyril continued. 'Pisano will guide the perfect being,' he read again.

'Excellent deduction,' said Borgia. 'All that remains is to determine the meaning of the term 'Beyond'.'

'The number following thirteen in the Fibonacci sequence is twenty-one. That would explain the term 'Beyond'. I think we have to take this number into account,' said the young woman.

'And what about the royal cubit?'

'We keep this notion by applying the same calculation as before. I suggest you go and test it! And if we really find ourselves

The Mystery of the Lost Crypt

at an impasse again, then we'll continue, but after a well-deserved rest, suggested the second in command of the Order of Malta.'

The two young lovebirds exchanged a brief glance and both consented.

'This seems to me to be the wisest proposal, yes. The night was, to say the least, restless. I must admit that a little rest would be welcome. So let's give it another go and if we don't succeed, there's always time later.'

'Perfect. So we have to look for ten to eleven meters. Let's go!'

'Do you think he heard what you just said to him?' Natasha asked Cyril as Borgia had already gone into the darkness of the tunnel.

'I doubt it. He seems to think only of that treasure. Like Visconti. I really hope it's worth the bloody treasure and that we don't do all this for nothing.'

'Gilles will curse us if we find out anything.'

'The poor guy. I don't even dare to think about it... well, in the meantime, let's follow him.'

Clyde and Bonnie quickly returned to the crypt.

'Abbiamo trovato Vittorio!' said Clyde.

'E poi?'

'Dead...'

The two carabinieri had paid a heavy price for this quest.

'Take his body down and put it in one of the burial niches. As for us, let's get it over with.'

This new death did not seem to affect the determination of the Grand Chancellor.

The trio went back into the underground, certain that they had all the keys in hand to decipher this piece of enigma. The frenzy of research did not go very far from the first one.

Less than fifteen minutes later, there was an explosion of joy. Borgia had obviously found it.

He pointed to a regular horizontal opening between two stones, in place of the mortar, about eight to ten centimeters wide.

Cyril approached and cleaned the top stone with his hand. A sign quickly appeared.

A letter Phi was engraved in the rock!

'The Golden Number!' exclaimed Natasha.

There was no longer any doubt. They had just found the opening to the room.

'Time for the truth, my children!'

Borgia thrust the blade in. But only halfway through, Cyril shouted:

'Stop it! Don't go any further!'

'What is it?' asked Borgia, frightened by the young man's sudden intervention.

'Remember the end of the riddle. Only his dagger will be able to sink into the mother rock and open the door to the Holy Room, whose breath of God will bring the final punishment to every infidel'.' He emphasized the last words by repeating them several times. 'Whose breath of God will bring the final punishment to every infidel'!'

'Something is bound to happen when the passageway opens!'

'You are right Cyril. But you didn't really know what to expect either, for the crypt, and yet there was no problem. Hopefully the mechanism is the same.'

'Or not. As I read this sentence, I was reminded earlier of the writings of the abbot who officiated in this parish before the First World War. I had been able to read the last few pages before the behemoth took them from our flat.'

'Get to the point Cyril, please.'

'It stated that two French soldiers had passed through his house a few hours before the official outbreak of hostilities in the First World War, they were scouts, I think. And it seems that they had found, by the greatest of chance, the opening of this treasure room.'

'But how could they have found that opening? And with what dagger?'

'Obviously the door to the treasure room must have been ajar, allowing them to force it open. The mechanism must have reset itself at that point and acted as if it had been closed. Finally, what is most important here is that the abbot wrote how the man who first entered the passageway went into convulsions, died very quickly and his comrade-in-arms who had returned to seek help from the cleric was also taken by madness before he was killed by a German patrol alerted by the screams.'

'Malaise. Convulsions. Delirium. Symptoms most likely caused by a gas. Many plants, minerals, and various liquids can be highly toxic, even deadly. Their uses and harms have been known to man since antiquity. Lead, mercury, carbon monoxide, even hemp or spotted hemlock. There is a plethora of them. Especially since the Templars competed in ingenuity in all areas.'

'There are accounts of a pungent smell.'

'A pungent smell you say? A nod to the defeat of St. John of Acre... very clever! Let's see, it could be sulphur, in the form of hydrogen sulphide. This gas can be found in nature, it comes from the decomposition of organic waste accumulated in very confined places. In wells or septic tanks. It has a characteristic rotten egg smell. And I can confirm that it is deadly!'

'So opening a hatch or a door would release a gas at the same time, right? We'd need masks to get in safely.'

'Unfortunately I don't have any on me. Not the kind of paraphernalia you'd think of,' Borgia quipped.

'Wouldn't it be better to wait to get some? What's the point of taking foolish risks?'

Borgia did not give him time to answer.

'If the mechanism was already opened a hundred years ago, a lot of this gas must have been released then. And in that case I doubt that the pocket still contains much.'

'Yes, well, there's a lot of uncertainty in what you're saying... what if this gas was produced naturally? The pocket would be constantly regenerating.'

'In that case, I propose to go first. I will be the guinea pig. So it's a done deal.'

Borgia pushed in the rest of the dagger.

And just as with the door in the crypt, there was a distinct clanking sound followed by a dull rumbling that made the whole underground vibrate. Anxiously, the three occupants had only one fear left, to be buried alive if these vibrations caused a cave-in.

Slowly a passageway opened up.

The excitement reached its peak.

Borgia, for his part, almost fainted.

But their adrenaline surged when, with a sudden jolt, the vault at the foot of the huge staircase leading to the ancient castle collapsed. What they had feared a few moments earlier had suddenly happened. All three of them rushed towards the crypt. It was the only way to find refuge.

A cloud of dust billowed throughout the tunnel and crypt before they closed the hatch. They waited for the cloud to partially dissipate and then returned to the gallery to assess the extent of the damage. At the bottom, the passageway disappeared entirely, blocked by large stones and mixed earth. There was only one alternative now for them to reach the surface, the crypt.

The new passageway had only opened up about twenty centimeters. Not enough to slip through.

Borgia pressed the handle of the dagger to try to restart the device, but nothing happened.

'Help me push, we'll try to open it up a bit more. If two soldiers succeeded, there's no reason why we can't.'

After much effort and the fear of another collapse, they managed to move it another ten centimeters or so, allowing them to finally squeeze inside.

As agreed, the Grand Chancellor went first.

The Mystery of the Lost Crypt

62

Marimont-lès-Bénestroff
Saturday May 17th 2014, 7am

Borgia disappeared behind the heavy stone door.
'There is no immediate smell of sulphur! No headaches or spasms. Miracle, I'm still alive,' he joked after a few minutes alone. 'I think you can come!'
His voice was drifting away.
He was already taking the opportunity to visit the place.
Curiosity prompted Natasha and Cyril to enter the cavity in spite of the potential danger still present.
The torch lights were beginning to show signs of weakness and the greatly reduced halos of light gave the room an almost spectral appearance, offering only a thin and timid visibility.
Cyril shone his lamp over the entrance. The ceiling height of the room was the same as that of the underground passage. An iron grate about fifteen centimeters thick was positioned between the opening and the vault.
'The gas must come out of here!'
'Our luck must simply lie in the fact that the opening mechanism has seized up. Let's be vigilant! It could reopen at any moment.'
He swept his torch across the wall to his left.

The Mystery of the Lost Crypt

A mummy appeared, sitting on the ground, leaning against a large bag. Its jaw was wide open and clenched, showing the horrible agony it must have endured.

Natasha screamed in fright.

Cyril approached and saw more clearly the discarded military clothing the corpse was wearing as well as a pack and a rifle.

'The French soldier! This must surely be the one the priest was talking about.'

He knelt down and looked at the small metal plate around the skeleton's neck. He deciphered it with great difficulty and read aloud: 'Jean Lestrades - 26/11/1889 - $2^{\text{ème}}$ army'.

'Yes, it's him,' he confirmed to Natasha.

'Come here,' Borgia said suddenly.

Further on, six large wooden crates, stacked in piles, lined the entire back of the room and were covered with burlap.

'I can't believe it... Children, we may have just found the Templar treasure! Or at least a part of it... This treasure so coveted for eight centuries and which has fueled all possible and imaginable rumors.'

'Let's maybe wait and see what's inside these boxes before we claim victory, right?'

'You are right. But we have to admit that the legend handed down from generation to generation in this village seems to be true! At least for the underground passage that connected the old castle. But surely they had no idea that the castle was connected to the church via this crypt.'

'All this is really incredible...'

'Incredible is really the right word... says Natasha, thinking about Clyde and his coming back from the dead.'

'Well, let's try to clear the top crates to inspect each one.'

Each of the large trunks had six large handles around the perimeter, four on the sides, two each at the front and rear. On the smaller ones only two in total.

The question was whether they had stood the test of time. After a quick inspection, they seemed to be robust and in very good condition. As the boxes were not identical in size, they were positioned in descending order, in the form of a pyramid, so that the larger ones could support the smaller ones.

This configuration was beneficial to them.

They climbed up the ends of the ones on the ground so that they could get a better grip on the higher ones. But the weight of the crate soon became a problem. Cyril didn't seem to have any trouble lifting it, but Borgia struggled.

'Damn, I can't do it,' he lamented. 'I didn't expect it to be so heavy. It must be full of lead, I can't see any other explanation.'

'Let's look for Pietro in the crypt. He can give us a hand.'

Natasha took on the task.

The three of them made everything easier. They took down the two smaller crates and then took care of the two medium ones. They were all lined up on the floor side by side. The configuration was more like a coffin than a chest. A good way to go unnoticed when transporting them. The lids were so well sealed that they did not yield to the pressure of their hands or feet, not even if one of them fell off while being moved. They had to find another way if they were to satisfy their thirst for curiosity. The dagger they had used to open the passage was still in place in the slot and they did not want to touch it for fear of triggering the door's closing mechanism or the spread of a possible gas. The same applied to the sword that had been inserted into the slot in the Madonna's picture.

Another solution had to be found.

They looked around the room for a tool that could be used as a lever. Cyril had an idea. He approached the soldier's skeleton and grabbed his bayonet, well aware that by doing so he was desecrating this sepulchre, thus abusing a century-old piece.

But great evils require great means.

It would fit perfectly.

'Well done young man!'

Borgia let him. Once again he was no match for the strength of the former soldier.

Cyril pushed the full length of the spike into a gap and pressed for leverage. The wood cracked. He repeated the operation a good twenty times all around the box at regular intervals, insisting on the edges of the nails that sealed the lid. This repetitive work was exhausting, but he finally managed to get the first large box. Once the lid was slightly loose from the rest, the five of them, with Bonnie also joining them, worked their fingers into the gap and pulled with all their might.

The lid finally gave way.

They laid him against one of the walls.

Their hearts were pounding.

After all these adventures, they were finally going to discover the contents of these almost thousand-year-old boxes...

But before they had time to look inside, there was a roar. All eyes and torches were directed towards the entrance.

The stone door swung open.

'What's going on?' panicked Natasha.

While everyone feared that the stone door would close, fortunately the opposite happened.

'Look, the door keeps opening. The opening mechanism has probably unlocked itself,' Borgia sighed with relief.

More fear than harm...

But something immediately intrigued Cyril.

'If I were you, I wouldn't be so quick to rejoice,' said the young man, pointing his beam of light over the door. 'If it opens fully, we'll probably be asphyxiated by the gases that will be released in a short time. If we smell anything suspicious, we'll have to get out of here immediately...'

The Grand Chancellor had obscured it. His face hardened.

Clyde approached it and put his hand in front of the iron gate.

Fortunately, nothing happened. No gas seemed to be spreading through the room at the moment. Nor was there any specific smell to report. Borgia asked Clyde to stay near the entrance. He would be the guinea pig. As with the door, there could still be a slight delay in activating the mechanism for releasing these toxic fumes.

'Let's always be vigilant,' says Cyril. 'These old gears seem to be getting the better of us... and the underground is in very bad shape. I don't know if it's safe to stay here any longer. There could still be more cave-ins and we could be buried for good. Especially as no one knows we are here.'

'Let's make haste, then,q' said Borgia hastily.

They turned their attention back to the crates. They were surprised when they inspected the contents of the first box they had just opened.

By clearing away some straw, Cyril uncovered the first pin. Then others.

'Look, skittles! It's incredible. So the legend was true!'

He took one in his hands. Its lightness surprised him at once. He slammed his fist into the object. The sound was characteristic.

The initial joy of the discovery was soon replaced by a huge disappointment. If the legend spread in this hamlet seemed to be confirmed once again with the presence of skittles in the chest, this first one was made of wood and not of gold. Its lightness left no room for doubt. The surface was covered with a vulgar, faded yellowish paint.

Borgia frantically lifted several more, but the result was the same. He clattered them together and still made the same damned noise. He even threw one against the wall, disregarding its unusual archaeological value. It broke into several pieces. And there was nothing inside.

Wood, nothing but wood...

'It's not possible... such heavy boxes for simple wooden skittles! So this is the famous Templar treasure? Mere entertainment!' he shouted in disappointment, revealing yet another side of his character that no one had suspected until then.

He hurriedly opened the other crate of the same size, while the rest of the group looked on in amazement and helplessness. But the result was the same. Dozens of roughly yellowed wooden skittles surrounded by a few pieces of straw still lined the box. Borgia then moved on to the other two intermediate-sized crates. In these, no skittles, but large round balls, still made of wood, painted in black or red.

'Logical... if there are skittles, there must also be the balls that go with them! The fodder cushioned the shock this time. I had so hoped to find something...'

'Find something'? But you're joking, I hope,' Natasha said. But It's the case, open your eyes! This altar dating from the Carolingian era, this exceptional crypt with the abbot's notebooks and the old codices, a Templar sword and dagger, a painting of the Virgin of Philerme that must be nearly eight hundred years old. And let's not forget the miracle that occurred with the apparition of the Virgin and the resurrection of your friend. Not to mention these ancient skittles which are, or rather were for the most part - Natasha lowered her gaze to the ground towards the skittles pulverized against the wall by Borgia - real archaeological gems and also confirm the truth of the equally ancestral rumor of their presence in this motte castrale. Personally, I think it is a source of pride to have discovered all these treasures.'

At first astonished, then stung by the young woman's tone, Borgia pulled himself together and finally resigned himself to it.

'You are entirely right in substance. It was stupid of me to focus on a purely pecuniary treasure.'

But Cyril was not satisfied with this result. Borgia's sentence had intrigued him. The wooden crates, thick and strong as they were, should have weighed much less than that with their current container.

'Wait... I think there's more in those boxes...' said the young man suddenly.

63

Marimont-lès-Bénestroff
Saturday May 17th 2014, 7:15

Cyril was not convinced by this half-discovery which left everyone wanting more. He had learned at least one thing from the late Visconti. Investigate to the end and only stop looking once all the leads have been analyzed and explored.

While Borgia was still leaning against the wall, feeling the pinch, Cyril took turns inspecting the inside of the crates. One detail intrigued him about all six crates. The bottom seemed to be systematically raised from the ground by about ten centimeters. Either these boxes had been found in a hurry and therefore their size was of little use, which could explain why this thickness of wood was absolutely inappropriate for its contents, or they contained another secret.

'I'm pretty sure these boxes all have false floors!' he muttered, still concentrating on his study.

'Did you say something, Cyril?' asked Borgia.

'I was saying that the bottom of these boxes could contain a cache. The height of the boxes seems far too suspicious.'

Borgia, interested, approached the young man to verify this hypothesis.

'Take a look. Between the inner plank and the floor, there would be an overhang of at least ten centimeters. You can't see anything from the outside. If the bottom was reinforced, I think a second, much thicker board would have been nailed to the first. Here we are dealing with a false floor that could house a cache,' the academic analyzed.

'Indeed, the explanation seems plausible!'

The dignitary of the Order of Malta was filled with hope.

They emptied one of the boxes completely. The intermediate one. This time Natasha took command of the operations, taking good care of its contents.

As they tapped on the wooded background several times in different places, they noticed that the board reflected different tones. Borgia smiled.

'It sounds hollow at times. So there is a gap between the two boards...'

'Yes, and these laths are nailed at the ends as well as in the middle. This would prove that a double bottom has been added.'

Cyril took up the bayonet and tried to free the two boards. Luckily, many of the nail heads were sticking out slightly and he was able to get the blade underneath to remove them. They cleared the first board by forcing the last nails that could not be removed.

They revealed, as Cyril had guessed, a compartment covered with a burlap cloth that covered the entire surface. Borgia withdrew it with a feverish hand, curious to discover what lay beneath.

The double bottom was filled with cotton cloths, yellowed with age, rolled into a tubular shape ten centimeters wide and thirty centimeters long. These long sausages of cloth were stuck together over the whole surface. Extrapolating the part still hidden, but which represented the same surface as the one exposed, and according to the size of the box of about one meter by two, their number must have been close to one hundred.

'What's this?' said Natasha.

'We will soon find out...'

Borgia took one.

He didn't expect such a weight.

The Mystery of the Lost Crypt

'Now I understand the weight of the case better by weighing even one of these samples.'

He handled it as gently as if he had held a newborn baby in the palm of his hands and then placed it on the board still in place. A far cry from the fate he had reserved for the wooden skittle.

As the cloth was unrolled, its contents were revealed, despite the dim light of the dying torches.

All five were amazed.

The unfolded cloth revealed a line of coins.

Borgia took one of them.

'Extraordinary! These are silver denarii stamped with the cross pattée and in an exceptional state of preservation,' said Borgia, completely charmed by this discovery. 'If all the tea towels contain the same number of coins as this one, extrapolating, there are no less than... thirty thousand silver coins contained in this one box! Do you realize what that means?'

'And there are five more boxes...' muttered Cyril.

The same operation was carried out with the other box of identical size. They removed one of the two boards and were confronted with the same configuration, namely a line of carefully rolled tea towels.

This time it was Cyril's turn to check one.

What he uncovered was even more extraordinary.

They were still coins, in the same number, but this time in gold and not in silver.

'Tell me I'm dreaming,' he cried. 'I have never seen so many gold coins!'

'I must confess that I am in the same situation as you...replied Borgia who was not far from syncope.'

'There are millions of them!' added Natasha, whose eyes sparkled.

'Most certainly. Not to mention what might be in the other four boxes. I suggest we check it out without further ado. We might as well enjoy ourselves. After all, we've earned it, it seems to me,' added Cyril.

No one contradicted him. And for good reason, after these first two cases, everyone was eager to find out what was hidden in the others.

There was a dull roar again and they felt the ground shake beneath their feet. The whole area seemed unstable. Successive wars with their share of bombs had weakened the whole underground structure and the archaic access mechanisms, put to the test the night before, only amplified this phenomenon of insecurity.

'Let's get out of here as quickly as possible...' said Natasha, not feeling very reassured.

They quickly proceeded to open the two larger boxes. In one of them, they discovered a panoply of jewelry and various objects made of gold and silver. Rings, signet rings, necklaces, bracelets, but also dishes, cutlery and other decorative objects. The second was filled with documents and writings, mostly bills of exchange not yet honored.

'Do you have any idea what these documents contain?'

'The Templars were, for some, the first to introduce the bill of exchange system, although this is strongly disputed by others who claim that the system was used by tribes long before them. When it was first introduced, it only concerned pilgrims who, wanting to travel to the East, deposited a sum of money in one of the Templar commanderies in Europe and collected it in another in the East on arrival, or vice versa. This allowed them to travel with the bare minimum and thus avoid being targeted by brigands along their journey.'

'Very ingenious, these Templars...'

'How do you think they amassed such a fortune? They lent huge sums to the kings of Europe for their crusades and other wars. And at the same time, they made people envious. Making them disappear eliminated their debts de facto.'

'But I had always read that they were not supposed to profit by receiving any interest on the various services provided to the pilgrims, according to the laws dictated by the Old Testament, namely *You shall not charge your brother any interest for money or food or anything that lends itself to interest.*'

'You are absolutely right, Natasha, but the operating costs of the Order were also colossal and the commanderies alone were not enough to meet their needs. They not only protected pilgrims, but also took part in all the battles and crusades, paid the ransoms of kings taken prisoner... and for all this, they had to circumvent these laws. Given that this money benefited the whole of Europe, I doubt that any reproach was made to them during their trial.'

'There are surely gems in all these documents. Historians will be delighted!'

Borgia ignored this last remark.

He did not want this discussion to become a conflict of interest. In his view, these documents were the property of the Order of Malta, since all the Templars' assets had been transferred to the Hospitallers, and therefore to the Vatican. And in this case, he doubted that the Holy See would allow free access to these papers. They would, as always, be dutifully filed in the Vatican's confidential archives. Few people had access to them and few authorizations to access them were granted.

Then it was the turn of the two smaller crates to be checked.

Leather purses were lined up side by side over half the floor. More than thirty of them in plain view. Borgia took hold of one of them and untied the cord.

He could not believe his eyes.

This discovery was even more striking.

Gems of all colors and sizes. Diamonds, sapphires, emeralds, amethysts and pearls were jumbled together. He took a handful and showed it to the others. Some of the stones were worked, while others were still in their raw state.

'All these stones!' said Natasha.

'In the Middle Ages, people believed in the powers of precious stones. They attributed to them both medicinal and... how shall I put it... mysterious, not to say magical, virtues! For example, the diamond is the stone of invincibility, the emerald of vision and the ruby of love.'

'And when you see the price of these stones nowadays...' she lamented.

On the other half, they again discovered a series of neatly folded cotton cloths, still in the same tubular shape. But when Cyril checked the contents of one of them, the astonishment was still total. A long, thin gold bar weighing between four and five kilos each and stamped with the cross pattée.

'And there are a good ten in all! What could be more beautiful in the last chest? Apart from the chalice of Christ, I don't know...' Cyril ironically asked.

'Who knows... we can expect anything now. The legend of the golden skittles has just been verified, so why not the Holy Grail,' smiled the Grand Chancellor.

They opened the last false floor of the box.

Unlike the others, the cache in the false floor was much deeper. This made it possible to accommodate larger objects. A layer of straw lined the top, then a string of tea towels.

'The objects hidden there must be fragile to have taken so many precautions,' commented Borgia as he cleared the largest piece of linen. 'God... no... don't tell me that's...'

64

**Moresperg
November 1320**

Beynac was playing with his son in the snowy courtyard of the castle under the tender gaze of his wife, Odile, pregnant with their second child. They had married five years earlier with the consent of the count, who died shortly afterwards without having had the chance to meet his grandchildren. Odile's older sister was married to the Duke of Lorraine's brother and had not lived in the castle for some years. The count therefore left it to his only other child, Odile, during his lifetime.

His decision to detach himself from the obligations of the Temple order had not caused any problems of conscience to his two companions and was even welcomed as a relief. There was no question of renunciation, their piety remaining intact, but they aspired to more flexibility and comfort as they grew older. However, each of his friends met with a tragic fate. Jean had been injured in an unfortunate hunting accident and died a few days later, but not without fighting valiantly against adversity. He left in peace, proud of what he had achieved alongside his companions. For his part, Guillaume married one of Odile's ladies-in-waiting, but died the previous winter of a bad flu. The steles were erected side by side at the back of the church, and

The Mystery of the Lost Crypt

Beynac later stored their bones in the crypt, wrapped in monk's robes. Their presence was necessary after all they had achieved.

Life was peaceful in the Lorraine region. Beynac was able to complete the mission that the Grand Master of the Order had entrusted to him while taking over the management of the seigniorial domain. There was only one step left to complete his work. The very last.

At the dawn of his fifties, still in full possession of his means, Beynac could not wait any longer before starting his journey to Rhodes. Once this final step had been taken, he would finally be able to devote himself fully to his family life. He had set a date. He would leave the following spring. The winters were harsh in these parts, especially this year, with storms much more frequent in the Mediterranean. There was no point in taking unnecessary risks, especially not in his position. As the roads to Marseille were infested with brigands ready to cut throats to rob merchants and travellers, Beynac would be escorted by two soldiers from the castle garrison. This decision alleviated his wife's anxiety somewhat.

The choice of Rhodes was not random. After their withdrawal to the island of Cyprus with the Templars following the fall of Acre, the Hospitallers had received permission from Pope Clement V to arm ships, without the permission of the King of Cyprus, thus increasing their rivalry. Their departure became a necessity and they conquered the island of Rhodes around 1310 where they established their new headquarters and created the first hospital on the island. It was also at this time that they began their hegemony at sea by practicing race warfare.

The winter was interminable and even harsher than the previous year. The former Templar even had to postpone his departure twice and it was not until the beginning of May that he was finally able to set off. A few months earlier, he had gone to the Saint Jean du Vieil-Aître Hospitaller Commandery in Nancy

The Mystery of the Lost Crypt

to ask the Commander, Brother Aubry, if it was possible for them to make the journey in an Order ship. This was immediately accepted. A galleon would be waiting for them in the port of Genoa on June 5th. They could not afford to delay. Time was of the essence if they did not want to miss the boat.

The passes of the Alps made inaccessible by the abundant snow, they bordered the valley of the Rhone to Marseilles then followed the coast to Genoa. A few skirmishes cost them precious time and they arrived just the day before departure. Their safe-conduct, signed by the commander of Nancy, allowed them to move about in complete peace and to take shelter at night in other commanderies of the order.

The glorious day had arrived.

The galleon was anchored at one of the harbor quays and the men were finishing loading food and horses. It was rumored that chests full of gold had been unloaded a few days earlier. It was the same as every time a ship of the order docked in a port.

Beynac presented himself to the ship's captain accompanied by his two soldiers. He handed him the letter. This safe-conduct allowed the three of them to sleep in a cabin close to the captain's. This was a very welcome luxury, as it meant that they did not have to share their bed with the rest of the crew in the stench and noise of the hold. The calm of the first day at sea allowed the soldiers from Lorraine to gently familiarize themselves with the marine elements. But it was short-lived. The very next day the storm reminded them of the harsh reality of life on board a ship. Three to four meters high waves were enough to make them sick for the rest of the voyage, under Beynac's amused and compassionate gaze. After a few stops in other ports and as many days at sea, they arrived at their destination, the port of Rhodes, thus ending their ordeal. The wet and mild winter period in these parts was coming to an end, giving way to pleasant weather before the dry heat of summer.

The Hospitallers had taken possession of the island a few years earlier at the expense of the Byzantines, who had themselves driven out the Genoese fifty years earlier, and were continuing to fortify the city. The Saracens were only a few cables away and this last bulwark of Christianity had to be dearly defended, which was the task of Helion de Villeneuve, who had been elected twenty-sixth Grand Master of the Hospitallers of the Order of St John of Jerusalem the previous year with the support of Pope John XXII. He was to consolidate their position in the region by strengthening their domination over the Aegean Sea while countering Saracen ambitions.

Having just disembarked and strolling through the streets of the city, Beynac instantly recalled the few years he had spent in Cyprus blackening the pages of the order's main codex on beautiful, sunny, peaceful days in the shade of the maritime pines. The light breeze carried here and there the scent of flowers and spices. He closed his eyes and breathed in deeply to better enjoy the sweet Mediterranean aromas.

Rhodes was in the midst of a major redevelopment and life was bustling in the capital. For the past three months, ships had been pouring in their steady stream of western settlers as well as Genoese and Venetian merchants to increase the population that had dwindled to nothing during the years of the island's conquest. The city walls were strengthened and the buildings renovated, built all over the island, in order to transform it into a gigantic fortress. The Hospitallers, who had just firmly established their position in the region thanks to the final victory of the great preceptor Albert of Schwarzburg against some twenty Turkish ships, had plenty of room to grow.

Renovation and expansion of the ancient Byzantine citadel built on the city's acropolis had just begun, to become the grand master's palace. A modest part of it was already habitable and the three men were invited to it. After a restful night, Beynac was received by Hélion de Villeneuve. At no time, not even during their tête-à-tête, did Beynac reveal the primary reason for his presence here. He was not yet ready. He could not wipe out two centuries of animosity between the two orders with a magic wand. Time would surely allow it. But it was still too early today.

After a complete tour of the city, the following days were devoted to visiting the island, between citadels and holy places. The Grand Master, who wanted to see for himself the progress of the various works, honored him with his presence.

They first went to the monastery of Mount Phileremos, dedicated to the Virgin Mary, to pray. The monastery had been enlarged and embellished. On one side of the monastery stood a large eight-pointed stone cross, the cross of the order. The Grand Master entered the chapel with Beynac.

'It was here that our Blessed Mother appeared to a desperate man who had climbed the hill, determined to end his life in the ruins of an ancient Greek temple. Then she appeared radiant with light and persuaded him by her grace and gentle smile to renounce his plan and enter into penance. Since then, the chapel has been erected in this holy place. This icon was placed here three centuries earlier. The date of the apparition is highly symbolic for us as it took place on October 13th, the same day as the feast of our Blessed Brother Gerard, founder of the Order.'

'And where does it come from?'

'The ancients report that the icon came from the monastery of Saint John the Baptist in Trullo in Constantinople. At that time, shortly after the coronation of Emperor Charlemagne, Pope Leo III was fighting the iconoclasm of some Byzantine bishops. To protect it, they transferred it here. It is said to have been painted in Jerusalem by Luke the Evangelist!'

'Saint-Luc himself? That's extraordinary,' replied Beynac, signing himself.

'It is considered miraculous. I believe it is the greatest treasure we can take from this earth. I don't know what will happen to the order in future years, especially after what happened to the Order of the Temple, but whatever happens, this icon will accompany us wherever we go!'

This sentence was like an illumination for Beynac.

He had just found the solution to his dilemma.

Beynac waited until everyone was fast asleep. He sneaked out of his room where his two traveling companions were sleeping undisturbed, passed the grand master's room, whose loud snores could be heard even through the heavy door, and then slipped away into the night.

The two large holm oaks on either side of the entrance to the chapel evoke guardians, giants, protecting the entrance or two gods. Probably a historical and mystical connotation to remind us that the ancient city of Lalyssos and the temple dedicated to the goddess Athena stood here in ancient times.

At night, the effect was accentuated.

Beynac had feared for a moment that the door was locked, but fortunately it was not. He entered the sanctuary and locked it behind him. Several candles were lit permanently at different points and he did not need to use the candle he had brought with him. The icon of Our Lady was at the wooden iconostasis on the left. He unhooked it and walked to the altar where he placed it face down on the stone. All his senses remained alert. Guards might be making the rounds or monks might be entering. He had to be wary. He untied the cloth, secured by two nails, to the lower inner part of the wooden frame, took out his dagger and marked ten hieroglyphs on it. After each new drawing he stopped and looked around feverishly. He was aware of the sacrilege he was committing by desecrating this icon. To be caught at this moment would condemn him to certain death. Once all the signs had been engraved, he meticulously replaced the two small nails to reattach the canvas and then put the icon back in its place.

The circle was finally complete.

He returned to the room, slumped back on his bed and let out a deep sigh, happy with the work done, and especially relieved of such an old weight. More than twenty-five years of work had come to an end with this final act. As soon as he returned to the West, all that remained was to pass on his secret to his son, who would do the same with his own, and so on down the generations.

The completion of his codex remained a mere formality. For now, he wanted to savor the moment.

The discovery of the island for Beynac and the inspection for the Grand Master took almost four weeks. The bastilles being restored or enlarged made Rhodes an impregnable fortress. They returned to their point of departure to prepare for their return journey. Beynac had accomplished his mission and could return home with peace of mind to his wife, son and the youngest child born during his journey. During their escapade across the island, he divulged to Hélion de Villeneuve a few snippets of his mission without revealing everything. In return, the hospitable man showed great generosity and an unusual friendliness. Beynac was not fooled. He knew very well that most of the Templar commanderies had been transferred, by papal bull, to the Hospitaller order and that everyone was still looking for the pecuniary goods that had mysteriously disappeared.

Before embarking, the Grand Master presented Count de Beynac with a gift, a true copy of the icon of the Virgin of Philerme created by the talented painter of the island, and invited him to join him as soon as he felt like it.

On the return journey, he engraved a sign on the back of the painting:

The Mystery of the Lost Crypt

65

Marimont-lès-Bénestroff
Saturday May 17th 2014, 7:30

'What is it?' asked Natasha.
Intrigued, they approached Borgia.
'A staurotheque!' stammered the dignitary of the order.
'A what?' asked Cyril.
'A staurotheque. Literally from the Greek 'staurós', the cross, and 'theke', a container. It is a reliquary containing a fragment of the True Cross! The one on which Jesus of Nazareth was crucified during the Passion.'
Clyde and Bonnie immediately knelt down and signed their hands.
'Wow!' exclaimed Cyril. 'Indeed, it calms...'
'As you say. The Louvre has one. The most beautiful is undoubtedly the one from Limbourg-sur-la-Lahn brought back from Constantinople by the German knight Heinrich von Ulmen during the fourth crusade at the very beginning of the thirteenth century. The reliquary is thought to date from the middle of the tenth century. But this one seems to be much larger.'
He placed it gently on a flat surface.
'Normally its lid should slide off like this... he said as he made the gesture.'

The finely carved wooden plaque, at first sight decorated with fine gold, gave way to a cubicle in the form of a Byzantine cross with a double crossbar. The entire space of the box was lined with five pieces of wood. The central axis of the cross measured nearly twenty-five centimeters.

'Straordinario!' said Clyde.

'Yes, I confirm, it is quite exceptional,' replied Borgia, who was very moved and had tears in his eyes. 'I don't think there is any greater relic of the Holy Cross in the world that I know of. We were talking about the Holy Grail, Cyril, we are not far from it after all...'

They unpacked the other objects and discovered more reliquaries. Borgia assumed that they were all relics of the Passion. A thorn, probably from the Holy Crown; a piece of rounded wood, possibly a fragment of the Holy Lance; a piece of cloth, a fragment that could have come from the Holy Robe; and a sample of spongy material that could only have come from the Holy Sponge.

'For a treasure, it's quite a treasure! There must be tens of millions of euros' worth of gold and silver alone, not to mention the priceless gems, documents and relics...' said Cyril, looking around at the six boxes. 'If I expected that. The owners of the lodge will be amazed when we tell them about our adventure.'

Borgia frowned and then retorted as curtly as firmly.

'No way! I'm sorry, but no one will know about this except the five of us! At least not about this treasure. It will be brought back to Rome as quickly as possible. As for the crypt, which for the moment looks more like a morgue, we may announce its discovery later, once it is restored and fit to receive people. Which seems unlikely. I am afraid that the openings of the various accesses have greatly weakened the whole, including the crypt.'

'But... but... not even our friend Gilles? He has more than contributed to the building!'

Borgia thought, embarrassed.

'I know, he deserves it as much as we do. But the fewer people who know about it, the less likely it is to leak out. The excuse for your friend is obvious. No treasure has been found and the underground has collapsed, so the subject is closed. On the other hand, he will be associated with you two for the discovery of the crypt. Let's give Caesar what he really deserves. In any case, publicizing the discovery of this treasure would only lead to political and legal imbroglios that would last several decades as to its ownership and sharing. And to tell you what I think on this subject, I believe that the French state, in the person of King Philip the Fair, has already taken its share in this story. I can assure you that these riches will be much better used at home in the Order of Malta than in the high political spheres. It is an unhoped-for financial mass for our Order. We will be able to build hospitals, old people's homes, orphanages and many other things throughout the world. The documents and the relics will surely be handed over to the Holy See and will thus constitute excellent means of pressure... they come at the right time!'

Such arguments could not be contradicted or discussed.

But the debate was brought to a halt again by yet another dull crack from the bowels of the mound.

'I suggest we slip away now, before we are buried alive for good. We have done enough for today and have all had our share of emotions. A little rest will do us all a world of good. And it will be well deserved. I would like to thank you both, or at least all three of you and your friend, on behalf of the Order, in my person and that of His Most Eminent Highness the Prince and Grand Master Fra' Bertrand de Villaret, who will not fail to congratulate you in person in the coming weeks. I am taking the staurotheque with me. You take the others,' he said to everyone. 'Clyde, you will take care of the Madonna painting. It is just as valuable, if not more so, especially after this miracle on your person.'

All five emerged from the underground with the precious objects under their arms. The deceased, Professor Visconti, Karl and his last victim, the Carabiniere, had been stored temporarily in the three lower vaults. As the tunnel was completely blocked on one side following the landslide, they had left the trapdoor of the treasure room open, preferring not to touch the structure which threatened to collapse at any moment. Props would be placed throughout the gallery by the team that would recover the six crates. On the other hand, the access hatch to the tunnel had been closed and the Templar sword removed.

This had no direct consequences.

'And how are we going to tell the gendarmes about each other's deaths? I killed a man...'

'Yes, but to save my friends. And your life at the same time. Only in self-defense. Nothing else. It was him or us. But that's an excellent question and one we'll have to think about soon. I haven't got a clue yet. As for the Italian policeman, he is not supposed to be in France. So his case is already settled. He will be immediately repatriated by the helicopter that dropped us off. He will be handed over to the Italian authorities. Officially, he will have participated in a strictly confidential operation. Everything was planned in advance, in case the mission went wrong. Which unfortunately was the case. His very seriously wounded colleague has already entered one of our hospitals at the same time as your friend and will also be evacuated to Italy when his condition allows, without the French authorities knowing anything about it. But I must admit that the case of the other two is much more difficult... I am afraid that we will have to improvise. Sleep is the best advice...'

It was high time for them to leave.

Cyril pressed on the cross at the bottom of the stairs to reopen the trapdoor leading to the church choir. As always, the square of stone sank into the wall.

But nothing happened.

No mechanism was set in motion.

The stone gradually returned to its original position.

He tried a second time. Still nothing.

A third and then a fourth time.

The Mystery of the Lost Crypt

No rumbling was heard.

The stone inexorably returned to its initial position without any further action. It was clear that the mechanism was no longer responding. They became anxious.

'What's going on Cyril?' panicked Natasha.

'It seems that the opening system of the passageway is jammed... perhaps a direct consequence of the collapsing...'

'After eight hundred years, it may also have given up the ghost permanently. We've probably operated it as much or more in one or two weekends than in its entire existence,' says Borgia, who had expected anything but that.

'And what do we do now?"' asked Clyde.

'Good question. It's impossible to get through the tunnel, which is completely blocked on the other side, and I doubt that the treasure room contains any way out. So we have to find another way to escape from here.'

Cyril wasted no time and was already scanning the walls and vaults of the crypt.

'Wait...' said Bonnie. 'We left the treasure room open. What if that action caused it?'

'What exactly are you thinking?' asked Clyde.

'That it has to be closed again so that this passage can be opened. Maybe they did it on purpose so that they never forgot to close the treasure room.'

'In this case, the tunnel would have to be reopened... with all the risks that this could entail...'

Cyril and Borgia looked at each other. The same thought crossed their minds.

'We'll try that as a last resort, if we really can't find another way out of here,' Borgia said as Cyril looked on approvingly. 'The whole structure has weakened and any further opening to the tunnel would risk total collapse. Let's first see what we can do from the crypt.'

Half an hour had passed and none of them had the slightest idea how to get out of this mess. The collapsed vault at bed level was thoroughly inspected, but they did not have the necessary equipment. Their search was equally fruitless on the back wall and the part on either side of the underground opening and the part opposite it where the enfeus were located. No back doors seemed to exist. Solid walls in all cases with probably a large depth of earth and stones behind. Impassable as it was.

All resigned themselves.

'We'll have no choice,' said Borgia, disappointed. 'We'll have to reopen the access to the tunnel and close the access to the treasure room. And for what result? Perhaps none...'

Cyril thrust the Templar sword under the icon of the Madonna without further ado. A small click was heard and the hidden stone door opened.

So far so good.

Before closing the other passage, he wanted to make sure that there was no other way out on this side of the tunnel. He preferred to go alone and asked the rest of the party to stay in the crypt. But Borgia did not hear him the same way and asked Clyde to accompany him.

Natasha was not reassured.

Clyde examined the collapsed part of the tunnel while Cyril inspected the treasure room. He looked first at the trapdoor above the opening where the gas once came out, but it was far too narrow to squeeze through anyway. He then looked at each wall one by one, finding nothing unusual. The vault of the room was intact and gave no reason to expect anything on this side, which did not surprise him. A vault could not have more than one access for obvious security reasons. Clyde had not been any luckier. The passage was completely blocked by rock and earth. Impossible to dig without tools.

So they decided to close the passage. Cyril removed the bayonet from its orifice. The door closed with another infernal din. They both ran to the crypt as fast as they could for fear that the vault would collapse in other places.

This was not the case.

The whole structure seemed to be resisting.

66

Moresperg
End of September 1338

The years had passed. Beynac's son, Amaury, the eldest of six children, had grown into a tall, robust young man. He would soon take over his father's title, which was slowly declining with the weight of years.

The passing of the torch was approaching.

And with it the secret that only the Count knew.

It was nearly 10 p.m., the entire Beynac family had attended the last service of the day and were on their way back to the château. The count had insisted on raising his children in the strict Christian faith, a remnant of his past that he was keen to preserve. It was a pleasantly mild day at the end of the day, the first official day of autumn, punctuating an exceptionally hot and dry summer that had taken its toll on the crops. Here and there they passed through cooler, wetter air currents rising from the surrounding forests. Beynac and his eldest son remained outside, sitting on the still warm stones, leaving the rest of the family to go up to their respective rooms.

After half an hour of talking about the management of the manor, the two men went down to the basement. Several cellars had been set up to store various foods, including dried and salted

The Mystery of the Lost Crypt

meats or dried vegetables such as lentils or split peas. The place was ideal, cool and dry. They went to the spirits room.

'You know my weakness, Father!'

'I didn't bring you here to get us drunk, but to show you something. Close the door and put the bar down.'

At the back against the wall stood shelves. He approached them and pressed a protruding stone above the bottles of brandy lined up. The stone rose to the level of the others, letting out a clatter. A trap door opened. The Count opened the back door which concealed an underground passage.

Amaury was speechless.

'How long has it been in existence?'

'I don't know about the origin of the underground, but your grandfather asked me to finish it with the help of my two companions when I arrived here.'

They soon came to a fork in the road.

'If you continue along this path, you will come to the entrance of the forest,' said Beynac, extending his left arm to shine the light as far as possible into the gallery.

But the glow of the flaming torch did not extend more than a few feet. They turned right and went down an endless flight of stairs. The steps were narrow and Amaury took his time going down.

'How long did it take you to finish everything, Father? '

'A few years. We worked on it day and night. But thanks to the great architectural skills of one of my two companions, everything was done without a hitch.'

The long vaulted tunnel echoed.

Their voices echoed, forcing them to keep their voices down.

At the bottom, they continued in a horizontal section and then climbed another staircase, much shorter than the previous one, to reach a dead end. This surprised Amaury. There was no detectable opening.

'Another back door?'

The Count drew his dagger and thrust it between two stones. The sound of a door being unlocked was heard. He hung his torch

The Mystery of the Lost Crypt

on the wall and pulled the stone door with both hands, using the notches in which he could insert his fingers.

Amaury discovered the crypt.

'Don't tell me you've also built it all!'

'Don't worry, it already existed. But it was abandoned, forgotten by everyone except the former vicar and your grandfather. We renovated it and added the various mechanisms you saw in action tonight.'

'And why all these precautions for a simple funeral room?'

'For the simple reason that it's not just a crypt. You already know that my first life was entirely dedicated to the Order of the Temple. When we lost our last stronghold in the East, the Grand Master entrusted me with a mission to which I devoted nearly twenty years of my life. Then Jacques de Molay, the last great dignitary, seeing the wind change, chose to secure the Order's assets. He was the only one who knew all the destinations of the convoys that had left the Temple house in Paris. I designed the main codex grouping together all his encryption codes for the chosen destinations. On site, once established, each knight would use his encryption to record everything in the secondary codex so that the information would never be lost. In case our order should rise from the ashes one day. Afterwards, of course, you would have to be in possession of both codices to be able to decipher them.'

Beynac showed his son the book reserved for Moresperg.

'He will have to stay in this crypt. In that little chest. With everything in it. It's very important.'

When he opened it, the gems glittered in the torchlight, as did the gold coins.

'Magnificent... is this the Templars' reserve?'

'Not quite. It's a tiny part of the treasure... let's say a tiny sample...'

'And where is the main codex?'

He whispered the information in his ear, as if someone could hear what he was going to say.

'Who is in the niches?'

'Probably the first parish priests of this parish. And one of my long-time companions. You know his two sons. No one knows we were Templars except the Duke of Lorraine and your grandfather. Not even your own mother. And no one must ever know again. Except your own son... is that clear?'

'Very clear, Father.'

'Next month, your brother will go to Metz to see the bishop. I will then show you the system for opening the crypt from inside the church. No one will disturb us. It will be safer that way.'

The two men returned to the cellar of the castle and closed the passage. The visit was over and everyone returned to their rooms. The handover of the keys to the treasure was complete.

That night, Amaury did not close his eyes, moved by what he had just seen and learned.

On this cold day at the end of autumn, Count Beynac, accompanied by his eldest son, was preparing to go hunting. The abundance of game would be used to prepare the Christmas pies. The last few nights had been freezing, which was rather unusual for the season. It was probably one of their last outings before the first snow, which was already covering the whole countryside with a thin coat. The frost deposited on nature sublimated the landscape of the Lorraine plateau.

The squires saddled the horses while father and son gathered the pack of dogs who, eager to stretch their legs and fight, howled to death in an indescribable cacophony. Wrapped in their bearskins, they galloped off surrounded by the dogs. Earlier in the morning, the beaters had gone to the edge of the forest to bring deer and boar in their direction.

The Beynacs were waiting patiently for the game to show itself when the oldest dog in the pack, who had stayed with them, stood still, ears pricked and eyes alert. He sensed a presence. Suddenly a deer leapt out of a copse, raising a veil of snow and frost around it, and darted over the helpless dog, who could only follow the beast's flight path. The deer passed between the Count's and Amaury's horses, which reared up and narrowly missed knocking their riders off their feet. A chase ensued. The riders could clearly make out the steaming noses of the beast, frightened by the barking of the pack, which sped through the forest, dexterously avoiding trees and branches on the ground. After a good quarter of an hour of intense effort, the deer, exhausted and losing speed, zigzagged to dodge the bites of the dogs on its heels. The animal defended itself valiantly, charging headlong at its assailants to face them with its huge antlers. He managed to rip open two dogs, who howled in pain, their guts in the air. But he was on the run and his fate would be sealed in the next few minutes. The deer, cornered in its last entrenchments, surrounded by the pack, had a last instinct to survive. He dashed to the side where the fewest dogs were gathered and, as before, made an extraordinary leap over the dogs, who tried, in vain, to seize one of his legs with their fangs. They were left empty-handed.

The indomitable wild animal passed for the second time between the two Beynac horses, which this time had come closer to each other. The ends of the stag's antlers brushed against the horses' flanks on either side. Frightened, they took off in a frantic gallop in the opposite direction. No matter how hard Father and Son tried, their frightened mounts no longer responded to their commands. There was nothing left to do but to let them calm down by themselves. The Count's mare left the woods and sped off down a forest path. Frozen puddles crunched under the hooves. Nothing seemed to stop her, not even the hand and soothing words of her master.

The foot beaters continued their work, gradually returning to the castle, pushing the game into the trap concocted by the hunters. The hordes of wild boar, roe deer and stags were running away, surprised by the surrounding noise.

The mare did not seem to be weakening, although she had already been galloping for more than thirty minutes with her bit between her teeth. The Count no longer recognized the place. But at a bend in the road, absorbed in the animal's mad race, a formidable boar blocked his path. The mare turned and her hooves skidded on a patch of ice covered with thin snow. The horse went down on its side, taking with it the Count, who was still firmly in the stirrups. The fall was so sudden that Beynac could not anticipate anything, his head hit the ground with full force, the horse crushing his left leg. The animal quickly got up, leaving its rider unconscious on the ground, and then continued on its way alone.

The weather at midday turned sour.

Low, grey clouds were looming on the horizon and would soon pour out their myriad flakes.

Amaury, for his part, had quickly managed to control his mount, calming the beast with strokes on its shoulders and neck. He returned to the troop, determined to chase the deer that had caused them to lose the trail. So they continued the hunt in spite of his father's absence and finally caught the stubborn animal.

Back at the castle in the middle of the afternoon, he did not hide his astonishment when he learned of his father's prolonged absence.

67

Marimont-lès-Bénestroff
Saturday May 17th 2014, 7:45

Their fate was now a toss-up.
Either the trap door mechanism would reset or this crypt would become their tomb forever.
The moment of truth.
Cyril put pressure on the stone again.
All were in a state of expectation, feverish, their senses on the alert, waiting for the deafening noise that would, for the first time, caress their ears, a sign of an unhoped-for deliverance.
Unfortunately, nothing happened.
No noise, no movement. Nothing.
Cyril tried several times without success.
It was now over.
Natasha sobbed as she cuddled in his arms. Clyde and Bonnie did the same. Borgia clutched his head with both hands. Tears rolled down his cheeks.
'To be resurrected only to end up like these two hours later...' Clyde lamented.
'If only Our Lady would help us again,' Bonnie grumbled. 'One last little push to ward off the bad luck.'
'It's my fault. I am truly sorry. I dragged you into this mess out of greed. I didn't think about the possible consequences. I acted

on my own behalf,' he told the two couples. 'I was obsessed with this treasure hunt from the beginning, just as the professor was.'

'We all made the choice to follow you. There is no one to blame. We had the option of returning to the lodge, but we stayed of our own free will, also attracted by curiosity and the lure of gain,' Cyril replied tactically.

Trying to find other ways out of this crypt, Cyril discovered next to the bed the debris of their mobile phones that the colossus had destroyed earlier. An idea came to him immediately.

'But I think about it, you still have your phone! You've got a signal,' he shouted, turning to Borgia. 'You could call on your acquaintances who could get us out of here.'

'But why didn't I think of that before!' he replied, taking it out of his pocket.

He turned it on and the battery icon appeared large on the screen. It was flashing, indicating that the phone needed to be plugged into the mains to recharge its battery. He turned it off and on again without any further success.

'So?' asked Cyril anxiously.

'It's discharged... I had been using it as a back-up light the whole time we were in the treasure room, using up the last thirty percent of the battery. I'm sorry...'

Silence enveloped the crypt.

An eerie, heavy, interminable silence.

Everyone was resigned, sitting on a chair or on the floor, lost in thought, with a blank stare. All except Cyril, who kept on sweeping the walls.

'I admire your tenacity, Cyril.'

'As long as there is life, there is hope.'

The young man lingered on the wall next to the staircase and the adjacent vault. He examined it from several angles.

Something intrigued him.

'Well, that's strange...'

'What?' asked Clyde.

'I hadn't noticed that the vault is incomplete at this point. It stops at two thirds...'

'You are indeed right. The wall seems to have been added afterwards,' says Borgia, joining the conversation.

Then Cyril directed the light beam to the floor. In the same way the stones had been laid directly on the tiles. If the wall had been in place from the start, they would have been cut out and laid against the wall. Here this was not the case. Some of the tiles were only half visible and extended under the stones. He could see this by sliding his finger into certain gaps.

'It's always harder to see what's in front of you...' he says.

'Maybe it's an antechamber, to hide the automatic opening mechanism of the hatch?' says Clyde.

'I was thinking the same thing...' replied Cyril. 'If we could access it, maybe we could unlock it... in our current situation, we really have nothing left to lose.'

They moved the table to the bottom of the stairs, against the wall. Cyril retrieved the Templar sword and climbed onto the table. He slid the blade between the arch and a stone. The mortar was so crumbly that the blade sank into it almost like butter. He quickly cleared the whole top and started on the sides. Once the first stone was almost completely detached from the others, he pushed it out with the help of Clyde who had come to join him. The stone must have weighed about fifty kilos. With no support on this wobbly table, the only possibility for them was to push it, hoping that there would be a gap on the other side. They had a lot of trouble, especially as some of the mortar was still attached to the rock at the bottom. But they finally managed to do so, inch by inch, after considerable effort. At the very moment when the final blow was delivered, Borgia intervened:

'Wait!' he shouted.

It was too late. The stone fell to the other side with a thunderous noise that shook the floor of the room, hitting a wooden object beforehand which, at the sound, seemed to break.

'What was it?' asked a surprised Cyril.

'The stone that triggers the mechanism must have been just below the one you removed.'

'Oh, I hadn't thought of that...' said a confused Cyril.

'We'll see... we'll clear the next ones on this side so as not to damage it further.'

Perhaps they had just wrecked their chances of getting out of this place again. They would soon find out.

But the good news at the time was that there was another room behind that wall.

This discovery put a smile on the faces of the whole group, who set about the task. Borgia took the bayonet they had retrieved from the rifle in the vault and proceeded in the same way as Cyril on a nearby stone. The hardest part had been removing the first one. The task would be a little easier for the next ones. After removing about ten stones, Cyril took his torch and had a look around.

'What do you see Cyril?' asked an impatient Borgia.

'Pietro was right. It is indeed an antechamber with the entire opening mechanism. It is impressive.'

'Let's clear a few more stones to make it easier for everyone to get in,' lied Borgia, who didn't dare reveal that he couldn't see himself squeezing through in the current state.

Once the wall was sufficiently open, everyone without exception went into the antechamber and they could only admire the magnificent work done eight hundred years before, a very ingenious tangle of wooden gears and pulleys filled the room.

'All this to open traps,' Bonnie said in amazement. 'E incredibile...'

'Quite a skill for the time. The Templars were ahead in many areas. In banking with bills of exchange and cheques, in cryptography with their method of replacing letters with symbols from the Maltese Cross, in the development of construction processes thanks to the literary and scientific knowledge they had acquired from the oriental populations, and in the development of agriculture in France by importing numerous varieties of vegetables from the East, Borgia explained.'

Cyril already had his torch and his eyes riveted on the wooden piece broken by the falling first stone. The faint ray of light projected was enough to conclude that a possible repair would simply not be possible.

'It's hard to get around the mechanism without this little cogwheel...' he says.

'We have until we die to think of an alternative,' the Grand Chancellor replied.

'Seen like that...'

'I'm not too far from the truth, it seems to me. This is really the only solution left...'

'Not quite...' intervened Natasha who had ventured to the back of the room.

The four beams of torches were immediately directed in her direction.

'Look up there! It looks like a trap door!'

They rushed towards it and discovered what indeed looked like an opening in the ceiling closed by a wooden board.

'And this may be our ticket out of here,' Borgia exulted.

Cyril saw a ladder lying on the ground along one of the walls. Would it still support his weight after all these years? He put it in place and began to climb. The first rung broke cleanly as he placed his foot in the middle of it.

'Ouch... this is not going well.'

'Maybe put your feet on the sides rather than in the middle, right?'

'Yes, indeed.'

He put his foot directly on the left of the second bar, pulled himself up and waited a few seconds, anxious. This time the step did not break. He continued on several levels before his head reached the arch. He gauged the plank with the bayonet. It was thick and seemed to be in good condition. The whole of its perimeter rested on a stone gutter. He climbed two more steps and tried to lift it by pushing with his upper back.

The board did not move an inch.

'We can only pray that the opening has not been condemned along with the marble altarpiece behind the altar,' said Borgia worriedly.

On the one hand Cyril needed more support, on the other the fragility of the ladder rungs did not encourage him to force his way up. Did he have any other choice? He lowered his right foot onto the previous step to spread the pressure further. He took a breath and pushed as hard as he could.

A cracking sound was heard.

He released the pressure to catch his breath and tried again. The third attempt was the right one. The wooden plank finally gave way and lifted up with shouts of joy in the general jubilation. Luckily, the trap door was right between the sacristy door and the altarpiece.

They all emerged from the depths, relieved. To think that a quarter of an hour earlier they had already seen themselves buried alive.

'Well done to all. It was a great team effort,' said Borgia, calmly, as if he never doubted that they would get out of this quagmire.

The board was put back in place as well as the tiles, all covered with a mat so as not to attract attention.

It was eight in the morning. Outside, the fog was beginning to dissipate. The sun's rays were breaking through in various places. The top of the hill seemed to be completely clear.

'The weather is completely out of control! It's like autumn,' grumbled Natasha.

Borgia was talking to the two couples about his plans to fly back to Nancy by helicopter when he suddenly had the sensation that a curtain in the house opposite the church had moved.

'I think someone is watching us!'

'If you're talking about the white house on the corner, don't worry, it's an old lady who lives alone. Poor thing, she must be a bit upset with what happened at her house last night,' Bonnie replied, looking at the building and waving.

The old lady replied in turn.

'Come and see her later today to check on her and to make sure she doesn't spread any information about what she saw. Of course, we'll compensate her more than enough for the damage done...' suggested Borgia.

'Yes, we will do that with great pleasure. It hurt my heart to have to leave her to the fate of that murderer.'

Borgia went back alone to the hill where the helicopter would soon pick him up, but not without giving some more instructions to the two Italians. Their mission was to clean up and erase any past presence of the dead. The others took the direction of the lodge. As the two groups walked away, Cyril called out to the Grand Chancellor.

'What is this thing you wanted to talk to me about?'

'We will see about this soon when you come to the Order's headquarters in Rome! I will contact you again to prepare your trip. See you soon and rest well!'

When they arrived at the B&B, the owners were up and about preparing breakfast, surprised to see them all coming through the front door. The manager couldn't help but make a remark.

'You're up early, aren't you? Where did you all go in such terrible weather?'

'Admire the interior of your church and everything about your altar. Which is beautiful...' Natasha says laconically.

'Oh well, it was the worst night I've had in a long time. I had some strange feelings. I even felt a presence in the room. It was really strange and then these tremors, they were like very light earthquakes...' she said.

'Don't listen to her, ladies and gentlemen, she's out of order,' the manager muttered.

Cyril and Natasha's eyes met, rolling their eyes. They knew his wife was right about everything... their lips burned to tell him. But Borgia had expressly forbidden it. So they would remain in total ignorance, and the husband would continue to denigrate his wife's claims while she would not budge, for the rest of their lives.

It was probably for the best.

'Well, isn't your friend with you? '

The lovebirds had not thought at all about finding an excuse for Gilles' hasty departure. Cyril thought it easier to tell the truth!

'He had a big sprain and was transferred to a hospital in Nancy... we will get his stuff back.'

The two managers looked at each other, worried.

Seeing the discomfort caused by this announcement, Natasha immediately added:

'And of course we pay for his room!'

They pretended not to care, but that was exactly what they wanted to hear.

The two students went back to their room to rest for a few hours. A warrior's rest. The night had been tough physically, psychologically and emotionally.

They all wanted one thing.

Peace and quiet.

In order to put the matter behind us for good.

68

**Moresperg
Early December 1338**

Amaury waited for another hour, but his father was still late in returning. No one had seen him since his mare, panic-stricken and wounded by the antlers of the cornered stag, had galloped off like a fury. The sun would be setting in half an hour and the snow was falling heavily.

And above all, the temperature dropped sharply.

'He should have been here a long time ago. Something must have happened to him. It will soon be dark and with this storm coming, it will be impossible for him to survive such temperatures. I have to go and look for him,'" he said to his mother before riding out of the castle gate with a dozen horsemen.

The group returned first to the scene of the incident. But unfortunately for them the snow that had fallen in the last few hours had already completely covered the tracks. They split up into six groups, with Amaury continuing alone. The pairs called regularly to inform the count of their presence.

But only their voices echoed in the immensity of the forest.

Despite their torches, visibility was poor. Each group went further and further into the forest until they lost sight of each other, despite the glow of the flaming torches. Only the muffled calls reassured them of a presence in this dark and disturbing immensity. Amaury had just reached a small path winding between the trees and covered with a good layer of snow. The gloomy whistling of the wind, which was intensifying in gusts, made the expedition extremely painful. The flame of the torch flickered more and more and the young man had to protect it to avoid it being extinguished permanently by the strongest gusts. He had to get out of this corridor where the wind was rushing in and go back into the forest to protect himself. At last he saw a gap and was about to slip through it when he heard the whinnying of a horse. He saw a horse trotting towards him, foaming at the mouth. He blocked its path and approached the animal, gradually calming it down. It seemed lost and terrified.

It was his father's mare.

But without his rider.

He shuddered, for this did not bode well.

He untied the horse's reins on one side of the bit and tied it to the back of his saddle, then rode on.

Long afterwards, Amaury heard grunts. As soon as he rounded a bend in the road, he saw several pairs of eyes glowing in the darkness. Wolves, visibly hungry, occupied the entire width of the path, devouring a prey, fighting over it in turn, even fighting over scraps of cloth.

His blood ran cold. He suddenly became aware that this was a body.

His throat tightened.

He imagined the worst.

The pack of wolves did not seem to be frightened by the approach of the two horses. On the contrary. The growling increased. These odious beasts certainly thought that they were in danger of having their providential feast snatched away from them or that new unconscious prey was coming to throw itself into their jaws. The young man got down on the ground and approached the carcass, threatening them with his flaming torch in great sudden gestures accompanied by heart-rending cries, which had the immediate effect of dispersing them. The wolves moved a few dozen meters away, howling to death and watching for any opening that would allow them to counter-attack.

Amaury approached the mangled corpse. A wolf attempted a first attack but he aborted it by putting his torch under its muzzle, which made it back away immediately. He had a short respite to check the identity of the corpse. He approached his smoking torch, which crackled under the many flakes that evaporated on contact with the flames.

He gagged and swallowed in horror.

The face was completely disfigured. It was difficult to recognize this person in these conditions. The throat, the hands and the most accessible parts of the body had been almost completely eaten away. The torso lay naked, the guts and ribs largely cut away, and fragments of clothing lay strewn about. It was not a pretty sight. As he continued to inspect the body, his gaze fell on a signet ring still in place on the stump of the middle finger.

He recognized it at once.

Spasms shook him, bile burning his throat, he vomited and angrily wiped his chin with the sleeve of his tunic.

The ring did belong to his father.

A lead weight fell upon him. He dropped to his knees before the corpse, in tears. A death is always premature, but this one was even more so than others. He had so much to learn about running the estate. How was he going to break the news to his mother and siblings? Given the current state of the body, it would be difficult to show them. All these questions were running through his mind as the wolves came dangerously close. They didn't seem to want to give up their feast any time soon, especially if they could accommodate an additional prey. Amaury faced the enraged pack and drew his sword from its sheath. He was ready for battle. Ready to return the favor and avenge his father's death.

The wolves gradually moved in an arc around him, the younger ones staying back to learn from their elders. The first attack of the canines came from his left. Two glowing yellow eyes popped out of the night and a robust male pounced on him with his mouth wide open and his fangs clearly visible. Amaury just had the reflex to aim his sword in its direction, holding it as firmly as possible with one hand, his other hand being taken by the torch, the beast came to impale itself with a chilling whimper. The momentum and weight of the animal caused it to topple backwards. He fell on his back in the snow and dropped the torch. He discarded the dead prey, tipping it aside, removed the sword and retrieved his torch, which was about to be extinguished. Without it, he too would succumb to the sharp fangs.

He barely had time to regain his senses when he saw two more pairs of eyes glaring at him in the night. He waved the torch to his right to push the wolf away temporarily and concentrated on the other animal. But the latter did not rush in like his companion. It seemed to have learned its lesson and adopted a more strategic approach. Amaury was surprised by his quickness and his ability to avoid sword blows. He was so busy on his left flank that he no longer paid attention to the wolf on his right, who took advantage of this, despite the presence of the torch, to get as close as possible. Suddenly he felt a strong pressure on his right forearm, causing him to drop his torch again, which stuck straight as a peg in the fresh snow. The beast had disregarded the danger of the flame to clutch at his opponent's arm with all its might. Fortunately for him, the leather gloves he was wearing were thick enough to temporarily prevent the fangs from piercing the flesh. But they would not hold for long and they did not prevent the sharp pain caused by the compression of the powerful jaw from spreading throughout his forearm. The young count brought his blade down and struck a blow into the animal's side before skewering it. The animal let go and collapsed to the ground, inert. At the same time, the second wolf, on the lookout, took advantage of this to attack. Amaury did not have time to free his blade, stuck between two ribs, when the dog threw itself on him. Probably the dominant male of the pack, given his impressive size. He was thrown to the ground, managing to hold the wild beast by the neck and thus keep its mouth only a few centimeters from his face. He could smell its foul breath and its drool ran down his cheeks.

Amaury had underestimated the power of the wolf and felt his strength draining away as the minutes passed. The beast's fangs were getting closer and closer and he would not be able to resist much longer at this rate. His fate seemed sealed. Just as his father's had been. He too would be a feast for this hungry pack. The animal's jabs at his face caused scratches here and there, but each time the young man managed to contain the attacks. Even through his clothes he could feel the nails of the two front paws on his chest. The flakes were falling hard and the torch was gradually fading.

The end seemed near.

The rest of the pack did not stop there. Another wolf came to support the dominant male. He grabbed Amaury's shin with his sharp teeth and shook energetically. Then one last wolf joined the fray. Neither the torch nor Amaury's cries frightened the damn creatures.

The lynching was going well.

Faced with these three ferocious beasts, Amaury's dark future seemed sealed. On the ground, facing the wolf, without a weapon in his hand - his dagger was attached to his belt and he could not loosen the animal's grip to try to grab it with one hand at the risk of having his throat cut - he could not fight them all. He felt the fangs of the other two wolves penetrate his flesh and lacerate his lower legs. They were applying such force with their jaws that they would soon dismember him.

The young count was weakening.

He was going to let go. Definitely.

He closed his eyes and said a quick prayer. But just as he was about to finish, he heard a hissing sound split the air and end in a thud.

The characteristic sound of an arrow.

Immediately the beast let go with a grunt of pain and fell over on its side. A second arrow hit the animal, which was straining at its right leg. It also fell on its side with a groan. The third one did not ask for more and ran like a rabbit, probably feeling his turn coming. One of the groups of men had come closer, attracted by the noises, and had dealt with the wolves just in time.

They both rushed to Amaury's aid to protect him from another attack. This was no longer the case. The rest of the pack left.

The young man was badly injured in the legs and could not stand up, let alone walk. They helped him to his feet and then, as best they could, picked up the Count's body to take it back to the castle.

A week of mourning was declared throughout the estate.

The funeral took place in the presence of the Duke of Lorraine and the many lords of the region. The stele was placed next to his Templar brother, at his request during his lifetime. Later, Amaury placed the bones, wrapped in a cloth, together with his sword and dagger in one of the crypt's vaults, as he had also requested. This was the sine qua non for reality to match the writings of the codex.

Amaury died a few days later of a devastating infection, probably as a result of the wolf bites.

Taking with him the secret of the Templars forever...

69

**Rome,
Monday June 9th 2014**

Natasha and Cyril had never been to Rome before.
This was a first.
The appointment with Borgia had been set for this Monday at five o'clock, so they had taken the opportunity to come a few days earlier to admire the beautiful transalpine capital and visit its ancient buildings and monuments, its museums, churches, squares, fountains and have a good time in this very special atmosphere in a city known for never sleeping, so eager are the Romans to please the tourists. Accompanied by Bonnie, who had transformed herself into a tour guide for the occasion, they had of course visited the Vatican, enjoying VIP access to the Holy See thanks to Borgia for all their services.
Both were Catholics and had grown up in very religious families, but did not approach religion in the same way. He was rather Cartesian, rational and attached less and less importance to the aspects of religion as the years went by. Natasha, on the other hand, was a fervent and practicing believer and did not deny her pleasure at being here. And for good reason. Probably informed by Borgia of the exceptional discoveries made a few weeks earlier in France, the Holy Father had wanted to see them and congratulate them himself. And to thank them, he certainly

offered them the most beautiful gift that many Christian couples would dream of.

The sacraments of marriage administered by him in the heart of St Peter's Basilica.

The insistent looks of Natasha, but also of the Pope who seemed quite annoyed, not understanding that he could hesitate so long before accepting, had put Cyril against the wall.

He had just fallen into a trap.

Although he was not at all put off by the idea of getting married, on the contrary, he had just been taken by surprise. His laconic reply 'it would obviously be an honor' was immediately interpreted by the Holy Father as a tacit agreement and a formal request for marriage.

He could not go back.

The young woman's double dream had been fulfilled.

A marriage to the man she loved in the Holy of Holies of Christianity and by the Pope himself.

What more could you ask for!

So it was a done deal. All that remained was to find a date.

Here again the Holy Father forced their hand. His overloaded calendar did not offer much availability.

On the fourth day, after a stroll through the old town in scorching heat, in stark contrast to the miserable weather of the last few months in north-eastern France, Cyril and Natasha met, as agreed, at 5 p.m. sharp at 68 Via Condotti, in front of the entrance gate to the Order of Malta's magisterial palace, the residence of the Grand Master and seat of government. The bells of the Church of the Trinità dei Monti rang out at the same moment.

Seeing neither doorbell nor intercom, only two surveillance cameras were present on either side of the entrance, Cyril knocked energetically three times on one of the doors of the large gate under the intrigued gaze of the tourists and locals. One of them approached the young couple.

'No entry here, no visit... It's the order of Malta!'

The door opened and they were invited in.

'Oh well, thanks anyway!' Cyril hastened to reply to the man who had called out to them before disappearing in his turn.

The latter remained motionless in the middle of the street, silent. His friends who were with him were laughing their heads off.

They passed through a wrought-iron gate into a small inner courtyard which revealed a large Maltese cross, still called the Cross of St John, with four identical branches and eight points. At the back was a fountain with the coat of arms of the Knights of Malta above it. Always a white cross circled in red. Two large black cars were parked there. The number plates caught Cyril's attention. They were atypical, to say the least. S.M.O.M 35 and S.M.O.M 36. They turned left towards the official entrance porch of the palace.

'What are these two plates for?' Cyril asked the doorman in English.

'Ordine di Malta,' replied the latter in Italian. 'E per 'Sovereign Military Order of Malta'.'

In the entrance hall, Borgia was waiting for them. The French couple almost had trouble recognizing him in his three-piece suit. The last time they remembered him was as a half-baroudeur, half-treasure seeker.

'My friends! You are most welcome. I have been looking forward to seeing you since our little adventure in France.'

'So do I! You still owe me an explanation. I haven't forgotten...' said Cyril.

'You won't have to wait much longer, I promise you. I see that your friend Gilles is not accompanying you. Nothing serious I hope?'

'He is doing very well, but is in a cast for another week. As he finds it difficult to move around, he preferred to stay in Nancy, to his great despair. He sends his greetings to you at the same time.

And he is especially disappointed that no treasure has been found...'

Borgia could not help but smile.

'The poor guy... if he knew... in any case I thank you for having preserved the secret. In the end, it is the inhabitants of this little village of Marimont who are the happiest.'

'And why?'

'The legend that has been circulating for so long has been transformed into historical reality! We did find some skittles. They were not made of gold, they were simply painted. They were a decoy. But the gold did exist. One day they will have to be told and shown their treasure in a specially prepared little scene in the crypt. But only on condition that we manage to secure the place. And if not, all this will continue to remain a mere legend in their eyes. Nothing more. We shall see.'

The three of them entered the Council Chamber. The same one where the Grand Master of the Order received the main heads of state of this world. The latter, dressed in a long red jacket adorned with numerous silver crosses as well as various medals and distinctions, was facing them in the middle of the room. He was surrounded by several people in ceremonial uniforms and clerics, many of whom were present in the upper echelons of the order.

The moment was most solemn.

Cyril, intimidated, moved forward, keeping to the right of Borgia, with Natasha following slightly behind.

'Your Eminence, I present Cyril de Villiers, direct descendant of Philippe de Villiers de L'Isle-Adam, forty-fourth Grand Master and first of the Order in Malta in 1530, and his companion, Natasha de Beynac, also a direct descendant of a member of the Order, author of the codices that you have seen. These young people and a friend of theirs, Gilles Prevnic, who cannot be present today, were actively involved in the fabulous discovery made in France last month.'

The pope had obviously been informed, as had his prelate within the order. What remained to be decided was the question of the distribution of all this wealth, which was bound to whet the appetite of certain prelates. This would not be an easy matter... the endless dissensions within the Vatican itself or within the Order of Malta, or even between the two, as well as personal interests promised bitter discussions in the months to come.

The young lovebirds faces showed astonishment and incomprehension. Neither of them knew of any such connections and had never even been interested in their family genealogy.

'On behalf of the Order, we would like to express our gratitude for all that you have done. It is in this capacity that you are admitted to the Order as a Donat and Donate of devotion,' continued the Grand Master after a long introductory speech, to the hearty applause of the assembly.

Cyril and Natasha had just joined the order. This honorary title was reserved for those who had rendered services to him.

The Grand Master concluded the ceremony with this sentence:

'Given the reputations of your respective families, if you wish to become more involved in our order, a place of choice will be reserved for you.'

Although many of the current knights were no longer descended from the nobility, a place of honor was still reserved for those who were, as was the obligation in the early days of the order and as some of its current members still claim.

A magnificent banquet followed to celebrate the induction of the two new members.

Their destiny would be forever linked to that of this age-old order and, for Cyril and Natasha, would be a worthy successor to their respective ancestors.

The Mystery of the Lost Crypt

70

Morsperg
1776

Henri Grégoire, newly ordained curate, was, after his first two years in Château-Salins, assigned to the small parish of Morsperg. His superiors probably had the idea of replacing the old man in place. This parish priest had served his parish selflessly, but his old age and infirmities no longer allowed him to celebrate services.

The church, damaged by successive wars and by the many bad weather conditions over the centuries, had never been restored and was in a state of near decay. Both the interior walls and the vault were seriously cracked. To such an extent that the vault was in danger of collapsing at any moment, the exterior plaster had long since fallen off, causing the inexorable crumbling of the stone. A major renovation was essential. But this would not be an easy task, many inhabitants had perished, decimated by disease, wars and successive famines. There were only a hundred souls left, at most. The hamlet had struggled to repopulate itself after the Thirty Years' War, when only nine villagers had remained. The feudal castle had been in ruins for almost two centuries and was used as a quarry, thus providing the new, more functional building with robust ashlars. The imposing residence combined grace and power. The owners of the manor had moved in twelve years earlier, but were not fully accepted being from the outside.

A cruel dilemma for the new curate.

The decimators did not want to take on the cost of the work, nor did the new lords. Once again, the peasants were going to be made to contribute, inevitably raising tensions between them, the lord and Abbé Grégoire. As soon as he arrived, he was already alienating the entire population, and his natural elocution, which was usually so effective and appreciated, did not help. When the money of his flock, already hard pressed by the heavy taxes on salt and wood, was being drained, not to mention the tithe levied by the church, which alone represented more than a seventh of the harvest, there was no way to trick them.

He had to find a solution to lighten the load and thus quell the winds of rebellion. This problem haunted his days and especially his nights.

One evening, when he was struggling to sleep, he decided to go back to the church to pace around, determined to solve the problem. Just the day before, pieces of plaster had fallen from the vault during mass not far from the lord's bench, luckily not injuring anyone. He had to act quickly if he did not want to see his parish deserted in the next few weeks. And he could not use any influence with his hierarchy, which did not intend to contribute a single penny to this church.

While wearing his sandals on the polished tiles of the nave, he regularly raised his head to glance up at the ceiling with concern.

Suddenly he stopped dead in his tracks.

An idea was brewing in his mind as he detailed the altar in front of him. He had heard from the native inhabitants of the village that the stone block dated from the Carolingian period, presumably donated by Charlemagne himself. If this allegation were true, he could probably fetch a very good price for it and thus cover a large part of the costs. An altar of this value could take pride of place in any cathedral in France and Navarre.

He approached it, knelt down and illuminated the front of the altar with the candlestick he had picked up in passing. Thanks to

The Mystery of the Lost Crypt

the lateral light projected by the flame and his erudition in this field, he immediately recognized the Emperor's monogram. The engraved letters and geometric shapes formed the word 'Karolus'.

'So they were telling the truth! This altar seems to be from that time,' he said loudly. 'It would be almost a thousand years old! It is extraordinary.'

He stroked the stone and rubbed the outline vigorously to remove the roughness that had accumulated over the centuries. He dusted so hard that for a moment it seemed that the stone had moved. Intrigued, he applied pressure and found to his astonishment that the part containing the monogram sank without him exerting the slightest pressure. A few seconds after the block of stone had stopped, the altar and the surrounding space suddenly began to shake. Streams of plaster and mortar came off the ceiling. Father Gregory shielded his head as much as he could with his arms.

The altar shifted and then stopped perpendicular to its original position, offering instead a gaping, dark and dusty hole.

The vicar sat on the ground for a long time, stunned by what had just taken place before his eyes, his legs still wobbly. He did not dare to come any closer. The darkness of the abyss, amplified by that of the church in the middle of the night, terrified him. But once he had recovered his senses and tamed his fear, he cautiously advanced to the edge of the precipice on his knees and noted with relief that there was a staircase, albeit very steep. He fetched an old piece of cloth from the sacristy, wrapped it around a piece of wood, spread wax on it and set it alight, then threw it down into the abyss. The torch stopped three or four meters below, illuminating what looked like a tiled room.

Reassured, he carefully went downstairs to inspect his discovery. He picked up the improvised torch and hung it on the metal torch holder fixed to the wall opposite the stairs. The mortuary niches present left no doubt as to the purpose of the room. It was indeed a crypt as the abbot had thought. He discovered the inhabited chambers. Two of them contained long swords and daggers. The vicar took one of each. The pommels had Templar crosses on them. This detail intrigued him. What could these two Templars be doing in this crypt and in such a small village? Especially since no Templar commandery was listed in the area. He continued his exploration by moving towards the opposite wall. A painting caught his eye. The icon bore a strong resemblance to the Virgin Mary, which was confirmed by the inscription in Greek at the bottom of the frame 'Η Παναγία της Φιλερήμου', literally 'The Virgin of Philerme'. Abbot Gregory had heard of this icon which belonged to the Hospitallers and whose current headquarters was based in Malta. Several commanderies in the region belonged to this Order, which had taken over those of the Templars when it was dissolved. To his knowledge, there were no copies left, the few that existed having all been destroyed in various fires or disappeared, and he thought he could make a very good price by selling it back to the Order, given its probable age. He rejoiced at this discovery.

Assessing the rest, his attention was soon drawn to two old chests stored in the darkest corner of the room. They were made of wood, without any embellishment. A single handle on the side. One was locked. He opened the other one where only two old codices were neatly stored. He then took the locked chest. The first indication was that it was heavy. Then, as he handled it, he heard the clinking of coins. His heart raced. The size of the chest and its weight suggested the best. He had to return to the rectory to find the right tool to open it. In his haste, he inadvertently hit the prominent stone at the bottom of the stairs, which closed the passage. When he barely made it into the church choir, more debris crashed to the floor and onto the pews, damaging them.

Opening the hatch would certainly be the final blow to the building. He did not want to take any chances and decided to leave it closed until the building was restored and reinforced. Far too risky.

The whole place was a mess. He now hoped that the contents of the box would make up for all this destruction. He placed the box on his table and looked in the shed for a flat-tipped iron bar that would act as a crowbar to pick the lock.

His hands were shaking.

He was eager to discover its contents.

After many attempts, he managed to break the locking mechanism. He just hoped that the noise had not woken anyone up. There was no risk from the old abbot, who was snoring upstairs and was deaf as a post.

He was about to open the safe when there was a knock on the door.

'Mr. Abbot!'

The noise startled him. An annoyance mixed with frustration showed on his face. He had to find a hiding place quickly. He couldn't pretend he wasn't there, the candle and the earlier metal blows gave him away.

'I'm coming, just a moment.'

For a moment he stood still in panic, not knowing where to store the box until he was free of the intruder. He put his thoughts in order and went into the adjoining room where he placed the wooden box under a table and covered it with an altar cloth. Then he returned to open the door.

He was the village blacksmith.

'Father, I heard a noise, I ran to see what was going on. Are you all right?'

'Thank you for your concern, Anselm, you are very good, but it's really nothing serious. I couldn't get any sleep and I was keeping myself busy. There is no lack of work!'

'You see me reassured. If it's ironwork, I can help you, Father. Time to light the forge. Didn't you feel the vibrations in the ground? It sounded like it was coming from here.'

'Strange, no, I didn't notice or hear anything in particular... you must have been dreaming.'

'Oh? But I could have sworn... well, I'm sorry, Father, I meant that I was convinced...'

Abbé Grégoire felt uncomfortable.

He stammered an excuse which did not convince the blacksmith by the pout he made, then slammed the door in his face, claiming he was busy. Having got rid of the intruder, he could finally devote himself to his discovery. He stayed next door in the shed, a room with no windows at all, for greater discretion, placed the chest on the small table and finally opened the lid.

His eyes were filled with wonder.

His hands were shaking.

Hundreds of gold coins and precious stones mixed together glittered in the candlelight. At this late hour of the night, he could have thought it was a dream, but it was not. His excitement was at its peak. He plunged his two hands into the candle and pulled out two beautiful handfuls full of gems and gold coins, which he immediately let slip through his fingers. He repeated the operation several times in a row with ever greater frenzy and wonder.

He couldn't believe it.

He inspected one of the coins more closely. It was stamped with the seal of the Order of the Temple. The stones, diamonds, rubies, agates, sapphires, emeralds of all colors and pearls were either already cut or left in their raw state.

He was looking for money to renovate his parish and he had just found more than enough. This providential windfall came at the right time. It could only be God's will.

The next day, various tradesmen were already on deck, under the forbidden gaze of the whole community. To each question that was asked of him, the vicar answered very laconically, explaining that the money came from generous patrons who had been won over by the historical value of the altar and who wished to preserve it.

This gift from heaven enabled him to obtain the graces of his hierarchy and to acquire new statutes. He became a member of the Philanthropic Societies of Nancy and Strasbourg as well as of the Masonic Lodge of the Nine Sisters in Paris, all three founded in the middle of 1776, providing him with new knowledge and access to the capital, which he had always aspired to.

Thanks to this treasure, his dream was taking shape.

A few years later, he left the region to go to the capital and take a leading role in the French Revolution, where he became a key figure by joining the Third Estate.

Epilogue

Rome, Aventine Palace
October 2014

Low clouds enveloped the transalpine capital in this early autumn and a fine drizzle fell, accentuated by a light cool breeze from the east, unusual for this period.

'This is a change from the thirty degrees of the last time...' Natasha pitied, looking at her umbrella.

'That's for sure. It's hard to predict the weather in advance. But it was impossible to refuse an invitation from the Grand Chancellor!'

Cyril and Natasha were in the Knights of Malta square on the top of the Aventine hill. They were facing the majestic gate of the Priory of Malta's villa.

'But where are you going? Borgia told us to report to the small door to the right of the big main door,' said Natasha as her husband headed for the big double door.

As suggested by the Pope during their meeting in June, the religious wedding between the two lovebirds took place at the end of August in St Peter's Basilica. This exceptional event, celebrated by His Holiness in person, was of course very well attended by both families, bringing together almost two hundred and fifty guests who had to be accommodated and fed. But the Order had taken care of everything, both in the organization of the wedding and its cost, which even included the booking of the plane tickets. All expenses had been paid in full at Borgia's request. It was certainly the least he could do for the couple who had discovered one of the most sumptuous treasures.

'I know, but I have to check something I saw on the internet first,' replied Cyril.

A couple of tourists were standing next to the big door and seemed to be taking turns looking through the keyhole. Cyril had read that on some days the waiting time could exceed half an hour. When the couple left, Cyril in turn approached the rounded hole whose edges the curious had polished over the decades. Despite the bad weather and the low clouds, he could see the majestic dome of St Peter's Basilica in the center of a deep cypress avenue and behind the tall pines...

'Come on Natasha, look! It's really great.'

She approached and admired the amazing view.

The small door opened just as the French couple approached it and Borgia appeared on the stoop.

'We are not leaving each other anymore my friends! How are you? This time reminds me of our first meeting. Some memories... Come in, come in.'

'The view through the lock is really original!'

'Ah the famous 'Il buco di Roma'. It is probably the most famous keyhole in the world and one of the most popular attractions in Rome.'

They made a diversion through the gardens of the villa. Borgia couldn't help himself. The view of Rome was absolutely fascinating. Then they entered the Chapter House where the main events of the order were taking place, including the elections of the last Grand Masters.

'This place is beautiful. There's something... timeless about it... it's as if everything has remained in its original state. All that's missing are the knights in armor.'

'I'm going to take you on a tour of the Villa Magistrale and our national church, Santa Maria del Prirato, where a mass will be held later on. As a future historian, you will appreciate the architecture and the history of this place.'

These visits excited Cyril. But he was not at all prepared to attend a mass. Natasha tapped him on the shoulder when she saw his pout.

'What is this important news that requires our presence today?'

'All in good time, my friend. You'll find out soon enough.'

'The last time you told me such a thing, I waited about a month before I got to the bottom of it. It was about my ancestry.'

Borgia smiled.

'But you have to admit that the wait was worth it!'

'Yes, of course. Besides, my father did not have the opportunity to thank you. No one in the family had managed to go that far back and knew of such a lineage. He was also delighted, not to say proud, to learn of it.'

'I am delighted with this myself. We have specialists in the field who have access to all the archives they want, including those of the Vatican. Well, it's time for mass, you can admire our church which dates back to 939! It was renovated and redesigned around 1765 by Giovani Battista Piranesi, whose remains rest here. It is probably one of the oldest examples, if not the oldest, of neo-classical architecture in Rome! You can admire its temple-like façade with its double fluted pilasters on either side of the entrance.'

'What's a pilaster?' whispered Natasha to Cyril so as not to appear ignorant in front of Borgia.

'It is a rectangular support ending in a base and topped by a cap and embedded in a wall, unlike a capital which acts as an isolated, distinct support. Its purpose is therefore purely decorative,' replied her husband.

'Bravo, I couldn't have explained it better,' concluded the Italian.

Once inside, they went to the back of the choir. In the middle of the tabernacle, just above the ciborium, was a painting.

'Do you recognise it?'

'Is that the Virgin of Philerme in the crypt?'

'Absolutely. What better place than in the villa's chapel, right? Experts have dated this copy to the $14^{\text{ème}}$ century. Maybe the one that disappeared two hundred years later... we will never know. The original that was stolen has just been returned to its place in Cetinje, Montenegro, after a small restoration. And in order to guarantee better protection and conservation of this jewel, the Order has offered the monastery the must of the must. An armored humidity cabinet.'

'Why do you value it as the apple of your eye?'

'Since this icon was discovered in Rhodes around the year 1306, it has followed the fate of the Hospitallers. When they were expelled from the island and wandered for some years on the seas, it was put on the mast of the great carrack, the Santa Maria, the ship of the Grand Master Philippe de Villiers de l'Isle-Adam, your ancestor Cyril, and served as a banner. She protected the order. It survived the fires, wars and revolutions of the last century and, above all, it was the cause of three miracles, including the one we all witnessed.'

'And what did you do with the various reliquaries found in one of the boxes?'

'For the time being, they are stored in the Holy See. But we are hopeful that they will be recovered one day. They are probably the most beautiful finds in this room. The significance is much greater than the coins or the gems...'

The mass was held in a small group.

They left the National Church an hour later and returned to an office on the first floor of the villa with a historian working for the Order who was introduced to them before the service.

'But by the way, how did your dissertation defense go?' asked Borgia as he walked along.

'I apparently impressed them. Especially with the illumination of the altar dating from the Carolingian era. If I had been able to talk about the crypt and the tunnel, I would probably have won the Nobel Prize or the Legion of Honor, but hey...'

'Well done and thank you again for not mentioning everything else. Two members of the Order went there last month and

The Mystery of the Lost Crypt

confirm the poor state of the foundations of the crypt and the underground as a whole. It is preferable for the time being that access remains forbidden.'

'A year after its disappearance, the icon was found by chance by the French police in a villa in the hinterland of Nice of an order competing with ours and also claiming affiliation with the original Hospitaller order.'

'But what good would it do them to have this icon?' asked Cyril.

'Owning this icon is totally anecdotal. It is not the possession of such an object that confirms anything. The Vatican only recognizes the Order of Malta as a true descendant. On the other hand, they possessed a very old codex dating from the end of the thirteenth century, beginning of the fourteenth, which was also stolen.'

Cyril recognized the book.

'But I've seen it somewhere before! He thought for a moment. I remember, on the desk of the Dean of the Faculty of Nancy, Professor Visconti. He was studying it.'

'This book was discovered in a crypt in the rue du Temple, on the site of the former Templar house. We studied it before it was stolen and it mentions the presence of a code on the back of the painting of the Madonna of Philerme. And indeed we took a picture of it before it was returned to Cetinje.'

'And what did you find out?' asked Cyril.

The historian showed him a sheet of paper with the following hieroglyphs in the middle:

'So I'm at a loss. I've never seen this type of coding...' said the young man doubtfully.

'It's a series of cryptic letters. Still not ringing a bell?'

The Mystery of the Lost Crypt

'Not at all. But from the tone of your voice, I'm guessing you already know the end of the story.'

'Indeed,' said Borgia with a broad smile. 'This is an old encryption method used almost a thousand years ago by the Templars. They used the Cross of the Eight Beatitudes, also known as the Maltese Cross, the emblem of our order as you have no doubt noticed, to make another encrypted alphabet. Look,' said Borgia, showing the couple a sheet of paper.

'They broke down the Maltese Cross into a whole series of symbols, always by four, in order to recreate an alphabet.'

He turned the sheet, revealing the encryption table.

'They were really strong, those Templars...'

'And in our case, if we apply this equivalence table to the series of ten symbols, we obtain the following sequence of letters:

DOUOSVAVVM

'I am well advanced! I must confess that these letters are just as foreign to me as the previous symbols. I suppose you know what they mean too?'

'Come on Cyril! Are these letters really unknown to you? asked the historian with a touch of disappointment.'

'Sorry. As well as hieroglyphs... never seen them before!'

Borgia took out of his pocket a photocopy of a monument in a park.

'This is the cryptogram of Shugborough Hall. An inscription carved in the 18ème century in Staffordshire, England, on a stele dedicated to the painting *Et in Arcadia ego,* better known as Les Bergers d'Arcadie, by Nicolas Poussin. Look, the inscriptions are the same as those engraved on the back of the painting of the Virgin of Philerme. One of the most fascinating enigmas ever solved!'

'A new legend?' exclaimed the young man.

'Yes! The adventure continues my friends...'

To be continued...

The Mystery of the Lost Crypt

The Mystery of the Lost Crypt

The Mystery of the Lost Crypt

Photo couverture : © iStock

Manufactured by Amazon.ca
Acheson, AB